TREASURED ECSTASY

"How could you have stayed away so long, Irene?" With a cry she rushed forward. He met her with arms outstretched, catching her to him and clamping his mouth down on hers as he whirled her around with him. She found herself swept into the farthest corner of the side room. Her unfastened coat was jerked down from her shoulders to fall to the floor, while his kissing took her breath away. Her blouse was parted, the buttons flying undone as his hands swept in to find their way past silk and lace to caress her ardently. His lips left hers and were everywhere.

"Oh, Derek," she breathed, exulting in the male scent of him.

He enveloped her in his embrace, burying his face in her hair, his breath warm against her ear as he sighed with frantic despair, so much yearning in him that it vibrated from his body into hers. "I know where we can be alone," he whispered. "Now . . ."

JEWELLED PATH

ROSALIND LAKER

ZEBRA BOOKS
KENSINGTON PUBLISHING CORP.

To Melba and Grahame.

One

Today was *the* day. In Irene Lindsay's opinion it was not an occasion for rejoicing, even though she was being allowed to wear her jade brooch in its setting of gold. The privilege made her feel grown-up, considerably more than her nine years. Normally, in spite of being a jeweller's daughter, she was discouraged from any personal adornment beyond the large ribbon that tied her tangle of copper-red curls back from her thin, bright face. But on this special November day in the year of 1890, her best clothes and brooch were in order, because her widowed father was bringing his bride home to London from their honeymoon. His bride was a Russian lady whom he had met while on one of his business trips to St. Petersburg and had since married in the cathedral there.

"Oh, oh!" Mounting nervousness had caused Irene to jab her thumb with the brooch pin as she fastened it. When it was secure, she stood on tiptoe to tilt the swing glass on the bow-shaped chest of drawers and regard her reflection in it. How prettily the jade glowed against the dark brown wool of her dress! She patted the brooch proudly, not caring that she would have been admonished for vanity if her father had been present. Many a time she wished he was less strict with her. It was almost as if he sought to banish by constant punishment any weakness in her character, and therefore it was no wonder she would dread the coming of his new spouse, who would align herself in upholding the iron discipline with which he ruled the life of his only child.

His first wife, Denise Lindsay, had died before their newborn daughter was a week old. It sometimes seemed to Irene that the house must have died on the same day. No redecorating had been done in the interim, and the flock wallpapers had darkened to dismal hues. The plush drapes that hung looped across the windows, keeping out so much of the light, had developed faded streaks in battles against the sun. The mahogany furniture, big and heavy and ornately carved, most of which had been new on her parents' wedding day, had the lifeless gloss given to it by servants' elbow grease and nothing more. Only the long table in the dining room glowed with the warm patina that comes to furniture through the use to which it was intended. There Edmund gave the occasional grand dinner party. More often there were splendid luncheons when he entertained visiting diamond merchants while conducting transactions too important to be confined to his office.

Irene sat at that dining table only for the roast beef after church on Sundays and for the turkey and plum pudding at Christmas. Otherwise she still ate in the nursery quarters at the top of the house. This day was to be an exception. She had peeped into the dining room before going upstairs to change into her best dress and had glimpsed the gleam of damask and crystal and silver. The youngest parlourmaid had given her a cheery wink behind the butler's back. Everyone in the house, even the lowest kitchenmaid, was keyed up to the importance of the occasion and agog to see the bride. Irene was painfully aware of being the only one not in a festive mood this day at Number 7, Milton Square.

There was a step on the landing. Mademoiselle Desgranges, the French governess, threw open the bedroom door, one hand pressed to her black bombazine bosom to emphasize the haste with which she had taken the stairs.

"Did you not 'ear me call?" she snapped in her high-pitched Parisian tones. "Come at once! The landau 'as turned into the square. Your father and 'is wife will be 'ere at any moment. Remember to recite your speech of welcome exactly as we re'earsed it."

"Yes, Mademoiselle."

Irene swallowed hard. The awful time had come. Fearful of stumbling over her words when faced with the dreaded newcomer, she had devised her own special welcome and hoped desperately that it would not go awry. Surreptitiously she pressed her hand

9

over her pocket to reassure herself that it held more than her best handkerchief and then realized that she had probably squashed the contents. But it was too late to rectify that now.

The governess was already out of the room and descending the stairs. Obediently Irene followed her down the three flights common to the tall terrace houses built for the well-to-do over a century before and still sought after by those who could afford the elegant addresses.

In the hall the servants were lined up on one side, all seven of them. The menservants in their dark coats and trousers were flicking cuffs into place and straightening ties, the women smoothing aprons and flinging back cap ribbons with a toss of the head that was almost flirtatious. Irene took the last tread of the sweeping stairs and went to stand alone in the middle of the black-and-white-chequered floor. A last-minute prod of unnecessary sharpness from Mademoiselle reminded her to keep her feet together, her spine straight, and her head high. The butler opened the door, letting in a shaft of wintry air at the exact moment that the landau came to a halt at the kerb.

Edmund Lindsay alighted first. He was a mature man of sturdy build with a patrician nose and a stern facial expression, his trimmed side whiskers and thick, brown hair a shade lighter than his formidable brows. Well-dressed by the best tailor in London, he wore a plaid travelling coat of Scottish tweed with a fore-and-aft hat known as a deerstalker, clothes that he found comfortable and practical for his many long journeyings. It was said that no man had a better or more varied collection of cravat pins than he, but this was his one small flamboyance, his cuff-links and studs always plain gold, a single, engraved sovereign fob the only attachment to his watch chain, and his well-kept hands were always bare of any jewellery except for the signet ring he wore on the marriage finger. He had worn it for his first wife and now for his second, whom he was assisting out of the carriage.

Sofia, the new Mrs. Lindsay, was tall and swan-necked, her moon-fair hair arranged in a curled fringe and drawn back smoothly from her oval, high-boned face into a large coil at the nape of her neck, her hat of Cossack style in cinnamon velvet ornamented by a topaz pin. The same lush fabric made up her fashionably draped travelling costume, the jacket of which was fastened with tiny buttons, the jabot of her silk blouse displayed through the opening of the rolled collar. Completing her outfit was a magnificent cape of natural sable, which had been designed for a Russian winter and swirled opulently about her skirt hem. As she adjusted the soft folds, glancing up at the house that awaited her, she gave no sign of the tremor of apprehension that ran through her veins. A strict upbringing had taught her that women of breeding never showed their emotions in public. At all times, even in the face of danger or in abject mourning, a composed expression was *de rigueur*. In her veins ran a faint strain of Romanov blood, her link with the present

Czar too remote to be of any consequence, but her family was an old, established one in its own right, and if her parents had been alive, they would never have condoned her second marriage. Nothing would have atoned in their eyes for Edmund's lack of distinguished lineage and his involvement with commerce, albeit his goods were precious stones. Yet in his own way, his attitude of superior self-satisfaction was no less than her parents' haughtiness towards those not of their social stratum. He classed himself as a connoisseur and a critic, not as a tradesman, his business premises being located in Old Bond Street, renowned throughout the world as the quintessence of elegant shopping.

Perhaps it was her destiny to be mated with arrogant men, although she loved Edmund as she had never loved her first husband, who had been chosen for her by her parents, resulting in the twelve unhappiest years of her life, from which she had been released eventually by widowhood. She believed implicitly that a woman should marry for love and love alone, even when in her case now it meant facing comparison with an adored first wife, a devotion of which Edmund had made no secret, and becoming stepmother to the offspring of that union, from whom she must expect the worst. Edmund had prepared her fully for the waywardness of his difficult daughter.

"Sofia, my dear."

Edmund was offering his arm, and she took it, going with him up the steps and through the stone porch into the house. The hall looked small to her. She did not doubt that it would be considered a good size by London town house standards, but to her its narrow confines were in complete contrast to the spacious, gilded entrances of the mansions in which she had lived until now. As for the line of waiting domestic staff, the lack of numbers would be laughable to anyone of her circle in the land she had left behind her. She had acquaintances of her own nationality in London, but since they lived as handsomely abroad as they did at home, not one had thought to forewarn her in their letters of anything except the English climate. What a mercy she had brought her own personal maid! She would have brought her chief chef as well if she had not feared to offend Edmund by disrupting his household before she had so much as crossed his threshold. Now she was thankful she had not embarrassed him by even suggesting it.

Disengaging her hand from the crook of Edmund's elbow, she went forward, letting her smile and her cornflower-blue gaze sweep along the row of servants bowing or curtseying to her. Then her stately pace slowed to a standstill as she came to where a child stood timidly alone. Astonishment smote her. Such marvellous red hair! Such fine features and a skin so pale as to be almost translucent, the huge eyes a dark sea-green. But those clothes! Apart from the jade brooch, it would be hard to tell that the little girl was not the kitchen scullion. She was clean and neat enough, the white collar crisp and spotless, but the brown dress hung on the narrow frame as though from a peg, fitting nowhere, and the thin legs were encased in black stockings, the shoes pewter-buckled. This waif, then, was Edmund's wilful and untame-able daughter.

"How do you do, Irene." Sofia was more ac-customed to speaking French than English, the Gallic tongue being the second language of educated Russians, and she was conscious of her accent and anxious to improve it, unaware that to English ears it enhanced rather than detracted from her melodious voice. No reply was forthcoming from the child, who stood staring at her dumbly. Edmund, who had discarded his hat and topcoat, came forward smartly, with considerable impatience, to prompt his daugh-ter.

"Come, come. What do you say to your step-mamma?"

Sofia noted that he had given Irene no kiss of greeting. As he gripped the narrow shoulder to propel the child forward, his fingers pressed deeply, as if to emphasize his expectation of good behaviour on this of all days. Seeing Irene wince, her face becoming quite ashen, Sofia was filled with compas-sion. Could Edmund not see that his little girl was in a high-pitched state of nervousness over this meet-ing? Sofia was reminded of a time some years ago when she had experienced the same paralysing terror that had taken speech and movement from her. Admittedly she had been in far worse circumstances, finding herself alone for the first time and in utter innocence with the bridegroom to whom she had been given in marriage by her father only a few hours before. How familiar the longing to run away that was revealed in the bravely compressed lips, how identifiable the desolation in the green eyes, for had she not seen the same expression in her own mirror on many occasions in days gone by? Wisely she resisted the impulse to embrace the child in the reassurance that she came as a friend and not as an enemy. It had to be done some other way, and what better way than one out of her own need? She regarded Irene directly.

"I hope I may seek guidance from you in my new country," she said before Edmund had a chance to prompt his daughter yet again. "You see, everything will be strange and new to me. I have travelled abroad, but never to England before now. Shall you be my link, a steadying hand when I am at a loss?"

Colour gushed into Irene's cheeks and drained away again until even her lips were white. She was completely overwhelmed by such an unexpected request from this elegant, romantic-looking woman, who might easily have stepped out of an illustration in a book of Russian fairy tales. Some sixth sense told Irene that the favour had been asked with all sincerity and not as flattery, which she would have despised. Incredibly, it seemed that she was not going to be pushed still further into the background of the household, as she had anticipated. Her father's fleeting and uncharacteristic expression of surprised uncertainty as he released his grip, stepping away from her, aided the quelling of her previous qualms. A feeling of trust towards the newcomer began to glimmer and then to glow deep within her.

"I'll do anything I can to help you, Stepmamma," she stammered shyly. Dispensing completely with the rehearsed and stilted speech of welcome, which had not been of her choosing anyway, she dived into her pocket and took out what was concealed there. Tremblingly, she held it out to Sofia, who took it from her.

Edmund glared, seeing the mess of crumbled bread and salt lying on the white leather spread of his wife's gloved hand. "What stupid prank is this?" But Sofia was smiling at Irene.

"I thank you with all my heart, dear child. How did you know?"

"I've been learning about Russia in my geography lessons."

Sofia stooped and kissed her stepdaughter affectionately on both cheeks. Then she turned to her husband as she straightened up, her eyes shining. "It is an old peasant custom in my country that a newcomer is to be welcomed with bread and salt. What better portent could there be for my arrival at this house, Edmund? Truly I have come home."

In time to come she was to remember her moment of optimism with a certain wryness, but happiness was hers that day, enabling her to face the future with renewed hope that all would be well.

As for Irene, she began to love Sofia as a second mother from that day forth and was ever afterwards to think of Russia as a place of sunshine and not of ice and snow, simply because her stepmother had come from there. For the first time in her life, she had someone to talk to and laugh with, and there were comforting arms if she fell and hurt herself or shed tears for some other reason. It was a great treat to lunch alone with Sofia, for Edmund was rarely home at midday, and the two of them chatted away together. Unfortunately from Irene's viewpoint, these occasions were not as frequent as she would have liked, simply because Sofia was swept into an intense social round from the start, renewing acquaintanceships with fellow compatriots as well as being much in demand in Edmund's circle.

Yet Sofia never forgot her commitment to Irene in the whirl of her own activities. Whenever she was going out in the evening, she never failed to see that her stepdaughter was tucked up in bed safely. In fact, she made a point of always allowing enough time to sit on the child's bed and talk for a while, knowing that apart from anything else Irene shared Edmund's respect and admiration for beautiful jewellery and liked to admire whatever gems she was wearing. Although Edmund had been lavish in his wedding gift of a diamond brooch, Sofia had already owned some magnificent parures, nearly all having tiaras to match the accompanying necklace, ear-rings, and bracelets. Irene loved to be told their history and to hear about the special occasions when they had been worn. Then, when time was up, Sofia would give the child's brow a good-night kiss and go from the room, the sparkle of her jewels vanishing with her, the fragrance of her perfume lingering on in the quiet darkness.

Sofia did not like having to limit these minutes with her stepdaughter, but she had soon discovered that Edmund would be irritable and ill-tempered if she kept him waiting. He rarely said anything but would stand with his gold watch open in the palm of his hand and snap it shut deliberately as she came from the direction of the nursery quarters. She thought it sad that he should be as jealous of his own daughter as he was of anyone else who took her time and attention away from him, however briefly. She had learned to make a point of looking towards him quite frequently in any social gathering to let him see she had not forgotten him in the company of others. His eyes were always waiting for her.

He was a passionate husband. She had hoped that out of his constant ardour a child might be conceived, but as the months went by, overtaking their first wedding anniversary and leaving her still disappointed, she began to accept that her second marriage was doomed to be no more fruitful than her first. All the pent-up maternal love in her found an outlet in caring for Irene.

One of her immediate actions after her arrival in London had been to buy her stepdaughter a wardrobe of new clothes, most of them abounding in ribbons and capes and flounces. Irene half suspected that there was trouble between her father and his new wife about it. Nothing was mentioned in her presence, but one day her stepmother's eyelids looked pink and puffy as if she had been crying. The next time they went shopping for a dress, Sofia instructed the assistant not to bring anything frilly or frivolous to show Irene but to keep to simpler styles.

"You have so many fancy frocks, Irene," Sofia said as if in answer to an unspoken query, her smile deliberately cheerful. "We must be practical about everyday wear, must we not?"

So from that time forth Irene wore plain, well-fitting garments in pretty colours and was compensated by an extra frill trimmed with torchon lace on all her petticoats. It was a gentle conspiracy, causing no harm and breaking no rules. Irene thought herself greatly blessed in having a step-mother who had perceived her yearning for a touch of feminine frippery that had previously been denied her.

Gradually Sofia began to make changes in the house, asserting her own personality. When no opposition was put in her way and she found herself free to do as she wished with one room and then another, she realized thankfully that she had established herself fully as Edmund's marriage partner, allowing the late, lamented Denise to slip into a rightful place of cherished memory. She sent for some of her own furniture from Russia, inherited pieces of timeless elegance that replaced the heavily ornate sideboards, bookcases, and corner what-nots, some of which needed six men to move them. She went to Liberty's in Regent Street, where silk curtains were made for her in dawn tints and other delicate hues to replace the ugly plush drapes at the windows. In the same establishment she wandered for hours, making careful choices to create a light and airy look for the house, aiming to banish forever the bobble-fringed mantel hangings, the wax fruit under glass, the clutter of bric-à-brac, and the black bearskins rugs with their fanged heads and yellow glass eyes. One of her favourite purchases was a set of a dozen Mackmurdo chairs for the long dining table, the backs of which were of a new, linear design in a wonderful swirling akin to reeds blowing in the wind. They gave a final touch to the refurbished room, the handsome proportions revealed at last by the clearing away of all clutter. The walls had been rehung with a William Morris wallpaper in his "Pimpernel" motif.

Whenever possible, Sofia took Irene with her on these domestic shopping expeditions, frequently doing battle beforehand with the temperamental Mademoiselle, who resented the loss of lesson time and never failed to report it to her employer. Yet in Sofia's company Irene received constant instruction, gaining knowledge and understanding of the aesthetic changes coming about in design and manufacture, which were pointed out to her. Sofia explained that traditional modes were being ousted by a new movement that aimed to enthrall all things in an elegant stylization taken from nature in all its forms, much of which she had begun to capture in the rooms of their own home. Not only had paintings and sculpture already come under its influence, but it had reached out to every kind of domestic item from a simple teapot to a bell-push or a fire-fender. Its principle was that everything, no matter how mundane its use, should be beautifully proportioned and pure in line, whether it came from a craftsman's hands or a factory bench. As Sofia talked about it all, Irene was able to grasp the fundamentals and to see how the new interplay of line was linked to the earlier influence of Japanese art and its simplicity, as well as to a later Celtic development.

Since the shopping trips always culminated in lemonade and cream cakes in Liberty's Arab Tea Room on the first floor, everything Irene had learned stayed with her as part of another wonderful outing with her stepmother. Without either of them realizing it, Sofia had set Irene's appreciation of all things beautiful onto a fresh path, which she was destined to follow as if she had been born of the new aesthetic movement itself.

In addition to these expeditions, Sofia took Irene to art galleries, special exhibitions, afternoon concerts, and many places of historical interest. For Sofia it was all a part of getting to know London as well as she had known St. Petersburg, and she considered it as educationally beneficial to her stepdaughter as any number of hours spent reading about the subjects in an attic schoolroom. On some days when there was time to spare, Sofia would call in to see Edmund at his business premises. She knew Irene liked to study the jewellery on display and that it made an additional treat for her. Even Old Bond Street itself was always a sight to see. Forbidden to wagons and horse-buses, nothing interfered with the passage of gleaming carriages with sleek, high-stepping horses driven by liveried coachmen that carried an aristocratic clientele to and from the establishments there.

Edmund's shop had a regal frontage of cream marble; the entrance was set back between two windows, each of which held no more than one or two handsome pieces of jewellery set against rich velvet. In the facia his name was carved and gilded in tasteful lettering, and to the side of it was the royal warrant, proclaiming that he was among the privileged few in the street who had served the palace well. Irene almost skipped with excitement whenever she followed Sofia out of the landau and into the showroom, which was large and spacious with crystal gasoliers suspended from an ornate ceiling that dated back to Regency times. Glass cases and counters held sparkling arrays; some rings and bracelets were displayed on pale wax hands which Irene thought looked faintly tomblike and macabre. Mr. Taylor, the head salesman, came forward to give his employer's wife the deep bow he reserved for the most noble of patrons who entered there. To him she was a true lady in every sense of the word, and he respected her greatly. His bow to Irene was less formal and was accompanied by a little smile, for he had known her since she was born.

"Good afternoon, Mr. Taylor," Sofia replied to his courteous greeting. "Is my husband disengaged?"

"Yes, he is, madam." After showing her through to the office, Mr. Taylor returned to where Irene was gazing at a pair of diamond ear-rings that would dangle from the earlobes to the shoulders. She never ceased to marvel at the infinite variety in the cut and colour of precious stones, and these were set to cascade like a dazzling waterfall.

"Aren't they beautiful!" she breathed.

"Yes, they are very fine," he agreed, opening the case to take them out on their stand for her to examine more closely. He had always been kind to her, being a family man himself and pitying her motherless state over the years. He could remember the times the first Mrs. Lindsay had come into the shop until she had ailed in her pregnancy, and Irene never tired of having her mother described to her. She had learned more from Mr. Taylor of her mother's gentle demeanour, her quiet voice, and her preference for modest jewels such as a cameo brooch or a string of pearls than ever she had heard from her father. It was almost as if he had considered his grief to be a private matter, exclusive to himself, and had never wanted to share his memories with anyone else, least of all with his daughter. She would never have had a keepsake to treasure if Sofia had not arranged for her to be given a single sapphire and pearl ring that had once belonged to the late Denise Lindsay. Since it was such an unostentatious piece of jewellery, Irene was allowed to wear it on outings with Sofia and on other special occasions, although whereas her mother would have worn it on a little finger, it only

fit Irene's middle one. As Mr. Taylor returned the ear-
rings to the showcase, he addressed her with a
conspiratorial air.

"There is something more interesting than these
pretty adornments for you to see in the workshop
today."

"Oh, good!" She clapped her hands excitedly. It
had been Mr. Taylor who had first taught her some
basic facts about gems and how to distinguish
between them. She knew that emeralds ranged
through all the greens of the ocean, that diamonds
could be pink or yellow as well as colourless, and that
except for their colour, rubies and sapphires were
identical stones. She was able to recognize the pure
robin's-egg blue or the sky blue of the perfect
turqouise, knew that pearls from Europe were
usually larger and heavier than those that came from
the Orient, and that amber, for all its wonderful
golden-red shades, was fossilized resin and not a
stone at all, although no less prized for that. She had
favourites among other gems for their glorious
colors: red garnets, azure-blue lapis lazuli, green
jade, golden topaz, shimmering opals, chrysoberyl in
dark chartreuse, rose quartz, and tourmaline in its
wide range of rainbow hues. The intricate settings of
gold and silver fascinated her almost as much as the
stones themselves, and she would question Mr.
Taylor about the workmanship involved. Recently,
however, she had found herself less enthusiastic over
the finished pieces than she had been before, wishing
they were not so traditional, her lively appreciation

of the linear designs of the new movement making her critical of anything that did not adhere to it.

Keeping pace at Mr. Taylor's side, she went out of the showroom into the corridor that lay beyond it, a crimson-carpeted and mahogany-panelled area with her father's office at the far end. To the left were three doors, two of which opened into good-sized ante-rooms, the third into a much smaller one, which because of its sparse dimensions was rarely used. The furnishings of all three would have complemented any drawing room, the furniture rosewood and upholstered in apple-green damask. It was in these quarters that customers of exceptional distinction were received and waited upon or transactions in need of utmost security took place. If esteemed customers sometimes found themselves in dire straits and came to sell and not to buy, only Edmund and the trusted Mr. Taylor knew of it, and everything was conducted with tact and scrupulous fairness in the settlement of a price. The whole of the right-hand side of the corridor was flanked by the major workshop, an ivy-patterned panel of clear and opaque glass in the door giving glimpses of the goldsmiths at work within and enabling Edmund to check without entering that nobody was idling his time away. Mr. Taylor turned the handle and opened what Irene thought of as the pretty door for her to enter. Unable to spare time away from the show-room, he told her who to seek out there for the sight of interest that she had been promised. She went forward eagerly.

A long bench dominated the room, set at right angles from the wall and shaped with horseshoe curves, a goldsmith seated on a stool at each of the five places. Each had his individual tools at hand, and each wore a leather apron known as a board skin, which was hooked to the underside of the bench and tied by cords about his waist to catch precious filings and scraps that might fall from the valuable metals on which he was working. Nothing was wasted, and when evening came even the dust sweepings of the day were sifted thoroughly for savings before being sold to those traders who still thought it worthwhile to buy for possible salvage. To Irene the workshop was an intriguing place, sometimes quiet when every craftsman was engaged in an intricate task, more often noisy when the gas furnace roared, melting metal hissed, bench guillotines sheared off lengths of silver or gold, and drills and files rasped to set any outsider's teeth on edge. A long skylight, heavily barred for security, gave plenty of light that was supplemented when necessary by gas mantels on the walls and globes suspended overhead.

Many a time she had lingered at the bench to ask the goldsmiths questions about the stages of the work in hand there. It was from them that she had become familiar with the terms for the way gemstones were cut. She knew that cabochon was the name given to a stone, usually nontransparent, that was polished but uncut or cut *en cabochon* to an all-over symmetry without facets. She had also learned that the earliest cuts were the rose cut and the mogol cut, which had developed over the past three centuries into the brilliant cut, with its many facets and variations of form that gave such life and fire to a beautiful gem. Today Irene did not pause by the bench as she hurried through to one of the small adjoining rooms where the head goldsmith, who was also the firm's jewellery designer, was at work on his own. She gasped, poising briefly on tip-toe in astonishment at seeing what appeared to be a vast pendant of jewels that half covered the individual horseshoe bench at which the craftsman sat at his exotic task.

"Oh, what is it, Mr. Lucas?" she exclaimed.

"What do you think it might be?" he answered her, taking off his spectacles as he shifted his stool sideways to allow her a better view.

She was completely at a loss. Riveted to a large triangular piece of hide was a pattern profusion of diamonds, rubies, and emeralds fanning out from a star-shaped jewelled boss, which itself culminated in a large ruby. The edges of the whole piece were encrusted with a wide border of gems, enhanced in turn by long tassels of gleaming pearls, which she could have measured from her fingertips to her elbow. "I've no idea what it is," she declared, "although I'm sure only a strong giant could wear it!"

He smiled widely. "You're not far off the mark. These stones were sent to us by Indian maharaja to be made up into a head ornament for his favourite elephant. Take a good look at them. In my opinion they have come from a treasure chest in a vault

27

somewhere and haven't seen the light of day for a long, long time."

"How can you tell?"

"There are various signs. Some of the emeralds have been carved with a shell motif, which suggests that once they were mounted in jewellery or worn as beads. Quite a few of the smaller rubies have drilled holes that indicate previous service. The diamonds give the strongest clue. All of them are an early mogol cut, the parallel faces broad and flat. I'm sure you can see that they lack the beauty they would have had if cut by the methods we use these days."

"Could they be recut?"

"Some could have been if the maharaja had requested it, but he did not. Perhaps he would have if they had been for personal wear. It happens often when people inherit very old jewels that they decide to have them recut, and the difference is breath-taking."

"My stepmother has some beautiful Russian jewellery, and she told me that many of the lovely stones have been reset into parures two or three times."

"That is what fashion does and why so few original settings survive for any length of time. So often ladies decide to dispense with the old-fashioned style and have the jewels reset in the latest mode. It is good for business, but many a time I have regretted having to remove gems from an antique setting."

Their conversation had to draw to a close at that point, for her father had brought Sofia into the workshop for her to see the Indian ornament. Irene stepped away from the bench to make room for her stepmother, whose smile and friendly pat on the shoulder in passing did nothing to ease her frustration at not being able to ask the rest of the questions that had come tumbling into her mind, but she knew better than to chatter in her father's presence. Yet there was so much she had to learn if she was going to be a jeweller when she grew up. How and when the ambition to work with gemstones and precious metals first grew in her she did not know. She had never received encouragement from her father, who rarely mentioned the business when at home, and he had no idea how she loved to study the illustrations, many of the early ones hand-coloured in acid tints, in his extensive library of jewellery books. One of her most exciting outings with Sofia had been to see the crown jewels at the Tower of London. Afterwards the two of them had made a replica of the Queen's coronation crown out of stiff paper, with sequins for jewels, Sofia sitting on the floor in front of the nursery fire with her, snipping away with scissors amid the mess of coloured scraps. For as long as Irene could remember, she had made herself necklaces and bracelets and rings; and those she thought particularly pretty, she never threw away, but kept them in a cardboard shoe box in the bottom of her wardrobe. She thought of it as her jewel case.

On the drive homewards along Piccadilly after leaving the shop and the maharaja's jewels, Irene brought up with Sofia a point that had been at the back of her mind earlier on. "Do you think my father will ever follow the new movement in his jewellery?"

Sofia shook her head without any hesitation. "No. He is a traditionalist."

"But he likes all the redecorating and refurnishing that you have done to our home, doesn't he?"

"That is a different matter altogether. He allowed your mamma to furnish to her taste, which was in the fashion of the day, and he has allowed me the same privilege. Remember that jewellery is your father's own special sphere, and the classic pieces that he sells will be admired and appreciated long after other modes of the moment have come and gone. Never cast away the past merely to embrace change for change's sake, Irene. Keep an open mind always. Welcome beauty in whatever form it comes."

"I still wish Father would be a little more adventurous."

"The new movement has yet to establish itself fully. Some people oppose it strongly. It would be a sad day if your father filled his shop with adventurous pieces and nobody came to buy them." Sofia smiled and gave a nod. "Trust his judgement as far as his own particular establishment is concerned. He is a businessman and a clever one. None can surpass his knowledge of stones. Why else would the great Carl Fabergé rely on him as a valuable source of supply?"

Sofia had first met Edmund during a musical evening at the private home of Fabergé, a kindly, intelligent, and cultured man whom she had long respected and admired, his wife as charming as he, their way of life gracious and refined in the best sense of the word. Although she was still in mourning at the time, it was the second year of her widowhood, which meant that she was no longer compelled to wear dreary *crêpe* on her garments. She had gone forth that evening in a Worth gown of black taffeta that had been cut to enhance superbly her full-bosomed, slim-waisted figure as only that masterful couturier knew how. It had arrived from Paris just a few hours before, delighting her with its low *décolletage* and jet-fringed, bustled drapery, coming complete with a tall aigrette of feathery black plumes to fasten upright in her pale golden hair. She had looked her best and known it, her spirits set to enjoy the evening to the full, never dreaming that she was to sit next to a foreigner with whom she was to fall in love almost from the first words he spoke. And such prosaic words! Why did the English always talk about the weather?

"What a warm and pleasant day it has been, Madame Shuiski."

"I agree, Mr. Lindsay. Is this your first visit to St. Petersburg?"

He replied that it was not, and she learned that he came twice or thrice a year on business, calling exclusively at the head establishment of the House of Fabergé at Number 24 Morskayo, one of the grandest streets in the city. It was Edmund's voice, so strong, so powerful, seeming to come from the very barrel of his chest, that had stirred latent depths in her as much as his general appearance, making her pulsate deliciously, her blood racing. Throughout the programme of music, it was hard for her to keep her mind from wondering how it might feel to be crushed in his arms and to have those slightly fleshy lips devouring her. Never before had she been so disturbed pleasurably in a stranger's company.

Another eighteen months were to pass, and he was to make four more visits to St. Petersburg before she was to know his embrace or his kisses, and then only after she had accepted his proposal of marriage. Throughout his courtship he behaved with absolute decorum, the perfect English gentleman, while she kept subdued the turmoil of love within her. Not until their wedding night did she discover the full extent of his lusty nature that was complemented by her own ardent response. Still, whenever the clock drew near a bedtime hour, she was filled with anticipatory quivers such as she had never known in her previous marriage.

It was her love that enabled her to overlook Edmund's many faults and imperfections. Like most men in his position, he was absolute master in his own home, his word law, obdurate and rigid in all his attitudes, and liable to lose his temper violently at the slightest provocation. By nature, apart from being excessively possessive, he was highly conceited, well aware of being well-built and extremely virile. In all, he was a far from easy man to live with, as she had soon discovered, but she was a forgiving woman, believing herself to be alone in knowing that beneath the bluff and bluster there was a deeply vulnerable streak in him. It was almost as if he harboured a raw nerve as far as Irene was concerned, and Sofia was at a loss to understand his severe treatment of his daughter, which he refused utterly to discuss or have mentioned. In Sofia's opinion Irene was no better and no worse than any other lively, healthy child of her age, well-behaved on the whole, and answering her father back only on rare occasions when goaded beyond further endurance by his faultfinding. How Sofia dreaded these times of confrontation between them, and how hard she tried to avert them with a tactful word, but Edmund was like a bulldog when he had a grip on something that annoyed him. The terrible scenes that ensued were played out until Irene was banished to her room in disgrace, sometimes for days on end, all privileges withdrawn and entertainments cancelled. There had been no way to comfort the child when Edmund had banned at the last minute her participation in an outing to the Christmas pantomime at Drury Lane simply because she had disobeyed her governess over a minor point, which had been immediately reported to him. Yet Edmund was fond of Irene. Sofia could tell. It was ridiculous to say that the punishments hurt him more than the child, for this was not the case; but there were times when Sofia felt his anger was directed at some point beyond Irene herself, although how that could be was a mystery impossible to solve.

It was not long after the viewing of the maharaja's jewels when one dark and rainy afternoon Sofia and Irene decided to play a game of charades. Mademoiselle was laid up with influenza, which had reached almost epidemic proportions throughout the country, and several of the servants had succumbed to it or were in various stages of recovery, leaving the house strangely quiet. For the same reason many of Sofia's engagements had been cancelled due to friends and acquaintances becoming victims to the spread of the illness, and, although sympathetic, she quite welcomed the brief freedom from all social commitments that had come her way. Conscientiously she supervised some lessons for Irene in the mornings but felt that after midday the time should be spent light-heartedly. They had painted pictures one afternoon, played Ludo and Snakes and Ladders and Snap another day, completed a giant jigsaw puzzle together, and on this fourth afternoon Sofia had turned out some feathers and shawls and fans to aid them in their acting and to add to the fun of the game. Irene played out the first charade, Sofia the next, and so on, their mood becoming more and more hilarious. The acting finery was spread all over the bed and *chaise longue* in Sofia's bedroom, and when suitable accessories were donned, each made her way downstairs again to the drawing room, where the other awaited the performance. It was unfortunate for Irene that Edmund decided to come home early that afternoon, having felt the first shivering onslaught and feverish headache that pronounced the oncoming of the current sickness. His one thought was to get his aching body to bed and to down a hot whisky toddy, his particular panacea for his own ills, but he forgot all else when he beheld Irene halfway down the hall stairs. She was draped in trailing yellow satin, her face rouged and painted, a pink ostrich feather skewered through her curls, and a fortune in his wife's jewellery on her person.

For a few seconds he stood transfixed in horror. Then he spoke in tones of rasping harshness, his face congested with fury. "What the devil do you think you are doing?"

Irene, suddenly terrified, shrank back instinctively against the balusters. "I'm being a grand duchess, Father," she whispered tremulously.

"A duchess?" he roared contemptuously. "You look like a trollop off the streets!"

Never before in his life had he used physical chastisement on her, but now he lunged forward and half dragged her down the rest of the stairs to thrash her unmercifully about the face, head, and body, causing rings and other jewels to fly from her under the force of his violence. Her hysterical screaming brought Sofia, white-faced, running from the drawing room, at a loss to know what could be happening.

"Stop! Stop!" she cried out to her husband, but he was deaf to all appeal. She threw herself forward, using all her strength to prise Irene away from him, making a barrier of herself between the rage-maddened man and the shrieking, sobbing child. Only then did he seem to return to his senses, all strength ebbing from him as he let his arms drop limply to his sides. Wearily he shut his eyes in a kind of despair at the shocked expression on his wife's face, and without a word he turned and went across the hall into his study, closing the door behind him.

Sofia spoke soothingly to her stepdaughter, trying to quiet the wild sobs, and took her upstairs to put cool cloths against her bruises. As Irene became more composed, Sofia sat her down on the *chaise longue* to bandage a cut on her brow that had been caused by Edmund's signet ring.

"Why does Father hate me?" Irene asked listlessly, rubbing her wet eyes with a damp handkerchief.

Sofia, knotting the ends of the bandage, was dismayed to realize that she had come close to hating him herself at the sight of his abandoned cruelty. Nevertheless she shook her head firmly. "He does not hate you. Never, never think that. It angered him that you had dressed up in my jewellery. I must say that it was remiss of you not to ask my permission. Why did you do it?"

Irene was deeply contrite, fresh tears flowing at her own foolishness. "I wanted to surprise you. I didn't think further than that. I'm so sorry."

Leaning forward from where she sat, Sofia kissed the child's brow above the bandage. "I understand, my dear," she said forgivingly. "It was a jolly game, and I'm partly to blame for not having thought to put out some less valuable trinkets along with everything else." She returned the remainder of the roll of bandage to the little basket on her lap in which she kept supplies in case of household accidents. Irene's next words made her stiffen as she was about to close the lid.

"What's a trollop off the streets?"

Sofia slotted home the fastening of the basket before she replied with another question. "Why do you want to know that?"

"Father said I looked like one."

Automatically Sofia replaced the child's soaked handkerchief with a clean one from her own pocket. "A trollop is a slut," she answered carefully. "A female who does not conduct herself with dignity and is immodest in her person."

"How dare he!" Irene spoke through her teeth, deeply offended, and clenched her fists on her knees. "I can't be dignified with my awful red hair, but I *am* modest. I am!"

"Hush." Sofia spoke quietly and consolingly. "People say things in anger that they do not mean, and your father is no exception. None of us is perfect. We must learn tolerance and patience as we go through life. As for your hair, it is a beautiful colour. One day when you are grown-up, it will be an asset to your looks in a way that you cannot yet begin to understand."

"Are you sure?" Irene queried hesitantly.

"I would never lie to you, my child."

Irene gave a little sigh. "I know," she said gratefully.

Sofia took her medical basket into her hands and stood up. "Now I'm going downstairs to see your father, and I shall mend matters. I want no rift to come between you."

Irene looked down to hide her pessimism. It is too late, she thought as her stepmother's footsteps went away down the stairs. Somehow a rift had always been there, almost as if it had been created on the day she was born. How that might be she could not begin to imagine. Her private conclusion was that her father did not like red hair, which was why the sight of her always seemed to offend him.

In the study Sofia gave an anxious exclamation, seeing her husband slumped in a chair by the fire, his head back on a cushion. "Edmund! You are ill!" She darted across to him and put her hand on his forehead to find it burning hot. "It is the influenza, to be sure. Let me help you to bed at once."

He pushed her hand away irritably, ignoring what she had said as if she had not spoken. "Irene must go away to boarding school." His voice held the note of an irrevocable decision taken. "You have been far too lenient with her. From the time she began to walk and talk, she has been a child who if given an inch would take a mile. It is entirely your fault that Mademoiselle's authority has been undermined, to say nothing of mine." His eyes blazed at her so fiercely that she drew back a step, never having had to bear the brunt of his direct and ugly displeasure before. "Since you came to this house," he continued, "I have witnessed a deliberate countering of all I have tried to stamp out of Irene in the way of her follies and disobedience and, above all, a too fanciful preoccupation with her own appearance. Today was the prime result of your foolish indulgence. I was appalled."

"You misjudge her, Edmund. All children like to dress up and play-act, and it was for a simple game of charades."

He sprang up out of his chair, his temper exacerbated by the temperature that racked him, every limb aching, his throat burning. "A game! She was wearing two or three bracelets as well as a necklace that I gave you. Are my gifts to be treated no better than tawdry playthings? I appear to have overestimated your intelligence, to say nothing of your sense of responsibility. It seems you are better suited to the nursery yourself than as wife to me!"

He would have thrust past her, but she blocked his way, her colour high. "I had no real childhood, Edmund. Nurses and governesses controlled my life, and I rarely saw my parents. Is it so wrong that I should want to capture a little late in life the sensation of being very young and carefree that I share with Irene at times? Yet she has never taken advantage of this companionship to flout me when I have had cause to reprimand her. She trusts me to be reasonable and fair, and she realizes that I love her as if she were my own. We are as mother and daughter."

Her voice choked, and her eyes swam with tears. "Sometimes I pretend to myself that she is the child I might have borne you."

He gave her a long look. "I wish to God she had been of your womb," he replied heavily, "but since she is not, nothing you say will make any difference. She will be sent away to school with the least possible delay."

"No!" It was a heart-cry. Sofia ran to the door and stood with her back to it, facing him in desperation. "She has known so little affection in her years of growing up. No one understands what this means more than I. If you deprive her now of what small amends I am able to make, how will she ever be able to judge in later life whether the love she meets is true or false? She will have no filial standards set by you to measure it by."

His fever-flushed face went white about the mouth, and his eyes glittered dangerously. "So you think me a poor parent? How dare you, madam! Again I say, how dare you! The sooner my daughter gets away from your sentimental coils, the better it will be. Now stand aside and allow me to get to my sickbed before I need aid to reach it."

She had forgotten, in her panic-stricken concern for Irene's well-being, how savagely intolerant he could be of the slightest implied criticism towards himself. "I beg you, Edmund. Do not go on trying to crush her spirit for something that was not her fault. I saw from the day I first came here that you have always blamed her for being the cause of her mother's death!"

For him it was the final straw, bringing his temper to the explosion point for the second time in less than an hour. With a roar he seized Sofia by the throat with both hands and shook her until her teeth rattled. "Never let me hear you say anything like that again! It is neither true nor just! You know nothing!"

He half flung her from him and went from the room. Dazed by his onslaught, she leaned back weakly against the wall and put a shaking hand to her bruised throat. Struggling against shock and an outburst of tears, she tried valiantly to excuse his behaviour on the grounds of his fever, but against her will she saw a first hairline crack beginning to run through her marriage as though through fine porcelain. A cold sweat of fright began to drench her, and she reached out to take hold of a chair and sink down into it. The memory of her own bleak childhood and the desolation of the years spent with her first husband seemed to engulf her in darkness, and out of it she saw that it was a hunger for love more than love itself that had propelled her into a union with a man who cared only for himself. She bowed her head and held her brow in her hand, momentarily overwhelmed by her disillusionment, her disappointment, and a despair that was almost beyond her endurance.

It took Edmund two weeks to recover from the influenza. Throughout that time Sofia nursed him solicitously. Although he was too proud and ar-rogant a man ever to apologize or admit to being in the wrong, he did regret the violence he had used on her, no matter that he did consider that she had brought it upon herself. No wife had any right to speak to a husband as she had spoken to him. Sometimes he watched her under his eyelids as she moved neatly about the sickroom, trying to detect whether or not she harboured any lasting resentment. He soon reached the conclusion that she did not, deciding that in her own mind she shared his opinion of the whole affair and was blaming herself for having riled him. Munificently, he tried to convey his forgiveness of her lapse by patting her hand when she smoothed his sheets and smiling bravely at her when she gave him the odious medicine left by the doctor.

It would have astounded him to know that apart from anything else, she thought him an irascible and inconsiderate patient, although she realized that he was probably no worse than any other normally healthy male laid low by unaccustomed illness. With all her heart she yearned for him to make the single, loving gesture of retracting his decision to send Irene away, which would have been a show of good faith on his part and would have restored much of what had been driven from their relationship. But it was not to be.

While still in his dressing robe in convalescence, Edmund wrote to the boarding school of his choice in the north of England, ignoring the fact that there were others of equally high educational standards much nearer London, where Irene would not have felt so far away. His first expedition upon regaining his health was to take Irene to it, travelling by train and then covering the last five miles through the countryside by hired cab. Sofia had wanted to accompany them, but he had forbidden it.

Irene's heart sank at the sight of the grey stone walls of the Academy for the Daughters of Gentlemen. In fact, everything about it proved to be grey, from the pupils' uniforms, relieved only by a white collar, to the hair colour of the austere-looking headmistress, who made it clear that she ruled the school like a despot. After Irene had said farewell to her father, she was shown into a deserted dormitory with twenty beds and was allotted one of them. Left alone to unpack, she sat down on the bed and contemplated her future. Sofia had begged her to work hard and do well at her schoolwork, both of them knowing that she had slipped the leash of Mademoiselle's dull instruction far too often, and apart from an excellent and idiomatic command of French, she had achieved very little else. So she would work to recover lost ground academically, gain whatever she could intellectually from her new environs, and let no one divert her from her ultimate aim to be a jeweller. In the meantime, the one consolation of starting school in the middle of the autumn term meant that in a remarkably short time she would be home for Christmas.

In this hope she was doomed to disappointment. Her father wrote that she must stay at school throughout the vacation. He needed a change of air to complete his recovery from the influenza, and he was taking her stepmother with him to Monte Carlo for some winter sunshine. Irene, who had not known how to endure another day of homesickness, watched the other pupils depart on the last day of the term, the friends she had made among them. She thought no crueller misery could have been inflicted on her. But she would survive.

Two

Irene's schooldays came to an end when she was seventeen. Her education had been rounded off by a year at a pleasant, although equally strict school in Switzerland. Its purpose was to give the final touch of social polish deemed necessary for a girl to make a good marriage. Nobody had asked her what her views might be on the matter, for it was taken for granted that she would not wish for anything else in life. Only Sofia knew that she had more immediate plans.

With the advent of young womanhood, Irene's tight red curls had eased into a wavy luxuriance, their glowing colour in no way diminished. In the evening of her homecoming, she put her hair up officially for the first time, parting it in the middle and drawing it back in its waves into a high coil, rebellious tendrils left dancing on either side of her face and at the nape of her neck. Sofia, thoughtful as always, had guessed that she would like something new to wear in celebration. It was a Paris gown from Maison Rouff in shimmering, bud-green damask, with high-shouldered sleeves in the latest mode that stood out in enormous puffs. Irene had found the lovely garment laid across the bed in the large room that had been allotted her on the second floor, the nursery room on the floor above no longer her domain. This was evidence again of Sofia's kindness, establishing Irene's position as the adult daughter of the household, her childhood behind her.

The flounced hem of the damask and lace gown danced freely about Irene's feet as she went downstairs with time to spare before the arrival of the guests invited to dinner that evening. She thought it a mercy that the bustle had long since gone out of fashion, banished by Paris some years ago to reach the present silhouette of an hour-glass figure, which in her case, her waist being exceptionally small, happened to be her natural shape. The graceful flow of the skirt echoed the movement towards liberty that women were beginning to exert for themselves in the business world and in the field of sport, and one of the most comfortable garments that Irene had in her wardrobe was a pair of knickerbockers, fashionable because of the current craze for bicycling. In the drawing room she found her father on his own, a distinguished figure in his evening clothes, his white shirt front gleaming.

"So you are home again, Irene." He gave her one of his rare smiles and an even rarer kiss of greeting on her cheek.

"Yes, Father." It struck her that his suave expression was akin to the one she had labelled to herself in childhood as his "brandy and cigar" look, which had denoted satisfaction with a well-completed business deal over a luncheon or dinner in the dining room. She supposed that he was seeing her in a similar light, her whole appearance combined with her academic achievements mounting up to a good return for the large amounts of money he had invested in her education. Their relationship had certainly reached a more settled state, if not equanimity, in recent years. It was as if he had come to accept after a certain time and a number of excellent school reports that some danger point in her development was past. He had mellowed towards her in a way she would once have imagined impossible, only becoming tetchy and short-tempered if she and Sofia chatted too much or laughed together to his exclusion, but then he was the same with anyone else with whom he had to share more of his wife's time than he would have wished, his possessiveness unabated, his jealousy easily stirred.

"How does it feel to be grown-up at last?" he asked his daughter indulgently.

"Most agreeable," she replied lightheartedly, pleased to find him in so genial a mood. "As a matter of fact, I was hoping for the chance to discuss my future with you."

He glanced at the Sèvres clock on the mantel. "We have a little time in hand before the guests are due. Well? What did you have in mind? A foreign tour

47

with a chaperone? Some of your friends from the Swiss school will be doing that, I hear. Did you wish to go with them?"

She shook her head firmly. "I hope to travel widely later on in my life, but not now. I have too much to do."

"Oh?"

Drawing in a deep breath, she straigthened her shoulders. "I'm asking you formally to allow me to attend a school of arts and crafts."

He was taken aback. "I had no idea you had serious ideas about becoming an artist."

She corrected him. "An artist in a specialized sphere. For as long as I can remember, I've wanted to design and make jewellery." Tilting her head, she regarded him anxiously. "Surely you remember that I spoke to you about my ambition quite a long time ago? I even made a special appointment to see you at the office in order to emphasize its importance to me."

He answered her with a quickening of irritation, never liking to acknowledge that he had forgotten anything. "Now that I come to think of it, I believe you did." His sweeping gesture was dismissive. "However, I could not be expected to take seriously whatever was said to me then. Young schoolgirls are full of passing whims."

She frowned incredulously. It had never occurred to her that he had been inattentive when she had revealed her dreams to him, although it did come back to her now that his answers had been noncom-

mittal and his eyes had strayed to papers on his desk.
"I put it to you so clearly, Father. I explained how
much I wanted to be trained, and you did not refuse
me in any way."

He shrugged. "I suppose I took it that you had
been temporarily inspired by something you had
seen in the showroom. As I said before, I thought it
no more than an idle fancy. If you had been a son
coming to me instead of a daughter, it would have
been a different matter altogether."

"Why?" she demanded, hurt and indignant.

"It is perfectly simple," he replied with an air of
strained patience. "I should have arranged for a son
to train abroad, probably at the Staatsgewerbeschule
in Vienna where I spent some time, and afterwards he
would have come into the business with me. You
have no need to be a bread-winner, Irene. Your future
lies solely in being a good wife and mother."

A protesting cry broke from her. "I may never
marry."

"It does not please me to hear you say that!" he
snapped. In his eyes there was a certain glare that she
had not seen for a long time, a blend of bitter
animosity and a wary watchfulness that he had often
directed at her when she was younger. It chilled and
frightened her, reviving memories of the days when
she had seemed to displease him simply by her very
existence. Then a rustle of azure silk in the doorway
diverted his gaze as her stepmother appeared. Sofia,
ever sensitive to atmosphere, could tell at once that
her arrival was timely and hoped to dispel whatever

trouble was brewing, but Edmund continued to pursue his theme, his tone becoming crisp and sarcastic. "Did you hear what Irene said, my dear? She has adopted one of these new emancipated-female ideas of a career being preferable to the role for which nature intended womankind."

Irene spoke up forcefully. "I didn't make any comparisons. I simply pointed out that the possibility of a marriage should not be put up against my ambition to become a jeweller."

He rounded on her sharply. "The right women know how to wear precious adornments. Take your stepmother as a perfect example. But the intricacies of the craftsmanship involved are beyond female intelligence or comprehension. You would be out of your depth completely."

Irene stood her ground. "All I ask is the chance to find out whether or not those skills are inherent in me."

Sofia longed to speak up in support of her stepdaughter, but the proper moment was not yet. She could do more harm than good by speaking out of turn to Edmund. Without being conscious of it, she drew her lower lip in marginally under the edge of her pearly teeth, a habit developed over the years when holding back a retort or a personal opinion contrary to his views. The marriage, of which she had originally expected so much, had been hard on her and was getting harder. Her anxious blue gaze went from Edmund to his daughter and back again. So alike and yet so unalike.

"If it should be discovered," he replied to Irene on a derisive note, "that you have some ability in goldsmithery, what then? Do you imagine I would lower my position by allowing you to don an apron in my workshop? And I tell you that no jeweller of repute would employ an amateur."

"I would not be an amateur," she argued stoutly, "if I completed the full training at the School of Handicraft founded by the architect and silversmith Mr. Charles Robert Ashbee."

"But that place is an East End den of socialism and anarchy!" he expostulated.

Sofia grasped the opening for which she had been waiting. "No, no, Edmund. It is not at all as you imagine. Quite the reverse. It is a most industrious and respectable centre. The only revolutionary movement there is centred in Mr. Ashbee's wonderful idea that theoretical training in art and design should go hand in hand with practical work. Hence right from the start, the pupils work some of the time at the benches under the instruction of the Guildsmen, who are cabinet-makers, blacksmiths, silversmiths, enamellers, jewellers, carvers, and modellers, and so forth."

"How do you know so much about the place?" Edmund demanded.

"I have been twice to Essex House, the present home of the Guild in the Mile End Road. On my first visit it was still a male domain, but since Mr. Ashbee's recent marriage, a feminine influence is already making itself felt—hence Irene's wish to be one of the first women pupils to be admitted there. Mrs. Ashbee is a charming young woman, cultured and intellectual, who shares her husband's belief that craftsmen and -women who are given the chance to create marvellous work make the best citizens and thus, with time, a better world. No harm could come to Irene as a pupil under their guidance."

Edmund was staring at her incredulously. "You have visited this centre more than once? When? And why?"

"The first time was to view the goods made at the school that are for sale in the showroom there. That is where I bought the silver lamp with the amber globe for your study, the one that pleased you so much. The second occasion was with Irene today after I had met her off the boat-train at Victoria Station."

He had forgotten the lamp. It would not have been his personal choice, but Sofia had a flair for finding what was best in the latest styles, and his professional eye had not been able to fault it. As for her going there with his daughter today, that reason was plain enough. He turned grimly to Irene.

"I suppose this fellow Ashbee had agreed to see you by appointment?"

"Yes. He liked the designs and drawings that I sent him from Switzerland and wrote that he would see me. We talked for about half an hour, and then he said he would take me as a pupil. I'm so lucky to be accepted, Father. Apart from anything else, my whole background weighed against me."

He was astounded. "Why?"

"Mr. Ashbee usually draws his pupils from the lower working classes, opening up opportunities to excel that would otherwise never come their way. I suppose he thought me equally bound by the social structure on another level and was compassionate enough in the face of my enthusiasm and ambition to give me the same chance. So you see, Father, I must have your permission without delay while there is still a vacancy for me."

His expression, which had been one of intense displeasure the whole time, deepened into a mask of total animosity to all that had been said. Her stomach lurched sickeningly. Wild schemes flew through her head as to how she might take the place offered her without his consent but were balked by the knowledge that until she was twenty-one there was not a move she could make unless he condoned it. He must agree to letting her become an Ashbee pupil. He must! But he was about to turn down her request. She could see the words coming. Almost of their own volition, her hands rose flutteringly in preparation to clap them over her ears, as if by refusing to hear what he said she could keep his decision at bay. In her agitation she did not hear carriage wheels drawing to a halt outside in the square.

"Our guests are arriving, Edmund!" Sofia, spurred by the same dread that his refusal would be given beyond recall, caught at his arm with haste and in an uncharacteristic flurry. "This matter concerning Irene can be talked about again tomorrow. Let us take our places near the drawing-room door. Irene, you stand by me. Everyone will want to have a word with you, particularly those whom you know and who have not seen you for a long time."

Irene, feeling shaky and upset, moved forward obediently. She had been granted a reprieve, but only just, and there was nothing to indicate that her father would be any better disposed towards her request by the morrow. Why, oh, why was life made so difficult for the young by the middle-aged? Only dear Sofia had managed to keep a girlish heart within her mature and still beautiful frame.

As if to bring home the isolation of youth still further to Irene, there was no one present that evening who was anywhere near her age. The dinner party had been arranged before the time of her arrival home from Switzerland had been confirmed, and the gathering was a cross-section of her father's and stepmother's friends and acquaintances. If she had been less wrapped up in her own anxieties while trying to appear smiling and at ease with those plying her with questions about her school year abroad, she might have taken more notice of the guest who was a stranger to all but Edmund. His name was Gregory Burnett.

Sofia noticed him and everything about him. Needing an extra man to make up the numbers, she had suggested to her husband that his new business and club acquaintance be invited. Edmund had welcomed the idea. The agreeable newcomer had recently inherited the family business in Hatton

Garden, London's diamond centre, and Edmund was hoping to carry through many a good gem deal with him in the years ahead. When a written acceptance of the invitation had been received, Sofia had given the man no more thought until suddenly he was standing before her, being introduced by Edmund. There flashed through her mind all she had heard about him. He was married but estranged from his actress wife. A man of driving energy and ambition, he was rich and successful and well-respected in gem-dealing circles. He was ten years younger than she. He was more closely associated with Fabergé than any other dealer in stones, was a personal friend of Louis Comfort Tiffany, and had had a splendid new London house built and furnished throughout by Voysey. He also had a deep and pleasing timbre to his voice, which she, with her particular appreciation of good diction, noted to the full in the first words that he spoke to her.

"How do you do, Mrs. Lindsay? It was most kind of you and your husband to invite me this evening. I am honoured to make your acquaintance."

Although she was tall, he was much taller. Like most women of above average height, she did not take looking up at a man for granted, and in his case she experienced a pleasurable reaction to his magnetic, intensely physical presence. He had a face not easily forgotten, attractive but by no means handsome, square and aggressively chinned, weathered by worldly experience and a certain amount of self-indulgence, with a strong nose and a big, well-shaped mouth. His hair was black and curling, his brows thick, and his dark brown eyes were alert and intelligent, humour and cynicism in the lines at the outer corners. He wore his evening clothes with an air of distinction, as doubtless he did all else in his wardrobe, having the kind of broad shoulders that set off expensive tailoring; and his stiff, white shirt front sported diamond studs that would not have been out of place in royal regalia. She could tell that he had observed her as closely and knew it was one of those meetings, brief, conventional, governed by circumstances, that dazzle for a moment or two and can come to all or nothing in the process of time. It flew through her mind that she had not seated him near her at the table, and she thought it was as well.

When the dinner was over, the cloth drawn, and the gentlemen left on their own to the port and cigars, Edmund was filled with a sense of well-being, knowing that once again under Sofia's able direction the evening was proving to be a thoroughly successful one. Drawn into conversation on one side of the table for a while, he turned a little later to the other in time to hear that a silver exhibition was being discussed. He was reminded with a stir of irritation of his talk with his daughter earlier.

"Do any of you gentlemen hold an opinion of this Ashbee fellow's Guild at Mile End?" he inquired smugly, ready to have his own ideas about it endorsed.

Gregory, who had been engaged in the discussion, twisted around in his chair to answer without the least hesitation. "I class the work produced there most highly. In fact, I would rate Ashbee as the best silversmith and designer in this country today. Why do you ask?"

Edmund was somewhat taken aback. This reaction was not what he had expected. "It so happens that my daughter has expressed a wish to become one of Ashbee's pupils in jewellery."

Gregory recalled the girl to whom he had been introduced. Magnificent hair setting off a lovely little face with large, brilliant eyes and an alabaster complexion. "Has she any artistic ability?" he queried, refilling his glass from the port decanter, which had just reached him again.

"Yes, she has, according to her teachers both here and abroad. She wishes to develop her talents in design and goldsmithery to earn her own livelihood as a jeweller. Apart from the fact that I disapprove entirely of well-brought-up young women hankering after careers, I have reservations about the Guild and the School of Handicraft on the basis of its politics."

"Dismiss your fears as being of no account," Gregory advised firmly, already giving his support to the ambitious girl with a mind of her own. "Ashbee is simply making an idealistic stand that is really part and parcel of the aesthetic movement. He has recruited a cross-section of society to his workbenches and his lecture rooms, and I admire him for it. In return he asks for the best that his Guildsmen and pupils can produce. Anything less and they must go. Ashbee may have suffered a crisis of conscience in earlier life about his own rich and comfortable circumstances, but he is not in the least sentimental about the laggards of this world."

"You know him personally?"

"He was at Wellington College when I went there. Later I met him when I was up at Cambridge." Gregory was inwardly amused to see that his host was duly impressed. Without doubt Ashbee had gone up in Lindsay's estimation. Gregory pressed the advantage home. "I am sure that you want the best tuition for your daughter, and at the School of Handicraft she would receive a solid foundation in draughtsmanship and design."

He meant what he said. Too many art schools were hidebound in their rigorous training but not Ashbee's Centre. Any lively talent that the girl possessed would not be stifled there. Moreover, it pleased him to give her a helping hand anonymously towards her goal. He wished he could have done something similar for Edmund's wife, a beautiful woman with sadness in the depths of her eyes. She looked in need of love and comfort, which he would have given her bountifully if the opportunity had ever come his way.

"I have to argue the point that I see training a daughter to be all to no purpose," Edmund persisted stolidly, still not wholly convinced. "In short, a waste of time and money."

"How can you be sure of that?" Gregory countered smoothly, thinking his host a stubborn bore. "The last time I visited Fabergé's Moscow workshop there was a woman enameller at work on one of the latest Easter eggs for the Czar."

"My dear sir!" Edmund exclaimed in protest, jerking his spine away from the back of his chair. "I would not see *my* daughter in a place of common toil."

Gregory metaphorically took a last trick from his sleeve. "Then let her study with Ashbee in order to make pretty trinkets for herself. That sort of feminine enterprise is much admired these days. Nobody could point a finger at you for allowing her to do that."

Edmund saw his dilemma solved. He was no fool, and realized well enough that it was better for Irene to be industriously engaged in what was to all intents and purposes a ladylike hobby instead of idling her time away in resentment. That state of affairs could lead to trouble of the worst kind. He gave a cautious nod.

"I shall take a look at this school tomorrow, Mr. Burnett. I thank you for your advice."

"Glad to have been of service, sir."

Gregory kept his grin to himself. He found it gratifying that he and the red-haired girl had won the day. Although his present background was upper middle class, his lineage was too diverse and varied for him to have any patience with petty snobbishness. If handed-down family tales were to be believed, he could trace his origins back through the family trade of pawnbroking and gem dealing to the Lombards, who were said to be the first pawnbrokers,

having come from the Medici estates in Italy
centuries ago to settle in England and lend money on
land and property to English nobles with wars to
fight. It was no wonder that the chief centre of
banking interests in London was located in Lombard
Street. One of his earliest memories was of being
taken to see the sign of three gold balls suspended
above the entrance to an old pawnshop about to be
demolished, the very one in which his forbears had
lent money on goods in the plying of their ancient
trade. It was generally accepted that the three gold
balls represented the three blue discs of the Medici
arms, and Gregory saw no reason to doubt it. His
own looks and colouring, quite apart from his quick
and passionate nature, suggested a resurgence of
long-dormant Italian blood, and in the right robes he
could have passed for a Lombard of the fifteenth
century.

He might have been born a pawnbroker himself if
his great-grandfather had not prospered through
dealing in gems as a sideline, eventually concentrating on diamonds. As a result his grandfather had
received a good education and moved up in the
world, later selling off the pawnshops, which by then
had numbered over a dozen, and moving the
diamond business into the Hatton Garden premises
where the Burnetts had flourished ever since. Gregory
himself had been brought up in a knowledge of
precious stones and had travelled extensively to all
parts of the world where specialized buying and
selling took place.

He had chosen to base himself at the Amsterdam office after the collapse of his marriage. His father would have preferred him to remain in London, but he had wanted to get away, at least for a time, never supposing that when he did return, it would be to that good man's funeral and to take on, far sooner than he had expected, the total responsibility for the business that he had always known would be his one day.

The rest of the evening passed pleasantly. He waited for a chance to talk alone with the warmly feminine Sofia and was lucky enough to get her to himself on a drawing-room window seat just out of earshot of the rest of the company gathered there. He had taken note earlier how she glanced far too often in her husband's direction as if compelled to it by habit, and there was a tautness about her that suggested her nerves were coiled tight and in need of emotional release. Without doubt Edmund Lindsay must be the worst kind of domestic tyrant to drive his wife and daughter to a stage where both were desperate to escape, although where Irene was beating at the bars, her stepmother had withdrawn into herself and become subdued and intriguingly elusive. Gregory marked it up as a point to himself that throughout his conversation alone with Sofia she did not once take her sapphire gaze from him, and he made her smile and even laugh several times.

He did not speak on his own with Irene until he was in the hall with other departing guests while thanks were being expressed and good nights said. "I wish you good luck with your future, Miss Lindsay. If ever I may be of any help to you, be sure and let me know. Now I bid you good night."

Irene stared after him. She was able to conclude only that he had had some word of her ambition from Sofia. At the last second before he went down the porch steps to his waiting carriage, he looked back over his shoulder at her. Her eyes were still wide with surprise at what he had said, and his own became suddenly intent. All the brightness of the hall and the drawing room beyond seemed caught up like gold in her fiery hair, and momentarily he was held spellbound by her. Strangely, her silhouetted image remained on the retinas of his eyes, so that when he closed them in the darkness as he was driven away, her form danced against his lids in reversed colour.

In the house Edmund poured himself a final nightcap before following his wife up to bed. Mentally he struck Gregory Burnett off their visiting list. He had observed jealously the attention that Gregory had paid Sofia, who had seemed to revel in it, appearing to forget completely that she had a husband as well as far more important guests in the room. He had never seen her behave so foolishly before, not that anything indiscreet or amiss took place, but it had been galling to see her pandering to the rascal. He would not mention his displeasure to her, for it would upset her to know she had angered him and, his jealousy having put him in a high state of desire for her, he wanted to waste no time in placating any tears of remorse on her part. She cried too easily at a sharp reprimand these days, which irritated him, for she was as dear to him as on the day he had married her. If she was less responsive to his love-making than she had been in the past, he did not let it worry him, for she never refused him and was as dutiful in bed as in all other wifely spheres. Unlike most of his contemporaries, he never felt the slightest need for dalliance on the side, no other woman having her appeal for him. He thought her fortunate to be so cherished in faithfulness after eight years of marriage, and for her sake he would remove completely any further chance of annoyance by Gregory Burnett. Any return invitation would be refused, and in the future he would wine and dine the fellow at his club when the obligation arose. Gregory Burnett would never cross his threshold again. Edmund prided himself on never retracting a decision.

Neither did he dismiss advice that might prove to be to his advantage, no matter from whom it had come. In the morning he rode out to Mile End, a part of the city that he did not normally frequent. From the upholstered comfort of his brougham, he looked out disdainfully at the streets full of market stalls, the gaudy façades of music halls and other places of questionable entertainment, the innumerable pubs doing a roaring trade, the barrows selling whelks and eels, the dirt and the squalor. As if that were not enough, his ears were assailed by the din of barrel organs, the bawling of vendors, and the barking of half-starved curs. Life thronged throughout White-chapel, and none of it was to his taste.

Therefore it came as a tremendous surprise when the brougham drew up outside Essex House. Instead of the mean building he had expected, he beheld an eighteenth-century mansion of grand proportions with graceful windows and an imposing entrance. Moreover, it stood in a sizeable garden in which blossomed such a profusion of white pinks that as he alighted from the brougham, the fragrance in the summer's air banished the more pungent aromas of the area and fostered the illusion of being in the country instead of the heart of the city's East End.

In the hall of Essex House, he signed the visitors' book, found his wife's name on a previous page, and was much impressed by the number of distinguished signatures entered there. Ashbee's enterprise appeared to have aroused considerable interest in the right quarters. As he put the pen back in the inkstand, a neatly dressed young woman in a craftsman's apron appeared. Obligingly she directed him to the nearest workshop.

Nobody questioned his presence. He strolled imperiously through the building, viewing all that was in progress from the leatherwork and bookbinding to cabinetmaking and carving. He finally located Ashbee, a dark-eyed, poetic-looking man with a moustache and goatee beard, at a bench in the silver workshop, having already passed him twice in the belief that he was a pupil. Edmund was greatly impressed by the brooch in silver that Ashbee was making. It was the size of a small plate, and its theme was based on the designer's own name with a spreading ash tree encircling a bee with its branches. The two men fell into knowledgeable conversation, Edmund more than prepared to commission some pieces if he could clear his mind on one particular point, which was also linked to whether or not he allowed his daughter to take a place at Essex House.

"So far I have seen nothing morally questionable in the designs being carried out here," he said approvingly, "and I want to know if it is your policy to veer away from what I consider to be an outflowing of degenerate eroticism in much of the new art being produced today."

Ashbee untied his leather apron from himself and folded it carefully across his workbench to preserve whatever might have fallen into it from his silverwork. "You are referring to the darker shades of a creature calling itself *L'Art Nouveau*," he replied, wiping his hands on a grimy cloth before moving away at Edmund's side. "It has a pure form, innocent as light, but it can be black as Hades on its counterside, hence the inference of opium in its popular use of poppies in design and its unashamed declarations of sexual excesses in its symbolic cavortings of twisted roots and gaping caverns. I will have no part of it. My Guildsmen follow the independent path that I have set, aiming through teamwork to achieve the highest feats of fine craftsmanship in a harmony of life."

Everything certainly seemed thoroughly above-board and wholesome in Edmund's judgement. He was too worldly a man to imagine that such idealistic aims could survive the vagaries of human nature for any great length of time, but he respected Ashbee for what he was trying to do. In the meantime it was far better for Irene to train in this environment than for her to hobnob with wild students at a more conventional establishment of arts and crafts. Before leaving Essex House, he enrolled his daughter there. He felt he was being noble and lenient in agreeing to her being trained at all, and he conveyed this opinion of himself to Irene when he announced what he had done.

"I can't thank you enough, Father!" She was astounded by this wonderful turn of events and grateful for it.

"One word of warning, Irene. If at any time I should see fit through reasonable cause to terminate your training, it would be done immediately. Do you understand?"

She understood and was unafraid. Nothing should prevent her getting the qualifications that would make her a Guildsman of Mr. Ashbee's school.

It was an important day beyond all days for her when she started her attendance. She was absorbed at once into a routine as utterly different as it could be from anything she had known before. With so many Guildsmen drawn from the heart of the East End, it was natural that the quick Cockney wit should prevail, surprising her to mirth within the first few

minutes and taking away the strangeness of everything. She also sensed the good comradeship encouraged by Ashbee, essential to working well
together, and in the case of the East Enders it
stemmed naturally from the neighbourliness of those
used to living closely for generations in slum terraces
and tenement alleyways. At the end of the working
day, which was longer than it would have been in a
conventional college, she went home tired and
happy.

There was a slight contretemps that same evening
with her father when he discovered that she had
travelled by horse-bus instead of being driven in one
of the carriages, but she explained that she wanted to
blend into her new life without the conspicuous
trappings of a rich man's daughter. Her suggestion
that she take weekly lodgings with a respectable
couple in the school's neighbourhood, thus avoiding
any daily travelling, met with such a vehement
refusal that Irene held her breath, fearing for the
moment that she had jeopardized her whole future.
Fortunately the danger passed over, leaving her with
the knowledge that she must never risk bringing up
that subject again. Eventually a compromise was
reached over her travelling. She would bicycle in
good weather, but not in knickerbockers, which did
not meet with Edmund's approval as feminine wear.
On wet mornings she was to be transported in one of
the family carriages and take a cab home at night. She
might be allowed to travel by bus only in an
emergency or any exceptional circumstances.

With the matter duly settled, one pleasing aspect began to emerge that Irene had not realized before. The time taken up on her journey to and from the school could not be judged accurately due to the congestion of traffic, which sometimes snarled up a whole street in a solid block of vehicles and horses; in addition, her hours of training fluctuated considerably according to whatever work was in hand and whether there were lectures to attend in the evenings. She soon found herself with some leeway at the end of each day that could be spent exactly as she pleased with no one to question those short spells of liberty. Before long, she and some of the younger trainees would congregate in the old kitchen in the basement of Essex House when the day was done. There they would sit around one of the long, wooden tables with one pot of tea among them, thinning it out with hot water to make it last, and would discuss all manner of topics of the day. A favourite argument was whether or not Ashbee's work was entirely free of the influence of Art Nouveau, consequently their own work as well. Many held that he and they were as deeply embroiled as most other artists of the day, and those in opposition made up in vehemence for what they sometimes lacked in numbers. At first Irene, very much a beginner, had to listen more than contribute to the subject, but after a while she became as excitedly verbal as everyone else in voicing her opinions in lively debate and discussion.

In her training she worked hard and diligently, receiving the best of tuition in design, goldsmithery, and enamelling; and when she was piercing out a setting, soldering collets, or making hinges and catches for a pin, which was far from easy, she could feel her own deep-rooted talent thrusting forth towards the still far distant time of fruition. If she had had the inclination, she could have had romantic involvements as well, but she was determined to steer a clear path, letting nothing distract her from her goal. As for her father, he never showed the slightest interest in any completed work she brought home; neither did he seem to care how she was progressing. His attitude was one of bored indulgence, as if he were simply waiting for her enthusiasm for what she was doing to fizzle out like a damp squib. Sofia, on the other hand, continued to encourage her at all times.

After a suitable interval, an invitation to dinner did come from Gregory Burnett. It arrived with the afternoon post. Sofia mentioned it to Edmund when he came home from the shop.

"Decline it," he said brusquely. "We have a previous engagement."

She looked at him in bewilderment. "But we are free that evening, Edmund. I thought you wished to further this acquaintanceship."

"Not on a social level. I have changed my mind about the fellow. And remember, if ever he should call, we are not at home."

Sofia did as he bade her, sitting down at her bureau to pen the conventional excuse. She supposed Edmund had taken offence at some real or imaginary slight, which was far from an uncommon occurrence, but her disappointment was acute. Wisdom told her that fate was being kind, gently turning her aside from possible temptation, and that she should be thankful. But she had seen a rare tenderness in Gregory's eyes, and the memory of it had lingered with her. As she sealed the envelope, she knew she was closing a door on what might have been, and all that was bright and shining and loving within her shrivelled a little more.

As the weeks went by, Irene realized that her irregular comings and goings at home were being taken for granted without comment. The entire household had become wholly accustomed to her early departures in the morning, which were always before her father left the house, she having much farther to travel, and sometimes, when she wanted to put in some extra work on a project, she was gone from the house before he came down to breakfast. In the evening, unless he and her stepmother were dining in or entertaining at home, she did not see them except if she was still awake when Sofia looked into her room like a guardian angel to whisper good night before retiring. She had no lack of social engagements herself; some she enjoyed and some she did not; mostly she tried to keep her acceptances to events at the close of the week, not liking to cut a day's studies short in order to get home in time to bath, titivate, and swirl out of the house in silk or tulle to present a smile at a festive gathering, her thoughts still held by her workbench and her drawing board. The fact that she was always chaperoned on these social occasions seemed ludicrous to her. Nobody seemed to realize that she was frequently alone with men at the school during the day and knew exactly how to ward off advances potentially more demanding than anything a young gentleman would attempt in a ballroom, a conservatory, or under Chinese lanterns on a terrace. Several would-be suitors called on her father for permission to court her. She wanted none of them and made it plain enough, but most of them seemed to become keener when rebuffed, which she found exasperating. Moreover, they were the unwitting cause of outbreaks of trouble between her and her father. He found it just as exasperating that she would not consider any one of these highly suitable applicants as a prospective husband. At times, facing his hostility over the matter, she trembled with fright that he would decide on a moment's ugly turn of mind to bar her from further studies at Essex House and confine her to the boredom of domestic routine in his house until she sought escape by marrying to get a home of her own. Never!

Irene had been at the School of Handicraft for six months when Sofia celebrated a special birthday. The latest fashion was one that had been set by the Princess of Wales of a collar of pearls about the throat, and Edmund gave his wife a five-strand one of rare pearls in a deep cream colour. She wore it that same evening when they went to the opera at Covent Garden with some close friends and to a supper of celebration at Romano's afterwards. It was during the performance, not long after the curtain had gone up on *Don Giovanni*, that he made one of his proprietary glances at Sofia, who was at the front of the box with the two other wives in the party. Normally he felt nothing but pride in her appearance, but suddenly he saw that she was wearing an item of adornment that he had not noticed earlier, a ring on the little finger of her right hand. He felt his blood freeze at its tawdriness in contrast to her magnificent pearls. In the glow from the stage, he could see clearly that it was of poor-quality silver, its stone an agate of sorts that might have been picked up by a shell vendor on the seashore and sold for a few pence. How dare she jeopardize his reputation by wearing such trash!

When the curtain came down for the interval, Sofia's first move was to glance towards him as he knew she would since it was what he expected of her. Under the cover of the talk being exchanged, he gave her one of those hooded looks of furious displeasure that marriage partners can convey so succinctly like secret telegraphed messages of voluble length. Only he saw the flicker of dismayed bewilderment before she lowered her lashes, turning her head with her serene smile unchanged to reply to some comment addressed to her. There was nothing in her expression to show anyone else that she had registered his wrath and was distressed by it.

The opportunity to give full vent to his pent-up fury did not come until they were alone together on the drive home. "Where in heaven's name did you get that fairground bauble on your finger?" he demanded wrathfully.

She gave a little sigh of comprehension, putting her left hand protectively over her right as if she feared he might snatch the ring by force from her finger. "So *that* is the trouble. I was not sure at first what it might be. I think the ring is a lovely one. Irene made it for me, and I am proud to wear it."

"Are you insane?" he shouted. "She is not a child any longer for you to dress up in a paper tiara or a tinsel bracelet to please her! She is a grown young woman fooling her time away at my expense on a madcap scheme that I permitted against my better judgement only in the belief that sooner or later she would tire of the venture. How do you imagine I felt this evening to see my gift to you degraded by a worthless gewgaw?"

"I admit it was somewhat out of place," she conceded quietly, "but I ask you to remember that I reached my fortieth birthday today. Somehow I needed the reassurance of wearing the gifts I received from the two people who love me the most. Your pearls and my stepdaughter's ring."

He was silenced. It had not occurred to him that Sofia should have found crossing the threshold into a new decade of age so disturbing. Not for the first time, he wondered how well he really knew her.

A similar thought was running through her head.

How could he have been so insensitive as not to comprehend what it meant for her to face up to the final and irrevocable loss of all hope of childbearing? Was marriage always a union of bodies and never of minds? How was it possible for two people to share everything of themselves while still remaining total strangers to each other? She still did not know the cause of the grudge he harboured against his own daughter, which always lay just below the surface and glinted with a bitter light from time to time. Her frayed feelings for Edmund had survived only through her realization that he had a great emotional need of her, which enabled her to forgive and forgive and forgive yet again his many petty tyrannies and ungovernable displays of temper. It was her fear that one day she would reach a point when she had no more forgiveness left in her. She shivered in her solitary thoughts, gazing unseeingly out of the brougham window at the passing lamplit streets. Never had she felt more alone or more bereft in her womb.

A little later, when they were getting ready for bed, Edmund came from his dressing room, a Chinese silk robe over his nightshirt, and asked her to show him Irene's ring. She was seated at her dressing table, brushing her long flow of hair, her silver-backed brush catching the light. At his request she paused in the graceful rhythm of her action, and with a wafting of swansdown sleeve she reached out to take the ring from her jewel case and hand it to him. He had fetched a jeweller's glass from the pocket of a daytime coat, and he went to the nearest lamp to examine his daughter's handiwork through its magnifying lens. A year previously he had installed electric lighting in both his home and his business premises, and he was able to get the best possible view of the little ring.

The agate had a setting of tiny silver leaves winding out of a stem that made up the hoop of the ring. The workmanship was by no means perfect; a host of amateurish faults was apparent to his experienced eye, but the effect was charming, the presentation original. Thoughtfully he returned the ring to Sofia, who put it away again.

"Is the design Irene's own?" he asked.

"Yes, of course."

He took a meditative pace or two. "Hmmm. She should be working with better stones. Particularly," he added tartly, "if you are to wear the results."

She appeared to concentrate on the brushing of her hair, not entirely sure which way the conversation was going to swing. If he was angry again, she was afraid that in her present raw state of nerves her self-control might snap, and she had no wish to answer him back. It would only make matters worse and would solve nothing. "Irene has to make do with whatever she can find on market stalls, in second-hand shops, or in the occasional pawnshop sales of unredeemed goods."

"Good God! Why?"

"Because that is all she can afford. You make her an allowance, and she is determined to keep to it with no financial assistance from me."

75

He continued to pace up and down. "Why has she not asked me for some stones?"

"How could she?" Sofia was amazed that he should even consider the possibility. "You have made it increasingly clear that she is receiving her training on sufferance and that your interest in her work is nonexistent. She is your daughter, Edmund. She has too much Lindsay pride to ask favours and is content to make beautiful pieces out of very little. To my mind it is all to her credit and makes a far greater achievement out of every success."

Edmund grunted, although he made no further comment. He took off his robe and got into bed. Sofia supposed the subject to be closed, at least for a while, but she was mistaken. The next morning at breakfast he lowered his copy of *The Times* to address his daughter across the table just as she was getting up to leave.

"I do not know if it is of any interest to you, but since my head goldsmith, Lucas, left to work in Paris, his replacement, Richardson, has been acting like the proverbial new broom, and a few boxes of half-forgotten stock have come to light. There are some opals that you might be able to use and a range of semiprecious stones that have been generally looked over and discarded as being of no use to us. If you need gold or silver, there are some broken clasps, pieces of watch chain and so forth, that can be put aside and melted down for you."

Irene could scarcely believe her good fortune and expressed her thanks. Sofia, pouring the coffee, wished she could believe that he had acted out of the goodness of his heart, but she knew his concern was totally for himself. He would not risk it being whispered about that the renowned Edmund Lindsay, court jeweller and prominent member of the Goldsmiths' Guild, allowed his daughter to scrabble for stones in the unsavoury nooks and corners of the city.

"When may I visit the shop to see what is available?" Irene asked him.

"Why not come today after you have finished your studies? I have an appointment and shall not be there, but I will leave word that you are coming. Take no more than a stone or two at a time, or whatever you happen to need for immediate use the next day. I should not want the temptation to steal put in anyone's way at the School of Handicraft."

"Poverty and dishonesty do not necessarily go hand in hand, Father," she pointed out forcibly, always defensive towards those with whom she worked. "I have heard you say many times that some of the thieves caught red-handed in your showroom could have afforded what they filched ten times over."

"Yes," he agreed, his face tightening as it always did when she spoke up against him, "and some ne'er-do-wells turn to stealing jewellery in order to maintain a standard of living they can no longer afford. I despise both types, but not the honest man faced with easy gain when he has a wife to feed and children without shoes. I should consider it my moral duty to protect him from possible downfall. Do as I tell you. Take the stones only as you need them."

Sofia, seeing that Irene was about to take up cudgels verbally against a society that allowed people to go hungry and barefoot, managed to spill some coffee to create a diversion. In the resulting pandemonium, with the mopping up and Edmund withdrawing hastily from the table to avoid getting his newspaper saturated, there was no more conversation on the subject. Sofia sighed with relief that the danger had been averted. Irene never seemed to realize how close she was sailing to the wind when in conflict with her father. If he suspected she was garnering socialistic views at the School of Handicraft, he would have no compunction in snatching her away from it.

After both father and daughter had left the house for their respective destinations, Sofia remained at the breakfast table, her elbows resting on the wooden arms of her chair, her fingertips pressing at the throbbing temples of her bowed head. She felt as if she were struggling physically to keep a darkness of the spirit at bay. More and more the daily tension of life with Edmund was taking its toll on her.

It was with great effort that she finally rose up and with straightened shoulders went to make ready for the first appointment of her busy day.

Three

That same evening Irene arrived at her father's shop to find the showroom still busy with customers. Her old friend, Mr. Taylor, not far from retirement, broke away briefly to tell her that since the hour was so late, all the goldsmiths had gone home, with the exception of one on duty for emergency repairs.

"His name is Ryde. Derek Ryde. He is new since you were here last. He will show you the stones you are to see."

There was no sign of the goldsmith in the main workshop, which was in darkness, but one of the adjoining rooms was fully illuminated, throwing a rectangle of light across the deserted workbenches and the silent tools of trade. She went across to it, her shadow falling behind her as she came to a standstill on the threshold and, unnoticed, observed the man within. Her approach had not been heard due to his intense concentration, which was not directed at some piece of work, but at the horse-racing results in an evening newspaper. With his chair tilted back precariously to accommodate his feet on the work-bench was a young man with a leonine mass of straw-coloured hair, a frown of concentration on his bony face. Engrossed in his studies, he was ticking off selectively in pencil any horse's name that was of some significance to him down the length of a column. Irene, her mouth twitching with amuse-ment at his preoccupation with the rise and fall of his fortunes that day, loosened the long scarf from about her neck in the warmth of indoors after the chill of her drive. Leisurely she leaned a shoulder against the door-jamb.

"Good evening, Mr. Ryde."

He gave such a start that for a second or two she feared he would go crashing backwards on the teetering chair legs. Fortunately he regained his balance in the nick of time, bringing his feet thumping to the floor while the newspaper and pencil flew from his grasp, pages scattering every-where. She clapped a hand to her mouth in a vain attempt to restrain her burst of laughter.

He was not affronted by her honest mirth, although his grey eyes were hard and steely in the first throes of surprise. Rising to his feet, he allowed himself to be infected by her amusement, his mobile lips widening in a smile that indented his cheeks and gave an engaging quality to his clean-shaven looks, which were neither handsome nor ugly, the nose and nostrils thin, the jaw reckless and more than a little pugnacious. An interesting, curiously appealing man to whom she warmed immediately because of his tolerant acceptance of her amusement.

Quickly she introduced herself. "I'm Irene Lindsay."

"So I guessed," he replied amiably. "You almost stopped my heart with shock for a moment or two, speaking to me out of the blue."

But for another reason too, he added to himself. In her green tam-o'-shanter, her scarf draped casually over one shoulder, and her red hair aswirl, she looked for all the world as if she had stepped out of an Alfons Mucha poster, the epitome of the Art Nouveau woman, all grace and beauty with an alluring sensuality that almost gave off its own erotic bouquet. He felt drunk with the impact she had made by bursting so unexpectedly upon his senses. And she had a rosy mouth that had been made for kissing.

"I'm sorry I startled you," she said not too apologetically, her eyes still dancing. "I was told you were expecting me."

"I had begun to think you weren't coming." He stooped to retrieve the fallen pencil and gather the newspaper pages roughly together before dumping them in a wastepaper basket.

"I was delayed," she answered, looking about her at the room and remembering when she had seen the Indian pendant being made on the bench there. "I never know from day to day at the School of Handicraft when I shall get away. The only blessing is that nobody at home worries about me, which would happen if I was at a more conventional place of training with a timetable that ended on the stroke of four o'clock."

"Before I get the gems out for you, would you like a cup of tea?" he inquired, determined to prolong her visit for as long as possible.

She gave a brisk nod. "Yes, please. That would be nice."

He went to where the kettle was kept, filled it from a tap, and set it on a gas ring. When he returned with two enamel mugs of steaming tea, she had removed her outdoor clothes, hung them on a peg, and was studying some designs pinned to the wall, her arms folded, her hip swinging her weight onto one leg, and her head tilted critically.

"Are these designs yours?" she asked, glancing over her shoulder at him.

He grimaced his dislike of them blatantly. "No, I'm thankful to say. The name of the new goldsmith-designer is Dudley Richardson, which happens to give him the same initials as mine." He ladled sugar into both mugs, stirred them, and handed one to her. "I have to admit that I'm not a designer, but I'm a craftsman able to judge good design."

She liked his frankness. "That sounds as if your taste runs along different lines to those chosen by this establishment."

There was devilment in his calculating gaze. "How freely may I speak out to my employer's daughter?"

"As freely as you like. I'm not a traditionalist myself."

"Thank God for that! I thought you couldn't be when I heard you were training at Ashbee's place." He pushed forward the chair for her that he had almost tilted over previously and perched on a high stool himself. "Not that his work is deep enough into avantgardism for my true appreciation. I like to see work with all bonds released. The late, lamented Beardsley did it with a pen. Tiffany is doing it with flowing, graceful lines in glass, often in a purely abstract composition. Jewellery by Gautrait and Vever and Fourquet is vibrating and alive. I sometimes feel I'm stagnating in this workshop with nothing new or exciting being created by these hands." He spread wide his young, strong hands with the long, tapering fingers. Then abruptly he dropped them to his knees, leaning forward with elbows bent to stare into her face. "I should like to see some of your work. Will you let me see it?"

She experienced a little quiver of excitement as his assumption seemed to imply this was by no means the last time they would meet. "Yes. I'd value your opinion."

"Don't expect me to be a kind critic," he warned wickedly, testing her.

She was amused. "I wouldn't show it to you if I thought you were."

He grinned his approval, holding up his mug of tea in a toast to her before taking a gulp from it. "Tell me what it's like to train at the School of Handi-craft," he said with a keen interest, setting the mug down again.

She was holding her mug of tea between her cupped hands, and she sipped it before telling him all he wanted to know. He had made the tea as sweet as syrup, not at all as she usually had it, but somehow it was all part of this amazing interlude, which was proving to be quite different from anything she had expected from her visit. He fired questions at her, animated and eager, although quick to scoff at anything that differed from his ideas of how things should be. It added to the excitement that he had already stimulated, for much of what he expressed echoed her own thoughts on total freedom in design. She had sometimes felt held back by Ashbee's adherence to his own particular line in his tuition, master and perhaps genius that he might be.

"I've done most of the talking," she said at last. "Now I want to ask you a question. How and where did you become a goldsmith?" She wanted to know everything about him. Everything.

"I served an apprenticeship in Manchester, where I was born. A Lancashire lad, that's me," he declared jauntily. "I was lucky not to go down a pit or into a mill when I left school, but my widowed mother had worked as a maid in a millowner's house before her marriage, and he left her a little nest egg when he died. It was enough for her to get me settled into a good training and for her to live in modest comfort for the rest of her days." He held back his private belief that it was the millowner who had fathered him, and not the man whose surname he bore. "When I had been accepted into the Goldsmiths' Guild, I worked for a time in Chester and then in Cheltenham—working my way south, you might say. When I came to London, I thought my credentials would get me into Garrard's or Cartier's, but I had to settle for Lindsay's of Old Bond Street."

His voice was spiked with mockery, his eyes watching her to see how she would react to his rating her father's business lower than the others. She retaliated in the same vein, knowing that he was only baiting her for the fun of it. "How fortunate for my father that you are here to lift his reputation to the highest rank."

He liked her retort and was well pleased with her. "I'll do that. Don't think I can't. A goldsmith of my calibre doesn't come to London every day." Pushing aside his half-emptied mug of tea on the workbench, he leaned an arm on it, looking intently at her. "Why haven't we met before?"

She let her shoulders rise and fall casually. "I don't come to the shop these days. I'm too busy. This is the first time for a long while. I used to call in with my stepmother in the past, but her visits are rare now."

"I've never seen her, but I've heard she is fine-looking. Is that true?"

"Yes, indeed. She is also the kindest person I've ever known."

At that moment Mr. Taylor came into the main workshop and appeared in their doorway. "So, Miss Irene," he said with a smile, raising his bushy white brows enquiringly, "what stones have you selected for your next project at Essex House?''

She gasped with consternation. "Goodness! I'd forgotten all about the stones. I haven't looked at them yet. Are you locking up?''

He sighed inwardly, tired and more than ready to go home. How thoughtless was youth with all its energy and self-absorption. "I have secured the front grilles, and the other assistants have gone." Taking out his pocket watch, he glanced at it. "You may have another ten minutes while I continue locking up. Then we must vacate the premises before the police start thinking that a burglary is going on here at the back of the shop.''

As he went away again, Derek slipped off the stool and went across to a drawer which he unlocked with workshop keys and pulled open. Taking out a stone-sorting tray, he brought it across to her. It held quite a varied selection of semiprecious stones in many colours. Turquoises and amethysts, jasper both banded and clear, amber, quartz, lapis lazuli, and a variety of opals among other, lesser stones.

"What exactly are you looking for?" Derek handed her a pair of tongs for picking out the stones for examination and selection. "Is it a gem for a piece in the making or one to inspire future work?''

"I'm going to make a brooch of my own design, which requires a colourful stone in the centre of it.''

He helped her decide on a quartz cabochon, which meant it was polished but uncut, and she liked its natural shape.Its smoky yellow colour told that it came from a source in the Cairngorm Hills of

Scotland, which was appropriate to the wild simplicity of her planned design.

"I'll wrap it for you," he said, folding it into a piece of tissue paper and then placing it in a small box. She signed for it in a ledger, and by the time Mr. Taylor had returned in his hat and coat, jingling his keys, Irene and Derek had made ready to depart. There followed an elaborate procedure of locking doors and securing bolts with padlocks as Mr. Taylor let them and himself out of the employees' door at the rear of the building. They bade him good night in the street. Then Derek hailed a cab for her.

"I'm grateful for your help and advice, Mr. Ryde," she said from her seat in the hansom.

He tipped his grey bowler to her from the pavement where he stood, his bold eyes holding hers. "A pleasure, Miss Lindsay."

It seemed to her that she had a smile on her lips all the way home. In her bedroom she unwrapped the quartz and studied it with satisfaction, looking forward already to when she would need to make another selection. During breakfast next morning she told her father what she had chosen.

"Good," he replied absently from behind his newspaper.

"Mr. Ryde was there."

Sofia prompted her husband's attention towards the food on the plate in front of him. "Your kedgeree is getting cold."

He put aside *The Times* and took up his knife and fork. Irene addressed him again. "Is he a clever craftsman in your opinion?" It was not that she had any doubts, but she was eager to hear anything she could about her new acquaintance.

Edmund looked blankly at her over the top of his pince-nez. "Who?"

"Mr. Ryde," she replied patiently. "He gave me advice about the quartz that I chose."

"He is an excellent goldsmith, exceptionally skilled as a matter of fact. Only the cream of the Guild is good enough for Lindsay's."

"Isn't he quite young to be so accomplished?"

"No. He's twenty-six or -seven. I was at the top long before his age."

He continued to tuck into his kedgeree, taking a sideways scan at the newspaper folded beside his plate. She did not question him further. Sofia gave her an enquiring glance, but only to ask her if she would like more coffee.

A week later Derek was waiting at the foot of the stone steps of Essex House when Irene emerged at the end of the day. She paused, with one hand on the balustrade, while other home-going students streamed past her and set off in all directions.

"What are you doing here, Mr. Ryde?" She was aware that colour had spread along her cheekbones, although it was doubtful whether he would notice it in the bleak, yellow light of the nearest gas lamp. Her pulse was racing wildly.

"I thought it was my turn to surprise you." He came up the flight to meet her, stopping on the step below where she stood, so that his face was on a level with hers. His eyes were very bright and penetrating, seeming to bore into hers as if to read her thoughts. "Are you pleased to see me?"

She felt choked and breathless. "Yes, I am."

"As pleased as I am to see you?"

"I'm no judge of your feelings."

"I think you are." He reached out a hand and took hers into it. "Have you finished the brooch?"

"No. I'm still in the early stages."

"That's what I expected. That's why I came to see you. It could be another month before you come to the shop again."

"Do you live near here?"

He shook his head. "No. In Islington."

"You've come miles out of your way home."

"I intend to do it again. If you'll let me."

Her little show of hesitation deceived neither of them. "I think I should like to find you waiting for me sometimes."

"That's all I want to know," he said softly. "Do you have to go straight home now?"

She was conscious of how tightly he was holding her fingers. His tension was as great as hers. "I can delay a little while."

"Long enough to have supper with me?"

She thought swiftly. Her father and Sofia were attending a banquet at the Guildhall that evening. Provided she was home before they returned, there was no reason why she should not accept his invitation. "Yes." She tried not to sound too eager. "Thank you."

His expression became jubilant and he relaxed into the more carefree attitude that had become familiar to her during their first meeting. "Wonderful! I know just the place."

It was a small, French restaurant, cheap and cheerful, with red-check tablecloths, excellent food, and bentwood chairs painted green. A Frenchwoman with hollow cheeks and painted eyes, her dyed yellow hair twisted into a Psyche knot at the top of her head, sang songs of the Moulin Rouge, accompanying herself on a tinny piano. Irene enjoyed every minute. She and Derek talked without pause, burst out laughing simultaneously at the same things, and knew that not only were they getting to know each other, but they were also drawing closer to loving each other at the same time. She felt she was drinking vintage champagne instead of the rough red wine in their glasses. He was unlike anyone else she had ever known. In his own way he was as ambitious as she, although where her aims ran to artistic achievement and independence, his sights were set on rich living and all that went with it.

"Is that why you gamble?" she asked him.

His eyes narrowed at her. "Whatever prompted that question?" he asked warily.

"I saw you were interested in the horses that evening I came to the shop."

He grinned unashamedly. "I admit to the occasional flutter. I'm often lucky. With my next big win," he joked, thrusting out his chest boastfully and looping his thumbs in the armholes of his waistcoat,

"I'll take you to dine at the Savoy."

"You had better not," she gave back with a mischievous chuckle. "We might find my father at the next table."

They laughed together, he reaching out a hand across the table to her. She put her own into his. As before, he held it tight, but this time it conveyed more than mere suspense. "Do you mind? Shall you mind?" he asked, his mood becoming serious.

"What?" She put her head a little to one side in puzzlement. "I don't think I understand."

"Our having to meet secretly. For as far as your father is concerned, that's what it amounts to, isn't it? I'm under no illusions. I'm well aware that he would never allow me to call on you at home."

She tilted her chin. "On principle you should be able to, especially since we are fellow goldsmiths or will be when I've finished my training."

"I fear principles would not come into it. Remember, I have seen the business side of your father, and although perhaps I shouldn't say it to you, he is a proud and ruthless man."

She sighed. "Oh, I know that only too well. But that's no reason why I shouldn't choose my own friends. I sometimes feel that I'm living in two different worlds. There is not the slightest link between Essex House and my home life."

"Then you will allow me to be part of your goldsmithery world?"

Her whole face reflected her fervent answer. "There is nothing I should like more. Whatever

happens, my father must never find out or else you
would never rise to the position of head goldsmith at
Lindsay's, which you want so much. I wish you had
been given that promotion after Mr. Lucas left.''

"I hadn't been in the workshop long enough then.
I couldn't expect as a newcomer to be promoted over
the head of a goldsmith-designer as senior as Dudley
Richardson, but the disappointment irked just the
same. I had thoughts of going to work abroad—on
the Continent or in the United States. There are
always openings for a highly qualified craftsman."

"Are you still thinking along those lines?"

He gave her a long and velvety look before he
replied very softly, "How could I think of leaving
London now that I've made a bond with you?"

She thought love came into her heart at that precise
moment. It was certainly true that nothing was ever
the same again.

They began to see each other frequently. He either
met her at Essex House, as he had done the first time,
or if she expected to be finished with her work fairly
early, a meeting was arranged halfway between
Mile End Road and Old Bond Street at a tea shop
where potted palms gave privacy to marble-topped
tables set in semicircular alcoves. There they would
become oblivious to all else as they sat talking over a
strawberry ice or a pot of hot chocolate, which she
was never to taste again without remembering the
tender days of discovering and being discovered,
seeking and being sought, loving and finding love in
return. She was innocent and trusting, he was quick-

witted and experienced, and both of them were dazed by what was happening to them. She saw desire in his eyes long before he spoke of it, read his yearning to kiss her long before the time came.

They always held hands when they walked, and they walked a great deal. Her route homewards through the wintry streets of London to Milton Square became their lovers' lane, and they always had to part a safe distance from her home. If it rained, they shared a large umbrella or took a horse-bus, which she felt came into her father's category of emergency rides in special circumstances. If he was affluent, they would ride in a hansom. Generous by nature, his attitude towards money being very much easy come, easy go, he would always pay for everything, even when he had practically to turn out the linings of his pockets to find enough for their bus fares. She longed to contribute, but the only time she had ever hinted at it, he had begun to bridle, so she had quickly changed what she had been about to say, able to see that his pride would suffer if he did not fulfil his masculine role of protector and provider to the full. She sat with a sovereign or two idle in her purse, heartsick that he would have to walk the long way back to his lodgings in foul weather afterwards.

She knew it was his betting that caused his bouts of penury, because her father, with all his faults, was not parsimonious in the matter of wages, and by means of bonuses paid slightly above the rates expected by West End goldsmiths. At first she did not take the matter very seriously. She had been brought up to think of horse racing as the sport of kings, and when at Ascot with her father and Sofia, she had placed bets herself on horses that had taken her fancy. Her first disquiet came when she learned to her dismay that whenever the chance came his way, he went coursing, a sport in which bets were placed on which of the unleashed greyhounds would catch a fleeing hare first. Once at a country house party, she had been near enough to hear the screams of the torn hare, and the cruelty involved was totally abhorrent to her. When she put this point to him, he took her face between his hands, smiling at her indulgently.

"Would you begrudge me a healthy tramp in the countryside? Don't you think I should get some fresh air into my lungs, away from the fogs of London that descend at this time of year? I have a friend who keeps greyhounds, and he invites me and a few other chaps down to Sussex on a Sunday, and we spend the whole day on the Downs. His wife cooks us a roast dinner at the end of it. It's the dogs that interest me, not the hare. In any case," he declared, tongue in cheek, "the hare usually gets away."

She shuddered, unconvinced. "I'm thinking of those that don't."

After that she began to concern herself very seriously over the extent to which Derek wagered his money away. She was sure that not only was he unable to ride the bus during a run of bad luck, but there were times when she was convinced he was existing on very little food. She decided she must try to win him over from his gambling ways with tact and gentle persuasion and with love.

Derek, like most betting men, never spoke of his losses, but would always boast of a win. Then he would be wildly extravagant, buying her armfuls of long-stemmed hothouse roses, which she had to stick into empty buckets at Essex House, picking out only one crimson bud each time to keep in a slim silver vase in the privacy of her bedroom until it faded. He bought her beribboned boxes of chocolates, which she shared gladly around the workbenches at the school, not daring in any case to take home anything that might cause comment or enquiry. There were hand-embroidered handkerchiefs trimmed with Valenciennes lace, silk sashes, a Dresden trinket box, and a glass perfume flacon with a lotus flower stopper designed by a Frenchman named René Lalique. She was further overwhelmed by bottles of French scent with which to fill it. All these expensive gifts she had to hide away out of sight in her drawers beneath layers of her underclothes. She used a dab of the scent only when out with him. When they dined together, he ordered the best champagne, and woe betide the waiter who knew by his accent that he was not a gentleman and tried to fob him off with something inferior, for he had developed an understanding of wines as well as a gourmet's appreciation of special dishes, seeming to have a natural affinity for the good things in life. At these times of affluence there was about him a dangerous exultance, as if he felt he had come into his rightful place in the world and a continuing run of gambler's luck would keep him there. It never did. Before long he would be pawning his extravagant new clothes, and once more the two of them would be back to bus rides or walking under the umbrella.

It was a cold, wet night early in their acquaintance-ship when he kissed her for the first time. Although the rain was drumming on the spread of the umbrella he held above their heads and making fountains on the pavement about their feet, she thought nothing sweeter had ever happened to her. She had been kissed before, but she would have termed those brief encounters as "mistletoe kisses," having no more importance or depth or significance. With Derek she was filled with an overwhelming desire to give and to share, something she had never experienced emo-tionally before.

"May I kiss you?" he whispered throatily, but it was an announcement of intention rather than a request, for already his free arm was about her shoulders, drawing her close to him under the tilting umbrella. Without hesitation she slipped her arms about his neck, the strap of her purse sliding down from her wrist to lodge swinging at her elbow, and stood on tip-toe to meet his oncoming lips. Firm, rain-cool at first, and then his warm mouth washed over hers, ardent and active, the passionate pressure igniting a glorious response in her. The force of his kissing almost threw her physically off balance, only the strength of his embracing arm keeping her clasped to him, while the lamps of passing traffic failed to reach the depths of the dark passageway into which he had drawn her. When finally they drew apart, it was to gaze at each other seriously for a few moments before she flung her arms back about his neck and they hugged each other fiercely and spontaneously, his cheek pressed against hers as if in silent acknowledgement that something marvellously out of the ordinary was about to mould their lives.

After she had finished the brooch with the Scottish quartz at her classes, Ashbee commended her work and suggested that her next project should be a set of silver buttons. She promptly decided to incorporate the opals she had already already seen, and since she would need one for each button, she could look forward to half a dozen meetings with Derek at the shop that no one would question. It was a bonus that they both appreciated to the full. If Mr. Taylor wondered why she always chose to come for the opals on the evenings when Derek and not one of the other goldsmiths was on duty, he probably concluded that having once taken the young man's advice, it was natural that she should seek it again afterwards. At least he said nothing and showed no surprise. All went perfectly smoothly.

Then quite suddenly, Sofia began to ail. Her vivacity had been in decline for a long time, but the change in her had taken place so gradually that it was not noticeable to those who saw her every day. Had Irene been less absorbed in her training and slightly less in love, she would most surely have become aware, in spite of Sofia's brave attempt to keep up a cheery front, that the ebbing of her stepmother's spirits had increased to an alarming degree. Everything came to a climax one morning when Edmund was abroad and Irene was engaged in her silverwork at Essex House. Word was delivered to her that she was wanted in the entrance hall. She went there to find one of the menservants awaiting her, the family brougham drawn up outside.

"Could you come home at once, Miss Irene?" he said anxiously. "Mrs. Lindsay has been taken ill. The doctor is with her."

Irene felt an icy fear quake through her. "I'll get my coat."

Never had the drive seemed longer between Mile End and her home. When the carriage drew up in Milton Square, she was out in a flash and went dashing into the house. The doctor met her in the hall and drew her in with him into the drawing room.

"What is wrong with my stepmother, Dr. Harris?" she implored anxiously. "Is it anything serious?"

He replied reassuringly. "Calm your fears, Irene. I have made a most thorough examination and have found nothing physical to give cause for alarm. Mrs. Lindsay is simply in a state of mental exhaustion. I believe that she has been doing too much socially and domestically, which means she simply needs rest and quiet to overcome what I have diagnosed as nervous debility. I understand your father is abroad. When is he due home again?"

"Not for four or five weeks. Do you think I should

send for him?"

"By no means." Dr. Harris was firm on that point. He had been doctor to the Lindsay household for many years, had delivered Irene, and had seen the first Mrs. Lindsay surrender all will to survive. It was not that he thought the second Mrs. Lindsay was about to follow suit, but the early danger signals were there, the classic case of a highly sensitive woman having reached the end of her endurance in her marriage to a bombastic, hard-headed, self-centred man. The last thing she needed at the moment was her husband's return. If Irene had not been a girl of exceptional backbone, she would have been crushed in childhood to a cowed shadow submissive to her father's dominating will, and he felt pleased that he could rely on her to carry out his instructions in a sensible manner. "I have given your stepmother a sedative. She will sleep the clock round, and that is what she needs. It appears that she had been sleeping badly for a long time, something I could have remedied if only she had come to me before allowing herself to reach the point of collapse. She has admitted to having no appetite, and her loss of weight has been considerable. Now this is what I want you to do."

It was a very simple procedure. Nothing was to upset the patient, who was to stay in bed for a week. During that time she should be persuaded to take light and nourishing meals, Irene eating with her on a tray. Then she must be encouraged to dress and go downstairs daily, receiving only when she was ready for them those close friends of a sympathetic nature able to lift her spirits and revive her interest in outside affairs. At no time must she be allowed to think herself condemned to a chronic state of melancholia, for that borderline had not been reached, and Dr. Harris did not intend that it should be. Most of all he relied on Irene to keep the routine of the house as normal as possible, which included a return to her studies when the moment was right. Sofia must not be worried by the belief that she was ill enough to interfere for a prolonged length of time with Irene's training.

Dr. Harris called daily. Being a friend of the family, his constant visits did not alarm Sofia into thinking she was worse than she was, and although privately she would have preferred the attendance of a Russian doctor from the embassy, she was always glad to see him. She welcomed the rest he had prescribed as much as the absence of her husband from her bed. She knew full well that a bout of homesickness was responsible for her present extra-ordinary state, a symptom of so many other unhappinesses that had been steadily dragging her down. Not going to St. Petersburg with Edmund this time had been the proverbial final straw.

She had been back there once with him a few years ago on one of his business trips. Everyone had made a great fuss of her, giving parties and balls and inviting her everywhere while Edmund seethed with jealousy, throwing temper tantrums as soon as they were on their own. Worst of all, he had made love to her quite brutally throughout their sojourn as if to emphasize his sole possession of her. He had ruined what would otherwise have been the happiest of holidays for her, and she had vowed to herself that she would never accompany him there again. Not that he would have allowed it. She understood that now, although it was not revealed to her until he had mentioned about a month prior to this current trip that he regretted having to confine his time in St. Petersburg to a mere two days. She saw her opportunity, but listened to him first. One thing she had learned was never to interrupt.

"The pressure of business here prevents me leaving England at an earlier date, and there is a sale of Hapsburg jewellery in Vienna that I do not wish to miss by any account. So after delivering a parcel of stones to Monsieur Fabergé and offering him some quite extraordinary rose spinels that have come into my possession, I must leave post-haste for Austria. After that I shall be in Berlin and Cologne, where some other sales are being held. Most important of all, I shall be returning by way of Amsterdam, where I may have to spend a considerable time seeking out the diamonds I need for a parure of great magnificence which I am to make for the new Battenburg bride." He had looked well pleased with his arrangements.

Then she had spoken up with as much firmness as she could muster in conversation with him. "I shall go with you this time as far as St. Petersburg, Edmund." She was seizing a unique opportunity to see everyone she knew there without the blight of his resentment. "I can stay on while you continue your journey to those other places, and our arrivals home again can be timed to coincide."

His face set into the obdurate expression that she knew and dreaded. "No, I cannot allow that. It would not be seemly for you to remain there without me. In any case, I could not consider allowing you to travel abroad at this time of year. The snow delays trains, and all manner of inconveniences occur."

"But I am used to hard winters from childhood," she persisted.

"Since then you have become acclimatized to the milder English weather. My concern is only for you, my dear. Be patient, and at some more suitable time of the year, I will arrange for you to go to St. Petersburg with me."

She knew when she was routed. He would never take her. There would always be an excuse. He would never willingly face up again to the agonies of jealousy he had endured in witnessing her innocently joyful reunions with those who had known her long before he had come into her life. Yet there was even more to it this time. He was as aware as she that their relationship had deteriorated, and she guessed that at the back of his mind there lurked the fear that if he left her on her own among old familiar places, she might take it into her head never to return to him. But that was not her intention. He would be lost without her, and she would never condemn him to the torment of being deserted. She wondered sometimes if his first wife had ever attempted to run away, for he had the unhappy knack of making a prison of his home and padlocks of his possessive love.

It had become her habit to endure disappointments without complaint, and at first she did not realize how deeply this particular denial of her wishes had seeped into her whole being. As the days before Edmund's departure went by, a kind of numbness settled on her, and all the colour and sound of everyday life began to edge away from her. As if watching herself from a distance, she went through the routine of each day like an automaton wound up with a key. When the time came to wave Edmund off on his trip, she had watched without the least sign of emotion his baggage being loaded into the landau for its first stage to the London Docks and the ship that would sail for her homeland that day. He was entirely oblivious to anything being amiss, her request to go with him already long forgotten, and she kissed him goodbye with calm good wishes for a safe journey, as she always did. She continued to carry on in the same detached way until one morning, when seated at her bureau, she saw by the date in her engagement book that it was the day that Edmund would be arriving in the city of her birth. A violent shudder went through her, and the colour drained from her face with a painful suddenness. She sank back in her chair, closing her eyes and seeing in her mind's eye the spectacular skyline aglitter with snow, the skaters on the frozen Neva, the faces of friends she missed as never before, and the awe-inspiring beauty of the golden-domed cathedral in which she had worshipped. How long she sat motionless in the chair she did not know. She had no wish or will to move ever again. It was a manservant who raised the alarm. Her own maid saw her into bed and sent for the doctor and her stepdaughter, both of whom she thanked silently for not recalling Edmund from abroad. As yet, she was not sure how to face up to the turmoil of his fussing and worrying about her that would occur upon his return. How different was the calm and sensible approach of Dr. Harris and Irene. Never before had her stepdaughter been a greater comfort to her; never before had she realized the extent to which she thought of the girl as her own beloved child.

Irene had written to Derek's address to explain her absence to him. Then, when Sofia could be left by day, she wrote again to let him know that she would be returning to Essex House. As she had anticipated, he was there to meet her on her first day back. What she had not expected was that he would be totally unreasonable about her having to go straight home.

"I have to," Irene argued desperately. "Please try to understand. My stepmother is still far from well, and at the moment it is only my company she wants. I read to her, and we play cards, and she is much better when I am there."

"She sounds like a spoiled woman to me," he snapped back, his chin jutting mulishly, his fists deep in his coat pockets. He had welcomed his employer's absence as the chance to see Irene whenever and wherever he liked, and this further wasting of the time they could have shared seemed intolerable to him.

"She is not," Irene countered. "If she knew about us and if it were in her power to condone our meeting, she would do it. She would never willingly keep us apart."

"Then tell her," he urged, suddenly hopeful.

It hurt her to disappoint him. "I can't. It wouldn't be fair to burden her with a secret to keep from my father. Moreover, she would start worrying about me, and I'll not put anything extra on her in her present state of health."

He let her go from him that evening without a kiss, turning away and stalking back down the lamplit way that they had come, an angry, lonely figure. Through registering his displeasure, his intent had been to make her feel as miserable as he did himself. She watched him out of sight, hoping that at the last second he would turn and look back at her, but it did not happen.

He did not come again to meet her at the day's end; nor did she expect him. Whether or not it was over between them as far as he was concerned, she did not know and tried not to think about it. She half hoped he might write to her, but no letter came. It was hard to appear bright and smiling to Sofia as if everything in the world were rosy, but the invalid came first and must be cosseted against any anxiety.

Gradually Sofia did make progress. Irene found

her with a book sometimes, and although the bookmark did not advance more than a few pages at a time each day, it was a move in the right direction. Some petit-point embroidery began to extend its motif of birds and flowers. Letters from Edmund, which previously Irene had had to open for her, were now read without postponement or visible effort. Most promising of all was the evening when Irene brought home a collection of her jewellery designs. Something of the old sparkle returned to Sofia's eyes as she looked at them in turn, making admiring comments and asking questions about them. All were too advanced technically for Irene's still limited ability, but she hoped with time to execute them on her own workbench.

Sofia had not yet reached the stage of receiving visitors when Edmund returned home. Irene had let him know that his wife was unwell, although the emphasis that it was not serious enough to cut short his important business travels had reassured him. It therefore came as a great shock to see Sofia so thin and wan; there was a transparent look to her that alarmed him greatly. He went straight to the telephone to demand a report from Dr. Harris, who did his best to calm him.

"All she needs now is some sunshine, Mr. Lindsay. Late February can be a treacherous time of year. Take her to the South of France for a spell of recuperation. Five or six weeks by the Mediterranean would restore her health completely."

"Otherwise?"

"Otherwise things may go the other way. That cannot be denied. It would only take a slight chill or a bad cold to go straight to her lungs with results of the worst kind. If you cannot take her yourself, I can recommend a trustworthy nurse-companion, a Mrs. Burridge, who would take excellent care of her."

Slowly Edmund replaced the receiver on the hook. He was willing enough for Sofia to go to a sunnier climate or anywhere else other than St. Petersburg, when so much appeared to depend on it, but he would have liked to take her himself. Unfortunately, having only now returned from abroad, he could not possibly go off again from his business immediately. Countless matters would be awaiting his attention at the shop. Harris must have realized that, which was why he had made the suggestion about the nurse-companion. It had all sounded very cut and dried, almost as if the Burridge woman had been put on the alert to await the summons. Well, Harris's fees were heavy enough, so no doubt the fellow felt obliged to do something extra to warrant them. With a sigh Edmund went to tell Sofia of what was to be arranged and to give his promise that he would come himself to fetch her home again.

The next day Irene went to the shop to choose an opal for the second button in the set she was making. She had let Mr. Taylor know that she was coming. He in turn would inform the goldsmith on late duty to have the gems ready for selection. Although it was the night of the week when Derek filled that place on the rota, she thought he would have changed his duties to avoid her. But he was there in the doorway of the side room, the light behind him, head high, feet apart, arms at his sides. As she faced him across the length of the deserted main workshop, leaning back against the glass-panelled door that she had closed behind her, he uttered a tortured groan.

"How could you have stayed away so long, Irene?"

With a cry she rushed forward. He met her with arms outstretched, catching her to him and clamping his mouth down on hers as he whirled her around with him. She found herself swept into the farthest corner of the side room. Her unfastened coat was jerked down from her shoulders to fall to the floor, while his kissing took her breath away. Her blouse was parted, the buttons flying undone as his hands swept in to find their way past silk and lace to caress her ardently. His lips left hers and were everywhere, but when he would have exposed her breasts fully to his gaze, she caught his hand and encircled his neck with her other arm.

"Not here, Derek. Not now."

He enveloped her in his embrace, burying his face in her hair, his breath warm against her ear as he sighed with frantic despair, so much yearning in him that it vibrated from his body into hers. "Where?" he implored huskily. "And when?"

"I don't know," she whispered emotionally. "You must think of somewhere for us to be alone."

He tensed as if not quite sure that he had heard her rightly before drawing back to cup a hand against her face. "I love you, Irene," he said softly.

"I love you too," she whispered—words that had never been spoken between them until this moment.

"Did you mean what you said about our being together?"

"Yes, I did."

"There's no need to be afraid that I'll let any harm come to you."

She lowered her lids in complete surrender to trust, turning her head slightly to kiss the palm resting against her cheek. "I know."

"It's been hell for me not seeing you all this time. I have a present for you. Getting it ready helped to while away the hours of missing you."

She was ashamed that she had misjudged him. Far from not wanting to see her again, he had had to seek diversion while waiting for her to return to him. As she tidied her appearance, refastening buttons and tucking back strands of her disarranged hair, he fetched his gift for her from a pocket. She unwrapped the tissue paper and was left speechless by what she saw. It was a pendant in the full glory of Art Nouveau, a piece that would otherwise never have found itself within the stronghold of traditionalism that was Lindsay's of Old Bond Street. It was the head of a nymph with green eyes, delicately enamelled, her swirling hair of coppery splendour forming a loop that suspended her from a fine silver chain. To Irene the resemblance to herself was unmistakable. It was a compliment beyond all compliments, a gift to be treasured forever, not the least for the love that had gone into the making of it.

"It's beautifully made and the most wonderful gift I have ever received," she breathed.

"Let me put it on you."

She bent her head, scooping her hair aside to aid him in the linking of the tiny catch. His fingers brushed the nape of her neck, sending delicious shivers down her spine, and when he sealed his task with a kiss on that very spot, an involuntary sigh escaped her. He put his hands on her waist and swivelled her around to face him again.

"I'll find a place for us, I promise you. I'd take you to my lodgings if I could, but my landlady is a dragon, and female visitors are not allowed."

This did not surprise her, since respectable lodging houses had such rules. As he tilted her chin with his fingertips and kissed her mouth lovingly again, she was sure that somewhere in London a special retreat was awaiting them.

Two days later Sofia departed for the Continent, accompanied by her maid and Mrs. Burridge, the capable nurse-companion. The Channel was rough, making the crossing uncomfortable for her, but she recovered quickly in the luxurious accommodation of crimson plush, silk tassels, and embroidered sheets offered by the Calais-Mediterranean express for the overnight rail journey. At Nice she was met by an enchanting vista of peach, apricot, and almond blossom, with the Baie des Anges glittering blue-green in the sunshine, sleek yachts anchored opulently within its shelter. It had been decided that since she needed continued rest and quiet in her convalescence, a villa would be more suitable than staying at a hotel. Normally it would have been impossible to secure one on such short notice at what was the height of the season, but one of her compatriots, a diplomat at the Russian embassy in London, had offered his private *pied-à-terre* in Nice for as long as she required it.

She felt relaxed as soon as she crossed its threshold. Set in a rich garden, completely secluded, the villa was furnished in the Russian style throughout. The servants were also of her own nationality, adding to the sensation of being in a familiar domain. During her childhood she had visited the Riviera with her parents, it being customary for wealthy Russians to escape the worst of the bitter winters. Although she had been confined to nursery circles, she remembered Nice quite well from those days, but for the time being she had no wish to venture beyond the grounds of the villa to see the sights again and was prepared to enjoy her solitude. Plenty of reading matter had been brought in her baggage, and in addition there were bookcases full of fine volumes on every kind of subject awaiting her selection and her pleasure.

As the days went by, she thrived in the balmy climate, her mind at peace, everything blissfully in limbo with no decisions to be made, no constant tension with regard to Edmund's unpredictable moods. She wrote to him out of a sense of duty, letting him know of her progress, and then deliberately put him from her thoughts in order not to let the worry of returning to him hinder her convalescence. To Irene she wrote gladly on scenic postcards that Mrs. Burridge bought for her in the resort; otherwise she did not enter into any correspondence. Invitations that came to local events were declined on her behalf by a secretary attached to the staff of the villa. Not even a picturesque battle of flowers tempted her out of seclusion, and she was content to let the brass bands and the exuberant crowds pass by unobserved in the distance. A few petals drifted on an easterly breeze into the garden, where she sat reading a book in a sheltered corner, and fluttered down around her feet. She did not so much as glance up from the page.

She had been in Nice three weeks when she forced herself to emerge from her isolation and take a drive in an open fiacre owned by her absent host. Almost warily at first, she glanced to the right and to the left of her at the pastel-washed houses with the colourful window boxes, the ostentatiously baroque hotels, the narrow streets and the wide boulevards, the cafés with their striped awnings, and the golden clouds of the mimosa trees. Along the Promenade des Anglais, well-dressed people strolled leisurely in a confetti stream of bobbing parasols that followed the curve of the sparkling bay. By the time the whole outing was over, she found herself revived and uplifted by it, although a strong reluctance to mingle with other people remained with her, linked to the immovable dread of the day when she must pick up the threads of her life again with the bombastic man to whom she was married.

Yet she held on to common sense, realizing that she must make the supreme effort to rehabilitate herself. Her health had improved sufficiently for Mrs. Burridge to return to England, and her time at Nice was gradually drawing towards its close. For Edmund's sake she must not return home in a renewed emotional confusion. Her daily drives became part of her routine, and she had reached the point of acknowledging from the carriage seat the nods and smiles of acquaintances from England who were also staying at the resort. Then one exceptionally glorious day, she decided she must take the plunge back into society. To boost her morale and soothe the quaking trepidation that afflicted her, she put on a new silk taffeta costume that had been hanging in the wardrobe since it was unpacked. Its colours were soft and pleasing to her, being all the shades to be found in the feathers at a pigeon's throat. It had a sash that encircled her still slender waist, and the high neck was of white satin with appliqué lace that matched the little burst of snowy ostrich feathers on her wide-brimmed hat.

She instructed the coachman to drive to a certain spot, and there she alighted resolutely to join those strolling along the great palm-fringed promenade. Hoping that she would not meet anyone she knew on this first walk in public again, she focused her attention on the entry of a handsome yacht sailing into the bay, keeping her parasol at an angle to shield her more from the glances of passers-by than from the sun. But she was seen and recognized by a tall man engaged in conversation with an elderly couple whom he knew from home and had met by chance. Out of the corner of his eye, he watched her almost disappear in the distance before he was able to extricate himself and follow quickly after her. His shadow fell into step beside her.

"Good afternoon, Mrs. Lindsay. This is a marvellous surprise to find you in Nice."

Her heart almost stopped at the remembered voice of Gregory Burnett. Gripped by a sense of destiny, she turned her head and looked up into his face. His eyes were showing a keen awareness of her that dispersed the ten years between them and made her feel vulnerably young again and beautiful.

"Mr. Burnett!" she exclaimed huskily. "How are you? Are you on vacation too?"

He shook his head and smiled mock-ruefully. "I regret to say that it was a matter of business that brought me to the Riviera. Is your husband similarly engaged here while leaving you to walk alone?"

She switched her gaze from his and looked ahead again as they continued their strolling pace along the promenade. "Edmund is not with me," she stated without a tremour. "I am staying on my own at a charming villa that has been loaned to me."

"That sounds most pleasant. Far better than taking a suite at one of these large hotels."

"I must admit that I like having the peace of a

whole garden to myself. It has given me a chance to catch up on some long overdue reading.''

"How else have you passed the time? The races? The opera? Have you driven over to the casino at Monte Carlo?''

She smiled, shaking her head, her eyes lustrous in the shade of her sweeping hat. "None of those things. I have been leading a quiet existence. As a matter of fact, this is the first walk that I have taken along this famous promenade since I arrived from London.''

"Then it's my good luck that I chanced to see you.''

They chatted on, light and easy conversation that was in keeping with the sun-drenched surroundings and the leisurely atmosphere that prevailed. When they left the promenade, it was to drink Russian tea at a round café table under a blue-striped awning, banks of flowers all around them. As at their first meeting in her own home, she found him dangerous and exciting company. She basked in the glow of his admiration, knowing that as before he considered her a ravishing woman. She felt exhilarated and wonderfully happy as if suddenly liberated from all ties and responsibilities. When the afternoon was at an end, they both knew that he would not be keeping his business appointment in Cannes the next day or for several days to come.

Her daily letters to Edmund ceased. In fact she gave up all correspondence. Even the picture postcards for Irene lay forgotten on the secretaire. For a brief, halcyon interlude, nothing else existed for her beyond the villa and its grounds; her seclusion was recaptured, although this time it was passionately shared.

The idyll came to an end when the outside world could be kept at bay no longer. Gregory departed for Cannes. After half an hour of being on her own again, Sofia received a telegram from Edmund to let her know he would be arriving the next day to fetch her home again, as he had promised. She stared at the telegram as if trying to remember who he was and what other life awaited her outside the villa walls.

By the time he arrived, she was completely herself again, serene and composed. No trace remained of the wildly amorous and abandoned creature she had become in another man's arms for a fleeting while.

Four

Irene could not remember when she had last seen her stepmother looking so well. The spell in the South of France appeared to have done Sofia an immeasurable amount of good. She had about her the kind of girlish bloom that Irene associated with her arrival at Milton Square all those years ago. Edmund, although relieved that his wife had made such a remarkable recovery in both health and spirits, nevertheless found something puzzling about such a transformation. Never an imaginative man, he found himself haunted by an uncomfortable feeling that in some indefinable way the wife he had brought home from Nice was not the same woman who had gone there. Yet she was more herself than she had been for a long, long time, her qualities enriched, her beauty restored by the warm sun and the change of air. Always patient with him, she was more patient than ever before. Where her loving had waned, so she indulged him with a response he had not met from her for a considerable while. Strangest of all, a sharp rebuke from him when he deemed it necessary no longer appeared to have any effect on her, for she scarcely seemed to hear him, and the weeping that had irritated him was a thing of the past.

Sofia was fully conscious of the change in herself and was overwhelmingly thankful for it. Where Edmund had been slowly destroying her as an individual, using her sensitivity as a weapon against her, his power over her had quite gone. She thought how strange it was that in both her marriages two entirely different but equally selfish husbands had each tried to break her unmercifully—the first because he had despised women, the second out of a tyrannical possessiveness. It was as if something vital and alive in her had presented a challenge that neither husband had been able to meet, and out of a personal inadequacy each of them had tried to crush it out of existence. With Gregory she had come to a true fulfilment in what had been much more than a mere physical relationship. He had made her feel a complete woman again, a person in her own right. She, who had always thought unfaithfulness the greatest of sins, was astounded that her conscience troubled her so little. Neither she nor Gregory had looked beyond their brief time together. Not once had either mentioned further meetings when Nice had been left behind them. What had happened between them had been sufficient unto the moment She did not wish to mull over whatever might lie in the furthermost corners of her heart. If any tender feelings were lingering on, they must be confined without examination or dissection to what was past and gone. All that mattered was that she was more than ever able to be a wife to Edmund, and nothing he could do or say would ever threaten her individuality again. If sometimes he seemed to become Gregory when he held her in his arms, it was surely only a transitional frame of mind, and with time even that involuntary fantasy would become relegated to those past hours of a sun-shuttered room and nights with windows open to the moon.

Edmund's social engagements had waned during his wife's absence. This was through his own choice, for except in the matter of business occasions he no longer cared to go anywhere without her. His staying home in the evenings had proved an inconvenience to Irene, for it meant that she must get back to the house within a reasonable time after leaving Essex House, allowing no delays with Derek on the way. It was a burden lifted from her shoulders when her father and Sofia resumed their social life together, setting her free to follow her own will once more.

As for Derek, he had used the extra time gained through this disrupted period to make the final arrangements for a special meeting place that he had been weighing up carefully for quite a while. If the choice had been left entirely to him from the start, he would simply have rented a room with a bed somewhere long since. However, common sense had told him that Irene, loving him romantically, would have shied away from such a blatant setting; and for that type of accommodation, he must wait at least until he had initiated her into the pleasures of love. He had no wish to lose her through a single false move. For that reason alone he had restrained himself unmercifully on countless occasions, although driven half mad by the response of her kisses and the shape of her firm, young body that mostly he had only been able to caress through her clothes. There had been occasions on those dark, homeward walks when he had undone her blouse buttons and touched her breasts, feeling but not viewing their lovely shape, the nipples rising against his palms, the perfume of her skin filling his nostrils and making his senses reel. He had almost lost his head that day in the workshop when they had been reunited after an absence, he having come to believe that she had finished with him, and what he had seen of her bosom had almost killed him with desire. He had never waited so long for any girl before, had never yearned so desperately to discover and possess, and now at last he had secured a place of tryst for them. He chose the right moment to break the news to her when he was walking her home with his arm about her waist. There was a touch of spring in the air, and she was holding a bunch of violets that he had bought with his last twopence from a roadside flower seller.

"I've found somewhere for us," he announced triumphantly. "It's perfect!"

She came to a halt, whirling about within the

circle of his arm. "Where?" she demanded excitedly.

"You must guess," he teased, well pleased with his own ingenuity.

She made several wild guesses, only to be told that she was nowhere near the mark. "Don't keep me in suspense any longer!" she demanded, pummelling his chest playfully in happy impatience.

He caught both her hands in his. "A kiss first," he demanded in a mock-lordly fashion. She obliged, as always melting inwardly at the special way he had of taking possession of her mouth. Her head came to rest against his shoulder.

"Where are we to meet?" she asked softly, having become as serious as he during their long kiss.

He answered her in the same tones. "The shop. After hours. I've made a full set of keys."

She drew away to regard him steadily if somewhat incredulously before they began to walk on again. "It's ideal. The only danger that I can think of is that we might be mistaken for burglars by a police patrol."

"There'll be no chance of that," he assured her. "I told you. I've thought of everything. All that remains is for you to say which evening it shall be."

She thought carefully for a few moments. Then she made her decision. It should be within a few days time when her father was taking Sofia and some other people to the theatre and out to supper afterwards. "Next Tuesday," she said firmly.

"Oh, sweetheart!" He pulled her to him in rib-crushing triumph, a new fierceness in his kissing that somehow signalled a note of doubt within her as to her own wisdom in agreeing to his daring plan, but she was not lacking in courage, and her doubt was forgotten almost at once.

Sofia was not looking forward to Tuesday. Her heart had sunk when Edmund announced that he had obtained a box for the first night of the latest George Edwardes show at the Gaiety Theatre. The famous impressario specialized in lavish and witty productions of magnificently costumed musicals with the emphasis on beautiful girls. Among their number was Gregory's wife, Lillian Rose. Sofia was not ready yet for any reminders of Gregory, not even through so distant a contact as viewing from a theater box this young woman whom she had never met and whose path she hoped never to cross. She thought with a pang of misgiving, which was uncomfortably close to premonition, that it was almost as if Fate had taken a deliberate move to ensure that she should not be allowed to forget that romantic encounter in Nice. The old adage of the piper having to be paid flickered disturbingly through her mind. Yet it had been a time of talking as well as amorous embrace, an exchange of quiet confidences as well as passion. She wished with all her heart that she and Gregory could have remained loving friends if not lovers. But that was not possible.

The evening came. To add to Sofia's disquiet about the whole outing, the wives of the two business associates whom Edmund had invited were not women with whom she had anything in common.

Eileen Harding and Clare Balfour had an insatiable appetite for gossip, most of it cruel, and Sofia was careful of anything she said in their company. Often the most innocent remark about someone was taken up and misconstrued. Her avoidance of their spiteful small talk had been registered by them over the years, and for that reason alone, she knew they did not like her. It made their effusive greetings all the more distasteful to her when they all met in the foyer of the Gaiety Theater in the Strand.

It was an extremely grand theatre and had come a long way from the modestly staged shows with which it had opened over forty years previously. It was all thanks to the "Guv'nor," as George Edwardes was known, with his unfailing judgement in blending together all the ingredients necessary to make his particular productions certain successes at the box-office. Although invariably the songs and dialogue in his Gaiety shows were laced with innuendo, it came under the term of "naughtiness," and there was nothing to offend any but the most prudish, which was why George Edwardes was able to attract respectable women into his theatre as well as their menfolk. Since he always gave the female element a display of marvellous clothes, he looked for girls able to wear them with panache and flair, ensuring at the same time that they had the sexual allure that made men train their opera glasses avidly for a closer glimpse of a bouncing cleavage and the shimmer of a well-rounded thigh. He was a master of titillation, knowing that what was hinted at and partly revealed was far more intriguing to the male eye than a blatant flaunting.

Girls flocked from all over the country to be auditioned for each show, every one of them with the single, burning ambition to be a Gaiety Girl. When a girl was fortunate to meet all the Guv'nor's requirements in looks, form, and talent, her lifestyle changed irrevocably. Gaiety Girls were groomed like racehorses and were taught how to walk, to speak, and to behave in society. They were given singing lessons, were coached until their dancing reached the high standards required, and were instructed in fencing, riding, and how to conduct their lives. It was no ordinary girl who reached the boards of the famous stage, so it was no wonder that almost every young man-about-town, as well as those not so young, wanted to revel in the prestige of escorting a Gaiety Girl. The ultimate in success for the stage-door johnnies was to take to supper any one of the cream of the cream, the elite band of girls, specially selected by George Edwardes out of the whole bevy, who were known as the Big Eight, a reference to their status and not to their voluptuous hour-glass figures. Flowers, jewellery, chocolates, and fur capes poured into the dressing rooms, but most of the girls knew their market value, holding out for a wedding ring and, wherever possible, a title to go with it. A good many achieved that goal, breaking into the ranks of the aristocracy on the strength of their beauty and charm and, sometimes, on the quickness of their wits. Their example encouraged others presently following in their footsteps across the Gaiety boards.

Sofia did not know why Gregory's marriage to Lillian had failed. He had not spoken of his personal life in that respect but had been a sympathetic listener to her problems, unraveling them with a physical tenderness and sensitivity that she had not known possible in any man. He had soothed away past hurts that she had endured with too much stoicism and wifely self-abasement. She could not believe that any woman in her right mind would willingly leave such a considerate lover.

Nobody could accuse Gregory of having called a halt to Lillian's theatrical career after their marriage abroad, a course of action which might otherwise have been a cause of marital friction. On the contrary, she had continued to play the music halls until eventually she reached the Gaiety. For reasons known only to the two of them, this had signalled the end of their marriage. They had never lived together again, although they were sometimes seen in each other's company. It was almost as if the thought of divorce had never occurred to either of them. Sofia wondered if Gregory still loved his wife. Because of that possibility alone, she knew it would be a poignant moment for her when Lillian came onto the stage.

When Edmund had settled his guests around her in the box, Sofia saw that a good number of seats in the stalls, the dress circle, and in the opposite boxes had been taken by people whom she knew. Smiles and nods of recognition were coming from all directions, and everyone was in a festive mood, for the first night of a Gaiety show was an important event. All were in evening dress; the whole auditorium was glowing with shirt fronts and asparkle with jewels amid a wafting of fans. Sofia herself wore a parure of emeralds complemented by her gown of sea-foam green *faille*, a boa of ruffled white silk *plissé* looped lightly about her in the latest mode. Her fan, which was also of white silk, had been a gift from Edmund on an anniversary, its sticks inset with silver and pearls. He, ever the attentive host, had opened a large, beribboned box of chocolates in gold paper cases, which he was placing on the plush-covered ledge of the box. Clare Balfour, already overweight, was unable to resist helping herself at once. She was on one side of Sofia, while Eileen Harding was on the other.

Opening her red-tasselled programme, Sofia looked down the cast and saw that Lillian headed the Big Eight, making her the prima member of the group. It was a tradition with George Edwardes that the word "girl" should be used in the titles of his productions, and there had been every kind of variation on the theme, from *The Circus Girl* to *The Runaway Girl*. In view of the tremendous current interest in horseless carriages, Edmund himself toying with the idea of purchasing a Daimler, the new show was called most topically *The Motoring Girl*. As Sofia was about to scan the rest of the programme, Clare leaned towards her to prod a white-gloved forefinger at the printed name of Lillian Rose.

"That is the wife of Mr. Burnett, the diamond merchant," she said, her breath sickly sweet with the aroma of strawberry fondant and chocolate.

"Yes, I know," Sofia replied evenly.

Clare sat back in her chair again, making a flapping gesture at her own foolishness. "Of course you would know. I quite forgot for the moment. Everyone knows it, and not only in our particular circle where our husbands do business with him. I believe Madam herself likes to flaunt her marriage as far as her theatrical career is concerned, although it does not seem to deter the mashers that flock after *her*!" She helped herself to another chocolate.

Eileen glanced sideways at Sofia. "Mr. Burnett is less fortunate in his state of broken wedlock, would you not agree?"

Always wary of being drawn into talk of other people with either of the two companions whom Edmund had inflicted upon her for the evening, Sofia appeared to be engrossed in her programme. "I daresay his successful business life gives some compensation. Ah! I see Seymour Hicks is to sing several songs. He has such a pleasing voice."

Eileen was not to be sidetracked. "Nothing can compensate for Mr. Burnett's invidious position at any gathering. He is that pariah of our society, the husband living apart from his wife. Other men are inevitably suspicious of him with regard to their own wives, particularly since he is such a good-looking man; and no single woman, if she values her good name, can associate with a man in such limbo."

Clare, who had been listening, raised her somewhat shrill voice to make herself heard, the orchestra having launched into a rousing overture. "He is luckier than you may think, Eileen. I hear that there are plenty of married women willing to offer him solace away from the public eye."

As if the remark had been a prearranged signal, Eileen gave her a nod and addressed Sofia again in deceptively dulcet tones. "By the way, I have been meaning to ask you, my dear. How did you enjoy your visit to Nice?"

Sofia thought her heart had stopped. She concluded that it must have skipped a beat or two by the rate it pursued immediately afterwards, pounding against her ribs and setting a pulse beating wildly in her throat and at her temples. There had been no subtlety in the probing barb. Somehow and somewhere it had been learned that she and Gregory had been at Nice at the same time. But where was the danger in that knowledge abounding? They had only met once in public; the rest of the time they had been shut away at the villa. None could know of their being together there. Be calm, she told herself. There was no real cause for alarm.

"It was a most beneficial sojourn for me," she stated quite casually. "My health was completely restored."

"I am sure it was," Eileen endorsed gushingly. "Everything was conducive to putting the roses back into your pale cheeks. I hope you will tell me all about it one day."

Rigidly Sofia kept herself from being further un-nerved. She turned her head and directed a cool gaze straight into the woman's eyes. "Have you never been to Nice? I should be glad to advise you at any time."

Eileen raised an eyebrow. "Oh, I have been several times, although not recently. However, my cousin by marriage, Amelia Harding, happened to be there last month and saw you on the Promenade des Anglais."

That explained everything. Eileen was trying to make a mountain out of that little molehill of the one public sighting of her with Gregory. Sofia felt com-pletely in control again. "Really? I do not believe I know your cousin."

"Neither of you has been introduced to the other, but I pointed you out to her at Goodwood and again elsewhere."

"What a pity she did not make herself known to me at Nice."

"She would have done so if you had been on your own. Naturally she did not wish to intrude."

"It would not have been an intrusion," Sofia gave back steadily, "no matter whom I was with."

Eileen smiled archly. "Whatever you say, my dear. Later Amelia did call at your villa, but you were not at home."

"The whole purpose of my being there was that I should have peace and quiet. I did not receive any casual callers."

"How wise." Eileen patted Sofia's arm in a faintly conspiratorial manner. "In your shoes I would have done exactly the same. Nevertheless I should like you to meet my cousin one day." The lights of the auditorium began to lower, and she gave a little twitch of her shoulders in simulated excitement, exchanging a glance with Clare across Sofia. "Any moment now! How I love a Gaiety show."

"So do I," Clare agreed.

Then, as the curtain rose on an opening scene of spectacular splendour, which brought a spontaneous burst of applause from the audience, Eileen chose the moment to put her mouth close to Sofia's ear so that no one else should hear what was to all intents and purposes a simple last-minute remark before settling down to enjoy the performance. "You and Amelia could discuss the rival merits of the views from your windows in Nice. Her villa was on the hillside above yours, and she could just see into a tiny corner of your garden amid the trees." She turned her attention back towards the stage, her sharp features masked in reflected light, her expression deliberately guileless.

Sofia sat still and statuelike, nothing to show outwardly the effect that those few, carefully chosen words had had on her. Her eyes were on the stage, but she could not begin to focus on the dancers, aware only of colour and movement, and was as deaf to the tuneful singing as if she had completely lost her hearing. Instead she was remembering that she and Gregory had spent many hours in the garden together, strolling arm in arm along the winding paths, talking with their heads together, and sometimes sharing a kiss or two when out of sight of any servants in the villa. Had the spying cousin caught a far glimpse of them passing across a patch of lawn unshielded by foliage? The villas all stood in spacious grounds, so there was some comfort in the knowledge that at such a distance it would be impossible for anyone to recognize the identity of a man and woman walking together. Unless field-glasses were used. Sofia felt the chill of this thought seep down through her veins until she might as well have been encased in ice for all the effect the swirling spectacle behind the footlights was having on her. The spiteful hint that more was known than had been disclosed about her stay in Nice had an awful portent. Scandal could ruin and utterly destroy all in its path. She could not begin to assess the extent of poor Edmund's jealous rage if so much as a whisper reached his ears. He had a total abhorrence of immoral behavior in any shape or form. Their marriage would be at an end. He was incapable of forgiveness, and she in this instance would be defiantly unwilling to be forgiven. It seemed that her head must split with the sorrow and terror of this dreadful turn of events that had been created in the most frivolous of atmospheres.

She did not register the entry of the eight elite Gaiety Girls in dresses of amber lace and chiffon that would have put Paris in the shade, Botticelli garlands entwined about their well-poised heads. Their graceful saunter was unashamedly sensual, their expressions faintly amused and condescending as if all should know that the homage paid to their ravishing femininity was their natural right. They sang, twirled their parasols, and were executing the lightest of dances before Sofia realized with a start that Lillian was on the stage. Since she was at the head of the line, it was easy to pick her out immediately. She was, Sofia decided, quite extraordinarily beautiful, her eyes a sparkling violet, her skin milky, and her hair the colour of champagne. Her dazzling smile, although perhaps no more dazzling than those of the rest of the girls, nevertheless made every man present her lover as she and they formed themselves into a picturesque group in and around a rose-covered gazebo at the end of their number. Then Seymour Hicks in a long driving-coat with goggles on his peaked cap came bounding onto the stage. A well-established actor and comedian, a favourite with audiences, he was greeted with applause as the girls clustered prettily about him.

"Girls! Girls!" he declaimed. "Who's coming for a spin in my motor car?"

The plot was set in full swing, bringing with it the laughter and the jollity that were another hallmark of a George Edwardes show. Sofia felt already as if the evening would never end.

At the time the curtain was going up at the Gaiety Theatre, Irene was on her way to Derek in Old Bond Street. As with many London streets of old property, a narrow alleyway, little more than a passage, gave access to the rear of the shops where the employees' entrances were located. Policemen on the beat made regular patrols along it at night, and Irene had to make sure that there were none in the vicinity before she sped along to reach the closed iron gate that barred intruders from illegal entry into Lindsay's. Derek loomed out of the darkness of the doorway behind it at the sound of her footsteps, drew her through quickly, and padlocked it again, all in a matter of seconds. Then the inner bolt of the door was shot home.

"Safe!" he exclaimed in a whisper. They were still in complete darkness, and he led her by the hand through the workshop, across the corridor, and into the least used of the three anterooms, which had no window and was lit by silk-shaded lamps which met them with a soft glow. The only lamp not alight was the bright one over a centre rectangular table with chairs on either side, at which business transactions occasionally took place. He shut the door after them, ensuring that no light glimmered through the glass panel of the workshop door to show a faint irradiation out of the skylight roof there. Then he and Irene faced each other, smiling.

"I'm so happy," she whispered.

"So am I," he declared on the same quiet note. He did not dare to touch her, fearful that if he started kissing her, he would lose his reason and be far too hasty at what he wished to accomplish with the finesse that he felt was due to this lovely, unawakened girl. Not normally given to gallantry at such times, he knew it to be a measure of the depth of his feelings for her. With an enchanting unselfconsciousness, she tilted her face close to his, her eyes

133

joyous and half-closed with incipient laughter.

"Why are we whispering?" she whispered. "There's no one here to hear us."

He chuckled then, answering her in normal tones. "I think on my part it's due to the marvel of having you all to myself at last."

"Aren't we lucky?" she agreed blissfully. "No passers-by or a bobby's lamp shining on us or tables full of people rattling cutlery all around us. We are alone."

"I love you, Irene."

Her whole face reflected her love for him. "I wish we could be together forever and ever."

"Why shouldn't we be?"

She looked suddenly shy as if she had put words into his mouth that should have come first from him. "You said once not long after we met that you valued freedom above all else."

"I must have been talking about freedom of expression in my work," he insisted swiftly, not able to remember what he had said but cursing the folly of such an ill-timed remark. It explained to him why Irene had let him take so few liberties with her, for "good" girls ever cherished the principle of keeping their favours for the marriage bed. He could not endure at this late hour to be thwarted of what he wanted above all else. "There are many kinds of freedom, Irene. The best that I can think of is that which comes when two people share love and each other in the understanding that nothing shall part them ever again."

She sighed gently, a tremulous softness transforming her lips, her pupils widening and darkening at his amorous words. "That is what I believe too," she breathed.

Then he kissed her, enfolding her in his arms at the same time, and there was such sweet loving in her mouth that he no longer hesitated but drew her across to the velvet-upholstered couch on one side of the room.

He had anticipated an initial reticence and modesty, so he was prepared, murmuring quiet words while seducing her with kisses until gradually she began to melt and become openly adoring. As he parted her blouse, he found she was wearing the pendant he had given her. She had told him a while ago that she never removed it. He did not remove it now, only pushing it aside with his lips to cover even that small area of her smooth white skin before moving on to the pleasing devouring of her breasts.

She felt she was drowning in sensual delights. Deliberately she was letting go in a conscious decision to allow him to make love to her, any previous fear of pregnancy dispelled by the practical precaution he had promised to take. She realized she had been naive in imagining that their being alone would lead merely to an amorous extension of their kissing and embracing. Neither had she known that she would want to entangle her fingers in his hair, caress his neck, or try to seek the smoothness of his shoulders beneath his shirt, which hung loosely upon him. He had thrown aside his jacket previously and ripped away his tie. Her clothes were in similar disarray, her skirt rucked up to her hips as his hands moved from her black-stockinged legs onto her bare thighs in an advance that she was too lost in love to halt or to want to halt, her submission blissful. Then somewhere in the tangle of loosened garments, his fingertips met on the fount of her womanhood, causing her to gasp aloud upon the ecstatic sensation that leaped under his touch. His love-making moved into a new phase, urgent, eager, and demanding. He no longer spoke, intent on other matters. She was beyond speech, her love for him without bounds. It transcended the excruciating pain he inflicted in taking her virginity, for at the last moment he was rough and frenzied and frantic. As the pain subsided and he lay heavily across her, spent and exhausted, she folded her arms about him, holding him within a hoop of love. For some reason she did not understand, her body felt curiously bereft. It was as if something had been glimpsed and then lost again. But there was no lack of warmth in her heart. She thought its glow must be radiating out around her like an aura. Turning her head, she put her lips against his brow in a soft kiss.

He stirred and looked at her under his lids. "You're lovely," he sighed contentedly. Soon afterwards he wanted to make love to her again, but she had to persuade him that time was running out. Reluctantly he acquiesced. As they made ready to leave there was a new seriousness about him as if he understood as intensely as she did that there was a special significance to the step they had taken together. He kissed her again and again, fondling her and seemingly unable to find the will to let her go from him. It was as difficult for her to face up to a parting, but it had to be.

"We must go," she said at last, exerting strength to keep his lips from hers.

He let his arms fall to his sides and gave a rueful nod. They went back through the dark workshop, he locking doors behind them. They kissed once more with a renewed rush of passion in the last moment before he looked out through the iron gate to make sure nobody was about. When they emerged into Old Bond Street, he hailed a cab for her, remaining on the pavement to watch her out of sight.

At Milton Square she rang the doorbell for admission. Her father was the only one with a house key. Fortunately the domestic staff was so accustomed to her erratic hours that even the lateness of this arrival home was accepted phlegmatically by the manservant who let her in. She went slowly upstairs, still in a trance of happiness and love.

She was sound asleep when her stepmother looked in at her before retiring. Sofia would have liked to chat with Irene for a little while, knowing it would have been therapeutic to have some friendly company after the ordeal of the evening that she had somehow managed to endure. Yet she felt she had handled the situation well by the time she had gathered herself together and thought out what she should do. During supper at Rules after the show, she had invited Eileen to bring Amelia Harding to tea one day. Then she had explained to Edmund in everybody's hearing that she and Eileen's cousin had been in Nice at the same time. "What is more," she related, "we were neighbours at our villas there. I must arrange the tea-party for a day when you can be home, Edmund. I know you will enjoy hearing as much as I whatever Mrs. Harding has to tell us about her sojourn on the Riviera."

That, she thought, was scarcely the attitude of a wife with a guilty secret. She had had the satisfaction of seeing a waver of uncertainty in Eileen's eyes before the invitation was accepted, the date to be settled at a later time. As Sofia chatted on, she was aware of Clare's penetrating stare and hoped that the same doubt had been cast in that greedy woman's mind. In the carriage coming home on their own, Edmund had announced firmly that he had no intention whatever of being present at the forthcoming tea-party, the proverbial wild horses lacking the strength to get him to listen to a lot of foolish women's chit-chat. Sofia, who had known that this would be his reaction, was too exhausted mentally and physically by the strain of the traumatic experience she had been through to make any reply. Luckily he did not seem to expect one.

She did invite Amelia Harding to tea on an afternoon when three good friends of long standing would also be present. The invitation was declined politely owing to a previous engagement. Eileen came but was given no opening for any of her usual spiteful remarks, and after tea she was the first to depart, bored by the good-natured talk and laughter. She actually met Edmund on the doorstep, he having forgotten that it was a day on which to avoid coming home early, and his appearance gave credence to the wish expressed by Sofia at Rules that he should be at the tea-party. When the other three guests had left, Sofia felt that everything had turned in her favour after all. She would not repeat the invitation to Amelia Harding, the gesture having been made. Now she must live with the hope that she had nipped a potential source of gossip completely in the bud. The alternative did not bear contemplation.

Five

Irene went with Sofia to the shop on the day of Mr. Taylor's retirement. Edmund had thought it fitting that they should be there for the presentation of a clock and a cheque to the man who had served the business faithfully for over forty years. Irene was glad to be there, not wanting the old man to leave without giving him her own personal good wishes. There was also a bonus for her at the sight of Derek in his white working overall, lining up with the other goldsmiths when the moment of the speeches and the presentation arrived. Because of the tremendous risk involved in meeting at the shop after hours, they had only dared to meet there once since that first, passionate encounter, the second time no less thrilling for either of them. Somehow the danger added spice to the whole adventure. Their third nocturnal meeting had been arranged for the following week. By that time Mr. Taylor's successor would be in charge, but they hoped there would be no reason to change anything.

To tease Irene with a shared joke kept secret from anyone else, Derek looked with comical alertness everywhere about the showroom except at her. She, knowing full well he was seeing her out of the corner of his eye, found it difficult not to let her mouth twitch with mirth. How dear he was to her, this man so consistent in love and so inconsistent with his own financial affairs. Having learned the names of some of the horses that he backed, and at which races, she had begun to try to follow his fortunes herself in the sports columns of the daily newspapers, her heart sinking whenever she saw that once again his luck had gone against him. If anything, he was always the more cheerful in adversity, putting on a nonchalant air which no longer deceived her as it had in the past. The more flippant he was, the more she knew he had lost. She was never quite sure which side of him caused her most concern—the devil-may-care Derek or the darkly exultant Derek with his pockets full of banknotes and gold sovereigns. All that she was sure of was that she loved him in all his moods, no less in this present humorous turn. Then her father began his little speech, praising Mr. Taylor's long and faithful service. The clock had to be symbolically handed over, for it was marble and ormolu, too heavy to be lifted about with any ease. Mr. Taylor was deeply moved by the occasion and made a modest speech of thanks.

"I came here as an apprentice-assistant in your late uncle's time, Mr. Lindsay. I well remember when the old gentleman passed on and you became the new owner of these grand premises. You proved to be as great a connoisseur of fine jewels as ever he was in his day, and it has been an honour to be part of this respected establishment for such a long time. I thank you most sincerely for this handsome clock. It will always remind me of some of the best hours and days and years of my life. Thank you again."

Irene did not shake his hand formally as everyone else did. Instead she kissed her old friend on the cheek, ignoring her father's sharp frown of disapproval at such a demonstrative display of affection towards a member of the staff, albeit a retiring one.

"I'm going to miss you, Mr. Taylor. The showroom will never be the same without you."

"I shall miss seeing you too, Miss Irene. It would have made your mother most happy if only she could have known what a fine and talented young woman you were to become."

Irene thought she had never valued a compliment more.

She heard from Derek about Mr. Taylor's successor before she met him. Her father had mentioned that he had appointed a young man, but since it was not his custom to talk business at home, she knew nothing more initially other than that the newcomer's name was Lester Ward. Derek's opinion was that he was brisk, efficient, knew his job thoroughly, and was not a man to be crossed lightly. One assistant in the showroom had already been sacked for some very minor matter that Mr. Taylor would have overlooked with a word of advice to prevent it from happening again. On the whole Derek had little to do with Lester Ward, although Richardson, the head goldsmith, had clashed with him from the first day and had had cause to remind the newcomer forcibly that the showroom and the workshop were two separate domains. It appeared to have made little difference, for Lester Ward was everywhere, impatient when emergency repairs took longer than he deemed necessary and critical of everything; and he was altogether succeeding in making his presence felt most forcibly.

"One particular point in his favour as far as we are concerned," Derek told her, "is that he is a stickler for prompt closing on the second. Old Taylor never minded how late he kept the shop open with all the showroom salesmen in attendance when he had a dithering customer unable to make up his or her mind. Ward knows how to settle their decisions to their entire satisfaction in a minimum of time, which means we don't have to worry that a lateness in closing might put all our plans awry."

Irene had designed a peacock brooch for her next project. It would need a large number of stones for the tail, and she was full of happy anticipation at the prospect of making many special visits to the workroom to collect them in turn. When she arrived at the shop for the initial choosing of them, she saw one of the salesmen identify her for Lester, who immediately hastened across the showroom towards her. He was at first glance quite an attractive man, with deep-set, greyish-blue eyes, his gaze keen and guarded, thick, brown hair brushed back immaculately in waves from its middle parting, and a slim frame tapering from shoulders made squarer by the good cut of his coat.

"Miss Lindsay, I believe. Good evening. I am Lester Ward. I am afraid Mr. Lindsay has gone home, but I am here to be at your beck and call. I hope you will allow this occasion to be the first of many when I may be of service to you."

She was not flattered by his approach, which she thought too silky and obsequious, although she did not doubt that certain women customers would be beguiled.

"How do you do, Mr. Ward. I expect you know that I come periodically to choose semiprecious stones for my work."

"I do indeed. Everything has been made ready for you."

Neatly he escorted her through the showroom into the direction of the corridor, waving aside her insistence that she knew her own way, and chatted with her about the mild weather and how it had brought on such a fine show of daffodils in the parks. Although he was giving every sign of wanting to make himself agreeable to her, the annunciary rise of dislike that she had experienced at first sight of him was strengthening steadily. She told herself that she was being uncharitable. He meant well and did not realize that it was hard for her to accept anyone else in Mr. Taylor's place. Neither did he suspect that his pale and flawless complexion, of which no doubt he was proud, reminded her of the wax-display hands that had always made her shudder inwardly. Yet in truth it was more than these minor things. She did not like the way he looked at her. Although she was as used as any girl could be to seeing that special flare of admiration and sexual awareness which came into men's eyes at the sight of her, there was something sly and furtive about Lester's attitude. It made her wish she had a cloak to cover herself from head to toe to keep his slanting glances from her figure. As he stood aside to let her precede him into the corridor at the rear of the showroom, she felt his eyes rove over her as acutely as if his loathsome, white hands had reached out and squeezed her buttocks.

With relief she reached the workshop door and took the handle firmly, determined to keep him from entering there with her. "Mr. Ryde will be waiting to assist me as usual with the gems," she said over her shoulder to him with a polite inclination of her head in dismissal. But he was not to be banished so easily.

"But I have had them put ready for you in this room," he informed her expansively, throwing wide the door of the largest of three ante-rooms. Looking through, she saw the multi-coloured array glinting and gleaming in the sorting trays on the table under the bright central light. She had no option but to enter there, Lester darting around to hold the chair for her.

"Please tell Mr. Ryde that I'm ready to choose my stones," she said, seating herself.

"It is my honour and duty to carry out that task," he replied. To her dismay he drew up the chair on the opposite side of the table and settled himself down. "Do you have your design with you?"

Anger mingled with her original dislike. She wanted to insist on Derek being the one to advise her but realized it would not be wise. There was something too sharp and wary about the man seated opposite her. She felt he would pounce on anything that struck him as unusual and worry it like a terrier with a rat. With some reluctance she took the design from her purse and unfolded it on the table. She had looked forward to showing it to Derek, eager for his opinion, and Lester's praise for its originality left her cold.

"I want turquoises and amethysts for the tail," she said, studying the contents of the sorting tray.

"What about the neck?"

"That is being enamelled. I thought I'd add something with a glow for the eyes."

She was determined to get her selection made with the least possible delay; whereas with Derek these times had been stretched out from half an hour even to an hour sometimes. For the first time she regretted her father's rule that no more than the minimum of gems be taken away at any one time, for if it had been up to her, she would have claimed all she needed for the peacock brooch and would not have come back again to waste time in Lester's company. In any case she could well imagine that he would have the remainder of her choice packed ready in individual boxes when she came again, depriving her still further of any workshop meetings with Derek.

Her choice was almost complete when Lester was called away to the showroom. Seizing her chance, she darted across the corridor into the workroom where Derek sat alone repairing a necklace at a bench under the lights. He had been hoping that he would manage to see her before she left, and sprang up at once to embrace and kiss her. Both of them spoke at once, each equally indignant that Lester Ward should have snatched away their time together.

"At least all will be well for next Thursday evening," Derek assured her.

With reluctance she withdrew from his arms. "I must get back before that man returns."

His eyes looked lovingly at her. "At least Ward didn't choose our room in which to set out the gems."

She gave him a smile from the doorway. "I was glad about that."

No sooner was she back in her chair than Lester came hurrying in, apologizing profusely for having had to leave her. She cut him short by pointing out her final choice of gems. There followed the usual procedure of signing for them and having the ones she was taking with her put in cotton wool in a little box and wrapped.

"When may I expect you again, Miss Lindsay?" Lester asked as he held open the street door for her.

"I have no idea when I'll be fetching the next batch of stones," she replied. "It depends on my progress with the brooch."

"I will be here at all times," he assured her.

She smiled to herself. He would be nowhere near the Lindsay premises when love was in charge again.

Derek possessed her no less violently than before, fraught with desire. He appeared to imagine that she shared some quarter of his intense gratification, and she basked in the joy of pleasing him.

They began to make plans and to talk of their future together. When her concentrated training at Essex House was complete, they would marry, for by that time she would be over twenty-one, and no one would have the power to keep them apart. They would go away and work side by side in a jeweller's workshop somewhere until the day came when they could set up in business on their own, she designing and he making the wares. She was perceptive enough to see that whatever feelings Derek had cherished for her before she became his, his love had increased since by a thousandfold. She believed there was nothing he would not do for her. He had promised already to cut down his gambling, and she had high hopes that with time he would conquer his obsession altogether. She would help him in every way.

Only Sofia suspected that her stepdaughter was in love. She noticed that Irene's bright, vivacious face had taken on a softer expression, dreamy and introspective, as if her thoughts dwelled on secret dreams. Sofia hoped that the young man in question was worthy of the girl and supposed him to be a fellow student at the School of Handicraft, for he was certainly not among the number who sought her out at the parties and soirées and balls that she attended from time to time.

For herself Sofia had no such tranquillity of mind, for recently she had begun to suspect that gossip about her trip to Nice had been revived, if indeed it had ever been as fully crushed as she had come to believe it had. She thought she knew the reason why the matter had not been allowed to rest. She was suspected of committing the most heinous sin in female eyes of taking a lover younger than herself. There was not a woman she had ever met, not even the most devoted and faithful wife, whose jealousy, whether conscious or unconscious, had not flared beyond all proportion when a middle-aged woman was known to have a younger man in love with her. Claws grew, tongues became vindictive, and such bitchiness prevailed that on many occasions in the past Sofia had looked about her in silent amazement at the unmistakably envious rage of some of the most tolerant women she had ever met. She truly believed that when women reached a mature age, they looked at their equally mature husbands and longed to be ravished again by youth and beauty. When other women were able to fulfil this fantasy, they could scarcely endure the torment and gave vent with the only weapon in their grasp, which was the provoking of scandal and disgrace.

At the moment there was nothing she could actually challenge or put her finger on, nothing that could be clearly defined; but her unease had returned, making it increasingly difficult to concentrate on other matters without being torn back constantly to the ever-present dread of exposure. With her heightened senses she was aware that now and again eyes shifted uncomfortably to avoid her direct gaze. At times smiles appeared false to her as if all tittle-tattle had been stilled at her approach. If acquaintances did not appear to notice her when their carriages passed hers, she found herself wondering what had reached their ears. Yet she did not harbour the least regret about that glorious revitalization of herself at Nice. Indeed, the experience had given her the very strength to face whatever might come in the whole of her life ahead.

Her greatest anxiety was for Edmund. He must not be hurt if it still lay in her power to protect him from gossiping tongues. Although it was hard to play a role of complete unconcern, she must continue to keep to her normal social routine, her composure unassailed by any slight, real or imaginary. She must trust that her path and Gregory's would not cross again until malicious suppositions had been forgotten and allowed to die away. For herself, she would prefer never to see him again, but she realized the chances were that sooner or later they would find themselves at a function in the home of a mutual acquaintance or at some other gathering. As long as sufficient time had elapsed, no harm could come of it, either for Edmund or, heart-wise, for herself. Then, in the midst of all she had to worry about, she had to console her stepdaughter for the loss of a pearl from the setting of a sapphire ring. If only, she thought with less than her usual sympathy, all troubles in this world were of so little consequence as material possessions.

"Do not distress yourself," she urged, getting down on her hands and knees to join Irene in a search of the dining-room floor. "I am sure we shall find it."

"I've looked everywhere," Irene exclaimed frantically, pushing a chair out of the way as she crawled about, running her palms over the pile of the Turkish carpet. "It was my mother's ring and means so much to me."

"I know it does. When did you first notice that the pearl was missing?"

"Upstairs, about an hour ago. Two of the maids helped me go through the room as if with a toothcomb. Then I remembered that I knocked my hand against a corner of the sideboard in here at breakfast yesterday morning and wondered if it was dislodged then."

"So really you are not sure when it vanished? With a ring worn every day, it is easy to slip it on and off without actually looking at it."

"I can't believe I wouldn't have noticed the gap in the pearls almost at once. I'm really clutching at straws by looking here."

"Well, let us hope it comes to light!"

They searched the dining room in vain. Finally Irene sat back on her heels with a heavy sigh. "I suppose wearing my ring all the time without having the setting checked regularly for any loosening is the reason why the pearl has gone. Who would expect a jeweller's daughter, quite apart from being an embryo jeweller herself, to forget that golden rule? I could have done it myself at my own workbench. Oh, I'm so angry with my own carelessness!"

Sofia got up from the floor to take a seat in one of the Mackmurdo dining chairs, which had all been pushed awry during the search. "At least the pearl can be replaced."

Irene frowned uncertainly. "I'm not sure that will be easily done. As you know, pearls may appear white, but in reality they echo all the shades of the rainbow when it comes to matching them. In my ring they are almost of a bluish hue."

"What a pity your father is abroad on business at the moment. He would have been able to tell us right away if there are any at the shop that might match. Would you like me to take it in for you tomorrow morning? I am going to my milliner's nearby."

If there had been any chance of seeing Derek, Irene would have said that she would take it in herself, but Lester Ward made a point of waiting on her each time, and she could barely tolerate his presence. "That is kind of you," she said, accepting her stepmother's offer. "I'd hate to be without the ring for any length of time."

Sitting in the landau next morning, being driven to Lindsay's, Sofia looked at the ring she was holding in her gloved palm, turning it absently. With Edmund being away, she had chosen to be out less in the evenings, and when she did go, it was to women's gatherings only, either to play cards or to discuss

some charity fund-raising effort. She was not taking
the slightest risk of incurring further gossip by going
into mixed company without Edmund. It meant that
she came home earlier than usual and realized fully
for the first time exactly how erratic Irene's home-
comings from the School of Handicraft had become.
Some days she was quite early; at others she was late,
giving the explanation that she had walked homewards with a friend whom Sofia concluded was the
lover in the girl's life and was pleased that Irene had
confided that much to her. Then, the evening before
last, Irene had been late beyond all bounds. It was
almost midnight when she came in. Sofia, unable to
sleep from worry, had met her on the landing. Irene,
who must have seen from outside that the bedroom
light was on, showed no surprise when she appeared.

"I'm sorry if you have been anxious about me,
Stepmother," she had said, speaking first. "To be
perfectly honest I thought I should be home before
you. I have spent the whole evening with the friend I
mentioned to you before. I love him. I would tell you
more, but I can't make you my confederate against
my father."

"Oh, my dear," Sofia had exclaimed faintly.

Irene, smiling with a pure happiness, had shaken
her head at such agitation. "I tell you, there is no
need to worry. I'm not planning to elope. I have my
diploma to get at Essex House and have to be
accepted into the Guild before anything more can
happen in my life. Good night. Sleep well."

Sofia, seeking to be reassured, had decided she

must speak to Irene again on the matter the following evening. But then had come the disruption over the missing pearl, and somehow the right moment had not presented itself. In the landau Sofia closed one hand over the other, holding the sapphire ring captive and out of sight. Thus she must keep from Edmund that small disclosure of a secret love made to her by Irene. Little did her stepdaughter know that she now had two secrets to keep from Edmund. What was more, her own was potentially far more explosive than Irene's romantic involvement with a fellow student, who was probably not of her social station, which was reason enough for the girl to keep him out of Edmund's snobbish way. For herself, Sofia held no such views about the unknown young man. If Irene loved him, that was good enough for her. It was a natural assumption that he would be as hard-working as Irene and fired with the same enthusiasm, or else it was unlikely that the girl would be attracted to him for any length of time. Sofia tightened her grip on the ring. No one knew better than she how to evaluate the gift of love.

In Lindsay's, the new head salesman could not have been more attentive and obliging to her. "It is my stepdaughter's ring, Mr. Ward," she explained, "and since the missing pearl appears to be lost without trace, I was hoping that you would be able to match a replacement with the existing ones."

Lester put a jeweller's glass to his eye and examined the ring keenly. "Hmmm. It might prove difficult. Apart from anything else, these pearls are unusual and quite small. Are you quite sure that there is no chance at all of the missing one being found?''

''I think not. A most thorough search has been made.''

He removed the glass from his eye and gave her a reassuring smile. He had splendid teeth, and liked to show them. ''Leave the ring with me, Mrs. Lindsay. If such a pearl is to be located anywhere, you shall have the ring back in pristine condition in the shortest possible time.''

She thanked him and turned to leave the shop, he moving forward with a swirl of coat-tails to bow her out of the door. It struck her that he seemed extraordinarily pleased with himself, quite as conceited as Edmund in his own way and without doubt no less efficient.

Outside it was a bright and sunny morning. Old Bond Street was full of well-dressed shoppers, with plenty of elegant traffic flowing by in a jingle of highly polished harness and gleaming wheels. Sofia turned in the direction of her milliner's, which was only three shops away. She had been undecided whether to go there first or to see about the ring, and she had taken no more than a few steps when she wished that she had reversed her calls. Then she would have missed seeing Gregory emerge from a cigar shop on the opposite pavement, and all that it did to her. Sighting her, he came to a halt, his eyes meeting hers across the breadth of the street. Then a *daumont* driving past sliced him away from her gaze, and she increased her pace sharply in the direction of her milliner's, fighting down a sense of panic. She felt as if a thousand eyes had witnessed that simple exchange of a single glance, and as many tongues were ready to interpret its significance.

Once inside the milliner's, she made the excuse that she was not feeling well and was shown into a private room to rest, smelling-salts provided. She sank thankfully into a chair, unable to control the shaking of her knees and the trembling of her hands. After the inevitable cup of tea, which never failed to appear at times of crisis in this country she now thought of as her own, she was to all outward appearances herself again. Yet she was unable to summon up the least interest in any hats that were shown her and left the shop without buying anything. Although there was little chance that Gregory was still in the vicinity, she looked neither to the left nor to the right as she got back into the landau to be driven home. She could not risk a second spasm of wanting to run blindly into a beloved man's arms.

Edmund returned from the Continent two days later. After changing out of his travelling clothes, he went straight to the shop to deal with whatever was awaiting his immediate attention. When he came home, he had Irene's sapphire and pearl ring with him.

"Here you are," he said to her, handing it over. "Ward tells me that he matched up a missing pearl for you."

Irene was delighted. It was impossible to tell where

the gap had been. Much as she disliked Lester Ward, she would give him the thanks he deserved for the care and trouble that he had taken when she was next at Lindsay's.

She had not yet seen him when she and Derek met again at the shop after hours. When he had made love to her, they talked of rings. Derek, never far from his dreams of when he would be as rich as Midas, described the ring he would like to make for her. He wanted to use a Golconda diamond from the famous fields of South India, pink, flawless, with a rare limpidity, which he would surround with emeralds from South America, choosing only those that exactly matched her eyes. It was all said in light-hearted tones, but at the back of his words there was the steel of his determination to make his fortune one day. She did not doubt that he could do it, although it was her hope that he had relinquished the belief that it might come by way of horses on a racecourse. Then, as if he sensed her need for reassurance, he took her right hand and slid off her sapphire and pearl ring to place it in reverse on the third finger of her left hand, allowing only the gold band to show.

"That's how another ring will be one day." He kissed her third finger as if to seal the pledge anew.

She sat up to lean over him. Her hair, which she had scooped to one side, made a coppery swathe that flowed down over the frilled disorder of her petticoat bodice, half veiling the full curve of one bare breast, and came to rest on his shoulder in a flat curl. He was resting an arm under his head on the cushion that

157

served them as a pillow.

"I wish it could be soon," she said yearningly, unusually wistful and restless. Subterfuge was totally alien to her nature. All her life she had taken every step openly and unafraid. There was no fear in her now, only a day by day increase of healthy indignation at being manipulated by circumstances over which neither she nor Derek had any control.

"You know you have only to say the word, and I'll get a special license for us to marry." He put his hand over her breast and fondled it, liking to see her shiver delightedly at his touch. This time what he had said had an import that outweighed the prolonging of a pleasurable caress, for she moved away almost at once, swinging her slim legs to the floor and standing up to shake her petticoat into place about her ankles.

"We have discussed that suggestion often enough, and there's no more to be said." She stepped into her skirt and drew it up to fasten it at the waistband. She and Derek had never been quite naked together. He had wanted them to be, but something more than shyness or modesty held her back. It was as if to be in nakedness with love was to surrender utterly to its power, and she alone would know when the moment was right. "I accept the responsibility for my own actions," she continued, pushing an arm into the sleeve of her blouse, "but I will not falsify facts about parental permission in order to become a wife. In any case, you know full well that if the secret came out, my father's first action would be to have the marriage annulled because I'm not yet of age."

It piqued him that for all her tender-heartedness she could be so thoroughly independent and self-willed when holding to a principle that she believed to be right. He loved her. God! How he loved her. And he felt the fact that she loved him in return should be reason enough for her to cast all other considerations aside. It was not that he was in any hurry to marry. Far from it. That, at least, was some consolation for the hurt her stubbornness inflicted on his ebullient male pride. All the while he had his freedom, he could do whatever he wanted to suit himself. Naturally he was fully prepared to give up the diversions of bachelorhood upon marriage to Irene, but no normal man would want to give up his liberty before time, particularly when a wedding just now would make no difference to his being with her. They would still have to go on meeting secretly if he was to keep his job at Lindsay's for as long as it suited their plans.

Perhaps she thought he looked a trifle glum, for she paused in pinning up her gleaming hair, smiling at him through the aperture made by her crooked arm. "All will come right one day. You'll see."

Just as they were about to leave the shop, she remembered to transfer her ring back to her right hand, asking him at the same time if he had had anything to do with its repair. He was locking one of the inner doors after them and glanced back at her over his shoulder. "No, I didn't know it had been in the workshop. What was wrong with it?"

ROSALIND LAKER

"I had a pearl replaced."

"I expect one of the other goldsmiths was given the job." He took her by the elbow to hurry her through the next door that he had to secure. "Ward would never let me do anything for you, however indirectly."

"Why do you say that?"

Another key clicked in a lock. "First of all, he keeps those gems set aside for you in a locked drawer of his own, well away from the workshop. Then I found out that he made enquiries as to how often you had come to choose stones with me, probably comparing the frequency of your visits then with how often you call in now when he is in charge."

"As infrequently as possible!"

"Exactly. It's my belief that he half suspects there has been something between us, even if he has no idea that it is still continuing."

"How could he have suspected that?"

"Perhaps he caught a glimpse of you returning to the ante-room after coming to see me in the workshop that first evening, and added everything up. As I said before, he's sharp as a needle."

She jerked up her chin. "None of it has anything to do with him anyway. Why should he concern himself?"

"There's only one answer to that. He fancies you himself."

She said nothing. She had known that from the start.

Her father happened to be in the showroom when

she went to collect her next consignment of gems. "Mr. Ward has put aside some more semiprecious stones for you, Irene," he said to her. "When you have taken a look at them and are ready to leave, we shall go home together."

She never liked being alone in the largest of the three ante-rooms with Lester, the door firmly shut on the rest of the premises. For one thing she felt it pretentious to sit there, her humble gems very different from the valuable jewels normally discussed and displayed on the table, and for another she had to guard herself the entire time from physical contact with Lester. His hand would brush hers when they were both selecting gems. More than once his knee had come against hers, and wherever she tried to put her feet under the table, one of his managed to come alongside. The contact was always so brief, to all intents accidental, for he made a point of moving away quickly as if in apology before she could draw breath to register her annoyance. Today, as they sat down opposite each other at the table, she tucked her feet well under her chair and, smothering her dislike temporarily, gave him the thanks for her ring that in all fairness was due to him. He spread his hands wide and clasped them again in front of him.

"It was simply a matter of luck," he said with a self-congratulatory air. "Sometimes it is easy to get a replacement; at others it proves to be virtually impossible to find an exact match."

"Nevertheless I'm extremely grateful." She fastened her attention on the new stones in the sorting

161

trays. "These look interesting."

"How grateful?"

She jerked up her gaze and stared at him, startled by the unexpectedness of such a question. "I beg your pardon?"

His expression was curiously elated, his lids narrowed and his eyes very bright. "Forgive me, Miss Lindsay. I was clumy in my eagerness. I wish to presume upon your appreciation of the small service I did for you by asking if I may escort you to the Gaiety one evening."

She answered him with firm politeness. "I'm afraid that wouldn't be possible."

"Why, may I ask? Have you see the show? Would you prefer a straight play, perhaps?"

His persistence, with its undercurrent of arrogance, astonished her. It seemed to her that her father's presence in the office only a few feet away was giving Lester the confidence to speak out to her in a manner that he would never have done otherwise. Was it possible that he had already sought her father's permission to invite her out, and that it had been given? Did Edmund Lindsay hold his new head salesman in such high esteem that he would uncharacteristically allow him to associate with his daughter? If that was the case, it gave her hope with regard to Derek. Perhaps their situation was not as hopeless as she had feared. This rise in optimism tempered her reply.

"I enjoy the theatre whether it is drama, farce, or a musical show, but I have little free time these days.

My hours at Essex House are elastic and not bound by rules that govern other places of study. There are lectures in the evenings on gemmology, Gothic architecture, the dignity of handicrafts, and so forth. The students are all free to attend them, whatever their particular crafts may be, and since there is a linking theme, most of us like to be there." As she spoke, she recalled how often Derek had had to pace the Mile End Road waiting for her while a lecture went on longer than anticipated.

"That should suit you. Not being bound by rules, I mean. I think you are a very free person, able to dispense with conventions that control the more inhibited. I see you as one who seeks new experiences in every field. Yet you are in need of a friend."

She was becoming increasingly uneasy. "I have many friends, Mr. Ward."

"No one able to champion you as I would do, guarding you, protecting you, keeping your secrets."

So Derek was right. This man did suspect that she and Derek were romantically involved, and he was having the gall to attempt a mild form of blackmail by issuing his own invitation to take her out. Far from her father knowing anything about it, Lester was using his proximity to give strength to the request. Her first impression of the man had been that he was sly and devious, and this had been totally confirmed. To her dismay he shot up from his chair and came around to her side of the table where he perched his weight on the edge of it. She did not look up, aware of him through her lashes. A faint odour of male sweat emanated from him, for he was in a state of high excitement, and as he leaned towards her, he slid a hand along the table, leaving a spot from his damp palm. She was suddenly afraid to move, fearful that she might spark him into a grappling embrace.

"You must have realized during our sessions with gems," he continued with a strangely pitched eagerness, "how my feelings have been growing for you. Say you will allow me to be your friend. Your *special* friend."

In the privacy of his own thoughts, he had long considered her to be easy game. She had inflamed him ever since he first saw her come swinging into the shop with her splendid figure and her marvellous red hair, a colour well known to be synonymous with a woman of a passionate, unbridled nature. Everything he had found out about her since that first meeting had confirmed that assessment. Not only was she a student at a highly unconventional place of study, but it was commonly known that her views were socialistic and rebellious. Then there was her lack of ladylike decorum in travelling around on buses and in cabs, facing the risk of every kind of proposition, which any decent girl in her social position would have avoided. He had not been more than a few days at Lindsay's when he had heard that she dallied far longer than was necessary when chosing gems in seclusion with Ryde, who was known among his fellow workmates to be a reckless fellow in both gambling and amorous pursuits. It showed that for her there were no barriers which would normally have divided an employer's daughter from an employee. No barriers at all. This and much else had come to his knowledge in a simple gathering together of facts and clues, some more vital than others. As for himself, he knew his own worth as far as women were concerned, particularly women of Irene's calibre, and he had not met one yet whom he hadn't pleased with his suave good looks or who had not been flattered by his overtures, however overt. From the start he had been able to tell that the highly charged atmosphere between Irene and himself had been suspenseful and dangerous to her. Watching her, he could see that she was only waiting for the next move that he would make, and he did not intend to disappoint her. He moved his hand from the table and slid it swiftly from her knee up her thigh, his hard caress wrinkling her skirt over the smoothness of her black silk stocking and her flesh.

Her reaction was not at all what he had expected. She sprang to her feet, swinging out an arm and giving him a great thrust that half knocked him off balance. Her face was livid with rage and revulsion. "Keep away from me! Don't ever put a slimy hand on me again or I'll kill you!"

With her blazing eyes and the fist she had raised to keep him at a distance, he could almost believe she would carry out such a threat. "You teasing bitch!" he retaliated coarsely, his fury equal to hers.

As she made to dash past him, he caught her across the breast. She brought down her fist, striking his hold away, and in the skirmish one of the sorting

165

trays, which had already skidded close to the edge of the table, was jerked to the floor, sending the contents scattering in a rainbow spread in all directions.

The crash brought Lester back to his senses. He looked with alarm towards the door in case the noise had been heard elsewhere. Irene snatched up the wrapped box of gems that she had originally come to collect. With her hand gripping the doorhandle, she looked back at him, high colour in her cheeks.

"In the future Mr. Ryde will help me select whatever gems I might need as he did before you came!"

She pulled open the door and went out from the room just as her father emerged leisurely in hat and coat from his office. He lifted his eyebrows enquiringly. "Did I hear a crash?"

With a shrug she turned slightly away, averting her face with its still angry colour. "One of the sorting trays fell to the floor. No damage was done."

He nodded, losing interest; his thoughts concentrated on the new blue-grey Daimler that he had recently purchased. Irene walked ahead of him out of the shop, thankful to get away.

Six

When Irene told Derek of the unpleasant encounter with Lester, his reaction was less than she expected. It was not that he failed to be riled by the man's presumptuousness, but he seemed to have something of greater importance on his mind. She guessed immediately that he had suffered a particularly heavy gaming loss that had plunged him into difficulties. The fact that he was not as defiantly cheerful as he usually managed to be in these circumstances was, in its way, a good sign. It meant that he bitterly regretted going back on his promise that he would try not to get out of his depth in the betting world again. Without referring to the matter, thinking it best in this case to make a renewed resolve on his own not to be as reckless again in the future, she gave him comfort in her arms. In return he made love to her with a wealth of new emotion as if she had never meant more to him.

Her conviction about his debts was confirmed when he missed meeting her at Essex House a couple of times, explaining that he was looking for new lodgings. She guessed he was behind with his rent and compelled to move elsewhere through no choice of his own. On the third evening, when he met her with a decidedly haggard expression, she slipped her arm through his and prepared to bring up the subject of a loan as tactfully as she could.

"I don't like to think of your moving into just any old place," she said as they strolled along.

"It has to be cheap," he stated edgily. "I'm afraid the Savoy is beyond my present pocket."

"I'm going to ask you something I've never asked you outright before. Please say you won't be cross with me."

He became tense, the muscles of his arm tautened under the sleeve on which her hand rested as if he had balled his fists in his pocket. "What is it?" he demanded with a sharp look at her.

"I have a little money in hand at the moment. Sofia was more than generous on my nineteenth birthday a few weeks ago."

"Well?" His voice was without expression. He had given her a book on emeralds, which had pleased her more than anything else she had received.

"Let me give the money into your charge for a little while. You could use whatever you needed from it, and give it back to me afterwards."

The outburst of offended pride that she had feared was not forthcoming. Instead, his shoulders lifted and fell on a great sigh. He stood still, taking her by an arm to turn her towards him. In the lamplight the lovely oval of her face, accentuated by her brushed-up coiffure beneath the straight brim of her sailor hat, glowed at him with an expression of fond anxiety.

"You're the best girl any fellow could have, sweetheart. Don't you worry about me." His two hands cupped her chin gently and he stroked her cheeks with his thumbs. "I don't need your money. I only need you. I only want you." He bent his head and kissed her lips softly and caressingly. She, warmly demonstrative as always, stood on tip-toe, the better to slide her arms about his neck in a rush of love, and swayed against him like a slender reed. Somewhere in the distance, rival barrel-organs kept up a discordant jingle, a buzz of voices came and went with the swing of a pub's street door, and wheels and hooves rumbled and clattered past with the occasional shout and crack of a whip. Always the city throbbed about them. They had never shared a day in the country or ambled along a seashore. The only quietness they ever claimed was in the room they had made theirs with a set of forged keys. In their kissing each yearned for the next time they would be there together.

It came in the early part of the following week. She had been delayed unexpectedly at Essex House. Ashbee had called her into his office to offer a constructive criticism of her peacock brooch, which she had finished that day, and to discuss future work with her. Mrs. Ashbee was also present, sharing her husband's belief that a personal relationship should be maintained at a family level with every one of their craftsmen and craftswomen, from early training to full Guildsmanship. Although sparing with praise, Ashbee made it clear to Irene that she was fulfilling the promise he had seen in her when she had first applied to become a student at the School of Handicraft. For her next project, he wanted her to design and make a necklace with matching bracelets.

"I am aware that you are accustomed in your own home background to seeing such pieces made up in valuable stones. Forget all that. There is a fast growing trend, which I have helped to foster, for the far greater use of semiprecious stones in jewellery of modern design. Beauty of colour and workmanship combined with originality can result in masterpieces of grandeur equal to any occasion. If in any doubt, turn your thoughts to nature. Remember the haze of colours in a dragonfly's wing. Picture a meadow red with sorrel. What is more breathtaking than the flash of kingfisher blue? No priceless diamonds there, but hues that can be garnered with your craftsman skill from tourmalines, aquamarines, amber, lapis lazuli, and so forth. Of course you would wish to work with the highest quality of these marvellous gems, but it is a rare student who can afford them. Instead, do as you have done before and make what is available a true challenge to you. A turquoise with a greenish hue or a mottling is graded as a poor stone, and yet it may help an imaginative designer to achieve exactly a special effect being sought. My wife and I look forward to something rather spectacular from you this time, Miss Lindsay."

She arrived at the dark passageway entrance to Lindsay's, buoyed up by the double happiness of Ashbee's encouragement and the anticipation of being with the man she would one day marry. Glorious designs were dancing in her mind's eye, and she felt that she was breaking through at last into a realm of workmanship that would lead her eventually to the peak of her chosen profession as jeweller.

"I've so much to tell you!" she exclaimed excitedly as Derek let her in through the door of the premises. They embraced and kissed wildly, she out of exuberance, he with a relieved intensity that sprang from having been brought to the point where he had thought she was not going to appear.

"Why are you late?" he demanded in a strained voice. Now that she was there, he was experiencing the not uncommon reaction of anger at having been put through unnecessary concern. "I thought something was seriously wrong."

"Not at all," she answered jubilantly, putting her hand trustingly into his to be led past the benches in the unlit workshop without knocking into anything. "Everything is wonderful. And you're wonderful! I love you, love you, love you."

He allowed himself to smile, mollified by her unstinted declaration, and was prepared to forget for the next hour or two all that was troubling him in the world outside. They reached the windowless ante-room where one lamp glowed in the corner, and he shut the door, enclosing them in their haven.

"I have a marvellous new project." She was radiant, her eyes shining. "A necklace and bracelets. I'm going to use a botanic motif, but in an entirely original way, the necklace to be based on the shape of a gorget that knights in armour used to wear at their throats. Yet it will be light and delicate in appearance. I'll be using gold, which I have been saving, and the stones shall be chrysolite in both green and yellow. They have such a mysterious and intriguing sparkle. What I should like as well would be at least half a dozen baroque pearls. There were a couple in the sorting tray that was knocked to the floor. I wonder if there were others. I didn't really have time to examine the contents properly that day."

It amused him to let her chatter on while he combed her hair free from its pins with his fingers, taking pleasure in its red-gold silkiness tumbling down about his hands. She did not always allow him to do it, because it meant searching for the dropped pins afterwards, but today she had so much else on her mind and was on such a crest of bliss that he was only hampered by her spinning away every few seconds with her skirt aswirl to illustrate her description of the jewellery she planned with quick and pretty gestures, her long fingers spread curved and fanlike.

"Come here," he said after a few moments, catching her by the shoulders and holding her still.

"You're like a will-o'-the-wisp this evening."

She was laughing at his words, her head thrown back, her chin uptilted, when the door of the ante-room was flung open. The wall-switch clicked, and the lights low over the centre table plunged on, throwing a white glow into every corner. Edmund stood in the doorway, his face convulsed with outrage, his hand still on the switch as if it had been frozen there. Irene's laugh had faded to a low gasp. Instinctively she caught at Derek as they stood there side by side.

"Irene!" There was such shocked disbelief in Edmund's roar that his voice rasped with it.

She spoke up swiftly. "Derek and I love each other."

"Love?" He thundered the word as if unable to comprehend its meaning. Temper, already in momentum, recoiled and struck again like a whiplash, making him feel as if his pounding head must burst. He hurled his hand away from the light-switch and stamped into the room to stand full-square, his whole body shaking with rage, his fists doubled at his sides.

"Irene is in no way to blame for being here." Derek spoke in a dry, almost wearied voice. He was thinking that of all people he should have known that when luck turned against a gambling man, catastrophes set in from all directions. "It was my idea entirely. I made the duplicate keys. I persuaded her that it should be our meeting place."

"The devil you did!"

Irene broke in. "I needed no persuasion."

Her father rounded on her furiously. "You be silent! I'll deal with you later. Ryde! Come with me." He stood aside to let the young man go past him. When Irene would have followed, Derek himself turned about to hold her back gently.

"It's best you wait here. Your father and I have to talk everything out." She hesitated uncertainly before drawing away from him, her face pale and agonized. As the door closed after the two men, her head bowed as if under the weight of the whole dreadful experience, and she clasped her hands in front of her waist, her elbows coming tight in at her sides as she stood paralysed by tension. Then she heard the key turn in the lock and the scrape as her father jerked it out to pocket it. He was going to brook no interference from her in the painful and traumatic interview that was about to take place.

As it happened, Edmund had no intention of discussing anything. If his daughter's lover had been less muscular and agile, he would have set about him with a vengeance, but after an ignominious scuffle by the workshop door when he tried unsuccessfully to push Derek through by the scruff of his neck, he realized he was only inviting retaliatory damage to his own face and person. Thwarted of physical revenge, he became if anything even wilder, giving forth in an almost demented rage his opinion of seducers in general and his own daughter's ravisher in particular. He used language that had rarely, if ever, passed his lips before, punctuating it with a violent pounding of his fist on a workbench and kicking furiously out of his way anything that stood in his path. Throughout it all Derek, white-faced and tight-lipped, went through the process of collecting up his tools of trade and putting them into a leather bag. When he was ready to leave, he stood holding it by its handle at his side.

"How did you find out that Irene and I met here?" he asked in the same tired tones he had used previously, cutting across Edmund's tirade of abuse.

"Haa!" Edmund's exclamation had come in wrathful triumph. "Someone a great deal smarter than you has used his eyes. Hairpins. A cushion not left as it had been the evening before at the shop's closing time on more than one occasion."

"And the discovery of a pearl lost from a ring, perhaps?"

Edmund's eyes glinted and narrowed. "Get out!"

"Irene had no fault in this affair. Don't let her suffer as a result of it. I'm entirely responsible."

"Go to hell!" Edmund bellowed, thrusting his congested face forward.

When he let Derek out of the rear door, he had one moment of total satisfaction. Bringing up his foot, he landed a great kick against his former employee's backside and sent him sprawling. The leather bag went flying, snapping open in the process and sending valued tools clattering and ringing over the cobbles. Edmund crashed home the gate and secured the padlock as Derek scrambled to his feet. Then the rear door slammed on the scene. Edmund gave a mirthless grin to himself. It would be a virtually impossible task to find some of those small tools in the darkness.

Irene had her shoes on and her hair pinned up when he opened the ante-room door on her again. He stared at her with something close to hatred. When he had been informed that from gathered evidence it appeared that clandestine assignations were taking place on his property, the finger of suspicion had been pointed at Derek Ryde with no inkling as to whom the woman might be. No pearl had been mentioned to him, but he did not doubt it had been instrumental in setting his head salesman's eyes to work. The janitor who cleaned out the premises would have found it and handed it over. Thus had two and two been put together. For himself, he had half expected to find Ryde consorting with a married woman well out of reach of her husband's jurisdiction. He had even thought she might be one of his own customers, for there was a certain type of wealthy woman, however well-bred, who preferred to take a lover from the lower classes. It was because of this possibility that he had decided to wait alone to catch the culprits, thus keeping the matter entirely to the couple and himself without subjecting the lady in question to the embarrassment of the presence of other witnesses. Nevertheless it had flayed his temper to find himself skulking like some grubby private detective in the darkness of his own premises. This had been his second evening of waiting. On the previous occasion he had sent Sofia on to a concert at the Albert Hall, making a pretext of why he could not join her until later, for he had wanted no one else to know what was in the wind. This evening he should have been at his club. Instead he had found his own daughter in the most compromising circumstances. In looking at her he did not see a warm-hearted girl swept away solely by love. He saw only immorality and licentiousness, the vices he most abhorred, and the fulfillment of what he had most dreaded since the day he had lifted her out of her crib and seen that the dark birth-hair was receding on the well-shaped little scalp, giving way to a red-gold down.

"Where is Derek?" Irene asked him.

"He has gone. Now no more questions. Let us go home."

She saw he was in too dangerous a mood to tolerate the least procrastination, his face working, his attitude bull-like. He let her out through the front entrance of the shop. Outside she glanced about quickly, thinking that Derek might have waited, but there was no sign of him. Throughout the drive home in a hackney carriage, not a word was exchanged. Edmund's hands, alternately clenching and splaying over the head of his silver-topped cane that was propped at an angle between his spread knees, gave full indication of the seething state of his temper and his mind.

Sofia had had a charity committee at home that evening. The members had just left, and the maids were carrying out the trays of teacups when Edmund preceded his daughter into the drawing room. One look at his purple face and another at Irene's pallid, drawn one alerted her to disaster. She sprang up and closed the double doors on the departing maids.

"What has happened?"

He glared at his wife. "Ask your stepdaughter if she is in the family way!"

Sofia, deeply troubled, looked wordlessly at Irene, who shook her head vigorously. "I'm not. I know I'm not."

Edmund breathed through his nostrils heavily. "At least one must be thankful for that, I suppose." He then proceeded to tell Sofia what had happened that evening, she becoming more and more distressed. He was not to know that she was blaming herself for not having been more concerned when Irene had revealed that she was in love. It simply had not occurred to her that the girl might have fallen under the spell of an experienced man able to devise such an insidious place of seduction.

Throughout her father's irate soliloquy, Irene felt faint at his besmirching of what had been wonderful and marvellous to her. Whether she swayed slightly on her feet, she did not know. It all seemed in keeping with the nightmare situation that the three of them had remained standing like chessmen on a board instead of sitting down in a rational manner. One thing became obvious to her. Derek had not mentioned a possible marriage to her father, and she thought that was wise. It would only have inflamed everything still further. With time even her father would come to realize that nothing was going to dim or alter in any way her love for Derek and his for her.

Sofia, her hands twitching agitatedly, put a question in some bewilderment. "Whatever made you go to the shop this evening in the first place? I do not understand."

"I had been alerted." He turned to his daughter. "Give me your ring." His hand was held out to receive it.

Irene, brought out of her daze of anguish, looked at him in puzzlement. "My mother's ring?"

"Yes, yes." He snapped his fingers impatiently.

Slowly she drew the pearl and sapphire ring off her right hand. He snatched it from her and shook it within a few inches of his wife's nose. "It is my belief that your stepdaughter," he began pithily, seeming to have relegated all kinship with Irene away from himself, "lost the pearl from this ring in the ante-room where she never normally entered on legitimate visits to the shop. When my head salesman was asked to find a replacement, he must have realized that a certain pearl given into his care was not only an exact match but was the very one missing from the ring!"

Irene spoke as if from a far distance. "So he set a trap for me."

"He believed, quite rightly, that the truth should come out," Edmund countered.

Sofia, watching her stepdaughter anxiously, tried to intercede for her. "Let Irene go up to bed, Edmund. She does not look well. This has all been a great ordeal for her."

The appeal brought him to a pitch of exasperation. "Do not waste your sympathy on her! I am the injured party. I have been deceived and my property used for immoral purposes. She is deserving of the most severe punishment."

There was incredulity in Sofia's eyes. "Irene is not a child anymore. You reminded me of that a while ago. She is a full-grown woman."

"I am only too aware of that," he retorted bitterly. "I also know that justice and punishment go together."

"So do justice and mercy! That is more commendable."

He was losing patience with her. The days of quelling his wife with a glance were no more. With a shrug that dismissed her opinion entirely, he crossed to the bureau, opened the flap, and pulled forth pen, ink, and paper. Then he drew back the chair and indicated to Irene that she should sit there.

She held back, not moving. "What do you want me to write? If it's a letter to end everything with Derek—"

He answered her callously. "That is already over. You will never see him again. The letter you are to write now is to Mr. Ashbee, telling him that you are terminating your studies at his School of Handicraft as from today."

Irene cried out, "No!"

"You cannot mean it, Edmund!" Sofia exclaimed in disbelief.

He regarded her with menacing scorn. "Have you ever known me to say anything I did not mean?"

Still Irene remained where she was. "Derek had nothing to do with my work at Essex House. He has never once taken time that I should have spent there."

"I accept that as the truth," Edmund acknowledged grudgingly, "but it makes no difference. I warned you at the start that if you gave me the slightest cause to withdraw you from your studies, I would do so immediately. You gave your full agreement to my terms, and therefore you will abide by them. You have proved yourself to be irresponsible away from supervision and not at all deserving of the concession I made in allowing you to attend the School of Handicraft in the first place. I would be an unnatural father if I did not wish to see you protected from further temptation, which is more likely to come your way at Essex House than if you are removed from it." He picked up the pen and held it out to her. "Delay no longer. This letter shall be written. I am giving you the chance to express your appreciation to Mr. Ashbee in your own words for whatever you feel you have gained from his instruction. I think it would appear less gracious in his eyes if you left the writing of the letter to me."

Irene went to the bureau and sat down. Although Edmund did not stand over her while she wrote the letter, she made two false starts and had to crumple the sheets of paper into the wastepaper basket. When it was done and sealed into its envelope, she rose from the chair and stood resting her hand on the back of it.

"You haven't stopped me from becoming a

jeweller," she said to her father. The lamplight, dazzling on her lashes, made her realize that she had been weeping during the writing of the letter without being aware of it. "I'll get there somehow. Now may I have my ring back again?"

He had been holding it ever since he had taken it from her. Deliberately he slipped it into one of his waistcoat pockets. "You have forfeited the right to possess anything that belonged to your late mother. I will not have it sullied further by you."

She flew from the room, her sobbing echoing back down the stairs. Sofia stared at him, aghast. "Edmund! How could you!"

For the first time in his life, he felt a need to justify his actions. There was a look in his wife's eyes that he had never seen before, and it disturbed him. "It is all for her own good," he insisted defensively.

She turned away from him and went hastening away up the stairs in his daughter's wake. He spent the rest of the evening with a bottle of brandy in his study. When he went to bed, Sofia was already under the bedclothes, apparently asleep. He did not disturb her. There was a rigidity about her back turned towards him that discouraged even a leaning over to give her a good-night kiss. Had it not been for the brandy, he doubted whether he would have slept well that night.

Irene was up and about long before dawn. In a carpet bag she had packed enough clothes for all her needs, and her purse contained the money that she had offered to lend Derek. It should be enough to see them through until he was able to establish himself in work again. There was always the hope that she might get taken on with him in a lesser, half-trained capacity. Her only worry was that she might not find him at his old lodgings, for she had been so full of her own news when they had met that he had had no chance to tell her if he had taken another room somewhere. At least he would have left a forwarding address, for he always boasted of settling his debts when money came his way.

The sky over London was lifting to a clear April day as she let herself silently out of the house, and there was an early morning freshness to the air. She hurried across the square and took the outlet into the street beyond to find traffic already rolling by. The city was well astir. Brass churns rattled in the milk carts, a postman slammed a mail-box shut after emptying out the mail, and a chimney-sweep whistled as he unloaded his brushes outside a house. Along the pavements people bound for the humbler jobs of the day hastened to get to their places of employment by six o'clock. She looked for a cab and was in luck.

Derek's address proved to be in a respectable street of tall, three-storied houses built originally for those with large families and moderate incomes. They were of plain, rust-red brick with some Gothic ornamentation in ochre stone and set with high, sashed windows. None had railed basement areas since the presence of servants beyond a single housemaid had not been catered for, and low walls enclosed narrow front gardens no more than a yard in depth, in which on the whole shrubs and small bushes had been allowed free range. Almost all the houses displayed "Bed and Board" signs, some with the additional card bearing the announcement "Vacancies."

When she alighted at the house second from the end of the street, Irene asked the cabby to wait until she was sure whether or not she had to extend her journey. The front door needed a coat of paint, but the brass foot-scraper was polished, as was the knocker, which Irene thumped twice. Footsteps approached at a sharp pace from within, and the door swung open to reveal a middle-aged woman with greying hair, her clothes neat, her apron starched. From a kitchen somewhere behind her there drifted the aroma of frying bacon.

"Yes?"

"Good morning. Is Mr. Ryde still living here?"

The woman looked her up and down. "You don't look like a debt-collector. So you must be one of his fancy birds. No, he is not still living here." She made to close the door again.

"Please! One moment!" Irene implored urgently. "I don't want to be a nuisance, but it's most important that I find him."

"Is it?" The woman kept the door partly closed, but one half of her continued to eye keenly the early morning caller, who had an educated voice and a genteel appearance.

"Would you tell me when he left? Was it yesterday

or the day before? And what is his forwarding address? You see, he and I are engaged to be married."

There was a long pause while the woman appeared to consider how she should answer. "Oh, you are, are you? Well, he left here three months ago. He left owing me rent, packing up his traps and doing a moonlight flit. When I called him for breakfast one morning, his bed had not been slept in. If I'd known where he worked I'd have gone to his place of employment, but he was cagey about his doings, probably because the bookies and others were always after him for money he owed. About two weeks ago my daughter happened to see him from the top of a bus and alighted in time to follow him to a room he had in the Edgware Road. He made a promise to see her again but never showed up. Needless to say, he had cleared out of that place when she went back there. Where he is now, the Lord only knows."

Irene was conscious of a sickening sensation at the pit of her stomach. It had been getting worse and worse with every telling word uttered from the doorway. Yet it simply couldn't be Derek whom the woman was talking about. "I can't believe that we are referring to the same Mr. Ryde. Derek Ryde is the man I'm looking for."

"Yes, that's right. Derek Ryde. Tall and fair-haired with grey eyes." A twinge of sympathy showed in the woman's expression as she saw the effect that the confirmation had made on the girl at her threshold. "I've told you bad news, haven't I? Not at all what you expected, I suppose. You'd best come in and sit

down for a few minutes. My name is Mrs. Pendle."
She stood aside for Irene to enter. "I'm busy getting
my lodgers their breakfast, but my daughter will bring
you a cup of tea. I think you should meet her."

Irene was shown into a front parlour that was stiff
and uncomfortable with shining horsehair upholstery, starched, white antimacassars, and an
aspidistra in a glazed, yellow pot that dominated the
window and threaded greenly the light that entered
there. She sat down in the nearest chair, set her elbow
on her knee, and rested her brow in her hand. It was
as if she could not grasp this revelation of another
side of Derek's life that had been hidden from her. He
must have moved from this address shortly after she
had written to tell him that with Sofia getting well
again, she would be returning to her studies at the
School of Handicraft. He had met her at Essex House
the next day, never mentioning that he had any
thought of changing his lodgings. As for his having
moved several times since, she had not the least idea.
In her stunned state she recalled something else Mrs.
Pendle had said at the door, which she, afraid that the
door would be shut before she could get further
information regarding Derek's whereabouts, had not
thought about until now. Before she could dwell on
it further, there came the rattle of a cup on a saucer as
the daughter of the household came with the
promised tea. As Elsie Pendle entered the parlour,
Irene had an impression of a pert, pretty girl with
dark curly hair and blue eyes. She was also at least
five months pregnant.

"So you're looking for Derek Ryde, miss," she said drily to Irene. "So am I." She patted her bulging figure significantly.

When Irene came out of the house, she saw with some surprise that the cabby was still waiting for her. She had forgotten about him. Forgotten everything that was present and immediate. She had no money left in her purse, having paid Mrs. Pendle, who was a widow working hard for a living, the rent that Derek had owed. The rest she had given to Elsie, asking her to buy some clothes for the baby. The girl had been grateful. In the moment of departing, Irene had asked her about her mother's reference to "fancy birds." "After he had left here," Elsie had said, "an actress from the Gaiety called to see him, and I heard later he was often in the dressing room there—or he was whenever he had one of his big wins and was in the money."

The cabby looked down from his box. "Where to, miss?"

She had no choice. The only place she could go in her state of penury was home. "Milton Square," she said huskily, getting into the cab.

Seven

Edmund, setting off to work far earlier than usual,
missed seeing his daughter's return and was never to
hear that she had been out of the house long before
him that day. He had a particular reason for wanting
to get to the shop before any of the staff arrived,
which was why he had breakfasted exceptionally
early. It had been quite restful to breakfast alone, for
he had not been in the mood to tolerate the coolness
towards him that Sofia seemed prepared to maintain.
The memory rankled still, her accusing eyes and her
barbed reminder that justice should be tempered
with mercy were not at all what he expected of her
attitude towards him. In truth, she had upset him in
her own way as much as his daughter had done, and
he did not like it. He did not like it at all.

He let himself into the shop. First he went into the
workshop and put to rights all he had knocked and
kicked about in his rage there the previous evening.

He also checked that Ryde had made no disorder in the collecting up of his belongings. Apart from shutting a couple of drawers left open, there was nothing else to do. Unfortunately the glass pane in the workshop door had been cracked slightly during the scuffle that had occurred, but it was lost in the lower half of the patterned surface and would go unnoticed until a glazier was called in to replace the pane.

Last of all he went into the ante-room, the janitor's broom in his hand. He swept up a couple of hairpins and looked about to make sure there was no dropped glove or a forgotten handkerchief to show that Irene had been there. All seemed to be in order.

After replacing the broom, he threw the hairpins away and opened the door into his clerk's office. There he wrote down some instructions, which he left in the middle of the desk blotter for the clerk to see upon arrival for work. Then he went into his own office. Taking a ring box, he put into it the pearl and sapphire ring that he had confiscated from Irene and sealed it. Later that day it would go into the bank for safekeeping. He had no intention of its being taken out again until her wedding day, when the bride-groom should be a man of whom he approved. Otherwise it would never be hers again.

Seating himself at his desk, he took up a pen and wrote again at slightly more length on a sheet of his headed paper. When it was signed, he slipped it into an envelope and sealed it. At the same moment he heard the premises being unlocked from the employees' entrance as Lester Ward, prompt to the second of eight o'clock, arrived to let in the waiting janitor and the rest of the staff. There was a low rumble of talk as the salesmen began to filter through to the showroom, their first task to remove the counter cloths and dust the shelves. In the workshop there was a laugh or two as the goldsmiths donned overalls and made ready to start the day. They were responsible for their own floors, the careful sweeping up and sifting having been done at the close of work. Within minutes it was as Edmund had expected. His door opened without a knock, and the janitor came in with polish, dusters, and broom. The man's mouth dropped open at finding his employer already at the desk.

"Beg your pardon, sir. I didn't know you was 'ere."

"That is all right, Thompson. Leave the cleaning of my office for ten minutes. You will still be able to finish by the shop's opening time. Now tell Mr. Ward that I wish to see him."

"Yes, sir."

Lester wondered immediately if Edmund Lindsay's early arrival had anything to do with the absence of Ryde's tools from the workbench and the fact that even the goldsmith's overall had gone from its peg. Intrigued, he approached the office, glancing sideways at the ante-room in which he had a special interest. It was the first place he inspected each morning, although today there had been no sign of occupation the previous evening. It was a tiny pearl discovered there that had made him turn detective with such interesting results. Nobody ever crossed him except to his or her loss. With time Irene would pay for the dance she had led him and the loathing he had read in her eyes.

"Enter."

Briskly Lester entered his employer's office. "Good morning, Mr. Lindsay."

Edmund looked up over his pince-nez. "Good morning, Mr. Ward. Do you happen to have your set of keys with you?"

"Yes, sir. They never leave my charge."

"Give them to me, if you please."

Somewhat surprised, Lester drew out the chain from his pocket, on which the key-ring was attached, and removed it, handing it over into his employer's outstretched hand.

"Thank you." Edmund pulled open a drawer in his desk and put the ring of keys away next to those he had retrieved from the workshop bench after Ryde had cast them down in departure. "I have called you into my office to inform you that I am giving you notice to leave my employment with immediate effect. You will receive a month's wages, which the clerk will be making up now, and a testimonial in my own hand that will guarantee you an appointment elsewhere without any difficulty."

Lester stood as though transfixed, stunned by the unexpectedness of the blow that had befallen him. "But why? For what reason? I am entitled to an explanation."

Edmund, sitting back in his swivel chair, put the

fingertips of both hands together and regarded him stonily. "In brief, I have not found you entirely up to the standard of service and civility that I have decreed for my showroom staff and for my head salesman in particular. You will be better off in another shop that has less exacting standards."

Lester's normally pale features flushed angrily. "Do not take me for a fool!" he snapped harshly, his temper never far from the surface. "I know what is behind this. Ryde has not turned up for work this morning, and his tools of trade have gone. You must have come back here last night after what I reported to you a couple of days ago and surprised him with the woman he has been having his way with under this roof time after time! What did you do when you arrived here before anyone else? Put the cushions to rights again?"

"I do not know what you are talking about," Edmund replied scathingly. "I feared for the stability of your mind when you gave me that odd report. I said to you then that as you and I were the only ones with a set of keys in our possession, an entry by anybody else could only be effected by a break-in. That has not taken place. It seems to me, Mr. Ward, that you are given to the most extraordinary flights of fancy. If Ryde has left my employ without giving notice, as you say, a simple check will soon establish if he has absconded with anything of value. Then, if all is well, it will only remain for me to appoint another goldsmith, and Lindsay's will be better off without an unreliable craftsman."

"Do you deny that you came back here last night?" Lester persisted savagely.

"Whether or not I choose to visit my property by night or day has nothing whatever to do with you," Edmund gave back grimly. "There is no more to be said between us. Collect your pay-packet on the way out. Here is your testimonial." He held out the long envelope that contained what he had so recently written.

Lester jerked the envelope out of Edmund's hand and slammed it back on the desk. "You are kicking me out for one reason only!" he shouted, pointing an accusing finger. "You know as well as I do that there is a third set of keys which has been in another's unauthorized possession. You're afraid that I'll undermine your authority and make you a laughing stock among your own staff by letting it be known that it was your daughter—"

Edmund sprang to his feet and brought his fist thundering down with such force on the desk that papers flew up in the air and the floorboards vibrated. "Do not dare to utter any libellous accusations in my hearing or in anybody else's!" he snarled, his temples corded with an excess of rage. "Should a defamatory whisper ever be perpetrated against the good name of Lindsay, I would drag you into court and have you exposed as a contemptible liar! What is more, it would need no more than a judicious word from me then or now to ensure that no business of repute ever employed you again. Now get out!"

Lester was left with no choice but to capitulate. He understood the threat to its full. A deliberate slur on his honesty, however falsely contrived, by a jeweller as highly respected as Edmund Lindsay, would finish his career. He had realized well enough that his employer was a ruthless man, but he had not suspected just how ruthless. This confrontation had reached its limits. If he uttered another defiant word, that testimonial would be torn up before his eyes, which was a far more alarming prospect than any threats of future vengeance. In his aim to bring retribution to Irene, he had overlooked her father's natural desire to protect her whatever the circumstances. He should have realized that Lindsay, being the proud man he was, would never tolerate the continued presence of one who knew of his daughter's disgrace. Far from gaining by informing on the lovers, which he had thought would be another point in his favour towards an eventual partnership, everything had been wiped out completely. Abruptly he snatched up the envelope. Determined to leave with some dignity, he choked out his final words with some semblance of civility.

"You are doing me a great injustice. I would remind you that I took a vow upon my appointment here that nothing private in the way of business or customers' disclosures on these premises should ever pass my lips. When the door of Lindsay's closes on me, all that I have seen or heard here remains locked within it. Good day to you."

Edmund watched him go from the office. It had all

passed much as he had expected, thoroughly unpleasant and yet with the desired results. Ward had been a truthworthy employee, but a trifle too susceptible to good-looking women. Female customers had been charmed by him, but male escorts, whether husbands of lovers, had on occasion been gruff and abrupt with the fellow. That was not good for a business when men were the main purchasers of fine jewels. It had been in the cards that sooner or later he would have to go, and the present cause, disagreeable though it had been, had merely accelerated his dismissal. Reaching out a hand, Edmund rang the bell on his desk. There was a great deal to get through before this day was over, and there was no time to waste.

At home, Irene spent the day in her room. She needed to be alone. Luncheon came to her on a tray, only to be removed again untouched. Later she did accept a tray of tea, which Sofia brought to her, and as they drank it she told her stepmother that she had gone to find Derek, and what she had learned there. As she had known, her stepmother did not sermonize but conveyed a loving support that was the only balm acceptable to her.

Before her father came home from the shop, Irene was downstairs with her dress changed for the evening hour, its colour a vibrant coral, for she was determined not to appear subdued or crestfallen. She had shed her bitter tears, and there should be no more. The inner hurt that love had left behind was another matter and could not be similarly dismissed.

On her own in the drawing room, she marvelled reflectively as she looked about her at the familiar setting that so much should have happened to her since she had first asked her father to let her go to Ashbee's school just two years ago. Taking stock of her situation, she counted that on the credit side she had received a sound grounding in practical work at Essex House. Admittedly the workbench skills that she had hoped would make her a Guild member had been left sadly in mid-air, but at least she had learned enough to go on designing jewellery with a full knowledge of how the work should be carried out. And she would go on designing, adding to those detailed drawings mounting up in her folio. All she had to do was to wait with as much patience as she could muster until she reached the age of twenty-one. Then she would be a free woman, able to live her own life without the domination of any man, whether her father or husband or lover. In this year of 1900, with such an exciting wave of new lines and shapes and colours sweeping all before it across Europe to America and back again, she would find some place for herself eventually on its rich crest. On that she was resolved.

Her back stiffened as she heard her father come home. She turned to face him with a swirl of her skirt as he paused in the open doorway to address her.

"Come to my study, Irene."

He was switching on the Ashbee lamp on his desk when she entered. As the glow illumined his face, Irene thought he looked strained and tired. All that had happened had taken its toll on him as well as on her. She thought it curious that in spite of everything they still had the power to hurt each other emotionally. The filial tie was strong, whatever the circumstances.

"I have been making plans for you," he said, taking a slow pace or two across the carpet.

She answered him straightforwardly. "I have to warn you, whatever your plans are, that when I come of age I shall leave home and earn my own living."

"Oh?" he replied cynically. "Then what I have mapped out for you should stand in good stead. Shops always have need of a well-trained counter hand."

"I don't think I understand."

"I have decided to take you on at the shop as my personal assistant."

She was astonished and angry. "You made it clear before I started my training that you would never permit me to work as a jeweller at one of your benches, and yet now you are prepared to allow me into the showroom. Where is the difference?"

"There is a great deal of difference. As I mentioned, you will hold a position of importance, or so it will appear to others. This will quieten any speculation about why you left the School of Handicraft so abruptly and will be taken as my further indulgence towards you as regards your interest in jewellery. Moreover, the title of the position I have created for you means that you will be absolved from being labelled as a member of the staff." He wagged a finger grimly at her. "Do not imagine that this makeshift arrangement of mending matters gives me the least satisfaction. Far from it. I am thinking solely of the good name of Lindsay and its protection against gossip of any kind."

"I can't work with Lester Ward," she said tightly.

"He has gone. I gave him notice today."

Her eyes widened. "Who is to fill his place?"

"Mr. Taylor has come out of retirement at my request to hold the fort until such time as a new head salesman is appointed."

"Then I should be working with him?" She began to see what this new prospect might mean to her. She would be able to learn about the commercial side of the jewellery world, not only the buying and selling at the counter, but by catching up every scrap of information she should be able to learn much of the markets at a wider level.

Edmund nodded. "Before I left the office today, an office was made ready for you. It will set you still further apart from my employees when you are not serving customers. In addition, I shall expect some secretarial work from you. If you can learn to use one of those newfangled typewriting machines, so much the better. I bought one for my clerk, but he is loath to try it."

She was quiet for a few moments. Then she lifted her head. "When do I start at the shop?"

"Tomorrow morning. Be ready to leave with me in the Daimler after breakfast. We shall travel to and fro together. If I should be abroad or absent for some other reason, your stepmother's maid will accompany you as chaperone. In other words, you will be subject to closer supervision than ever before." His implacable mouth grew thin. "For all your wanton ways, I will see you into an honourable marriage yet."

It chilled her to see the old rancour showing savagely in his eyes. That undefined grudge had been given renewed impetus, and she found it frightening. "Where is my office located?" she asked bravely, wondering if a stockroom had been refurbished for her.

"Where else but in the particular room that you appear to have favoured above the rest?" he replied with derision, coldly intent on wounding her. "It was rarely used for customers. You will have ample chance to repent of your folly within the four walls that encompassed it."

He thought he had broken her then. There was such stark anguish in her sensitive face, and a tremour seemed to pass through her body. Then she folded her hands together as if gathering strength and inclined her head. "I'll be ready to leave for the shop with you in the morning."

In the hall she met Sofia, who saw by her stepdaughter's pallor that there must have been some further crisis. "What has happened now?" she enquired anxiously.

Irene managed a smile of reassurance, putting her hand on the woman's arm. "It's all right. Father is going to take me into the business as his personal assistant. At least I'm not being cut off completely from the world of jewellery. I'm thankful for that."

"I am thankful too." Sofia was intensely relieved. It appeared that Edmund was not totally incapable of mercy after all. Without going back on his decision, he had taken some heed of what she had said to him. She went on into the study and met him as he was about to go upstairs to change for dinner. Swiftly she put her arms about his neck and pressed her face into his shoulder.

"Thank you for giving Irene an alternative path towards her ambition," she said gratefully.

It was to be a long time before she learned of the exquisite punishment he had inflicted on his daughter, Irene being unable to bear speaking of it, he wishing to avoid a return to coolness on his wife's part when all was well between them again.

"What are you going to wear tomorrow at the shop, Irene?" Sofia asked as the two of them went upstairs to bed, leaving Edmund still reading in the drawing room. Since he had never employed a woman on his staff before, no precedent had been set.

"I'm not sure. Let's have a look through my wardrobe. You can help me decide." It was hard for Irene to concentrate on anything. She was haunted by the prospect of the room she must face the next day, her feelings fraught and desperate.

"It will have to be black," Sofia said, sorting through the dresses. "Simply because when you are selling jewellery it is the best colour for setting off all kinds of stones. And you must be chic. That is most important.''

''I only have two mourning dresses kept for funerals,'' Irene spoke listlessly from the dressing table stool where she had seated herself.

Sofia had already found them and held each one at arm's length in turn, studying them critically. Both garments were of silk, simple and classic, the collars throat-high.

''Put on this one.'' She handed a self-stripe to Irene.

As the girl put it on, Sofia took the velvet sash from the other dress. With her unerring eye for fashion detail, she tied it expertly about Irene's high collar and arranged the ends to fall into a graceful cravat, which was the latest mode newly come from Paris. The effect was as she had known it would be, elegant and dramatic. All that was needed was a striking brooch to secure it and give the final touch. Irene fetched her jewel case, and together they went through it.

''This one!'' Sofia picked out the jade brooch that Irene had had from childhood. ''The green will compliment your eyes, and the gold filigree setting will show up against the velvet. Do you have any earrings to go with it?''

Irene had a pair that were suitable. When she had secured them, she surveyed her full-length reflection in the cheval-glass.

''Father will approve my array,'' she observed

wryly. "I look every inch the proprietor's daughter."
Her chin tightened determinedly. "But I'll work
harder and sell more than anyone else already at
Lindsay's."

Sofia, standing a little distance behind her, gave
her reflected image a slight smile. "I knew you would
be courageous. You always have been."

Irene answered her in a choked voice. "I'm not at
heart." She put a faltering hand across her eyes. "I
don't know how to bear the pain."

Sofia went quickly to her. "It will ease, my dear
child. Believe me, with time all things heal, even the
heart." She did not add that it was the hope that she
herself was clinging to, wanting to erase a romantic
love that she had never wanted to harbour.

The next morning it was as Irene had foretold.
Edmund looked her up and down before approving
her attire with a curt nod. After that he did not speak
to her until they arrived together at the shop. First in
the showroom and then in the workshop, he
presented her as his new personal assistant. Then he
left her in Mr. Taylor's charge.

"My word, Miss Irene," her old friend said to her,
"whoever thought that you and I would come to
working side by side? You will do well in the
business, I know."

"You have taught me so much in your time, Mr.
Taylor," she replied, "and I gained a lot from my two
years at the School of Handicraft, but I'm insatiable
for knowledge." Her tone held a frantic eagerness
because work, work, and nothing but work was all

she wanted now as an antidote to heartache and to prepare her for the future. "Turn me into a jewellery expert. You can do that better than anyone."

He chuckled. "That is a tall order, but I shall do my best. I knew years ago that you were one of those rare people with an instinctive feeling for stones and their quality. What is more, you began to acquire knowledge when you were very young and receptive, which should stand you in good stead. However, first of all I have to follow Mr. Lindsay's instructions with regard to settling you in here. After you have seen your office, I am to show you where stock is kept. Then I am to teach you how to sell with courtesy and efficiency, which should come naturally to you. Later Mr. Townsend, your father's clerk, will explain the paperwork to you."

She tensed herself as she followed Mr. Taylor into the ante-room that had become her office. To her overwhelming relief, it was completely transformed. The lime flock wallpaper was unchanged, but the couch and gilded chairs had been removed to allow cupboards and a filing cabinet to take their place. Instead of the table under the centre light, a mahogany desk took up the space, well stocked with writing materials, its leather-upholstered chair matching a pair set at angles to the front of it. A Turkish rug in more garish colours replaced the sombre-hued Persian one that had previously been spread on the polished floor. Her attention was caught by the typewriting machine on a side table. She thought it would be a little like playing the piano, and she had only to master the setting of keys, which should not prove too difficult. Mr. Taylor pointed out that bells had been installed connecting her office with her father's when she should be wanted there, and others would allow her to summon Mr. Townsend or be alerted to a need for extra assistance in the showroom. A place of love had become a place of work. As she went from her new office to be shown where stock was kept, she made up her mind never to recall the past there or to think of it in its former light.

Eight

Irene had been at the shop seven months before she served her first important customer. Many distinguished people had been into the showroom, but Irene was too much a beginnner in the eyes of her father or Mr. Taylor to be entrusted with a specialized sale. After Mr. Taylor finally and reluctantly made a second retirement, the same attitude towards her lack of experience was held by his replacement, Robert Symington. She liked Mr. Symington. He was fortyish, just and fair towards members of the staff, strict when necessary, and encouraging of her passionate interest in stones. When there was some spare time, he even carried on the tests that Mr. Taylor used to set for her, putting out a variety of one kind of stone—either diamonds or emeralds and so forth—and she would try to identify by colour, size, and brilliance their place of origin and approximate value. Since she had excelled in gem-

mology at the School of Handicraft, quite apart from
the curious empathy she had with stones, she often
surprised him with her remarkable accuracy, which
he checked from shop sales sheets. He knew a great
deal about gems, but he was more a salesman of good
jewellery than an expert in the definitive quality of
them, unlike his predecessor, but this in no way
diminished his interest in Irene's steadily increasing
ability. If any stone that was the least unusual came
into the shop, he always made a point of letting her
try out her knowledge in identifying it. One day he
showed her a pair of ear-rings that had been designed
and made in the workshop, using the customer's own
stones, which were a rich blood-red in colour.

"I should like to hear what you have to say
about these," he invited.

She studied their magnified splendour through
her jeweller's glass. She knew that with cut stones
only an expert was able to distinguish between a true
ruby and other red stones known as spinels, which
could be equally magnificent and valuable. Thus the
element of guesswork was there with her from the
start. Nevertheless she looked for the hint of purple
common to stones that came from the Mogok area of
inland Burma, a source of the rarest and most
beautiful rubies in the world. It was not there, which
did not surprise her, but she was following the rules
of observation that had been laid down for her. She
looked for the flaws and inclusions that were often
found in true rubies, and these were wonderfully
clear, with what seemed to be an orange glint in their

depths. Having studied so many handsome stones since childhood, her eye seemed to have acquired a keen appreciation of infinite shades. She removed the glass from her eye.

"The stones are faceted with a step cut and set in gold. I would say they come from Ceylon."

"That is correct. The owner has a tea plantation there. The ear-rings are to be a gift to his wife. Are they spinels or rubies?"

She compressed her lips in earnest contemplation as she weighed up the evidence, her own unique intuition playing no small part. Then she made a firm decision. "I believe them to be balas rubies." She had used the other name for red spinels.

"Well done!"

Another and more mundane field of progress for her was the typewriting machine. She had had some lessons from a woman "typewriter," as qualified operators of the machine were called. With her retentive brain and nimble fingers, she had soon begun pounding away at a good speed, with remarkably few errors. It gave added prestige when business letters were typed, although correspondence with customers of distinction still went out in Mr. Townsend's best copperplate, anything else amounting to a discourtesy. He gave her some basic instruction in bookkeeping, and when he was away ill for a week, she took over his work and managed better than she had expected.

When it came to serving, Mr. Taylor had kept her at his elbow in order that she should observe the process of selling expensive wares to customers who ranged from being comfortably well-to-do to being possessed of enormous wealth. She fetched and carried the shallow leather boxes of midnight blue embossed with gold, which were the hallmark of Lindsay's and which contained the beautiful adornments on beds of silk or velvet. It gave her particular pleasure when, at a sign from Mr. Taylor, she lifted the lids to reveal the sparkling displays that irradiated over the faces of the beholders. Sometimes she found herself to be more the object of attention of male customers than the jewels. She had taken to piling her hair high up in the new fashion of a pompadour, which showed her ears and enhanced her long neck in the high collars. Her father did not pay her a wage, apparently considering it unseemly that payment to his own daughter should go through the books. Instead, he had increased her dress allowance quite handsomely, wanting her to cut a dash with her clothes in the shop. She kept to black, but no longer wore any of her own jewellery, having discovered what an impact was made on a potential buyer when she picked up an ear-ring to hold to her ear in display or placed a brooch or some other rich adornment against a frothy black jabot or across a plain silk cuff.

Her favourite customers were young couples buying engagement or wedding rings, and these she had been able to serve on her own almost from the start. They were usually so happy, holding hands and gazing at each other, the girls transparently in love, the young men fond and proud. At first their joy in each other had speared the great aching emptiness within her with memories she had no wish to recall, but after a while she was able to subdue all else except an interest in what she was selling and a wish to produce the right ring for the couple concerned. Quite often the man would be in an officer's uniform, for war had broken out a while ago with the Boers in South Africa, and for many couples London was a place of farewells at the railway stations when troop trains left for the ports. It did not take her long to discern when a wedding ring was being bought to cover a few snatched hours together in a hotel room before a heart-torn parting.

She was putting a tray of wedding rings away after one such couple when an elderly woman with aristocratic looks came into the shop, a female companion in tow. Irene recognized her instantly from pictures and photographs that she had seen. It was the deposed Empress Eugénie of France, widow of the late Napoleon III, who had once reigned over the glittering Second Empire until his retreat into exile in England, where he had died some years ago. Irene looked quickly about her. All the salesmen were busy, and Mr. Symington, who should at that moment have been coming forward, was engaged in consultation with her father in the office. It was her chance.

The Empress, in spite of being in her seventies, still walked as if on wheels with the gliding step for which she had been famous. Clothed in an elegant black from head to foot, she was Paris personified in elegance, the filmy veil of her hat passing under her chin to keep her jawline firm, a single plume curling along the brim to waft against her snowy hair. Irene came swiftly from behind the counter to give a bob of respect. A pair of intensely blue eyes between softly wrinkled lids regarded her graciously.

"I have just broken the clasp of my bracelet. I would like it repaired immediately. I am prepared to wait if it will not take long." She held out a diamond bracelet.

Irene examined the clasp and could see where a vital link had become detached. "It should only take a little while, ma'am." She gave her decision expertly, thinking that she could have done it herself if nobody else had been available.

"Good. I shall wait."

Irene showed the Empress and her companion into an ante-room and saw them settled. Then she took the bracelet into the workshop. Richardson set to work on it. As soon as the clasp was mended, she returned it to its owner.

"Would you like me to fasten it on for you, ma'am?"

"Please do. Eugénie folded back her glove and held out her thin wrist. She watched as the girl bent a bright head to fasten the bracelet. Such burnished hair! Once she had surrounded herself with beautiful women at the Imperial Court, and she herself with her Titian tresses had been the most beautiful of them all. In a way she was reminded of herself when young in the colouring and slenderness of this handsome girl and was amused by her flight of fancy. It took a great deal to make her smile these days.

"What is your name?" she asked when the clasp had been snapped into place.

There was a reaction of wide-eyed surprise. "Irene Lindsay."

"Are you Mr. Lindsay's daughter?"

"Yes, I am."

"How interesting. You may wait on me the next time I am here."

Irene saw the Empress out to her carriage and stood for a few moments looking after it before going back into the shop. Although she had known suffering in Derek's deception and desertion, how much greater was the unfortunate lot of that lonely woman. Eugénie had lost her country, her husband, and her only son, the Prince Imperial, who had died valiantly in the Zulu wars while serving with a British regiment. The daily news from the present battle areas most surely stirred poignant memories for an Empress who had never come out of mourning.

One of the ways Irene filled her own time was in continuing her designs. Sometimes she took sandwiches to the shop, and during the lunch hour she drew and painted at her desk. If the facilities of the workshop had not been forbidden to her, she would have executed some of her designs to the best of her ability, and at times the frustration was almost more than she could bear. Occasionally Edmund would catch sight of some of her drawings. He thought the designs bizarre and made no secret of his contempt. It made no difference to her. She continued to feel as one with the curvilinear patterns and natural motifs of Art Nouveau, which had become to her the expression of her own forceful youth and hope for the beauty of life.

She had not forgotten Derek. The hurt still jarred excruciatingly whenever her thoughts drifted to him. In Oxford Street one day she stood looking into a shop window, numbed by what she saw there. On a display stand were half a dozen enamel and gold pendants of a nymph's head that were exactly the same as the one he had given her. They were handmade in Germany to a design by Obrist. She had thought Derek had made the one he gave her, and he had never countered that impression. One more deception in the midst of so many, and yet it caused no less pain than the rest.

In January of the year of 1901 and shortly before Irene's twentieth birthday, the aging Queen Victoria died. An era was at an end. Irene was among the thousands who stood in silent respect as the cortège went by to the throbbing of drums and the mournful funeral marches. It was a deeply moving occasion. Men and women wept openly. In the midst of it all, Irene spared a thought for the tragic Empress Eugénie, who in the Queen's passing had lost a dear and personal friend.

All those in society were to be in full mourning for an allotted time. Among them was a well-dressed woman named Mrs. Duncane, who came into the shop the following week by appointment to buy a certain ring. It was extremely costly, being a Cape diamond from South Africa with the characteristic golden colour created by its size. A rounded brilliant cut, it was set classically in gold. The customer was shown into one of the ante-rooms, where she sat down at the centre table on which the ring was placed on a velvet cushion for her inspection. Although Mr. Symington and Irene were in attendance, Edmund himself had brought in the ring, its great value demanding his personal supervision of the sale. As it was the customer's first visit to the shop, he had taken the precaution of making discreet enquiries as to the lady's social and financial integrity, with satisfactory results.

Irene watched the whole procedure of the sale alertly. It was not the first outstanding transaction she had witnessed; nor was the diamond ring the most valuable item that she had seen purchased, a parure of rare Golconda diamonds heading the list. But such was her feeling for jewels that she never failed to speculate on the reasons, apart from personal taste, why one particular piece appealed to a purchaser more than another. Squandermania, avarice, and vanity were the basest reasons for purchase; generosity and love were the finest motives. What made this woman come on her own to contemplate spending a fortune on the ring of her choice? Investment? No, men thought more along those lines than women on the whole as far as jewellery was concerned. Fondness for a beautiful stone? Definitely not in this case. Women showed that pleasure in their eyes and expressions, whereas this customer's face could have been made out of marble behind the spotted black net that veiled her flatteringly. Self-glorification? No, she was not admiring the effect of the diamond ring on her hand; the action of displaying it at arm's length was almost automatic. She had even glanced at the watch she wore on a long gold chain around her neck almost in the same instant as if allowing herself an allotted amount of time in which to acquire the ring. Irene's curiosity grew. She began to wonder what lay behind such a cold-blooded attitude. Was Mrs. Duncane so rich that one more diamond, however glorious, meant little to her? Without meaning to, she found herself staring fixedly at the woman.

Mrs. Duncane gave a faint sigh of indecision, pursing her lips and tilting her head critically as she drew in her hand again to look down at the diamond which was putting forth a golden radiance that danced about the room.

"It is a faultless stone and a magnificent one." Edmund never pressed a sale, speaking almost casually. Yet he was a master at dropping a favourable comment at just the right moment, and this was surely no exception.

The woman straightened her shoulders as if brought to the point of purchase, and she rested the fingertips of the ring-adorned hand against her other palm. "I agree, Mr. Lindsay. It *is* superb. I think—"

She was cut off in mid-sentence by the sound of

smashing glass in the direction of the showroom, followed by an uproar of shouting and confusion.

"What the devil!" Edmund expostulated, forgetting the presence of a lady. "Go and see what is happening, Mr. Symington!"

"Yes, sir!" Symington hurried out of the room.

The customer had sprung to her feet in alarm. "Is it a fire?"

"No, madam, no." Edmund reassured her hastily. "It cannot be that. There is no smoke." He gestured with confidence towards the door that Symington had left open.

"I'm terrified of fire!" Mrs. Duncane had become completely agitated. She thrust the ring back at Edmund. "Take this if you please. I cannot possibly make a decision now."

Just then the head salesman reappeared in the doorway. "Somebody threw a brick through the window."

"A smash-and-grab?" Edmund was outraged.

"It would have been, but the rogue must have taken fright and made a run for it."

Edmund turned back to his overwrought customer. "Everything is all right again, madam." His smooth tones thinly disguised his private fury with the villain who had dared to cast a brick through his auspicious window. His daughter would have found his falsely benign smile amusing if circumstances had been otherwise.

"Nevertheless I am leaving, Mr. Lindsay." Mrs. Duncane was adamant. "I am quite upset."

Edmund was full of profuse apologies. He cared more that a prospective customer had been distressed than for the loss of a sale, his shop's impeccable service having been assailed by the unfortunate incident. Then, as if that were not enough, his daughter stepped forward to bar the way when he was about to bow the lady at his side out of the room and through the shop.

"I will have the Cape diamond ring before you leave," Irene said, holding out her hand with palm uppermost to Mrs. Duncane.

"How dare you!" Behind the soft veil dark eyes flashed imperiously. "This is intolerable."

Edmund thought for one highly charged moment that his daughter had lost her wits. "Mrs. Duncane gave the ring back to me!" he ground through his teeth, attempting with his hostile glare to make Irene back away.

Irene remained resolutely in the doorway, her position unchanged as she continued to regard Mrs. Duncane steadily. "I repeat what I said before. If my father cares to look a little closer at the ring he is still holding in his hand, he will see that you, madam, switched a substitute most cleverly!"

Her direct accusation was like a signal for pandemonium. Edmund needed only a swift glance to see that his daughter was correct. At the same time the woman with all her strength gave Irene a great thrust aside, which sent her reeling, cracking her head against the door. Edmund threw himself after the attacker, shouting for assistance, and managed to grab her before she was halfway into the showroom. But she had got out of tight situations before and, wriggling free, she doubled back down the corridor as goldsmiths came from the workshop and salesmen from the showroom to give chase. There was no further struggle. They found her clasping the stout bars of Edmund's office window, her chest rising and falling with exertion, her head bowed in resentful defeat.

The police extracted the true ring from a secret pocket in her skirt and returned it to its rightful owner before hustling her away. She was known to them. Her name was Ruth Williams, although she had several aliases, and one of her tricks was to use the name of a respectable member of society to gain access to highly valuable jewels, an element of surprise always being used to cover the switch. Her accomplice on this occasion, a short, stocky youth according to witnesses, appeared to have escaped in the crowd after throwing the brick through the window, but a search would be on for him.

"Why did you suspect the woman in the first place?" Sofia asked when she had been told all about it. Edmund had sent Irene home, for she had suffered a cut on her head from the door-jamb that had needed his wife's expert first-aid administrations.

"I didn't suspect her," Irene answered frankly. "It was simply that there was something about her lack of personal reaction to the ring that I found puzzling. It is such a beautiful stone, enough to take anyone's breath away when seeing it for the first time, and yet nothing seemed to register with her. I suppose she was so tense that she only saw it as the object she intended to steal."

"How did she switch the rings?"

Irene chuckled softly. "I don't know. I truly don't know, and yet I was watching her all the time, even when the commotion occurred outside. I just happened to spot that when she drew off the ring and handed it back to Father, it was as if the stone had died. All the light had gone from it. If Father's attention hadn't been distracted, he would never have been deceived. It was a clever ploy to smash the window and the boldest plan I've ever heard of to try to filch such a securely guarded ring from under his very nose!"

Sofia thought to herself that Edmund should reward Irene in some way for her quick-witted intervention that had prevented the theft and fully expected him to do it. When several days went by and nothing was forthcoming, she brought up the subject with him. He answered her gruffly. "Irene was only doing her duty within her capacity as my personal assistant."

"But you would have rewarded any ordinary member of your staff!" she protested.

His brows contracted in a fierce frown. "Irene forfeited all right to privileges in any shape or form through her own wanton behaviour last year. She should be grateful that I did not turn her out of the house instead of taking her into the shop for her own salvation. No other parent would have been as *merciful* as I." He put special emphasis on his words, wanting to impress his wife again with the concession he had made for her sake, even though unbeknown to her he had turned some part of it into punishment for his daughter at the same time. "I have absolutely no intention of granting any favours that might lead Irene to suppose that all was forgiven and forgotten. It will never be. Never!"

Sofia's cherished hope was dashed. She had thought that Edmund might have allowed Irene re-entry into the School of Handicraft. He was the most intractable man she had ever met.

Edmund had his wife very much in mind on the day a tiara of exceptional splendour was completed in the workshop and brought into his office for inspection. Alone with it, he thought Sofia should see it before it was packed and boxed in readiness for him to take it to Paris whence it had been ordered, for it had been made up from stones that had once been part of the crown jewels of the French Imperial Court before reaching private hands. Three rows of yellow, pink, and colourless diamond brilliants of immense worth dazzlingly supported a cresting of nine marvellous sapphires enclosed in frames of still more diamonds.

Sitting back in his swivel chair, not taking his appreciative eyes from the sparkling piece, he reached automatically for the afternoon mail that had been placed by his clerk on his desk. He was thinking that he would take Sofia to Paris with him this time. She would enjoy buying some clothes while he attended to his business, since after handing over the tiara, he would be delivering some rare stones he had acquired to Fabergé, who would be in Paris at the same time. His fingers encountered an envelope among the letters he was drawing forward, and glancing towards it he saw that it was marked "Private and Confidential." Taking up his ivory-handled paperknife, he slit it open and took out the enclosed sheet of paper. Unfolding it, he saw that it bore no address or signature beyond some indecipherable initials. The first line leaped out at him with his wife's name incorporated into an accusation of extraordinary and terrible dimensions.

One part of his brain told him he should tear it up and throw it away. He despised anonymous letters and all who wrote them, but against his will his gaze remained riveted, travelling with speed along one line and then another until he came to the end of the defamatory account of his wife's alleged infidelity with Burnett in Nice last year. The writer knew all the details. They had been seen in intimate conversation on the Promenade des Anglais. For a whole week they were secreted away together in the villa, only to emerge for strolls interspersed with passionate embraces in the grounds, all of which had been observed from a point of vantage by someone who had felt compelled to pass this information on to the injured party. Dates were given. Edmund, racking his memory in vain, threw down the letter on the blotter before him and snatched a diary from a drawer. The pages fluttered wildly as he dashed through them to find the month and the day for which he searched. He groaned deep in his throat. According to the writer of the letter, Burnett left Nice the day before he arrived to fetch Sofia home. The telegram! He had sent a telegram. He groaned again. He should have gone there unannounced, and then he could have crumpled the letter into his wastepaper basket and thought no more about a vindictive pack of lies. Now, try as he might, he found it impossible to dismiss the poisonous seeds of suspicion.

Setting his elbows on the desk, he dropped his head into his hands in a kind of wild despair. His temples were throbbing and his heart was pounding. Who could have sent such a tale to him? Who might be harbouring a grudge? He thought of Lester Ward, wondering if he had overheard two women gossiping, for it was amazing what females divulged to each other in a jeweller's ante-room, seeming to forget that sales assistants had sharp ears. Then he dismissed the possibility. Ward was working for a reputable business that would rely on his trustworthiness in all matters, and the fellow was not likely to jeopardize his career with a letter that might be traced. In any case, it was more a female trick to pen such a letter, vitriolic spite with an awful eyewitness authenticity inscribed into it. Who among Sofia's acquaintances aimed to destroy her as a wife and his marriage to her with the same deadly stroke?

He leaped to his feet, feeling that his head would explode, such a rage mounting up within him that every sinew in his body was growing taut, every nerve stretched to the breaking point. Try as he might, he could no longer think logically about the matter. The truth, although used to evil purpose, weighted every word in the letter. Coming back to him now were any number of things he had not known still lurked in his inward eye. There was the attention that Sofia and Burnett paid each other in his own house! He recalled his own pique when her letters ceased from Nice, the time exactly coinciding with the information given in that detestable letter! Then there was that extraordinary sensation he had had when bringing her home again that somehow she had changed completely during her sojourn there. He realized with rising gall that since that time Burnett had done no business with him and had declined a couple of invitations to lunch at his club, severing further contact. Did the two lovers meet secretly in the afternoons when he was at the shop? Or did they engage in more extended trysts when he was abroad on business? Was it not enough that he had had to suffer the ebbing of his first wife's affections, albeit she was never unfaithful, without having to go through it a second time and in the light of far more sordid circumstances? It had been hard enough to endure Irene's inexcusable escapade, but that his cherished Sofia should have betrayed him and brought disgrace upon herself was more than he could stand.

He made to seize the infamous letter, unaware in his blind fury that it was only the empty envelope he shoved in his pocket. Grabbing his hat from its peg and ramming it on his head, he snatched up his cane, unconscious that he held it at an upright angle as if ready to attack. All he knew as he strode from his office was that he would get a full confession out of his wife if he had to flay her flesh from her bones. As he passed Irene's office, he heard her at the typewriting machine and thought it was as well that she would not be at home when the confrontation took place. He would brook no interference of any kind. By God! Sofia should pay for her misdeeds if proved guilty and should be shown no quarter!

"I shall not be back today," he snapped at Mr. Symington before slamming out of the shop. It was too early for his Daimler to be waiting for him, but the hansom cab rank was not far away. He picked one with a tough-looking fellow on the box and a horse in the shafts which looked more able than most of the docile nags.

"A sovereign if you get me to Milton Square in ten minutes!" he shouted, flinging himself into the seat.

"Yes, sir!"

The whip cracked and the horse bounded forward, its eyes rolling and ears back. Another crack, and it was off into the congested street. Edmund sat forward on the seat, gripping both ends of the cane that he held horizontally across his knees, his fingers jerking spasmodically, with waves of savagery and hatred passing through his body as a violent lust for vengeance consumed him.

"Faster!" he yelled to make himself heard. "Get out of this damn traffic!"

The flap in the roof lifted, and the cabby looked down at his passenger's hard, flushed face. "There's always 'old-ups at this time of day, guv'nor. I'm trying to get through."

Edmund's teeth glinted ominously between his thin, drawn-back lips. He was reaching the edge of his endurance, and if he did not reach home in the minimum amount of time, he feared his self-control would snap completely when he finally confronted his erring wife, for all doubt had now flown. "I am paying you to get me home. Lay your whip about other men's horses if you have to! For every minute you save in getting me to Milton Square, I'll match it with a five-pound note!"

The cabby accepted the challenge exuberantly. He had not been driving a cab in London for thirteen years without learning a few tricks when there was a need to use them. Wheel hubs scraped as he drove his horse through narrow apertures. Other cabbies and drivers swore at him as his whip stung snorts and whinnies from neighbouring nags as well as his own, allowing him to bowl through. All was going well when a highly polished brougham pulled out unexpectedly. There were warning shouts and a resounding crash of wheels. The cab and the offending vehicle smashed alongside, the latter teetering over to the scream of frightened horses. If Edmund had been sitting back securely in the seat, he would probably have escaped serious injury. As it was, he was shot forward by the violent impact, unable to save himself, and went head-first into spinning wheel spokes.

When he was extricated, his features were unrecognizable. He had died almost instantly. His coat had been ripped to shreds, and the only means of identification was the torn piece of an envelope caught in a scrap of lining. A policeman went at once to the shop.

Irene was in her father's office where she had taken to his desk the letters she had typed for him to sign, not knowing that he had gone from the premises. Through the door she had left open behind her, she saw Mr. Symington coming from the direction of the showroom, a policeman at his side. Their grave expressions forewarned her that something was terribly wrong.

"What is it?" she asked, filled with apprehension.

She listened to what the policeman had to tell her, staring at him, her face stricken. As Mr. Symington saw him out again, she bowed her head, putting a hand over her eyes as she struggled to come to terms with what had happened, aware of feeling ice cold. Around her a quietness was taking over as the goldsmiths ceased work at their benches and voices became hushed in the showroom. Forcing her limbs into movement, she went to her father's desk, stooping automatically to pick up a crumpled letter lying on the floor. Without glancing at it, she locked it away with the papers from the top of his desk, knowing that it would be her responsibility to go through everything later. She did not leave the office until she had secured everything, following her father's custom. She was ready in her hat and coat to depart, her face gaunt with distress, when the head salesman returned to her.

"Have you closed the shop and pulled down the window blinds, Mr. Symington?" she asked him.

"That has been done, Miss Irene. Is there anything else you would like me to do?"

Already she was in charge. She shook her head. "I shall communicate with you tomorrow." Then she left, acknowledging the murmurs of condolence of those from the workshop and the showroom who had gathered to watch her leave. None of them doubted that she was the new head of Lindsay's.

When Irene arrived home, Sofia was upstairs getting ready to go out. She was spearing a pearl-headed pin through her hat before the dressing table mirror when her stepdaughter appeared in the bedroom doorway. Her eyes met Irene's reflected gaze, and her whole frame became frozen, both hands stilled in the feminine action of securing headgear, her elbows at angles, her spine very straight.

"What is wrong?" Sofia whispered in dread.

"Father met with an accident. A terrible accident."

"Oh, no!" Sofia sprang up as though propelled from the velvet stool. "I must go to him! Where is he?"

Then she saw by Irene's torn expression that there would be no going to Edmund. He had already gone from her. As the realization sank into her conscious-ness, she began to shake from head to foot, her jaw quivering, her throat too constricted for speech. She reached blindly for Irene, and they clasped each other tightly in the sudden awfulness of bereavement.

Edmund had no close relatives, although Sofia notified two distant cousins of his passing. She also telegraphed her own family of her loss. It was a great comfort to her that her elderly Uncle Vladimir, spare of frame, with white hair and a clipped beard, travelled all the way from St. Petersburg to arrive in good time to attend the funeral and with every intention of staying for a while afterwards. He had brought with him his only grandchild, Maria, who was the light of his life since he had lost a wife, son, and daughter-in-law in the same fever epidemic that had taken Sofia's first husband from her. Maria was seventeen, tall and slim with enchanting elfin looks, her eyes a dreamy grey under winged brows, and a mass of fair curly hair aglow with golden lights. Irene thought her striking and unusual in appearance, and it was not long before she discovered that by nature the girl was as kind-hearted and generous in spirit as Sofia, whom they both shared respectively as an aunt and stepmother. Maria did much to cheer with her sweet personality a house steeped in mourning, and Sofia found her a great help in dealing with the letters of condolence that came pouring in. Irene did what she could, but the shop made first demands on her time, and Sofia was merely thankful that her stepdaughter was able to take charge so ably in the interim before the funeral. Maria was most impressed by Irene's business aptitude.

"How I admire you, Irene. You must be exceptionally clever."

Irene smiled, shaking her head. "Not at all. From my first day at the shop, I interested myself in all sections of the business, and now it is standing me in good stead."

"I have no understanding of commerce. The nearest I ever came was when I was being taught how to manage a large household, approve menus, and so forth."

"Do you run your grandfather's house?"

"Goodness, no!" Maria's English was as flawless as her French, which was expected of any well-reared Russian girl. "I was being prepared for the time when I shall marry." Her eyes danced romantically. "And marry I shall! A tall, handsome man who will adore me for the rest of my life."

Since Maria had been loved and cherished and cosseted by everyone else in her life, there was no reason to doubt that the man of her choice would do likewise. Irene smiled. "I hope you find him soon."

"When I do, you shall design my wedding tiara. That is a promise."

Irene blushed with pleasure, seeing that the promise was meant sincerely. In the friendship strengthening daily between them, she had shown Maria her designs, something she never did to anyone these days. Her father's constant disapproval had made the filing away of them an automatic process, which was the reason why Sofia had not been shown them, Irene having no wish to involve her inadvertently in any discord with him.

The day of the funeral dawned. The service was heavily attended. Black-plumed horses pulled the hearse, and a thick carpet of wreaths covered the new grave in the north London cemetery. Sofia had borne herself with the extraordinary courage that frequently sustains a widow through the long and awful days leading up to the funeral. Even then, her rigid training enabled her to bear her grief privately, although she leaned on Irene's arm when the time came for her to throw a bunch of violets onto the coffin at the last moment of farewell. Her tears beneath her thick veil were not hypocritical. The accidental cutting short of Edmund's life when he was still in his prime would always haunt her. Nobody knew why he had left the shop that day or where he was going, and it was assumed that he had suddenly remembered an urgent business matter. She had shared many difficult years with him, but she had always understood his temperament and his obsessive need of her. Apart from a clash of differences over his treatment of Irene after the affair with Derek Ryde, they had moved into a new harmony together in recent months. Not even an unexpected meeting with Gregory had disrupted it. She had come face to face with him at a charity function being held at Eileen Harding's house—a sweet, brief meeting, he courteous and gentle, she trying to keep all she was feeling from showing in her eyes. She had drawn away from his company as quickly as she could, knowing for certain that other women would be observing them, Eileen in particular, for he was there at her invitation, and such hostesses resented the monopolization of a special guest by anyone else, particularly since Gregory had donated a diamond ring to the charity's cause. Again her fears had become acute that malicious, newly revived talk would drift hurtfully to Edmund's ears. She had even feared that Eileen, vindictive and jealous, might drop a spiteful hint to Edmund out of resentment that Gregory had never fancied her. Again and again Sofia was struck by the irony of fate. Never had she thought that Edmund was to be the one to bring such hurt to her with his untimely and tragic death. She grieved for him. Her only consolation was that all she had feared most had never come between them. In his own way he had loved her in peace of mind until the end.

The funeral guests had departed, and Maria and her grandfather were elsewhere in the house when Irene and Sofia sat side by side in the study while the lawyer read the will to them. It had been made on the eve of Edmund's marriage to Sofia, and nothing had been changed since. He had bequeathed everything to her, apart from setting aside an adequate marriage endowment for Irene, who would receive her mother's jewellery on her wedding day. There was a special clause with regard to the shop in Old Bond Street. Lindsay's was to be sold, lock, stock, and barrel. Sofia was dismayed. Although neither she nor Irene had spoken of it, she had assumed that her stepdaughter would take Edmund's place in the business and reshape it to follow new styles and ideas.

When the lawyer had departed, Sofia returned from bidding him farewell in the hall to find Irene at the window, looking out into the garden. "My dear," she said compassionately, "are you very disappointed?"

Irene turned slowly. She was quite composed. "Not at all. I think I've always known that the business would never be left in my hands. All Father ever wanted for me was that I should marry well; hence his provision of a generous dowry. It was to please you that he allowed me to have a ring from my mother's jewellery. Now it may never be mine again, and that causes me the greatest disappointment."

Sofia kept to herself the belief that her stepdaughter would marry one day, but this was not the time to discuss that possibility. "What do you wish to do? You are free to return to the School of Handicraft and take up your training again at the point where you were forced to leave it."

Irene shook her head. "There would be no vancancy for me a second time. I was granted a privilege by being accepted in the first place. In any case, I hear that before long the whole school is to be removed from London to a village in the Cotswolds. It was always Mr. Ashbee's aim to create from a country setting, but I need to be at the commercial hub of jewellery circles."

"You are still hoping to design and sell your own work one day?"

"That is my ultimate aim. I have a little money saved. Father was excessively generous with my dress allowance in recent months. But I cannot make any decision until I have been to Paris. Father was due to deliver two packages by arrangement next week, one of them to Fabergé himself. The great man is to be in France while a special exhibition of his work is being held there. You knew him, didn't you?"

Sofia nodded, although her thoughts seemed to have drifted elsewhere. "I met your father at a musical soirée given by the Fabergés," she answered almost absently. Then she gripped the back of the chair by which she was standing. "I have something important to tell you, Irene. Something very important indeed. Your speaking of France makes this an opportune moment to introduce the subject."

"Yes?" Irene observed her closely.

Sofia moved around to stand by Edmund's roll-top desk, which was open. One of the duties she had taken upon herself in the last few days was the clearing out of all that had been kept there, a result of her need to be busy all the time. "As you know, I have been going through your father's papers. He was a methodical man, and it presented no difficulties until I found a letter right at the back of one of the pigeon-holes. It was unopened, the ink was faded, and the envelope had yellowed during its storage. The postmark was French and not easy to decipher, but it appeared to have been posted about twenty years ago."

"Well?" Irene was puzzled as to the cause of her

stepmother's worried expression.

"I did not know whether I should open it. I actually threw it into the wastepaper basket before I reconsidered and rescued it again."

"It couldn't have been an important letter, or else it would have been opened at the time of its delivery."

"That is what I told myself. Then I wondered if it had simply been overlooked. Perhaps Edmund had been about to open it and had then been interrupted, never to give it another thought, although that was not like him. I felt he had always known it was there."

"So you decided to read the letter."

Sofia nodded. "I came to the conclusion that if he had kept it, there must have been some purpose. I could not believe that it would hold any significance, whatever it was." She linked her fingers and twisted them together. "How wrong I was!"

Irene stepped nearer, completely bewildered. "What could possibly hold any importance over so many years?"

Drawing a deep breath, Sofia looked Irene straight in the eyes. "Prepare yourself, my dear. It was a letter from your maternal grandmother."

Irene stared at her in astonishment. "But my grandparents died years and years ago. My mother was brought up by foster parents. My father didn't often talk about her; but he mentioned that fact occasionally."

"He told me the same story, and yet this letter is written by your mother's mother. I suppose he recognized her handwriting and, for reasons of his own, decided against opening it.''

"But why?''

"Who can say? I should imagine from the lack of any fond salutations that Edmund and his mother-in-law were not on good terms. Nevertheless it is a very sad letter, and you should read it.'' Reaching into the desk, she found what she was looking for and handed it over.

Irene sank down into a chair as she studied the fine writing on the envelope. Then she took out the letter, finding a banker's draft enclosed. She glanced at it before reading the letter, which bore the printed heading of the Hotel Meurice in Paris. It opened without any preliminaries, as Sofia had said. It was simply a touching and heartfelt request that Edmund should use the enclosed draft to purchase a wreath of the most beautiful spring flowers available as the writer's loving tribute to Denise, her only child. The signature was that of a Gabrielle Roget. Irene lowered the letter to her lap.

"Those flowers were never bought,'' she said tensely. "The banker's draft was never cashed. I knew my mother's maiden name was Roget, but never once was I given any idea that she was French. Why did my father keep this information from me?''

Sofia sat down beside her with a little sigh. "I can think of only one explanation. Your mother may have been illegitimate. That would link up with her being raised by foster parents. Knowing your father's attitude, it is not hard to see why he should wish to keep your mother's origins a secret, even from you."

"I still can't understand why he should have kept the unopened letter."

"Perhaps his conscience would not let him throw it away."

Irene accepted that explanation. It was in keeping with her father's extraordinary character. She wished that there had been a private address on the letter that would have given her a clue as to where her grandmother might still be found, if she were still alive. There was always the bank from which the draft had been issued, although it might have been one used temporarily since Gabrielle Roget was staying at a hotel at the time.

"May I keep this letter and the banker's draft?" she queried.

"Yes, do." Intuitively Sofia knew the reason behind the request and felt compelled to give a compassionate warning. "Twenty years is a long time. Anything may have happened."

Irene filled in what Sofia had refrained from saying. "And if Madame Roget should be still alive, she may not wish to see me. I realize that. I'm going to write anyway."

She sent the letter off the next day, giving her home address and the name of the hotel at which she would be staying in Paris. Then deliberately she concentrated on other things, determined not to harbour any false hopes. In any case, she had much to keep her occupied. There were still many matters that needed her attention at the shop, and when she was free from it there was Maria eager for her company. As they were in mourning, no place of entertainment could be visited, but they always had plenty to talk about, and they went for walks and drives together. Both knew that each would miss the other when the day came for Maria to return home with her grandfather. The two visitors had tried to persuade Sofia to go back with them on an extended vacation, but she could not leave home until Edmund's affairs were settled and the sale of the business had gone through.

"Write to me, Irene," Maria urged when the time came for farewells.

"I will," Irene promised.

"Remember what I said. Try to come with Aunt Sofia when she is able to visit us."

Irene smiled. "I can't make any promises. So much depends on the outcome of my visit to Paris."

When she in her turn left London for France the next day, accompanied by a burly escort from the shop to guard the precious jewels, she felt as if her whole future were hanging in the balance. It was an exhilarating challenge. Moreover, she was experiencing freedom for the first time.

Nine

Paris was everything Irene had ever heard about it, beautiful and spacious and voluptuously elegant. On the evening of her arrival, she delivered the tiara of diamonds and sapphires to an address in the rue de Rivoli. The next morning she walked from her hotel along the sun-drenched Champs Elysées to the Grand Palais where a private exhibition of Fabergé's work was being held in one of the galleries. It was strictly for connoisseurs, and Irene was entitled to admission on the ticket that had been sent to her when she had notified Carl Fabergé that she would be coming to Paris in her late father's place. It was an event and a privilege, for several of the Imperial Easter eggs were to be displayed. Although the famed jewelled eggs of the House of Fabergé were by no means restricted to ownership by the Russian Imperial Family, those made for the late Czar and his reigning son, Nicholas II, were of exceptional interest and beauty, and had only been put on public display once before, at the Exposition Internationale Universelle of 1900 in Paris the previous year. Edmund had visited it, Irene never imagining that the chance to see some of the same marvellous eggs would ever come her way.

Quite a number of well-dressed people were already in the long, silk-panelled gallery when she arrived, but there was ample room to study at leisure the contents of the glass showcases, and the other pieces that were set openly on display. Almost every aspect of the great goldsmith's craft was represented. There were ikons, chalices, clocks, and bowls; coffee sets and fans and parasol handles; figurines and cigarette cases; models of animals in chalcedony, jasper, and quartz, with jewelled eyes and flowers of enamel on gold. There was some jewellery, handsome brooches, and an abundance of pendants and tie-pins, but Fabergé made little pure jewellery, his interest lying far more with ornamental art objects.

Irene was a critical observer. Much of the work on display was absurdly ornate and ostentatious and over-decorated, bordering on the vulgar and as far removed from the simple, flowing lines and shapes that she favoured as it could be, but it was impossible not to be enthralled by the superb craftsmanship which filled her with awe. As if that were not enough, she found herself succumbing to the enchantment of the fantasy articles for which he had become so famous. She stood dazzled by a three-inch-high sedan chair of pink, translucent enamel on gold, with windows of rock crystal that showed tasselled furnishings within of mother-of-pearl. A table of white jade mounted in gold was even smaller, as were chairs of pale apricot enamel and cabinets of dark red cornelian with inset enamelled medallions. These lovely objects of minuscule detail, and many more, made her linger before them with a loss of all sense of time. It was with a start that she realized she had yet to reach the showcase at the far end of the gallery where the famous eggs were the main centre of attention.

If she had not yet fallen under Fabergé's special spell, the Easter eggs would have won her over completely. To begin with, they were love gifts, which set them apart from all else. Nearly twenty years ago Czar Alexander III had consulted Fabergé as to the creation of a special gift for his wife, wishing to cheer her after a period of trouble and desolation. Fabergé had suggested an Easter egg of gold and translucent white enamel, which would open to reveal a miniature hen with enamelled feathers, surely guaranteed to return a smile to the Czarina's sad face. It had done more. It had made her laugh softly with sheer delight. Thereupon a tradition had been established that each Eastertide there should be an egg with a "surprise" hidden within it, and not only had the custom been passed from father to son, but it had spread throughout the Romanov family and beyond.

Irene, viewing a selection of the eggs displayed, tried to decide which one would have appealed most to her as a gift on Easter morning. She was unaware that she was being observed in her turn through the glass from the opposite side of the showcase. Gregory Burnett was trying to place where before he had seen this striking girl in the plain, black silk mourning dress and wide-brimmed hat that she wore with such style, her hair flaming back from her oval face, her lashes presently downcast as she studied the egg nearest her in the velvet-draped showcase.

She had chosen it as her favourite one. Standing six inches high, it was of pink enamel and decorated all over with lilies of the valley in rose diamonds and pearls, the elongated leaves of the flower forming legs of gold. An Imperial Crown as a finial had been lifted to reveal the "surprise," which consisted of miniature portraits of Nicholas II and two of his children. To Irene's mind it outshone with its theme of love the superb, lime-green enamelled one trellised in gold, which had no mount and lay on its side, its "surprise" a working model of the Coronation Coach in yellow-gold and red enamel, which had taken Nicholas and his Czarina to their crowning. The rest of the eggs were all equally magnificent. Her gaze travelled swiftly over them once more at the varying heights at which they were arranged in the showcase. An egg clock of strawberry enamel rotated with the dipping beak of a gold swan pointing the hours. Another egg was encased in a colonnaded temple of love of palest green bowenite with a pair of exquisite platinum doves. Yet another was of milk-white agate latticed in gold ribbons, and it opened to reveal a basket of enamelled spring flowers in delicate hues. So many glorious colours, so much ingenuity and perfection of skill. With a deep sigh of appreciation, she swung away from the showcase and left the gallery, returning to the Paris sunshine. She was looking forward even more than before to meeting Fabergé himself at an appointed hour that same afternoon.

Gregory watched her go. He had recalled her identity in those last few seconds when she had taken a final glance at the rest of the contents in the showcase, and he had seen her eyes. How could he have forgotten such green eyes? Irene Lindsay, Sofia's stepdaughter. If the connection had not been there, he would have gone after her and made himself known. As it was, he merely smiled to himself and continued his tour of the exhibition.

Irene prided herself on never being late for an appointment, and Fabergé's own good manners did not allow him to keep anyone waiting. Thus they met on the first stroke of three o'clock as she was shown into the drawing room of his hotel suite. He was on his feet in readiness, grey-haired, balding, with a well-groomed beard, kindly eyes, and a restrained smile that was almost shy. Quiet, cultured, he cared nothing for fame, liked best to be with his wife and family and good friends of long standing, and yet never stinted hospitality to others. In spite of his French Huguenot ancestry, he did not care very much whether anyone in France or anywhere else beyond the borders of his beloved native Russia purchased his exotic wares, and he was totally unmoved by flattery. Commitments sometimes compelled visits abroad, this short sojourn connected not with his own exhibition, which had been coincidental, but with the invitation to judge the entries submitted to another exhibition by young goldsmiths and lapidaries below a certain age and from several competing countries. He believed implicitly in the fostering of new talent. People visiting his workshops at his St. Petersburg and Moscow and Odessa branches of the House of Fabergé often commented on the number of young craftsmen at the benches, but he never turned away an applicant of outstanding promise. A good workshop needed constant replenishing, the new arrivals and those of long standing blending together into new strengths. Over the years he had seen many a raw apprentice develop into a workmaster of esteemed reputation.

"*Bonjour*, Mademoiselle Lindsay," he greeted the young woman, bowing from the waist in the courtly way that was natural to him."

"*Bonjour*, Monsieur Fabergé."

"Please be seated. First of all, allow me to offer my condolences on the tragic death of your father." He took a chair opposite her.

"Thank you. Madame Lindsay, my stepmother, appreciated the letter you wrote her."

"So she said in her kind reply. How is she?"

They continued to converse in French. When the social preliminaries were over, she produced the parcel of stones for him, and he took them to the light, sitting down at a table by the window. When he had examined each one through his jeweller's glass, he nodded approval, sitting back in the chair to look across at her.

"What price do you have in mind?"

She quoted the one that she had taken from her father's notes. There was no haggling. He opened a drawer, took out writing materials, and wrote out a draft immediately. When he handed it to her, she thanked him and folded it away in her purse.

"There is one more matter I should like to present to you," she said.

"Yes?" He sat down again to put her at her ease.

"In dealing with my father's correspondence, I learned that you are planning to take a suite at Berner's Hotel in London at intermittent periods for the purpose of the display and sale of your work."

"That is correct." It had not been his idea. He had no intention of visiting London himself if he could help it, preferring to leave foreign ventures to his South African-born business partner. However, the selection of who was to be employed under the banner of his name was always his. He liked to know exactly who was engaged in the making and also the selling of his wares, which resulted in the whole of his seven hundred employees working as a complete team. "As you will know from the same correspondence, it is with a view to opening a branch of the House of Fabergé in London later on."

"My father was to shoulder certain responsibilities on your behalf during that intervening span." She felt amazingly calm and composed. "I'm asking you to let me take his place."

He neither smiled nor frowned, but simply continued to regard her levelly. Young, beautiful, and ambitious, he thought. Courageous, too. She was asking for a position of authority that men of repute would vie for against each other if it should be publicly advertised. "What makes you think you have the qualifications to fill that post?" he questioned out of interest.

She told him, filled with a confidence that had become unassailable. She knew she had proved herself competent in business, both on the clerical and selling side, quite apart from her basic jewellery skills, her soaring ability to design, and her knowledge of gems. The experience of working for Fabergé would establish her in the right sphere, enabling her to go forward on her own when the time was right. The master goldsmith heard her out. Then he made his reply.

"I regret having to disappoint you. When news of your father's death reached me, I had to turn to my second choice immediately, and he accepted."

She blanched, biting deep into her lower lip, but admirably her spine did not sag, and her chin remained high. Her voice came forth firmly and distinctly. "He will need an assistant, Monsieur Fabergé."

He felt tempted to applaud her, although that would not have been seemly. "Two have been appointed already, and he has his own clerical staff."

If anything, she became even whiter. Yet still she

did not succumb to defeat. "He should have a personal aide, which is the role I filled for my father."

He allowed a few contemplative seconds to tick by before he gave a slow nod. "That is precisely my opinion," he commented drily. "Would you be prepared to fill that vacancy?"

Her face became radiant, her eyes sparkling. "I accept with pleasure."

"Good. Details of your salary and other matters will come to you through my partner's brother, Mr. Bowe, who is leaving the Moscow branch to become my representative in London. He will be head of the Berner's Hotel sessions. No doubt you will have some tasks to carry out for him from time to time."

"Then he is not the one with whom I shall be working?"

"That is correct. It is Mr. Burnett who has taken your late father's place. It was essential to be able to draw on the advice of a man with his finger on the current pulse of commerce in the London realm of ornamental art and jewellery. There is no question of his taking over the new branch if it should be opened. He is kindly bridging a gap."

"Did you say his name was Burnett?" she inquired, her brows drawn together in uncertainty.

"Yes. Gregory Burnett. Is it possible that you know him already? He was acquainted with your father in business circles."

Her expression was one of startled disquiet. "He is a diamond merchant. What can he know about selling Fabergé wares?"

"His position is one of supervision, not of selling. So you do know him?"

"I met him once, a long time ago," she said quietly, her tone ruminative.

"That is fortunate. It means you will not be meeting a stranger when I present you as his new personal assistant. He is in Paris at the present time and is due here at four o'clock." He took out his gold watch and glanced at it. "Only nine minutes to wait. Allow me to offer you some refreshment."

He sent for the tea, which came in an ornate silver pot on an engraved silver tray with Sèvres porcelain cups and saucers. There was also a plate of pastries thick with cream and exotic fruits. Appropriately grand, she thought. The hotel was sensitive to the refined importance of its distinguished guest. He invited her to pour. As she did so, Gregory arrived. Fabergé welcomed him, although by their conversation it was apparent that they had had several business discussions over the past few days. Without looking up from where she sat, she continued to pour the tea, filling the third cup that had been provided. Out of the corner of her eye, she could see the two men drawing near her across the room.

"I have appointed a personal assistant for you, Monsieur Burnett," Fabergé was saying. "You knew her late father, and you have met her on one previous occasion, I gather. Here she is! Mademoiselle Lindsay."

She set down the teapot and turned from the waist to look up at the man she had last seen departing

from the house in Milton Square after a dinner party.
It had been on the same evening as her return home
from Switzerland, when her wish to attend the
School of Handicraft was still hanging in the
balance. Then he had looked back over his shoulder
at her as if seeing her for the first time, a look almost
of being mesmerized by her in his eyes. There was a
very different expression on his face as he regarded
her now, annoyance and exasperation in the set of his
features, the glint of hostility in his gaze.

"It must be three years since we last met,
Mademoiselle Lindsay," he said a trifle brusquely,
keeping to French. "How are you?"

"Very well indeed," she replied evenly. "You seem
taken aback at hearing of my appointment. Do you
have any objection to women in business?"

He became aware that he had given away something of what he felt. He did not need a personal
assistant; it was as simple as that. Even less did he
wish her to be involved. If it had been any other
female, he would have stated the fact openly and put
an end to the matter. Fabergé would have respected
his decision. Unfortunately, jarring his memory,
there was that half-remembered promise made to the
girl on the evening at her home. What was it he had
said? All he knew was that it had been a promise
made to help her if ever it lay in his power, which
meant he could not in all conscience deny her the
once-in-a-lifetime opportunity to work for the court
jeweller to the Czar. For himself, it made little or no
difference, the name of Burnett long established in its

247

own right; in fact, in his father's time it had been Fabergé who had first sent to Burnett's for a supply of the particularly rare and beautiful rose diamonds that the great goldsmith preferred to all others, and which had been supplied ever since. Therefore, for himself, it had been a small step to take over the organization of the forthcoming London sessions at Berner's Hotel, no personal glory involved, although for Irene it would open doors in jewellery circles for the rest of her days. He knew himself to be trapped by his own word given to her, and it added to his intense displeasure. He attempted to modify his tone as he answered her, but it remained curt.

"There is a place in business for any woman able to match a man in wits, endurance, and the perseverance to put work before everything else throughout long hours."

She would not let herself be riled, at least not openly. There was too much at stake. Her angry thoughts were her own. "Then you will be able to find no fault with me," she stated crisply. "Tea, Monsieur Burnett?" She held out the cup with a cool smile.

She saw him three times during the next two days when she attended board meetings with a number of other representatives of the Fabergé entourage, several of them connected with the current exhibition. Her presence was deemed necessary in her capacity as personal assistant to Gregory, although not once did she sit next to him, and except when he glanced over the notes she had made for him during the meeting, they exchanged no conversation. She spent the time she had to herself in exploring Paris. She also called on Arthur Lucas, the goldsmith who had once worked for her father and now held a position of some importance in the workshop of *La Maison de l'Art Nouveau*, which had been opened by Siegfried Bing, an enterprise leading the way of the new movement in France as Liberty's carried it forth from London. Not knowing Mr. Lucas's private address, she had had to seek him out at his place of work, and as she approached it along the rue de Provence she was impressed by the eye-catching façade of the building, which abounded in floral and fruit forms in the flowing style that was becoming recognized as one of the most imaginative innovations ever conceived throughout the history of design. Within the showrooms she found treasure that rivalled in its own field all the magnificence she had viewed at the Fabergé exhibition, and yet it could not have been more different. Not for the first time she recalled with gratitude her stepmother's wisdom in opening her eyes in childhood to beauty in all its forms, enriching her life from every quarter so that her personal preference for Art Nouveau in no way diminished her appreciation of the magic of Fabergé's fantasies. Here was fantasy of another kind. Stained-glass windows by Louis Comfort Tiffany poured light of pure colour, which was caught up in turn by group arrangements of his Favile glass vases and bowls and lamps in light yellow, rose, violet, apple green, and delicate orange swirling out of a smoky white. More glass by Gallé, furniture by Gaillard, bronze clocks by De Feure, silverware studded with opals by Thiéde, and tapestries by Obrist. And the jewellery! Bees and Medusa heads and curling snakes and flying nymphs by Lalique and Derosiers and Veazey. She was resolved that one day her designs would take their place alongside these and others signed by such famous names.

"Monsieur Lucas?" the sales assistant said in answer to her query. "Yes, I will fetch him, mademoiselle."

Arthur Lucas came with a look of pleased amazement on his face, his bald head ashine. "Miss Irene! What a splendid surprise! My, my! You had just started at Ashbee's School of Handicraft when I left England. Is all going well?"

He had not noticed immediately that she was in mourning, and when she told him the reason, he was shocked that such an accident should have happened. Lindsay had been a good employer, albeit a hard one, but he did not hold that against him. They talked for a short while and then, feeling that he should not be too long away from the workshop, he invited Irene to dine one evening. His wife was French, which was why he had moved to Paris, for even after fifteen years of their marriage in London she had never been able to overcome her homesickness. Irene had met her once a long time ago, and accepted the invitation gladly.

She made other visits to *La Maison d'Art Nouveau* without disturbing Mr. Lucas from his work, for there was so much to see. Most of the merchandise was beyond her purse, but she did manage to afford a Tiffany vase in one of his purely abstract designs, which was of a glorious blend of red-gold hues as if the sun itself had been trapped within the moulding of it.

It was after the fourth and final meeting around the boardroom table that Gregory approached her. She had just said farewell to Fabergé and others who would be returning with him to Russia, where they would split up to travel to the respective branches of the House of Fabergé.

"When are you planning to leave Paris, Miss Lindsay?" Gregory enquired, not speaking in French when they were on their own.

"Tomorrow morning by the ten o'clock boat-train." There was nothing to keep her in France any longer. No reply had come to the letter she had written to Gabrielle Roget through the bank, and if there was nothing when she arrived back at Milton Square, she could be almost sure that there would never be one.

"I suggest we travel together if you are agreeable. We still have many matters to discuss between ourselves with the opening session at Berner's not many weeks away."

"I thought I heard you say that you were staying on in Paris," she remarked.

"So I was. I shall have to return here as soon as possible, but in the meantime my London office had cause to telegraph me about something needing my

attention. It would be better if instead of leaving all
discussions until tomorrow, you could dine with me
this evening."

"I'm afraid I have a previous engagement," she
answered truthfully, for it was on that evening that
she was to dine with the Lucases. She saw his eyes
harden. He did not believe her and had taken her
reply as a snub. She did not think women would
normally snub him, either unwittingly as she had
done herself or deliberately, for he was far too attractive with his buccaneer looks and his relaxed air of
being completely in command of himself and of any
given situation.

"Then shall we meet at the Gare du Nord
tomorrow?" he said coldly. "I have booked a first-
class compartment."

"I'll be there in good time," she replied with a nod.

She thought about him as she dressed that evening
in readiness to meet Arthur Lucas and his wife. It was
not surprising that Gregory should resent her
appointment. First, at an ordinary level, it was
obvious he would have preferred to chose his own
personal assistant instead of having her thrust upon
him out of the blue. On a far more personal level
there was the fact that she was Sofia's stepdaughter
and that he and her stepmother had had an affair in
Nice.

She would never forget the shock of that discovery.
A letter sent with scurrilous intent to her father had
come to light when she had been sorting through his
business papers and documents after the funeral.

Distressed amazement and disbelief had been followed by a wave of such fury at the vindictiveness of
the unknown writer that the letter had trembled in
her hand, the paper rustling. She realized that she
herself had gathered it up from the office floor on the
day of her father's death, its creased state releasing a
chord in her memory. It was not a letter he would ever
have left about for other eyes to see, and she could
only conclude that he had dropped it accidentally
when going out that dreadful day.

It would have been a strange letter for him to keep,
although he had been equally odd about keeping the
unopened one from his mother-in-law. At least she
could be sure that nobody else on the premises had
had access to the defamatory material, for she alone
had kept the key to the locked drawer.

At first her reaction was that her stepmother was
the last person imaginable to indulge in an affair.
Then the more she thought about it, wrathful
indignation subsiding to allow more logical con-
sideration, the clearer the possibility became that
something untoward had taken place. Sofia's unhappiness had been transparent enough at times to one
who knew her well, and she had been oppressed at
every turn by her husband's moods and demands.
What was more likely was that when she was away
from every responsibility in a sunnier and more
romantic clime, the emotional, gently sentimental
Sofia should succumb to the inducements of a
charming philanderer. Irene felt old and wise. Her
own experience in a similar situation erased any

thought of standing in judgement over her father's wife. Derek and Gregory were two of a kind—dangerous, self-centred men who used women for as long as it suited them. She did not hate either of them; in fact her own heart's painful sensitivity was proof that in spite of everything, what she felt for Derek still lingered on, which showed how foolish and lacking in all reason love could be. She felt sympathy for Gregory's estranged wife. No doubt the poor woman had been driven to leaving him. Her main hope was that Sofia had not been harmed by the affair. Her father had had his own exquisitely cruel way of punishing people, and with such knowledge against his wife in his possession, there was no means of telling what misery he had caused her. Yet it was a subject that could never be broached. Irene had burnt the defamatory letter in the desk ashtray. She hoped that she and her father and the writer of it were the only people who had ever seen what had been set down on paper.

She enjoyed her evening with Arthur Lucas and his wife, Yvonne, who had worked as a court dressmaker in London and who was extremely elegant in spite of a buxom figure. They lived in a tall plastered house, one of a row, with pots of geraniums in the windows. Irene was made most welcome and immediately felt at ease. As they talked, it soon became obvious to her that whereas Yvonne was content to be at home again in France, in spite of the fact that she and her husband had three married sons living in England, Arthur himself had become the homesick one. He did not care very much for working in an establishment where jewellery was a small part of the merchandise sold, although the new designs that he had to execute were a challenge to his skills, his own days of designing along classical lines having become a thing of the past.

"If ever you need a goldsmith to make up your designs, let me know, Miss Irene," he said, half in jest, half earnestly. She promised she would not forget his offer.

It was late when she arrived back at her hotel. She collected her room key and was moving away from the reception desk when the hotel clerk spoke after her. "One moment, Mademoiselle Lindsay. There is a letter for you."

She seemed in a single, heart-stopping moment to know from whom it had come. The clerk handed it to her, and she held it close as she went up on the escalator to the fifth floor. In her room she tore it open. The paper was delicately scented. It had been written that same day, and the address was an elegant one. There was a single sentence of invitation: *Madame Roget will be at home to Mademoiselle Lindsay at noon tomorrow.*

She read it through several times as if seeking some clue to the writer's personality. Imperious? Commanding! A take-it-or-leave-it attitude. If she did not attend at noon tomorrow there would be no further invitation. It was not promising.

Her first move was to telephone down to the reception desk and cancel her departure next morning. Although the hour was late, she then made a call to Gregory's hotel. He was not in. She concluded that he had found someone else with whom to dine or otherwise spend the evening hours and left a message to say she would not be leaving Paris with him as arranged.

She slept little that night due to excitement and trepidation, trying to imagine the visage of the grandmother she was to see on the morrow. If her mother had lived, she would have been forty-three years old, having been only twenty-three when she died. Therefore Gabrielle Roget could be anything from her mid-sixties to almost eighty, according to how late in life she gave birth to her daughter. It was dawn when Irene finally fell into a deep sleep thinking of the image of a white-haired, arthritic old lady in high-necked black silk, who would regard her haughtily through raised lorgnette.

A telephone call from Gregory just after seven o'clock awoke her with a start, sleep still heavy upon her. "What is all this about your not leaving Paris today?" he demanded fiercely.

She had propped herself on one elbow, the polished brass receiver to her ear, and she brushed back with one hand the fall of her long hair out of her eyes. "I've changed my plans," she explained firmly, resenting his tone of bristling hostility. "Something extremely important has come about."

"More important than your job with the House of Fabergé?" he snapped back.

She answered honestly. "Yes. On a personal level."

"I'll remind you of my stipulation that a woman may only take a man's place in business when she puts work before all else."

Her anger began to burn. "Allow me to remind you in turn that you had no intention originally of leaving Paris today, and if you had not been called back to London for your own interests, we should not have been meeting again for another two or three weeks at least. If I am kept in Paris longer than a few days, we can cover all you would have talked about on the journey home when you return here."

He breathed deeply. "Very well, Miss Lindsay. But let this be the last time that you do not fit in with my change of arrangements. Good day to you."

He hung up. She took the receiver away from her ear and returned it to its cradle. How dare he imply that she had a flibbertigibbet attitude towards her work! His surprise would come when he discovered how hard she applied herself to any task and how conscientious she was to detail. Meanwhile the time had not yet come for her to run at his beck and call, which he knew well enough, or else he would have given her no option about accompanying him today. It was as well, for she would have had to refuse, and then that would have given him the chance to rid himself of her. He really was a most difficult man!

She did not wear full mourning dress when she set off in good time to arrive at her grandmother's residence by noon. It was such a glorious summer day that she had chosen a high-collared, white silk blouse with a skirt of black-pleated silk and a matching

257

straw hat. The house when she reached it was dignified and impressive, lying back with its own forecourt behind high gates and a screen of trees. She gave the bell-pull a tug.

A manservant admitted her. He showed her through a plant-filled vestibule into a hall that was richly carpeted with a grand, sweeping staircase; the walls were hung with Italian paintings in ornate frames. She was only able to take a quick glance, but she thought she recognized several as the work of Caneletto. Then double doors were opened for her.

"Madame Roget will be with you shortly, mademoiselle," the servant said before leaving her alone in a long salon with a decor of ostentatious splendour that had been fashionable at the height of the Second Empire thirty and more years ago. Her first thought as she stood glancing about her was that the tragic Empress Eugénie might once have held court in such a room. Mist-blue blinds were drawn down against the sun over tall windows swagged in gold-fringed drapery, which ran the length of one wall alternating with magnificent pier-glasses, console tables displaying fine pieces of porcelain beneath each one. The walls themselves were hung with figured silk in a deep magenta hue, the mouldings gilded. At the far end was a huge, white marble fireplace flanked by large sculptured female figures, which were presently flecked with reflected light from the chandeliers sparkling in the diffused sunshine. On all sides the upholstery of the furniture glowed a cerulean blue, the cushions tasselled and pigeon-plump.

Footstools and occasional tables and silk-shaded lamps added an extravagant clutter to the flamboyant setting. There was so much bric-à-brac taking up every inch of polished surface that it would have been almost impossible to put down a commonplace pin between the silver rose-bowls, the sweetmeat glasses, the Dresden shepherds and shepherdesses, the Sèvres candlesticks, the Chinese bowls of every shape and design that were unmistakably of the Ch'ing Dynasty, and all the other costly little ornaments that nudged each other so closely. Somewhere in the room a clock began to chime melodiously. It was noon. Suddenly Irene knew she was no longer alone.

"So you're Edmund Lindsay's daughter!" accused a female voice in English spoken as only it could be by a Londoner born well within the sound of Bow Bells.

Irene whirled around in astonishment, looking up to see for the first time that a narrow gallery spanned the double doors through which she had entered the salon. Standing at the gilded balustrade looking down at her, having come through an archway from an upper room, was Gabrielle Roget. For a few stunned moments, it would have been impossible to judge which of them was the most astounded as each stared at the other. The wide brim of Irene's hat had hidden her face and hair from above until her gaze had been alerted upwards. Red-haired granddaughter and red-haired grandmother gazed at each other speechlessly. For Irene it was a time of revelation. At last it was made clear to her why her father had always cold-shouldered her. He had been unable to look upon her without seeing a likeness to her mother's mother, a woman he had loathed to a point of denying her existence and failing to open a letter that he must have guessed was connected with his young wife's death.

"I am also your daughter's daughter," she declared clearly.

"So I can see," came the dry reply on a completely changed note, from which all hint of enmity had melted away.

Slowly Gabrielle began to descend the spiral staircase that led down from the gallery, turning her head continually to keep the girl within her view. She could not have been less like the white-haired old lady whom her granddaughter had pictured. She was tall and voluptuous-looking, with a huge, swelling bosom and wide hips, her hair dressed in the latest mode of a large pompadour twirled into a Psyche knot at the top, dyed to a glaring brilliance that nevertheless echoed its original colour, proof lingering on in the arched brows. Her face was that of one who had lived well and lived hard; even the throaty quality of her voice was an indication of a hedonistic existence. Her complexion was of the ivory translucency with which redheads are frequently blessed, except that hers had freckled thickly over the years, and defying the masterly application of paint and powder, the tiny, brown flaws spread from her hairline down to the high-boned collar of her dress, its plate-sized lace frill seeming to hold her whole head upon it and hiding whatever age had done to sag her jawline or crease her neck. Similarly her cuffs came to a point with a film of lace to hide the liver spots on the back of her beringed hands. She was sixty-five years old but passed herself off as fifty if ever her age was called for, and no one doubted her. Only her doctor knew the truth, and she hated him for it. Coming to the last tread of the stairs, she stepped from it with a swish of amber satin to regard her granddaughter with dark, intelligent eyes in which a glimpse of incipient amusement showed itself between the softly wrinkled lids.

"I've surprised you, haven't I, Irene? You didn't expect a Cockney, did you? Oh, I can speak la-di-dah when the need arises, but this is no time for pretences of any kind. My real name is Roget, which has a French ring to it, but I was baptized Gertrude, which is not so fancy. It was a small step to change to Gabrielle when I had been long enough in France to pick up the lingo. Well? Do I get a kiss of greeting, or are you going to leave again?"

Irene did not hesitate. She stepped forward and kissed her grandmother's cheek. Then she withdrew a pace, and they looked at each other watchfully.

"Oh, come here!" Gabrielle exclaimed, holding out her well-rounded arms. "Let me give my own granddaughter a hug!"

Irene responded willingly. When they drew apart again, it was with laughter at their own tears, each drying her eyes with a handkerchief, Gabrielle's taking on streaks of black from her painted eyelashes.

"Am I at all like my mother in looks?" Irene asked.

"Not very much," Gabrielle answered, tilting her head and leaning backwards to study her granddaughter. "But then, you're not like that late father of yours either, thank God! I was afraid you were going to be the spitting image of him."

"I heard that in your first words to me."

"Did you? You're a sharp one."

"What's more, I believe now that is why you did not make up your mind whether or not to see me until it reached a point of now or never."

Gabrielle let her head waggle sideways, neither denying nor affirming the quite accurate assumption. "I'll tell you one thing. If you hadn't answered me as you did after I spoke to you, I might have turned on my heel right there on the gallery and never come down the stairs at all."

"I must say I doubt that."

"Oh? Why?"

Irene's lips twitched on a smile as she put up her hands to draw the jet-beaded pin out of her hat. "You wouldn't have been able to resist taking a closer look at someone so like yourself." She swept the hat from her head, revealing the full glory of her hair.

Gabrielle burst into rollicking laughter. "Damn it! You're right. I could have been knocked down with a feather when I saw from the gallery that you had hair the colour of mine. And you *are* like me when I was your age. I'll show you a picture of myself in my young days later on. Now we're going to have luncheon together. There's so much to talk about, so much to hear." She took Irene's hand and brought it up to clasp it between her own, her bent arm folding over the girl's at the same angle, so that they walked closely side by side at a quick trot towards the double doors that led out to the hall. Their steps must have been heard approaching, for both doors parted for them and they swept through, Gabrielle full of questions. Then, in the midst of the wall-hung Canalettos, she brought the two of them to a halt, twirling apart to face her granddaughter eagerly.

"Send to the hotel for your baggage," she urged. "Stay here with me. There's days and days of talking ahead of us. I've dozens of rooms in this house and nobody in them. What do you say?"

"There is nothing I'd like better," Irene replied happily.

The telephone call was made. Then Irene and Gabrielle sat down to luncheon at a round table in a cool, green-hued circular room with glass doors opened to a shaded veranda and a view of the garden beyond. It was a light and delicious meal. While they ate and sipped a superb wine, Irene did most of the talking, not through choice, having many questions of her own she longed to ask about her mother, but because Gabrielle wanted to know all about her years of growing up and what she had done with her life so far. Her grandmother became as proud as a peacock upon hearing that she was to work for Fabergé, which seemed to impress her more than Irene's aim to design jewellery of her own.

"I have no end of pretty things made by him!" Gabrielle exclaimed. "You must let me know when you start selling at Berner's, and I'll come and buy something from you."

"How often do you come to London?"

"I haven't been home for many, many years." Gabrielle gave a wry little shrug, touching the corners of her mouth with her napkin. "You see, England is still home to me even though I've spent the greater part of my life in France."

"What brought you to this country in the first place?"

"Ah, that is quite a long story. I suggest we take coffee on the veranda, and I will relate it to you. After all, it is linked with your mother coming into this world, and I realize you will want to know everything I'm able to tell you about her."

Gabrielle talked openly of her humble beginnings, deliberately lapsing into the East End accents of her childhood to conjure up more vividly certain incidents during the first thirteen years of her life. Joe Roget, her ginger-haired father, had had a fruit-and-vegetable barrow that he trundled about the streets, and Kath, her dark-haired mother, had been in domestic service. They had married and had fourteen children, bringing them up in a slum dwelling of two rooms up and two down, sharing an outdoor privy with a dozen other families. Gabrielle, or Gertie as she had been called then, was the youngest, born when her mother was worn out and her father had taken to the bottle, which had brought to the surface the full violence of the temper that matched his hair. Out of all his offspring, Gertie was the only one who inherited his colouring, although in a richer hue. He was proud of this likeness, she being the first of his children he had ever dandled on his knee, and he made no secret of preferring her to anyone else in the family, even to his wife. As she grew older, she still remained his favourite child, but as his imbibing became worse, it did not spare her from his brutality when he was crazed with drink. In spite of everything she loved him, she alone sensing without comprehending the frustration and misery that lay behind his outbursts. Sometimes she was the only one able to calm him down, whereupon he would sob with maudlin self-pity, and Gertie would see her mother's face become a mask of loathing for the husband she had come to despise. His grown sons never came home and would have nothing to do with him, slipping their mother whatever little bit of money they could spare whenever they happened to see her. His daughters got into trouble of one sort or another and did not dare come home. Out of it all grew a resolve in Gertie that things should be different for her. Somehow or other she would get out of the squalor that had dragged all the others down. She knew she had the best looks in the family, and her hair had drawn glances for as long as she could remember. Later, when she came early to young womanhood, she began to realize that she had more than looks; there was something about her that aroused men to her presence with a persistence that embroiled her in several frightening situations until she learned to look after herself and deliver a kick in the groin if need be. She and her youngest brother, Archie, who with her was the last of the Roget offspring still living under the family roof, helped Joe with his barrow. More often than not they found themselves completely in charge when he was drinking in a pub or lying insensible somewhere. Then brother and sister came home one day to find that their father had reeled there on his own ahead of them. He sat slumped in a chair, his head in his hands, far from sober, but shocked into some kind of sensibility by what he had done. Gertie gave a terrible scream. Kath lay dead, with her staring eyes blackened by punches, her head at an unnatural angle where her neck had been broken when he had struck her back against the wall. Neighbours had already informed the police. He was taken away from the house in a Black Maria van, and none of his family ever saw him again. He hanged himself the same night in his cell.

Apart from Archie, whom Gertie had pitied because he was a weak-willed creature unable to keep his hand out of the day's takings and as destined as their father to end up in prison, she felt nothing for any of her other brothers and sisters. They may have been fond of Kath Roget in their own way, but there was no sign of it as they quarreled between themselves over the few sticks of furniture and over the cheap little knick-knacks that their mother had treasured and that each wanted only to sell. She watched them contemptuously, leaning against the wall with her arms folded, for already somebody had swiped all the chairs.

"You'd better move in wiv me, Gertie," one of her married sisters said disagreebly, "but I ain't 'aving Archie as well, the thieving little toad. One of the others can 'ave 'im."

"I ain't coming," Gertie replied. "I've gotta job. Wiv a widow in Edgeware Road what 'as a grocery shop. She used to buy from Dad's barrow sometimes, and she knows I'm a 'ard worker."

That was how a start in life was made. Gertie scrubbed the stone floors of the shop and the storerooms, washed shelves, carried heavy cheeses, packaged up orders, ran errands, and generally made herself useful. She received no wages, only her food, a supply of aprons, and whatever cast-off garments Mrs. Jones cared to give her to be cut down. It was harder and more grinding work than being with the barrow, and she would probably have had a better time in domestic service where at least she would have had some company when at ease from her labours, but she had a particular purpose in electing to work for Mrs. Jones. The woman had a pleasant speaking voice, good diction, and above all else Gertie wanted to "talk proper," as she termed it to herself, seeing it as the key to advancement. She had a quick ear and a quick mind. Before long she was leaving her Cockney accents behind, and they were only ever to return involuntarily to her in moments of rage or great stress, which was why her origins had shown forth so clearly when she had first addressed her granddaughter from the gallery.

"By my fifteenth birthday, I was serving full time at the counter and receiving a small wage," Gabrielle continued. "As time went on, Mrs. Jones began to rely on me more and more. She was being courted by a widower and it quite turned her head, for she was at a foolish time of life. I didn't fiddle her out of one penny, but I developed my own sidelines, buying in fruit and tomatoes and so forth from barrows at cut prices and then selling them over the counter for my own profit. She had no interest in the shop anymore, but her suitor had. He began to look into things in readiness to take over. And he saw me. Then for what he thought he would get on the side from me, he kept his mouth shut, and that gave me the chance to increase my profits until I had quite a little nest-egg tucked away. When he wasn't prepared to wait any longer for a bit of slap-and-tickle, getting quite nasty, I went to Mrs. Jones, got her to write me a tip-top reference for another job I had lined up, and departed. I worked in a flower shop next. That's considered genteel shop work, which was what I was aiming for, but I had to work in the backroom first, learning to make nosegays and wreaths and bridal bouquets. Nevertheless, it wasn't long before I moved to a posh West End florist's, and there I began to meet gentlemen—real gentlemen, I mean, by status if not always by manners. Many of them used to call in daily for a flower, such as a rosebud or carnation for their buttonhole, which was as fashionable then with dandies and swells-about-town as it is today. I used to make a point of tucking the flower into place for those I fancied and, to be honest, knew to be well to do. I began to be asked out and then to the theatre and expensive restaurants. I had invested some of my money in my wardrobe, and, although I say it myself, I've always been able to wear clothes with flair, and I did my escorts credit with my appearance when they took me around. Then what happened?'' Gabrielle shook her head meditatively at her own folly. "I fell in love with one of those gentlemen and he with me. I began to dream of wedding bells and living happily ever after and all the rest of it. Then I opened a newspaper one morning to read in the society news of his marriage the day before to a baronet's daughter.''

"Oh, Grandmother!'' Irene exclaimed sadly, sitting forward. "You must have been broken-hearted.''

"I was. I made myself so ill with weeping and wailing that I had to stay away from work for three days, keeping to my bed.'' Gabrielle paused for a moment in her tale, regarding her granddaughter closely. "You've been through the same sort of heartache, haven't you? There's a stark look in your eyes that I recognize.''

Irene lowered her lids and leaned her head back in the cushioned wicker chair. "It's over. I've almost forgotten him. At least, I think I have. It's strange to realize that you went through a similar experience.''

Gabrielle smiled as if to herself. "The young always imagine that they are the first to know and discover everything about love and sexual encounters. Believe me, it is the same for each generation in turn."

Irene turned her gaze towards her grandmother again. "How did you get through your unhappiness? Work was the antidote for me."

"Well, I had help from an unexpected source. My absence was noticed at the shop. An elderly Frenchman, who was one of those most particular about his buttonhole, asked where I was. On being told I was indisposed, he had flowers sent to me that day and the next. The third day he called with a bouquet himself. I dragged myself from my bed, put on a silk robe, and opened the door of my room, never expecting to see him there. My room was a shambles, and I looked such a fright with my eyes swollen and my hair in a tangle to my waist, but he doffed his topper, bowed, presented the flowers, and walked in. He had to push things aside to find a place on the only chair to sit down. I never saw a more incongruous sight than that little Frenchman with his thin, waxed moustache and goatee beard sitting there in his natty clothes and white spats amid all the confusion that I had created in my misery. He had found out my address by bribing someone in the shop and admitted to me later that he had had his eye on me for quite a while. He was kind and sympathetic. I poured out everything to him, even something that nobody else knew about. It must have given him the opening he had long awaited. He offered to take me with him to France, to set me up in an apartment, and when the baby came, he would pay all the bills and cover the

cost of fostering the child with a reliable couple."
Gabrielle flicked out her hands from the wrists
expressively. "So that is how I came to France. When
your mother was born, I was still suffering from
homesickness, which was why I decided she should
be brought up in England. The couple who took her
were good Christians in every sense of the word. They
had no children of their own and would have
adopted her, but I could never bring myself to sever
the bond, even though I never saw her after she left
my arms. Unbeknown to Denise, her foster parents
wrote me an annual report on her growing up and
her educational progress. Then, when she met your
father and wanted to be his wife, her foster parents
sent him to me to ask for her hand. Denise never knew
he came. He hated me on sight. It was as if he saw me
as a defiler of his beloved simply by having given
birth to her. It was not enough that I gave him my
word that I would never under any circumstances try
to contact Denise, but he had to have a legal
document drawn up then and there to make him her
guardian until their wedding day, when she would
automatically come under his jurisdiction as his
wife. I think he was afraid that since our dislike of
each other was mutual, I would try to prevent the
marriage, but I had made up my mind long ago never
to interfere in my daughter's life. I could tell he was
devoted to her, and I put my trust in that. I never saw
or heard from him again. Her foster parents let me
know I was a grandmother and that my poor Denise
had died. That was the only time I ever wrote to him,

asking that a wreath be placed anonymously on her grave as a tribute from me, and now I have learned from you that he never opened the letter." Gabrielle passed the fingertips of one hand across her brow as though unconsciously soothing away painful memories. Then, with a deliberate shift of mood, she rose lithely from her chair and stretched out her hand in invitation with a dazzling smile. "Come! I told you earlier that you are in looks a lot like me when I was young. I'll show you a portrait of myself to prove it."

"Why did you name my mother Denise?" Irene asked as they went side by side from the veranda into the house.

"It was to please my little Frenchman. His mother's name had been Denise. As you must have realized by now, he had a wife, which was the reason why we never married."

Upstairs Irene was shown the bedroom that would be hers; a maid was already unpacking her baggage, which had arrived from the hotel. Then they went on to Gabrielle's own bedroom, which was graciously proportioned with classical pillars supporting an arched ceiling painted to represent a bower of roses. Pink chiffon swathed the windows on one side of the room, veiling the summer brightness to a romantic glow, which in turn gave a rosy lustre to the gilded furniture. Yet it was the bed that completely dominated the scene, having the look of Cleopatra's barge. Set on a dais, swagged in garlands of silk flowers caught up by gilded cherubs, it was topped by a coronet canopy from which draperies of filmy lace flowed down seductively on either side of it. On drawing closer, Irene saw with a start of surprise that the underside of the canopy was lined with mirrors that would reflect in entirety the bed beneath and whoever might be lying in it. She dragged her glance away as her grandmother drew her attention to the large portrait on one wall.

"Well? What do you think?"

The painting was not what Irene had expected, although she was becoming a little more used to the unexpected in this house. Gabrielle had been painted naked with her red hair unbound, lying asleep with her arms reposing gracefully above her head. Facially there was a strong resemblance; physically Irene's own breasts were more firmly pointed, and she knew herself to have a much narrower waist than the young woman in the portrait, who had had a baby by the time it was painted. In shapeliness there was nothing to choose between their respective figures.

"You could have been my sister instead of my grandmother," she agreed seriously. When they had discussed the painting, Gabrielle had more to show her. There was the bathroom *en suite* of Carrara marble walled with panels of embossed silver, and a room that Gabrielle referred to casually as her clothes closet, although in fact it was a spacious area lined with fitted wardrobes in which hung scores of expensive dresses for every occasion, furs, coats, and capes, shelves of hats, and tier upon tier of shoes. Lastly she opened her jewel chest. It was no ordinary chest designed to be placed on a dressing table, but one that stood breast-high to her as she pulled out each of the shallow drawers in turn to display the contents lying on quilted silk. Some drawers were allotted entirely to parures of diamonds; others to rubies, emeralds, sapphires, and pearls. The last of all held a collection of stones that had never been mounted. She scooped out half a dozen beautiful emeralds and pressed them into her granddaughter's hand.

"Please accept them as a little gift from me. Get that jeweller at Bing's whom you told me about to make them up into a piece of jewellery of your own design and to send the bill to me." She silenced Irene's protest that it was far too extravagant a gift. "No, no. I want to see how creative you can be."

"I can't thank you enough." Irene was almost at a loss for words.

"It gives me such joy to find exactly the right memento to give my own granddaughter."

As Gabrielle locked up her treasure chest again, Irene took the emeralds to her own bedroom and put them in a safe place, her mind already racing with ideas. When she went to rejoin her grandmother, she found her waiting at the head of the stairs.

"How your Frenchman must have loved you, Grandmother," she said impulsively. "Surely no woman has ever been so lavished with things of beauty."

Gabrielle gave her a long and penetrating look. She saw that the remark had been made without guile and in the genuine belief that her elderly benefactor had been a millionaire. "He did love me, Irene. Generous in all things, he taught me how to look after my savings and to invest through the Bourse. In addition he guided me along the path I was to follow, having identified a special quality in me that would provide security for me long after he was gone and would keep me in the luxury that had long been my aim. He loved me more unselfishly than any man I've ever known. Unfortunately our relationship ended sooner than I had expected, even though he must have had warnings himself. He suffered a stroke that paralysed him, and he spent the last months of his life in the dubious care of his unloving wife, who never allowed me to see him." She read the question revealed in the girl's bewilderment and then saw comprehension dawn. "Yes, you are drawing the right conclusion. I thought you had guessed when you came here, just as your father recognized me for what I was as soon as he set eyes on me. I truly assumed that you knew. I am a woman whose profession is love. In my prime I was the most sought-after courtesan in Paris, one of *les grandes horizontales.* These days I have one dear man to whom I give all my affection." She gave a wry half-smile. "I suppose you think me too old to know pleasure in a man's arms. I will tell you that on my fiftieth birthday I ran through the Bois de Boulogne to meet a lover half my age. Well? Have I shocked you?"

Irene leaned against the balustrade, resting an arm and hand along it. "No, I'm intrigued."

Gabrielle's eyes began to twinkle mischievously. "I will tell you something else. That distinguished gentleman, Louis Tiffany, heard of my romantic tête-à-tête in the Bois, and it put his handsome nose quite out of joint. He went back to America without visiting me again, but the next time he was in Paris, his first call was at my door. I made him call three times before I would receive him. Then he gave me a diamond necklace worth a fortune!" She threw back her head in her throaty laugh that was full of rich cadences.

"May I ask if you cared for him at all?"

Gabrielle answered frankly. "I was fond of him. I could say that I loved him for his generosity, but then, men who pay court to a *demi-mondaine* of my standing are expected to be generous." She glanced at her fob watch, which was suspended on a silk ribbon at her waist. "I have an appointment with my financial advisor, who will be here at any moment. Shall you be able to amuse yourself for a little while?"

"I'll explore the garden."

"Take a parasol. You mustn't spoil your lovely complexion. A woman's first duty is to be beautiful, you know."

As Irene strolled between the formal flowerbeds and the playing fountains, her thoughts drifted to her father. It had been so much more than her resemblance to Gabrielle that had set him against her. He had interpreted the likeness as a taint already upon her, and everything he had done had been with the sole aim of preventing her from slipping by any path into what he thought of as Gabrielle's evil shadow. Poor man. He had created barriers between them that need never have been there.

When at last she retraced her footsteps in the direction of the house, she realized how significant this visit to Paris had become in her life. First of all she had gained this valuable insight into her father's long-held concern for her. Secondly she had found her grandmother, who had given her a welcome beyond anything she could have pictured. Then she had achieved the triumph of being accepted into the employ of Fabergé. What was the other development dancing just out of mental reach? Almost instantly the answer leaped at her. She had met Gregory again.

Her brows drew together in a frown of annoyance. He was of no importance to her. It was Sofia who might well let thoughts linger after him. With a shake of her head to dismiss all thought of the man, she went into the cool and shaded interior of the house.

Ten

Irene discovered that her mornings were always to be her own in her grandmother's house. Gabrielle never made an appearance before noon. This enabled Irene to carry out certain written instructions that came from Gregory, although he was unaware that she collected the mail herself from the hotel where she had been staying when he left Paris. The reason was that she hoped to avoid contact with him before she had to meet him again in London. Any replies she had to send him went out from the hotel's writing room on its headed paper. She smiled triumphantly to herself each time she sealed an envelope.

Writing to Sofia was a different matter. There had been the first difficult letter, informing her stepmother that she would be working with Gregory in London for Fabergé, but since she was not suspected of knowing anything about the romantic encounter in Nice, she kept her reference to him casual and impersonal. Sofia sent warm congratulations; there was nothing in her letter to hint at what her private feelings might have been at the news that once more and indirectly she was being linked to an incident in her past.

Irene had lost no time in drafting out an idea for a design to incorporate the emeralds she had been given into a brooch. She delivered the design, drawn out in every detail, to Arthur Lucas, meeting him by appointment. He had a small workshop at home and promised her that he would complete her order as quickly as possible. "Allow me two weeks," he requested.

"That will be near the end of my extended stay in Paris. I'll have to leave soon afterwards."

"You shall have it to take home with you, never fear."

That same afternoon Gabrielle took her shopping, brushing aside her protests that she had more than enough clothes with her. "Nonsense! No woman can have too many hats and dresses. It's only husbands who think along those lines for their wives, although not for any female they happen to be pursuing, needless to say! In any case, I don't like to see you in mourning clothes. Never wear it for me! Wear scarlet or orange or flame, anything that will pronounce a thanksgiving for the life of the departed and for the joy of having known that person. That's what I do. Black should be confined to dresses of truly refined elegance, a setting for one's finest jewels. I once went in black to the races at Longchamps, holding a daffodil-yellow parasol above my head, and I created a sensation. For weeks afterwards black and yellow held sway in the fashion world."

She chuckled at the memory. She was full of tales of the *demi-monde*, which had emerged from the decadence of the French Empire before its fall and continued to thrive on the fringes of society, a glittering, witty, and sexually exciting circle to which flocked men of high rank, wealth, and distinction from every country. It was a point of pride with her that she was still at the heart of it. Scandal and intrigue, lust and avarice and sheer *joie de vivre* were woven into the experiences she related. There was a French nobleman whom she had so exhausted with her youthful passion that his wife, out of concern for his health, had asked her not to allow him any more visits. She had not particularly liked the wife, but she had noticed the increasingly purple tinge of her lover's complexion and his shortness of breath, so for his sake she agreed to the request. Practically, she and the wife had found him a less demanding *belle-petite* to divert him in gentler ways. Once, wishing to tease an ardent young man, she told him that he could only make love to her for as long as it took for a stack of twelve thousand franc notes to burn. He took her by surprise, arriving with the money, which he set fire to leisurely, note by note! Then there was the case of a rival who, upon arriving late at a party for the Prince of Wales, threw off her gown in supplication to reveal her entire nakedness, meeting with royal approval. Another courtesan, similarly proud of her figure, had had herself served up on a silver dish at a banquet for Cossack officers when visiting Russia. The Czar had had her deported.

Gabrielle dismissed out of hand all present-day courtesans, unaware that it was a sign of age that she should imagine all was so much better in the past. In her opinion, none of them could compare with those of her hey-day, not even the two whom she grudgingly admitted to be rated higher than the rest. These were the daughter of a Spanish gypsy, known as Le Belle Otèro, and the equally exotic Diane de Chandel. Gabrielle detested them simply for being in their prime, fearful of her own reputation being overshadowed. Nevertheless this did not stop her from inviting them to her house whenever they were in Paris, for either of them enlivened any gathering. It would never have done to ask them together, for the rivalry between them was deadly.

As the days went by, Irene was continually amazed by the brilliance of the company that came to dinners, receptions and grand salons at her grand-mother's house. Musicians, writers, artists, and sculptors mingled with those of political fame, as well as many more known by distinguished titles and of royal birth. It was noticeable that the women were always beautiful or vividly attractive, sparkling like jewels in the midst of predominantly male gatherings, for all of them without exception were established *demi-mondaines*.

Irene was not surprised when she was propositioned, losing count of the number of times it happened. It was almost always voiced with charm and a practised ease, which was in keeping with the atmosphere that Gabrielle maintained. She became adept at turning aside these advances with a smile that left no animosity. Sometimes she was quite amused, knowing those men could never have understood her sense of personal liberty that enabled her to come and go wherever she liked and to mix with whomever she liked. In no way did she blame them for attempting to compromise her, for it would never occur to any of them that Gabrielle's grand-daughter would not be following in her footsteps. Some of them even voiced the supposition that Irene was being coached to take over the high place that Gabrielle had long held in the *demi-monde*. It was as well that none of these particular remarks reached Gabrielle's ears, for when she was presiding over these cultured and sophisticated gatherings, she felt young again and was her most scintillating self. She knew that other courtesans would like to see her fade into oblivion, particularly her most virulent ene-mies, Otèro and De Chandel, both of whom coveted her throne, but it would have been a shattering blow to her self-esteem to know that there were others present who considered the time had come for her abdication. And that her own granddaughter should be considered as her successor would have been more than she could endure. She was still seeing Irene's look as a candle to her own. What she did not see in her mirror was that she was comparing a painted visage to the natural bloom of youth.

Arthur Lucas delivered the jewellry he had made to Irene's design on the day he had promised. She was alone on the veranda when he was announced. She set aside the book she was reading and went to meet him. One look at his face told her that he was more than pleased with the work he had done.

"Oh, show me!" she cried excitedly, clasping her hands together.

He put the package down on a veranda table and opened the folds of the tissue paper almost reverently. "There!" he exclaimed. "What do you think of that?"

She was speechless. It was a true work of art. Although she had made up her own designs at the School of Handicraft, it had been beyond her to attempt anything so elaborate; therefore, since she had become reconciled to a halt in her practical training, she had given full rein to her imagination in her designs, and the present result was stunning. With the fingertips of both hands she picked up the large brooch that had been made. Set against a swirling foliage of translucent white enamel was a dragonfly, its body composed of the most magnificent emeralds, its wings of gold filigree so delicate that they quivered on the tiny mechanism that she had devised. As if it had rained gold upon the brooch, tiny droplets clung to the leaves of the foliage, the whole shining and gleaming as if it had a life of its own. Unaware that she was holding her breath, she pinned it to the bodice of her striped dress. Then she ran indoors to view its reflection in the nearest mirror, which happened to be in the hall. Arthur followed to stand a few feet from her.

"Let me know when you need a craftsman in a business of your own, Miss Irene," he said to her.

She smiled and spoke on a note of promise. "One day, Mr. Lucas."

"Don't leave it too long. I'm not as young as I used to be, and my eyesight is not what it was in your father's employ."

"Come, come! You're not anywhere near retirement age."

"Well, it would have to be this side of the Channel if you should ever consider a serious arrangement. My wife would never go back to England now."

There was no further discussion. The clocks throughout the house were chiming noon, bringing Gabrielle to the head of the stairs for her first descent of the day. Irene went swiftly to the foot of the flight. "Look, Grandmother! Mr. Lucas has brought the brooch."

Gabrielle paused on the stairs. The brooch on the girl's bodice was spectacular. She felt her whole face tighten with avarice. It was always the same when she coveted something that could not be hers, an involuntary reaction that for a few painful seconds took her back in time to her wretched childhood. "It's handsome," she praised, recovering herself to let pride in her granddaughter's achievement come through. "I don't know when I've seen a more eye-catching piece. Congratulations, Irene. And to you,

Mr. Lucas, for your workmanship. I trust you have brought your bill with you."

She never owed money to tradesman. Again memories of the past with what it meant to have empty pockets made it impossible for her not to settle promptly the accounts of humble folk. This side of her character contrasted with and yet was related to her ruthlessness with rich men, from whom she had gathered in everything she had ever wanted to enhance her material status throughout her years in the practice of pleasure.

That same evening Gabrielle held one of her salons. The rooms glowed with candlelight from the chandeliers, for she would not consider having electricity installed, believing that it gave off a crude light that was unflattering to a woman's complexion. People thronged everywhere in full evening dress, and musicians played on the gallery above the drawing room. Irene wore one of her new dresses with the latest neckline of dropped sleeves with a strap over each shoulder, the material cream lace over pineapple chiffon, her new emerald brooch her only piece of jewellery. She was aware of it drawing sideways glances from the women from the moment she began to mingle in the gathering, greeting people whom she had begun to know.

Then she felt someone staring at her. It was almost a tingling at the back of her neck. She turned her head and met Gregory's hostile eyes from across the room. He must have just arrived. She found his gaze compelling, igniting a resentment in her that she should be so angrily aware of him. Somebody was repeating a question to her, and with a strained effort she gave her attention back to those with whom she was engaged in conversation. She could feel his gaze still upon her and knew he was wending his way through to her. He spoke at the back of her ear in a voice that vibrated in its harshness.

"What the hell are you doing here?"

She withdrew from the people she was with to face him. "I was invited," she replied coldly.

"Invited! By whom?" He glared about as if to locate the culprit. "This is no place for you!"

She feigned innocence. "Why?"

"It happens to be the house of one of the most notorious *demi-mondaines* in Paris. All the women here are nothing more or less than expensive tarts! No honourable man would have brought you here under any circumstances. When I arrived back in Paris today and telephoned your hotel, I was told you had left. I naturally assumed you had returned to England. If I had known you had cancelled your arrangements the day you were supposed to go back there with me simply to continue an association with someone debased enough to bring you under this roof, I would never have allowed it."

She gasped aloud at his audacity in assuming he could control her actions. "I don't have to answer to you for anything!"

"You do if you don't want to let the chance of working in London slip through your fingers. Men who chat with you here certainly don't want to meet you again when they are with their wives buying trinkets from Fabergé!"

Her eyes flashed defiance. "Are you giving me the sack before I've even started?"

"No, I'm giving you a second chance. Now get your wrap and leave with me at once."

She made no move. "Where are you planning to take me?" she goaded.

"Since it appears that supper has not yet been served here," he answered with barely controlled impatience, "I will take you to dine somewhere and then back to whichever hotel you are staying in now."

She decided that the time had come to end the little masquerade. "I have no hotel. I'm staying in this house until I leave Paris the day after tomorrow. My grandmother is Gabrielle Roget."

His eyes stretched wide and then narrowed, an expression of stupefaction hardening his whole face. Before he could make any comment, a young woman, a pretty, doll-like creature with a beaded dress and a feathered aigrette adorning her bright yellow hair, bounced between them, cutting off Irene's immediate sight of him.

"I must ask!" the intruder cooed to her. "I've been dying with envy. Is it a Lalique?"

Irene, dazed for the moment, looked at her blankly. "What do you mean?"

"Your brooch. It's a René Lalique piece, isn't it?"

"No, it isn't."

Another *demi-mondaine* who had drawn near

added her opinion. "Then it must be by Fouquet. It's divine! Every woman in this room wants to claw it from you."

Another female voice piped nearby. "You're both wrong. It's a Henri Vever design. I'd know his work anywhere."

Irene knew she should have been flattered that they imagined her work to be that of any of the three leading Art Nouveau designers, but the situation was taking on a nightmarish quality. Now that the opening on the subject of the brooch had been made, women were drawing towards her from all corners of the room. Gregory had disappeared, and she was being steadily backed into an alcove by the feminine pressure around her. She felt half suffocated by the invisible cloud of the blend of their scented bodies and their paint and powder. All of them were clamouring at once, some reaching out to finger the brooch, a few becoming aggrieved that the wearer of it appeared reluctant to reveal the name of the designer, a secret each one of them would have kept to herself to spite the rest, but they knew this girl was not of the *demi-monde* and therefore should be easy prey. To Irene's relief, Gabrielle came to her rescue.

"Stand aside, ladies. I'll tell you the name of the designer if you will only give her a little air."

She cleared a path for Irene and hustled her through the renewed clamour. Gregory was waiting for her. As she reached him, he put his arm about her waist and hurried her from the room, Gabrielle barring the way of the flock that would have pursued them. In the hall he whipped her wrap from the maid who had brought it from her bedroom, swept it about her shoulders, and hastened her out of the house to a waiting cab.

"Maxim's," he said to the cabby. Then flinging himself down on the seat next to her, he said drily, "And you had better remove that brooch if you don't want to get lynched."

Leaning her head back against the upholstery, she began to shake with mirth, he joining in her laughter, both of them overcome by the absurdity of the scene that had taken place.

"Are they mad?" she asked at last, getting her breath back.

"No. Just greedy," he said with a sigh, serious again.

"If that is your opinion, why do you go to that house?"

"I've known Gabrielle for a long time. Never intimately, I hasten to add. A friend of my father's, Louis Tiffany, took me under his wing when I was a boy in Paris for the first time. He introduced me to her, and ever since I have attended her salons if they happened to coincide with my having time to spare. They vie with those held by some of the city's richest and most cultured families, such as those I particularly enjoy at the home of Comtesse de Loynes, whose gatherings have a definite influence on French politics. As a matter of fact, my original plan for this evening was to go on there later. After we have dined, perhaps you would like to accompany me?"

"It would be interesting for a little while." She wished to clarify matters. "I have to tell you I intend to return to my grandmother's home and not to any hotel for the rest of my time in Paris. You have not removed me from her residence for any longer than it takes for her salon to come to a close and the *demi-mondaines* to be gone."

"Kidnapping is not my intention," he retorted pithily. Now that those brief minutes of shared amusement were over, the tension between them was seeping back. "I had a few words with your grandmother before she plunged in to reach you in the midst of that voluptuous swarm, and she told me when you would be leaving. This time we shall travel back to England together."

Irene's nostrils quivered as she breathed hard, and she clenched her hands in her lap. He *did* take matters for granted. She could only suppose that for Sofia's sake he was assuming such a proprietory attitude towards her, quite apart from having anything to do with her working for Fabergé.

The cab had turned into the rue Royale. "Here we are," he said.

She had seen it from outside when going about Paris, an eighteenth-century town house built of grey stone, with a fringed, crimson awning over the entrance, a doorman in brass-buttoned livery. She had heard that it had been completely redecorated and refurbished quite recently in the full style and spirit of Art Nouveau, and the gaiety of the atmosphere enveloped them as soon as they had entered. Champagne corks were popping, music came from a tuneful orchestra, and oranges, lemons, and swirling foliage patterned the stained-glass roof that bathed everything in incandescent tints. They were shown to a table in the shimmering, soft-hued glow. Here the younger, brighter element of refined society mingled with *demi-mondaines* and their escorts, the jewels of the women irradiating from all sides, some female heads adorned with nodding plumes, sparkling hair ornaments, and twisted pearls. Laughter and talk buzzed merrily.

When Gregory had given their order and the menus had been whisked away, he remarked on her brooch for the first time. "I want to congratulate you. It is a beautiful design. I've never seen emeralds more finely set in a contemporary piece. Is it all your own handiwork?"

"Not beyond the design on paper. It was executed for me by a goldsmith I know in Paris, who once worked for my father."

"Is your practical work to his standard?"

"No," she answered honestly. "He is a master craftsman with years of experience. My design was so intricate that it needed a goldsmith of his aptitude to execute it. I left the School of Handicraft before I reached the level of Guildmanship." She did not tell him how or why the termination of her studies came about, simply saying that her father had decided she should assist him in the shop. They talked on for a while about her time in the office and behind the counter at Lindsay's, he questioning her on various points, which she could tell were related to all she would have to do under his direction. She also told him, again without going into certain details, how she had found and met her grandmother for the first time. He listened with interest while his seemingly lazy gaze took in the pleasing sight she made with her gleaming, red-gold hair afire in the diffused light, the pearly curve of her shoulders, and the deep shadow of her cleavage where the extraordinary emerald brooch, aquiver with gold, was drawing glances from every woman who passed their table, no matter how abundantly bejewelled each happened to be.

Meanwhile, the food served to them was superb. *Cole Madrilène à la Mimosa* was followed in turn by *Campanile des Crêpes* and *Canard à la Marengo*. Irene had the appetite of the young and healthy, doing justice to each course. It was actually the first time since she moved in with her grandmother that she was having enough to eat. Gabrielle, like so many wealthy people, especially those unable to forget their humble origins, was as parsimonious in small, unexpected ways as she was generous in others. She did not stint her guests but seemed to consider that Irene, now a member of her household, should eat as sparsely as she did herself. She actually revealed that she expected leftovers from a dinner or supper party to keep her servants fed for a week. Only in the matter of chocolates and bonbons did Gabrielle indulge herself, which was a rational explanation for her ample figure. Many a time Irene had risen from her grandmother's table still hungry.

Gregory approved of and was quietly amused by Irene's appreciation of the food. He liked her naturalness, her lack of false airs, and the lively look about her of being ready to cope intelligently with whatever came her way, good or bad. He thought she knew as well as he did that the abrasive sparks which were always on the point of flying between them had roots in a sexual attraction that neither wished to pursue for individual reasons.

"Have you ever given thought to going into jewellery designing?" he asked her. They had just finished a ginger sherbet with champagne to clear their palates, and she was welcoming with renewed enthusiasm the garnished baron of lamb which the waiter had just displayed to them on a silver dish before the succulent slices were carved.

"All the time," she replied. "Once I might have considered applying to get into one of the Cartier workshops or with a jeweller of similar standing, but I don't want to be confined to the rules of the house. Briefly and for the first time in my life I have tasted independence. That is how it has to be for me from now on. Somehow and somewhere I'm going to open my own place. In the meantime, I'm going to gain valuable experience by selling for Fabergé. It may give me enough prestige to encourage a bank to advance me the necessary funds to launch my enterprise."

"I see one great barrier against that chance."

"What is that?"

"You're a woman."

Her green eyes flashed angrily. "That should have nothing to do with it."

"In your case, I agree."

"Why only in my case? All women should have an equal chance."

"It's a fact of life that in business matters the female sex lags far behind."

"That's only because there are not equal educational opportunities for women to prepare them for competition with men. One day that situation must change."

"Is that your recipe for perfect co-existence?" He deliberately drawled his query.

"Don't mock! You're biased! Men always are. Their ego demands that women be kept subservient to them."

He had taken a sip of wine, and he looked into the glass for a moment or two as if into a crystal ball before he set it down again. "I have to disagree with you. When my wife made her decision to go back to the stage, the choice was entirely hers. She and I both knew it was the end of our marriage, but that was the price that had to be paid. I would never have kept her against her will, because subservience in any human being is totally abhorrent to me."

Irene had blushed uncomfortably. "I'm sorry. I forgot when I spoke out that you have been married."

He looked at her sardonically. "I still am. The knot has never been untied. Simply stretched by a civilized state of separation, which suits me well enough. I

294

never intend to marry again."

"You sound extremely positive."

"I have reached a stage of mature wisdom where I recognize love for what it is. A brief spell of delicious insanity that sets mind, heart, and body at variance with all that is commonsensical. When the ecstatic mist clears from the brain, the reality is harsh and uncompromising."

"That's a cynical viewpoint. I don't agree with it at all."

"I should be saddened if you did. Romantic dreams should be cherished for as long as possible."

"I'm not talking about ephemeral illusions. I happen to believe that it is possible for two people to love each other all their lives. Few of us are fortunate to be blessed in that way, but it can happen."

He smiled suddenly. "Momentarily I'll allow you to convince me. For the duration of this evening, anyway. Let's drink to love. May it be yours. For always."

She paused before she lifted her glass in response to his, suspicious that he was taunting her as he had done before. Then she saw that for once there was nothing disturbing and indecipherable in his eyes, only a clear look that praised her eloquently for being pleasurable to his gaze.

"To love," she said, replying to his toast.

They drank, smiled at each other, and smiled again as the waiter refilled their glasses. It was as if they had let the atmosphere of Maxim's take over at last. From that moment they kept to lighter, less controversial subjects all through the cheeses, the wild strawberries dusted with sugar that were sweeter than nectar, and the steaming coffee in gilded cups with accompanying liqueurs.

As they were leaving Maxim's they came face to face with one of the *demi-mondaines* from Gabrielle's salon, her escort in tow. "I'm calling on you tomorrow," she hissed fiercely at Irene in passing. "Don't see anybody else before me."

As Irene looked back after the woman in surprise, Gregory summarized her reaction for her. "It seems that if you wished it you could have clients waiting in line at your grandmother's house, all demanding your designs. I think that settles when we should leave Paris. We'll take the first train in the morning."

She was stepping ahead of him into a cab and almost bounced down on the seat inside. "I don't want to cut short my time by two days," she protested indignantly. "And if my designs are going to be in demand, I'd be foolish to leave."

"You'd be foolish to stay," Gregory replied crisply, ready to crush any argument. "You have no workshop, no goldsmiths, no place of display."

"Mr. Lucas, who made up my brooch for me, is eager to do my work."

"It's my guess he wouldn't be prepared to give up a secure position at Bing's to chance his luck on the whim of half a dozen *demi-mondaines* wanting expensive trinkets from you. Don't try to run before you can walk, Irene. Your day will come if you give it time."

She realized he was giving her sound advice, and yet she resented it, for it was given almost as an order that brooked no argument. Every nerve in her bristled against this reassertion of male domination. The short truce between them was at an end as far as she was concerned.

"If I'm to think over what you have said," she stated coolly, "I had better return home and leave you to go on alone to the De Loynes salon. I can always enter the house by the servants' entrance if the place is still full of people."

"As you wish," he replied, following his own line of thought. "You'll need your sleep with a day's travel ahead of you. Be ready by seven-thirty. We can catch the eight o'clock boat-train."

"I haven't said yet that I'm coming!" she burst out.

He had been looking unseeingly out of the cab window at the passing streets, concentrating on certain messages he would leave with regard to the business matter he had completed earlier in the day, and he slewed his eyes round towards her. "If you are banking on support from Gabrielle, forget it. Her attitude towards your designing for the *demi-monde* will be the same as mine, although for a different reason."

Irene bit her lip. How had he guessed she had been thinking that she would get backing from another quarter? "I happen to believe otherwise," she declared stoutly.

He made no reply. They did not speak again until they arrived at Gabrielle's house. There were still plenty of lighted windows but no carriages outside. All the guests had gone. He saw Irene to the door.

"Let's make no pretense about it having been a wonderful evening," he said as he rang the bell for her. "You and I can dispense with conventionalities."

"I can say truthfully it was an unforgettable one," she answered.

"I'll endorse that." As he spoke, the door was opened wide and the light from within fell full upon her, accenting all that was lovely and feminine and desirable about her. He was reminded of the time when he had glanced back over his shoulder and seen her in the hallway of her father's house. There stirred within him such a force of feeling that it was almost as if the original spell she had cast over him momentarily in the past had swept back to reach the very core of his being. There was no question of his leaving her behind in Paris a second time. "Good night, Irene. I'll be back at half past seven."

Her sharp pace as she entered the house revealed her irritated mood. She found the servants tidying up and removing trays of glasses in the direction of the kitchen. "Where is my grandmother?" she asked.

"Madame Roget has retired. She left word that you should go and see her."

Irene hurried up the stairs. Gabrielle was ensconced in her extraordinary bed with its black satin sheets and pillows, an incongruous elderly woman without her cosmetics, her figure sagging under the silk nightgown without the support of her daytime stays, her dyed hair hanging down over her shoulders. She removed her spectacles and put down the book she was reading. Her expression was grim. Irene drew the obvious conclusion.

"Am I late? Did I keep you awake?"

"Late?" Gabrielle slammed the book aside to give emphasis to her contemptuous tone. "In Paris? Dawn would not be too late to come home in Paris. How like your prudish father you are at this moment, Irene!" It was the most scathing insult she could deliver.

Irene sighed, crossing to sit on the edge of the bed, facing her grandmother. "I've displeased you somehow. What have I done?"

"You ruined my evening with that brooch of yours! I have never had one of my salons fall apart so disastrously. The women were in such tantrums over my getting you out of the house that they made the rest of the evening as unpleasant as possible. Some left quite early. I've never been more humiliated."

"I met one of them when Gregory and I were leaving Maxim's. She said she was calling on me in the morning."

"Did she?" Gabrielle was quite white about the mouth with temper. "I suppose she won't be the only one. They shall not be admitted. I'm not having my house made into an agency!" She wagged a painted, taloned finger at her granddaughter. "You're not to design anything for any of them under my roof!"

Irene jerked up her head involuntarily under the blow of disappointment that had been delivered to her. As always in times of stress, she reminded herself fiercely that she had come through setbacks before, and she would again.

"You'll have no need to keep the door barred, Grandmother," she said, managing to keep her voice clear of any tremor. "Gregory wants me to leave for London with him by the early morning boat-train. My stay with you is over a little sooner than I had expected."

Gabrielle's whole expression changed to one of distress. "But you'll come back! You'll come and see me again!"

"Of course I will. And I'll write, I promise." Irene took the trembling hand that had been reached out to her and was drawn closer. They kissed each other on both cheeks.

"You're a dear girl." Gabrielle found a wisp of lacy handkerchief and wiped her wet eyes. "I'm going to miss you."

"I'll miss you, too. This is *au revoir*, because I'll not disturb you in the morning."

"*Au revoir*, my dear." Gabrielle used the handkerchief once more. Then, as Irene reached the bedroom door, she spoke again on a new and wheedling note, her eyes holding an almost cunning glint. "One second more, Irene. If you should think of a nice design for a brooch for me, using some of the unset gems I showed you, I would be pleased."

Irene nodded without hesitation. "I will design one and post it to you. Let Mr. Lucas carry out the work."

"Yes, yes. I'll look forward to receiving it from you."

On her way to her own room, Irene thought over her grandmother's request. She was glad to be able to do something in return for the hospitality she had received, but at the same time it had become obvious to her why Gregory with his knowledge of the women of the *demi-monde* had been sure she would get no support from her grandmother to stay on and design for them. Female jealousy was at the root of it. Gabrielle in her own mind still felt rivalry towards those younger women following her age-old profession. The manner in which they had ruined her evening was typical of the spite and bitchiness that prevailed in their circles. Gabrielle was taking subtle revenge in denying them access to the designs they coveted. Her triumph would be complete when she could display a unique piece of jewellery that would be the envy of them all.

Irene was on the steps of the house, her baggage beside her, when Gregory arrived at the hour that had been set. He leaped out of the cab and came to her. "I'm pleased that you decided to travel with me," he said.

She compressed her lips in a rueful smile, tilting her head in temporary submission to circumstances. "I had no choice," she admitted frankly.

"Don't be downcast. As I said to you last night, your day will come. It's inevitable."

She was not ungrateful for his encouraging words, but she could not help thinking that men were invariably magnanimous when they were getting their own way. If she had not fallen in with his wishes this day, his attitude to her would have been entirely different.

The journey was a strange one for her, making her feel that it would not be easily forgotten. They travelled first class and in comfort all the way. At the Gare du Nord he had bought a whole armful of magazines and some English newspapers for her, which proved to be instrumental in making her aware that he was taking a particular interest in her that she found oddly stimulating. As she read or turned the pages of a magazine, she could sense his gaze switching from his newspaper towards her, but when she turned her head he was looking down again, and their eyes never met. It seemed that he wished to study her as though he had never truly seen her before, yet did not want to embarrass her with his scrutiny. When they talked together, it was in a perfectly ordinary manner. He told her that a selection of Fabergé's wares was to be sold in Paris in the same way it was to be offered for sale in London. Whether or not the Russian goldsmith would decide to open a shop in the French capital was another matter. They touched on other subjects related to the time they would be working in each other's company, and for her it was in these more level and quite bland areas that she was able to be at ease with him. It was only when they lapsed into silence while taking a stroll around the deck of the Channel steamer or resumed their reading in neighbouring deck-chairs, as well as on the train from Dover to London, that an electric current seemed to dance between them. It made her so attuned to his every movement that it seemed to her that if they took each other's hand it would seize them with a riveting force which would strike forth a shower of white-hot sparks. It was an image that should have made her scoff, but the impression remained. Quite ridiculously, it made her avoid even the most accidental contact with him. When the train deposited them at Victoria Station, she pretended to fuss with her purse and her gloves, deliberately avoiding as if not seeing the hand he held out to help her alight from the carriage to the platform.

As they walked toward the ticket barrier, porters following with their baggage, he said he would see her to her door, but she declined his offer. "There's no need. We'll take separate cabs. I asked my grandmother's housekeeper to telegraph Milton Square that I would be home today, so I'll not be returning to an empty house."

It was more than being tactful not to mention her stepmother being there. Somehow it had become impossible to speak of Sofia to him. But she might just as well have done so. As she preceded him through the ticket barrier, she saw Sofia waiting with a happy smile to meet her. Even as they walked towards each other, Irene saw Sofia's eyes go beyond her to Gregory and become quite unconsciously transfigured by a look of love.

"How kind of you to meet me, Stepmother," Irene

303

said faintly.

"I was so excited that you were coming home that I had to be here," Sofia replied as they embraced. Then she turned to Gregory. "How are you, Mr. Burnett? Irene wrote to me of her good fortune in being accepted for a post by Monsieur Fabergé and mentioned that you are to be in charge."

"It's good to see you again, Mrs. Lindsay," he replied. "Allow me to escort you two ladies to your carriage."

"I have the Daimler today," Sofia answered. "I use it most of the time. May we give you a ride to your destination?"

"I wouldn't dream of taking you out of your way. Thank you all the same." He went with them to the parked Daimler where the chauffeur, wearing a new, cream-coloured uniform with a black-peaked cap, awaited them. Irene recalled that Sofia had never liked Edmund's choice of slab-grey for his driver. It was a small but positive sign that Sofia was beginning to make adjustments to her life in widowhood. When they were both seated and the chauffeur was taking his place behind the wheel, Sofia expressed the hope to Gregory that he would dine with them quite soon.

"You are most kind," he said conventionally. "Goodbye, Mrs. Lindsay. Goodbye until tomorrow, Irene."

As the motorcar pulled away, Sofia looked askance at Irene. "Tomorrow?" she repeated on an inquiring note.

"I'm to meet Gregory at Berner's Hotel. We are to view the suite where Fabergé's wares are to be sold."

"Oh." She seemed satisfied and patted Irene's hand affectionately where it rested on the rug over their knees. "Now tell me all about Paris. Needless to say, I'm agog to hear more about your grandmother and everything else you wrote about in your letters."

Perhaps a little more about Gregory too, Irene added to herself. She was heart-heavy. It had been transparently obvious to her that Sofia had come to Victoria Station in the buoyant hope that Gregory would be arriving back in London at the same time. It made her afraid for the kindly woman who was so dear to her. Somehow it also made her afraid for herself at the same time. It was proving to be a most wretched homecoming.

Eleven

Three weeks later the suite at Berner's Hotel had been
opened up to allow ample space for the display and
sale of Fabergé's wares. Irene finished some last-
minute written work in the room set aside as
Gregory's office and then emerged to join the
salesmen who stood ready and waiting to receive the
first customers. She would be serving only if the
pressure of demand necessitated it; otherwise she was
dealing with any problems that might arise. The
suite had been quite transformed since she and
Gregory had first viewed it. Cabinets, showcases, and
glass counters had given it the look of an exclusive
shop, which indeed it was temporarily.

She had worked extremely hard with Gregory in
preparation for this opening day under his super-
vising control. Domestically, it had been an up-
setting time for her, because whenever she went
hurrying off to meet him at some appointed place,

Sofia had had a wistful look in her eyes that spoke unconsciously of a wish to see him herself. Irene could only guess at her stepmother's state of mind. Sofia had come to terms with her widowhood, and in reestablishing her life it was not unnatural that she might wish to regather the strings of a brief love affair that had been curtailed by circumstances for a considerable while. There had been no question of the invitation to dine being settled to a definite date, simply because he was working to all hours on last-minute preparations, and usually Irene was with him. It was a point of satisfaction to her that he had come to rely on her completely, her efficiency having been proved to him over and over again. Although he had a clerical staff, he had designated much of the written work to her, and she had shouldered it willingly, wanting to gain every scrap of experience available to her towards the day when she would supervise a business of her own. Now and again he gave her a word of praise. More often he was abrupt and impatient. Sometimes they clashed fiercely.

Since he had only stepped in to organize the month-long session as a result of the crisis caused by her father's sudden death, there was no question of his taking on the next selling session in a few months time, which meant she would be working with his successor. She thought it was as well that they should go their separate ways again. There was too much vibration for her in a room when he was there. She even felt it on this soft, autumnal morning when he was far across the suite from her, his dark head bent in concentration as some lists were being discussed, a tall figure almost in silhouette against one of the windows. She did not attempt to analyse her reaction to his presence, telling herself that she had come to a stage where she neither liked nor disliked him, a bland enough state of affairs; it was simply that she was constantly far too aware of him as a man and herself as a woman whenever they were in close proximity. Whenever she did allow her thoughts to dwell on their strained relationship, she accepted that although the journey from Paris had brought her tingling sensitivity towards him to the surface, it must have been deep-rooted ever since he had walked into Fabergé's suite to find her there.

"Somebody's coming!" The whisper alerted everyone. Who would be first? A member of a European royal family? A titled personage? Someone of taste and distinction in another sphere? An attendant outside the double doors opened them wide and stepped aside. The woman who entered was a vision in a street costume of olive green silk, huge, peach-coloured plumes and ribbons ornamenting a hat the size of a cartwheel, which was set at an angle to enhance her bright golden pompadour. Irene recognized her immediately from any number of picture postcards of Gaiety Girls that were all the rage to collectors. It was Gregory's estranged wife, Lillian Rose.

"Good morning, Gregory," she said blithely. "I thought I should be your first customer."

Irene saw his eyes narrow on a smiling look as if

her appearance was not all that unexpected. "You will also have the best choice of what is available, am I not right?"

She made a little face at him, not displeased. "I have to set the scene. Where I lead, others follow."

"What did you have in mind?"

"A cigarette case. For a gentleman." It was as if she relished the flaunting of a conquest with all the guilelessness of an indulged child.

"Nothing for yourself?"

"Ah. I'll probably want everything I see." She pivoted around theatrically, her hat plumes wafting outwards, her gaze taking in the individual arrangements of the spectacular wares, large and small, that had been transported there. As it happened, Irene was standing by a display of cigarette cases. Lillian promptly came across to her. "Show me the best that you have."

Irene followed Fabergé's established usage in the serving of customers. She turned to the cabinet behind her, opened one of the mirrored doors, and selected two of the pure white holly-wood boxes within. All of Fabergé's wares had these unique presentation boxes, each lined with silk, with the double-headed Russian eagle marked on the inside of the lid together with his name. She placed both the boxes on the counter facing Lillian, released the catch of the first one, and lifted the lid to reveal the cigarette case for a few moments before lifting it out to display it between the fingertips of both hands. It was steel-blue enamel and gold, and she turned it a little, setting alight the tiny rose diamonds on the border. She then repeated the process with the second one. Since it was unwise to dazzle the customer with too extensive an array at any one time, the lids of both boxes were closed again on the cases before more were shown. Irene had chosen a mid-way price range and took her guide-line from there. She found that Lillian was not prepared to go anywhere near the highest price, settling finally, after much deliberation, on a case in ribbed red gold with a cabochon sapphire as a thumb piece. All the time Lillian was making her choice, Irene found herself wondering what had caused the break-up between Gregory and his actress-wife. With his blasé attitude to love, had he simply wearied of her after a short span of time and, to console herself, had Lillian returned to the stage? It must have seemed to everyone at the time of the marriage that they were perfectly suited, he with his sensual good looks, she with her chocolate-box beauty. Their attitude towards each other appeared to be amiable, he chaffing her agreeably, she decidedly flirtatious. He had even come across to her once while she was being served by Irene to enquire how she was getting on in the new Gaiety show.

As Irene took up the presentation box for the cigarette case, she was able to take a quick glance around. There were plenty of customers now; all the salesmen were busy. Then she froze. Sofia was there. Gone were her widow's weeds. She had emerged dramatically into half-mourning in a rich, violet silk with a matching toque, her face covered by a spotted veil that gave her an air of romantic mystery. She was engaged in talk with Gregory. My dear Sofia, Irene cried silently to her, don't pursue him. He has a philanderer's heart. He loves for no longer than it suits him. It would never stretch beyond a few amorous days in Nice.

Lillian's voice broke in on her thoughts. "Do you intend keeping me waiting for my purchase all day?"

"No, Miss Rose," Irene replied quickly. Afterwards, Lillian wandered off to gaze around. Irene, putting the boxes away, looked for Sofia again and was surprised that there was no sign of her. It seemed odd that she should leave without a word or two. A little later, when given an urgent message to deliver to Gregory, Irene went to the room set aside as his office to knock and enter, only to find that Sofia was there. He was leaning his weight on the edge of his desk, talking to her stepmother, who sat facing him. They both looked at Irene as she came towards them. Sofia was smiling a trifle artificially as if her thoughts still lingered on the private interview that had been interrupted.

"I was just coming to see you, Irene," she said.

Gregory, having received the message from Irene, needed to deal with it immediately. "Perhaps you would be kind enough to show your stepmother the Easter eggs?" he said to her. "I think they would be of particular interest."

Sofia gave him her hand. "I enjoyed our discussion, Mr. Burnett. Then we shall see you at Milton Square on Saturday evening."

"I shall look forward to that occasion, Mrs. Lindsay."

Irene's backbone was stiff as a board. She was illogically furious with Sofia for her folly in chasing him with a dinner invitation and with Gregory for accepting it. She could not remember ever being angry with her stepmother before.

"Do you like my new outfit?" Sofia asked as they came into the showroom once more.

"You look wonderfully elegant," Irene answered truthfully, her voice taut.

Sofia did not seem to notice that anything was amiss. "I needed to come out of full mourning. Three months is quite acceptable these days. That is why I want to start entertaining again."

"Is it wise to have Gregory on his own?"

Sofia glanced sideways at her through the spotted veil. "I have already invited Dr. and Mrs. Harris as well as Mr. and Mrs. Cummings. He will not be the only guest. Why should you have thought he would be?"

Irene answered awkwardly. "I had assumed it, that was all."

In any case, she thought, the fact that others would be present was small consolation. The dinner party was still being used as a lever to open the way to a deeper renewal of close acquaintanceship. There was every indication that Sofia was emerging from the initial stages of bereavement into a reassertion of herself as an individual with a life of her own to lead as she pleased. Thoroughly commendable in many ways, but not when a path was being set towards further sorrow from another source.

Sofia enjoyed seeing the Easter eggs which, unlike those in exhibitions, were all for sale. Some, housing elaborate "surprises," were as costly as those made specially for the Romanovs, but others were less elaborate, and all were beautiful. Some tiny ones were mounted as pendants. Sofia was tempted to buy one but decided instead on a photograph frame of dark mauve enamel. By the time Irene returned home that evening, its oval aperture held a picture of Edmund, and it had been placed on the grand piano. It was almost like an offering of atonement to his memory. That same night Irene thought she heard sobbing in her stepmother's room. Still half asleep, she hurried from her bed, only to find when she reached Sofia's door that there was no sound from within. Thinking she must have been dreaming, she went back to bed. It was not until next morning that she wondered if the sobbing could have come from somewhere downstairs.

Irene completed the sketch design for her grandmother and posted it. Having remembered Gabrielle's drawer of pearls, she had based the brooch on the shape of a bunch of grapes, the leaves of gold and the pearl grapes of white, cream, and grey to descend from bosom to waist. A letter of rapturous approval came almost by return post. Irene was pleased that the design had been so well received, and she knew she could rely on Arthur Lucas to carry out the work exactly as she wished it to be done.

Saturday evening came. Sofia, graceful in lilac lace, was unusually nervous as the hour drew near the time when her guests would arrive. She kept adjusting cushions and rearranging a flower here and there in the vases about the room. Irene, watching her, wanted to cry out that Gregory wasn't worth such a torment of anticipation. When the doorbell rang, Sofia became motionless, putting a hand to her throat, her eyes fixed towards the open doorway where she could see through into the hall. Gregory was the first to arrive. At the sight of him, she came vibrantly to life, sweeping through to meet him out of Irene's earshot. There was a low-voiced exchange of confidences before they resumed normal tones, turning together to enter the drawing room where Irene waited, torn between animosity towards him and exasperation with Sofia.

"We meet again, Irene," he said agreeably to her. Less than three hours earlier, she had been sorting out a complicated order with him in the suite office.

She swallowed hard, clasping one hand in the other behind her back as if the urge to strike the smile from his handsome face might overwhelm her. She hated him. It was a hatred that agonized her at the same time and left her trembling. What superficial reply she made to his greeting she hardly knew.

It should have been an entertaining evening. It was, for everyone except Irene. Sofia had a gift for inviting people who she knew would enjoy and be stimulated by each other's company. Apart from Gregory there were seven other guests, and from her place at the head of the table she was a radiant hostess, holding sway for the first time since Edmund's death. Dr. Harris, who understood and knew her better than anyone else present, was of the private opinion as he spooned up his consommé that Sofia Lindsay had become liberated by her widowhood, whether she knew it or not. He did not expect to see her professionally for a long time. It was amazing how many female aches and pains had their origins in an unhappy marriage.

As if by unspoken consent, Gregory and Irene kept their distance from each other throughout the evening. They had come to know each other well enough to recognize a volcanic state of mind or turn of mood as he saw in her since his arrival. At times their violent disagreements during working hours were almost pleasurable to them both because they provided a clearing of the air, a momentary banishment of tensions that had been building up. Present surroundings were not conducive to that kind of explosive confrontation, but shortly before the evening came to an end, his curiosity got the better of him. Irene went to her father's study to fetch a book that Sofia had offered to lend to one of the guests. Gregory followed her. As he reached the study, she was taking the volume down from the shelf. The only light in the room came from an amber lamp on the desk. He closed the door behind him and leaned against it. She must have seen him coming after her in one of the hall mirrors, for she spoke to him coldly without turning around.

"Do you want to borrow a book too?"

"No, I want to know why you're in such a hell of a mood. You weren't like this when you left Berner's earlier. Do you resent my coming to this house?"

She spun about to face him, holding the book like a breastplate to her with folded arms. "Yes. Yes, yes, yes!"

"That's not very hospitable."

"I don't feel hospitable. You're Sofia's guest, not mine."

He came across to her. "Tell me the reason why you don't want me here."

She could not back away, for the bookshelves were behind her. Her shoulderblades were pressed against them defensively. "I don't want Sofia hurt any more. She has been through too much and endured too much to be given any more heartache."

His face was without expression; only his eyes were searching for hers. "Why should you imagine that I would ever want to hurt her?"

"I know you were with her in Nice."

"So that's it," he said contemplatively, almost to himself more than to her.

"I found out. By chance. She has no idea that I know, and you must never tell her."

He rested a hand against the bookshelf on a level with her head, bringing his face nearer hers. "I wouldn't dream of it. You have my word. Was she unhappy when she came home from Nice?"

"No. Quite the reverse. But it's not the past that concerns me, it's the future. You don't care for anyone for any length of time. You told me so yourself. Sofia is exceptionally vulnerable just now. I won't have her destroyed.''

"Why don't you have me banned from this house?''

"I have no voice in who comes here. In any case, she would start asking questions. She would want to know what I have against you.''

"How would you answer her?''

Her eyes glittered at him angrily. "I would say that any woman who cared for you would be out of her mind.''

His gaze was resting on her piercingly. "Would you be referring to her or to yourself in that particular context?''

Her furious reaction was to slam the book at him with both hands. He jerked it from her clasp and tossed it aside. Then he had her in his arms, his mouth on hers, hard, blazing, and almost overwhelming her on a cry in her throat. She clung to him, lost in an obsessive wildness of response, his mouth marvellous and dangerous to her. The very violence of their kissing welded them together as if they could never be prised apart, each seeking to assuage the long-held, long-denied desire for such a time to come upon them. Their blood raced, their hearts pounded, and their breathing was quick and urgent. Each was totally attuned to the contours of the other's body as if in a matter of seconds they had been created solely for love. When it seemed that their kissing must go on to new depths, a faint sound from the doorway cleaved them apart as abruptly as if the world had stopped rotating. Sofia stood there with her hand on the brass knob of the opened oor. Her eyes were dilated to appear quite black, her face ashen.

"I thought you were unable to find the book, Irene." She spoke with difficulty, the effect made all the more ghastly by her brave attempt at a smile as if she had witnessed nothing of their fiery embrace.

"I have it." Irene took the book up from the chair on which it had landed.

Together and without exchanging another word, the three of them returned to the drawing room. The evening proceeded as if the short, shattering incident had never occurred. Only Dr. Harris noticed that Sofia looked drained as if not far from the point of collapse. He concluded that she was tired. After all, it was the first social event she had held since her bereavement. He signalled to his wife with a glance. She rose to her feet obediently, causing the rest of the guests to stir. The evening, which had become horrendous to Sofia, came mercifully to an end.

Gregory bade Irene good night. She replied without looking at him, conscious that his gaze lingered on her as he turned to go out into the hall where Sofia was seeing her guests on their way. What he and Sofia said to each other in the few moments before he departed, Irene did not know and did not want to know. She heard one of the servants close the front door. Then Sofia's footsteps came back into the drawing room.

"I think it all went off very well, did it not?" she

said vaguely, looking about at the emptied coffee cups and the indented cushions, which were the only signs that a gathering had taken place.

Irene realized that Sofia intended to make no reference to what she had witnessed in the study. It was not hard to guess that she could not endure the anguish of recalling it. "You are always a perfect hostess, Stepmother," she said quietly.

Sofia made a self-deprecating little gesture to brush aside the compliment. "I am going straight to bed. I feel quite tired. Good night, my dear." She kissed Irene fondly on the cheek as she had done every night since she had come to the house as Edmund's bride. Then she went upstairs to where her maid waited to help her undress.

Irene followed at a slower pace. In her own room she went across to the fireplace and stood looking into the dancing flames that took the chill from the dark night. She had never thought that she herself would be instrumental in destroying whatever illusions Sofia had harboured about Gregory. She wished she could comfort her stepmother, but that was impossible without revealing that she knew of the liaison in Nice. Neither could she inflict the further pain on Sofia by the spoken confirmation that Gregory had had no other woman in his thoughts they had met in Paris. She had not realized it until this evening and had not comprehended the source of her own emotional turmoil when near him. At least it was not love. He was not capable of loving as she understood it, and nothing could persuade her that her reaction to his powerful masculinity was anything more than a natural yearning of her own female body for a renewal of physical loving such as it had experienced during her time with Derek. Armed with this knowledge, she could guard herself from any such encounter with Gregory again. She shivered suddenly and rubbed her arms through their thin covering of pale yellow chiffon.

She was too restless to sleep. With a silk kimono over her nightgown, she sat at her drawing desk and worked on a sketch design she had prepared earlier. When finally she put down her pen, closed the cap of the India-ink bottle, and shut up her paintbox of watercolours, she still did not move from her chair. From a drawer she took out a ledger and entered into it the sum of the weekly salary she had drawn that day. The total of her savings still fell short of what she would like for the enterprise she had been mulling over for a long time. Originally she had hoped to start in a small but exclusive way somewhere in London. She had pictured a tiny shop in a commercial area where she could do repairs for jewellers whom she had come to know through the trade, a steady if moderate income to back up the initial selling of modestly priced jewellery of her own design. Her early days at the School of Handicraft had taught her that beautiful objects did not have to rely on expensive components, Ashbee himself having used semi-precious gems for choice, revelling in their rich colours. She had estimated that she should be able to pay the wages of a craftsman to work with her after a short time and be able to make ends meet. Now she had not discarded her plan or the certainty that her efforts would eventually be crowned with success, but she had changed the location for the opening of her own business. Somehow she must place herself within reach of the *demi-mondaines* complete with her little shop, a workbench and, if she could possibly manage it, the skills of Arthur Lucas. For a while she would have to make up customers' own stones, for she would have no money for the kind of stock that those of wealth would expect her to keep. But with the *demi-monde* decked in her designs, she should eventually get through to the *monde*. Her jewellery would be everywhere. The only shadow that she could foresee was that of Gabrielle's jealous outrage that she should take up designing for the women whom her grandmother regarded as rivals for her reputation as queen of the *demi-monde*. But surely, if Gabrielle continued to receive designs for exceptionally outstanding pieces from her, then that opposition would eventually be withdrawn.

Sitting back in her chair with a sigh, she lifted her arms and combed her loosened hair away from her face with her fingers. One more Fabergé session after the current one, and then she would be ready to take a chance and try her luck. By then Gregory would be gone from her life.

Her expression clouded, and she pressed her fingertips lightly against her temples. Whether he would be gone from Sofia's life was another matter. She did not for one moment imagine that this evening's incident would have severed Sofia from her devotion to him. A woman in love did not give up when she found her man kissing someone else, not even when the female in question happened to be her own stepdaughter. Irene began to feel more and more distressed. It was impossible for her to regret the experience of being kissed by Gregory, except in the context of causing hurt to Sofia. The truth was that she had liked it. Loved it. Felt split asunder by it. In age he stood approximately halfway between her years and Sofia's, an older man to her, a younger one to her stepmother. With a flash of insight she saw that they were fond and unwilling rivals for a man whose aim was conquest and nothing more.

Her conviction that nothing would deter Sofia from her pursuit of Gregory was confirmed in less than twenty-four hours. With such an able Fabergé manager in charge at Berner's, Gregory was able to deal with his own business in Hatton Garden quite freely, which meant that he often did little more than call in and leave again. Irene did not see him when he did arrive that morning, for she was busy with an important customer, and if he did look in her direction, she was too occupied to notice. The customer in question was Empress Eugénie.

The dignified old lady in her customary black, her companion with her, had glided into the suite, the manager bowing to her. Then suddenly she had spotted Irene on her way to the office with some papers in her hand.

"Miss Lindsay! You shall wait on me."

Irene, amazed that the Empress should have remembered her face and her name, had come forward. "I'm honoured, ma'am."

"You have lost your father since I saw you last," Eugénie said in sympathetic tones, seating herself in the chair that was offered. "My condolences."

"Thank you." Irene was touched by the thoughtfulness of the royal lady, who had been through such sad bereavements herself. Then the conversation turned to the Empress's needs, which resulted in the sale of a *bonbonnière* in rock crystal with a gold lid.

By the time Irene reached the office on the errand that had been interrupted by the Empress's arrival, Gregory had left again. Later, checking through his appointments, she saw he had filled in a luncheon engagement himself. The Savoy, 1 P.M. No name, which meant it was strictly social, and it had been entered simply in order that track could be kept of his whereabouts if he needed to be summoned in an emergency, which did happen occasionally. That same evening Sofia innocently showed her a new hat she had bought earlier that day.

"I went out in my velvet toque, decided I was going to be too early for my luncheon engagement, and whiled away twenty minutes at my milliner's. The result was this new hat, which I wore out of the shop." She laughed merrily, putting on the wide-brimmed concoction to display it, its osprey feathers curling bewitchingly. "Do you like it?"

Irene hesitated, drawing in breath. "I have always considered you to be the best-dressed woman I know. I would say that it concerned you more whether Gregory liked it when you lunched with him today."

The resulting silence fell between them like a stone. Sofia opened her mouth to reply, closed it again, and turned away rapidly to remove the hat with trembling hands. "Why should you imagine his opinion would be of any interest to me?"

"I know you well. I have been able to see that you're drawn to him."

Sofia's head jerked up, her back still turned. "Since when did you begin to deduce that?"

"I saw how you looked at him when you met us at Victoria Station."

Sofia's shoulders sagged. "I find him an extremely attractive man," she said wearily. "That cannot be denied, even though I am older than he. Ten or eleven years at least."

"You are still beautiful."

"And you are being kind to me." Sofia took a pace towards a chair and sat down to face Irene, the hat still in her hands. "Gregory has been equally generous. He helped me once before when I needed understanding more than ever in my life before. If afterwards I choose to read more into his concern than was ever there, the fault is entirely mine. More recently, I should not have used the seeking of his advice as a means of re-establishing contact, but as it happened I could think of no one else able to give me the information I required. If I am to be truly frank, I must admit I hoped that through it our relationship might develop along new lines. In my foolishness I had convinced myself that my widowhood would open the way. It took me a little while to face up to the fact that nothing was more unlikely."

Irene remembered the night she had heard the desperate sobbing. "Why are you telling me all this now?" she ventured.

"Because I do not want you to feel guilty towards me about allowing him to kiss you in this house. There is nothing between Gregory and me except friendship." Sofia looked down at the hat, playing absently with one of the feathers. "I hope you believe me, or else you are not going to accept what I have to say next."

"I believe that a state of friendship exists between you," Irene conceded. It was clear to her that her stepmother was still struggling to crush down far tenderer feelings, but they would never be voiced or demonstrated again. If she herself was questioned as to whether she still loved Derek, she would say that it was over, which was the truth, no matter what deeper emotions might still linger unacknowledged below the surface.

Sofia's suddenly direct blue gaze on her was full of anxious appeal. "Do not fall in love with him, Irene. He is married to someone else, and you are young and free, with all the world to choose from when you wish to love again. I have thought of you as my daughter ever since I came here, and I speak to you now as if you were truly my own flesh and blood."

Irene answered decisively, standing very still and resolute. "I have no intention of complicating my life by any involvement with Gregory. I'm cutting myself free of him just as soon as he and I have finished working together for Fabergé. That kiss meant nothing at all, Stepmother. Nothing at all beyond a momentary attraction."

It struck Sofia that the girl's denial was a shade too vehement, almost as though she were trying to convince herself. "You are bound to meet him again in the realms of work, Irene," she pointed out tentatively.

"No!" There was no trace of doubt in this exclamation. "I don't want any dealings with him whatever. When the day comes for me to get stock from gem merchants, there are plenty of others in the trade. I met quite a number personally when I was working in Father's shop."

"Are you so against him?" Sofia queried, not yet wholly convinced.

Irene moved forward to crouch down beside Sofia where she sat, taking hold of her wrists and looking up into her face. "I've loved once. Disastrously. I don't want to love like that ever again. That's why I have to rid my life of Gregory once and for all while there is still time. You did right to warn me. I believe I could slide into love with him if I didn't cut myself away. I will not love someone again who is incapable of loving me forever." Abruptly she dropped her forehead onto Sofia's arm as if close to despair.

Sofia lifted a hand, freeing her wrist from Irene's

loosened clasp, and held the girl's head protectively as if she were a child again. Perhaps it was too late already. Maybe the seeds of love were already sown. Deliberately Sofia crushed down her own personal anguish at the possibility and let all that was maternal in her soar towards the girl and her well-being. For herself, she did not know whether or not Gregory could love the right woman for a lifetime. He was not to be judged by a few days in Nice, which had been passionate and caring, although not of the true depths of the heart. But he was married, and scandal could destroy. She would not let that happen to Irene if it lay in her power to prevent it. It meant a revision of the plans she had been making with him towards a partnership, backing Irene financially when the girl was ready to launch out on her own. He was as keen as she herself that Irene should have her chance, and his advice had been invaluable. Her own lawyers in St. Petersburg were attempting to tap various financial sources on her behalf, so much of her money there being tied up in trusts. Edmund had been no less canny about how he had left his money, even the sale of the shop and its stock being channeled into controlled investments, which meant she was a rich woman with security and no readily available funds to follow any inclination of her own. Until the money was raised, she was unable to say a word to Irene, guarding against disappointment. It seemed now that she must find a partner other than Gregory to back Irene. Her thoughts went to Gabrielle Roget. She had heard about the *demi-*

mondaines' attempt to overwhelm Irene at the party and of Madame Roget's jealous fury, but she could not believe that if the whole case of giving Irene a great chance was put to the woman in a proper manner, she would not agree to give her support.

It did not prove as difficult as Sofia had feared when she explained matters to Gregory. They had achieved that unique harmony which can exist when former lovers become friends. For him it had been there since they parted in Nice; for her there had been the setbacks of false hopes, the first tentative acceptance of the situation, and then the traumatic experience of seeing Irene in his arms. She doubted if the sensation of excitement that always assailed her before any meeting with him would ever be totally banished, but at least since her talk with the girl, she had come to terms quietly and resignedly with the only possible relationship between Gregory and herself. She was thankful that at least it had the qualities of warmth and lasting endurance.

"I have reason to believe that Irene would never accept a half-share of financial backing from you, Gregory," she said. "She is strong-willed and independent, as you know, and has made it clear to me that she wants to follow her own path, free of any male involvement."

They were in his Hatton Garden office. Leaning back in his leather chair, he looked at her across the desk. "I'm not surprised by what you say. Naturally I'm disappointed. However, are you able to raise enough to back her on your own?"

"No. That is why I have a favour to ask you. You know Madame Roget well, and you are going to Paris again as soon as the Fabergé session is over. Would you approach her on my behalf with a view to putting up a half-share of the necessary finance?"

He considered before he replied, not through any hesitation about doing what she had asked, but because he had doubts about the outcome. "I'm sorry to say that courtesans are a breed of their own. They care only for themselves and rarely for anybody else, least of all for the men to whom they grant their favours. Wealth and possessions are everything to them, and whether Gabrielle would be prepared to gamble a great deal of money on Irene's future remains to be seen."

"She was generous to Irene with her gift of the emeralds," Sofia reminded him.

"It was out of character, I would say. An emotional whim of the moment." He smiled at her. "You think I'm being uncharitable. Perhaps I am. Leave the matter with me. I'll do my best."

Sofia did not doubt his success. She preferred to believe that Gabrielle was more soft-hearted in her old age than she had been when she cut herself off completely from her own child and later allowed her to marry a man whose character had caused her misgivings. She left Hatton Garden in an optimistic mood.

The demand for Fabergé's wares continued unabated. The list of orders grew daily, the most important of all from Buckingham Palace, for

Queen Alexandra was an avid collector of Fabergé
wares. Then the last day came, and the doors of the
suite closed. Within it the process of packing up
began. Irene and Gregory went through the last of
the orders together.

"I'm going to miss you, Irene," he said when she
closed the final ledger. They were on their own.
Everyone else had gone home. It was the first remark
he had made to her of any personal significance since
the evening he had kissed her. The rest of the time
when they had spoken, it had been of the work at
hand. "This is the last time we shall meet here. I'm
leaving for Amsterdam tomorrow. Then, by way of
Paris, to Monte Carlo."

"A holiday?" She was stacking the ledgers.

"No, business."

"Even in Monte Carlo?"

"Oh, yes. There is probably no place anywhere in
the world where money flows more freely or
diamonds are in greater demand."

"Really?" She was alert and interested. "More than
Paris?"

"In a concentrated sphere. Think of the Casino
and the fortunes that change hands nightly. The
Vanderbilts, the Rothschilds, representatives of every
royal house, and many more."

She sank down slowly onto a chair as if overwhelmed by a thought that had occurred to her. "Is
property very expensive there?"

"If you wanted a prime site, it would be exorbitant.
Otherwise there are still narrow streets and steep

passageways that are virtually untouched commercially, remnants of the quiet place that the township on the slopes once was before the Casino took over."

"Would I be able to rent a couple of small rooms there, do you think? One as a showroom for my designs, the second as a workshop?"

"I daresay you could if you don't leave it too long. In my opinion it's only a matter of time before every inch of the resort is developed, the old parts as well as the new. I happen to know through personal contact that there are half a dozen jewellers' shops there already. It is a sign of its growing importance that I often meet fellow diamond- and other gemmerchants at Monte Carlo. I get called upon many a time to provide a unique stone for a client there."

She listened keenly, warming enthusiastically to her growing idea. "I'm certain Arthur Lucas would be able to persuade his wife to live at Monte Carlo. It was being across the Channel from her native land that she did not like. So with time I could bring him in to work for me."

He came and leaned an arm on the back of the chair, looking down at her. "You are preparing the ground wisely. To have stayed in Paris when you were first tempted to do so would have been to rush your fences. Now you can take your time. The *demimondaines* will not have forgotten you. Monte Carlo is their favourite hunting ground. Why not meet me there in ten days time? I know it well. I could help you find what you require."

She looked up quickly and her gaze met his with

such impact that each was conscious of a passionate upsurge between them, leaving neither of them in any doubt about what such a meeting would bring forth. They would find themselves on the brink of their yearning for each other, and there would be no going back. He saw her whole frame stiffen, and she rose swiftly to her feet, bent on escape while there was still a chance to evade the magnetism that was drawing them closer and closer together.

"That's impossible. You forget that my work continues here until all the special orders are through from the Moscow branch. That's why I'm being paid a retaining fee until the next session. I might just get to Monte Carlo for a few days in the lull before this suite is made ready again." She held out her hand to shake his in a brisk, businesslike manner. "It has been interesting working with you. Goodbye."

"Goodbye." He took her hand but did not release it. She tugged it free, not far from panic. Snatching up her coat and hat, she almost ran from the suite.

He went to the window and saw her emerge from the hotel entrance. As she hurried away down the street, her head was bowed as if she wept. He watched her until she was lost from his sight in the far distance.

Irene did not get to Monte Carlo before the next Fabergé session. Just when the anticipated lull came her way, she received two important letters from her stepmother's birthplace. One was from Maria to say that she had become engaged to Count Leon Romanov, who was young and handsome and everything she had ever wanted in a future husband. The second letter was from Maria's grandfather, commissioning the design for the bridal head-dress, which would be made up by special concession in Fabergé's workshop.

Never before had Irene tackled such an enthralling project. With Maria's face and colouring fixed firmly in her mind, she sat for hours making preliminary design sketches until the ethereal, Titania look for which she had been aiming crytallized at last. She had been told that the choice of stones was hers, and her directions would be followed to the last facet. She wished she could have handled the stones, for then she could have arranged them on wax pads and with coloured paint filled in the details of the precious metal that would enhance the gemwork, which was usual when doing a design for a client. It gave a clear impression of how the finished piece would look. She felt it was a compliment to her that both Maria and Grandfather Vladimir were prepared to accept whatever she chose to send them. Crown-shaped, it had a sunburst of diamonds within each of its six flaring points, which in turn terminated in pink pearls *tremblant* and drop-shaped pale rose spinels. From it the wedding veil would swirl in a mist of lace and tulle.

"It's exquisite!" Sofia exclaimed, studying the sketches, which showed the bridal crown from every angle, inset drawings giving details of the mounts and other aspects of the piece that would be needed by the craftsman who would create the work. "I hope the day is not far distant when you will be designing such a headdress for yourself."

"I think that is most unlikely," Irene answered firmly. She went out socially less and less, devoting herself to her own studies and designs when she was not engaged in daily work for Fabergé. Sofia, on the other hand, was blossoming forth, no longer in mourning, and her engagement diary was always full. It worried her that Irene declined so many invitations, although that was not the only matter of concern on her mind. Her lawyers were taking an interminably long time to raise the money she required to back her stepdaughter, who still knew nothing of the financial support that was in the offing. Gregory had been unable to get a franc out of Gabrielle. He had been right in supposing that she would not allow sentiment to come before financial risk. She was already thoroughly disagreeable when he arrived to see her, having had a letter from Irene that mapped out her intention of setting up a little workshop in Monte Carlo, where she was hoping once more to attract the attention of the *demi-mondaines* and other wealthy women. Gregory suspected that it was pique as much as anything else that had made Gabrielle refuse adamantly to invest in her granddaughter's future.

In the hope of hastening her lawyers' activities, as well as the chance at last of visiting old friends in complete freedom, Sofia made plans to go to St. Petersburg. It also meant that she could take Irene's drawings with her instead of their being consigned to the mail. Right up until the last day before her departure, she hoped that some word would come through that the money was raised, but when it did not, she was forced to fall back on a loan to cover the interim.

"Irene," she said that evening as she and her stepdaughter sat alone, "I have something to ask you. Indeed, I trust you will forgive me when I tell you that I have presumed from the start of my idea that you would not refuse me."

Irene regarded her smilingly, putting aside the book she held. "We have never fallen out yet except over very minor matters. I can't imagine that we'll ever begin now."

Sofia was of the same opinion, although in this life it was impossible to be sure of anything. How would she herself have felt if she had had to watch Gregory and Irene falling in love, which might easily have happened if the girl had not chosen through the experience of previous disappointment to make her head rule her heart. The strain might have been beyond the power of her own endurance if put to the test. Briskly she returned her thoughts to what she had to say.

"If you had not been leaving for Monte Carlo before I get back from St. Petersburg, I would have waited until my return to bring this subject up. You see, I don't want you to rent meagre premises in

Monaco. I want you to find the right shop in the right street to attract the customers you seek. That does not mean it will be any easier for you to establish yourself beyond the fact that you will be on a firmer footing financially."

Irene was looking puzzled. "I have to keep within my means for a while if I'm not to go bankrupt. More expensive premises would only hasten that end."

"Not if you will allow me to back you financially. I want to be a sleeping partner, never interfering or having any control over the running of the business. Let us say that I am asking you to let me share your ultimate success."

Irene stared at her stepmother with incredulous delight. "Is it true? Can you really manage it? I thought you had only an income from trust funds."

"There are always ways and means," Sofia answered indirectly. "In the meantime, an account has been opened for you at Smith's Bank, which looks after the interests of English people in Monaco. You will be able to go ahead with redecoration of the premises you choose, the fitting-out of a workshop, and so forth. I have the necessary papers ready for you, and the manager of the bank has promised to help you in any way he can."

Irene could hardly speak, her expression radiant. "How shall I ever thank you? This means I can engage Arthur Lucas immediately. He did say in reply to a letter I sent him with an eye to the future that he and his wife would not be averse to moving to Monte Carlo, provided I could offer him security of employment." She sprang up from her chair and went to hug her stepmother where she was sitting. "Come and see me in Monte Carlo before you return to London from St. Petersburg."

"That is what I planned," Sofia replied, smiling at her. If the lawyers failed her, she could always sell her jewellery to repay the munificent loan that Gregory had made available to launch unsuspecting Irene on the greatest phase of her career.

Twelve

When Irene arrived in Monte Carlo, it was late summer. She could not think why the resort was not so fashionable during the warmer days as it was in the winter, for she did not find the weather excessively hot, and there was plenty of shade from the trees. For herself, she was quite glad to have the chance to find premises and get them ready before the season changed again. When the cold weather descended on Europe and the first snows began to fall in Russia, the rich would return to Monte Carlo like migratory birds. She planned to have wares waiting for them that would dazzle far more fiercely than the sun touching icicles in the lands they had left behind.

Some of the hotels were closed at this time of year, the season not opening officially until the sixteenth day of November, when it would last through until May, but there was no problem about immediate accommodation for her. In her purse as she was driven from the railway station there was a set of keys to an apartment. It had come into her possession through her breaking her journey for a day in Paris. There she had called on Arthur and Yvonne Lucas as well as her grandmother. At first Gabrielle had given her a cool reception. There had been cutting remarks about pandering to the vanity of the younger *demi-mondaines*, sulks, and a pouting mouth that was ill-becoming to a woman of considerable age.

"I've told you I will continue to design for you, Grandmother," Irene said patiently. "As a matter of fact, I've brought a drawing with me that you may like to have made up by a Parisian jeweller of repute. As I explained, Mr. Lucas will now be in the process of leaving Bing's and packing up to follow me to Monte Carlo."

Gabrielle grabbed at the drawing and was somewhat mollified. It was of a high collar of sapphires rimmed by butterflies. She had never seen anything quite like it. That Spanish gypsy, La Belle Otèro, had been vicious with envy over the brooch of pearl grapes. This would rub her arrogant nose even harder into the dust.

"Then you had better make this collar your first commission in your new surroundings," she said, speaking more graciously than she had before.

"That will make a splendid beginning," Irene answered with pleasure.

Gabrielle did not mention that Gregory had been to see her a while ago on Irene's behalf, able to tell that the girl knew nothing of his visit. In view of the fine design sketch that had been done for her, together with the assurance of the first choice of others to come, Gabrielle felt a trifle shamefaced about not having agreed to invest even a small sum in Irene's courageous venture. Then, when Irene was about to leave to catch the overnight southbound express, she thought of a way to make amends.

"Wait a moment," she said, going to an escritoire. She took a set of keys with a label from a drawer and handed them to her granddaughter. "I have an apartment in Monte Carlo where I spend the winter months. You may use it throughout the summer and longer if you wish."

Irene could scarcely believe her good fortune. When the cab drew up at the address on the label, she was even more overwhelmed. The apartment was on the second floor of a lavishly baroque building with balconies and awnings and an abundance of flowers. She was admitted by her grandmother's resident housekeeper. Every room of importance, including the luxurious bedroom into which she was shown, had a direct view of the sparkling sea.

It did not take her long to get her bearings in the resort, which was screened from the north winds by the steep slopes of the Alpes Maritimes into a natural sun shelter, the harbour with its pale yachts glimpsed constantly through a veil of palms and other exotic foliage. In a lacy straw hat to keep the bright sunshine out of her eyes, a cool cotton dress, and comfortable shoes, she strolled past the Palace with

its Saracen origins, traversed the Gallerie Charles III
where she drew some money from Smith's Bank at
one end of it, and passed the fashionable corner of
Ciro's famous restaurant. She went into every
jeweller's shop to pinpoint their location and assess
the competition. Some very fine wares were being
offered for sale, Cartier jewellery arousing her
unstinted admiration for its sheer perfection. She
noted that each shop, in keeping as she had been
informed with everything else in Monte Carlo, from
the Casino through to the best hotels and restaurants,
was furnished in the ostentatious style of the Second
Empire, which was not what she had in mind for her
shop when she had found it. The hotel that interested
her the most was the Hermitage. It was closed for the
summer, but she knew of its pink marble pillars and
ceiling paintings and medallions of exceptional
artistry from Gabrielle, who had told her about a
unique facility advantageous to the benefactors of *les
grandes horizontales*. Gabrielle had stayed there
herself many times until an admirer had given her
the apartment in return for her favours and was ready
enough to talk about it.

"When a gentleman goes on vacation to Monte
Carlo, it is naturally that he should want to enjoy
himself to the full. He will have the Casino, the
promenading, the pigeon-shooting, and yachting,
the sea-bathing from an enchanting pavilion, the
salle garnie, and the Opera and other theatrical
delights, but he will also desire more erotic pleasures.
So, if he is to be on his own, he will take his mistress

or his favourite courtesan with him, and they will stay in adjoining suites at the Hôtel de Paris. If, however, he is encumbered with his wife and perhaps with his family as well, he will install his other lady in a suite at the neighbouring Hermitage Hotel. A convenient underground corridor leads sumptuously to the Casino *and* connects the two hotels, enabling the gentleman in question to visit his paramour nocturnally without embarrassment to his wife. She might not even know about it and might assume that he is sitting late at the gaming tables!" Gabrielle had thrown back her head and given forth her noisy, infectious laugh.

In a corner cigar shop, which sold everything from postcards to books on gambling systems and was sliced into the side of the opulent Café de Paris, Irene bought a guidebook to the principality. She read that it was comprised of Monaco, the Condamine, and Monte Carlo, the whole of it not more than three kilometres and 500 metres in length, its width a mere one kilometre and 400 metres. So much fame out of so small an area. It made her smile.

She climbed the narrow streets where the ordinary folk resided, interesting little stores catering to their needs with wine, bread, fruit, and vegetables, and a limited choice of meat chopped up by blue-frocked butchers. Now and again a pair of ponies in the shafts of a *voiture* went clattering by her, the driver almost always with a companionable dog on the seat beside him. Finally, although she had seen it from several angles already, she came to the very symbol of self-indulgence on which the wealth of the principality depended. It was the Casino. Standing with her hands on her waist, she viewed it in the perfumed air of the terraced gardens, her gaze travelling up and over its pinnacled towers and elaborate façade that gave it the appearance of a giant wedding cake, its windows looking beyond her to the port below.

During the next few days, she visited agents and viewed property. On her walking tour she had observed the number of well-to-do middle-class people taking advantage of the lower, out-of-season prices, and she saw them as potential customers. If she sold to them as much as to the richer clientèle of the winter influx, she would have a year-round business. She had also noticed where new businesses were opening up and looked out for the rebuilding of premises and expansion. She finally decided on a small shop with one display window and a door beside it in a street leading a little way off the Casino square. Not only was the ground floor adequate, but on the floor above there was living accommodation that she could make comfortable. A small, sandy courtyard lay to the rear.

When everything was signed and sealed, she gathered in workmen and set about making alterations to the property upstairs and down. Her theme throughout was to be one of simplicity, with softly tinted walls. As she had resolved, the traditional chandeliers and Louis Quinze-style chairs, the swagged mouldings and lavish ornamentation, were not for her showroom. Instead she aimed for a tranquil atmosphere with a changing of light and shade through a decorative, stained-glass panel that she had put into the entrance door, its muted colours of silver, lilac, and mauve echoed in the wall-frieze of her own design. It was picked up in turn by the mother-of-pearl inlays in the straight, high-backed, thin-legged furniture that was pure Art Nouveau. The exterior of the shop was painted white, and the fascia above repeated the frieze within; her two forenames, Irene Denise, were incorporated into it. To have used her surname would have linked her to her father's well-respected reputation, whereas this venture was to be entirely hers. She would stand or fall by her own achievements.

Arthur and Yvonne Lucas arrived in the early stages of the alterations, he to supervise the fitting out of the workshop, she to find a small house to suit their requirements. As to the question of stock, he and Irene were able to decide between them what they would need for immediate requirements. Although she had notified her own contacts, he in turn had let gem-merchants of his acquaintance know that he might need special stones on short notice for instant delivery. Priority had been given to the workshop, which was ready in a couple of days, enabling Arthur to settle down at his new bench at once. He wanted to complete Gabrielle's new sapphire collar without delay in order for it to be displayed in the window on the shop's opening day. Irene donned an apron and worked at his side on enamelled pieces of original design but low in cost. At times they both sat at the bench for such long hours that Yvonne Lucas would appear with a big dish of food under a cloth, which she carried herself all the way down from the house that she and Arthur had rented on the outskirts. She would reheat the food on the workshop's gas ring, and the two workers would eat heartily together while the cook watched them with satisfaction.

Irene heard from Maria, who took two pages of a long letter to extol ecstatically the design for her wedding head-dress. Grandfather Vladimir sent lavish payment, which was most welcome at this time of heavy expense, particularly when Arthur interviewed a goldsmith fresh from his apprenticeship, a thin-faced, dark-haired Frenchman named Jacques.

"Can I afford him yet?" Irene queried.

"He's good. I can tell. I think it would be a false economy not to take him on."

"Very well," Irene agreed. It did not take her long to see that Arthur had been right. Jacques proved to be a keen worker with skills of a remarkable standard. Her designs appealed to his own contemporary tastes, and he executed them with enthusiasm and a craftsmanship that could not be faulted.

As soon as the builders had completed their work, she left Gabrielle's apartment and moved into her own quarters, knowing that sooner or later her grandmother would return. The blinds were being kept down over the entrance door and window of the shop until all was ready for the day of opening. Irene was on her hands and knees unpacking some boxes in the showroom one morning when Arthur admitted an unexpected visitor by way of the workshop at the rear of the building. She was busy removing wood shavings and layers of tissue paper from the first of the Tiffany lamps that had just been delivered. As she sat back on her heels, examining with pleasure the leaded-window effect of the opalised glass shade, the visitor entered the showroom. Her whole being responded to the knowledge of his identity. The back of her neck tingled, and the *frisson* slipped deliciously and frighteningly down her spine.

"How are you, Irene?" Gregory asked from where he stood in the draped archway.

Not moving from where she sat, she turned her head to look slowly up at him. His eyes welcomed hers, dark, tender, and eloquent as if the separation between their last meeting and this day had been too acute for any further pretence. She gulped in a breath, still clutching the bronze base of the lamp that was balanced in her lap. Any belief she had cherished about getting over her attraction to him was instantly dispelled. If she had had some warning of his coming, it might have been different. She could have been alert and on her guard, totally on the defensive. But not as now. The unexpected soar of excitement at seeing him again made her stare mutely at him, the power of speech and movement stunned out of her. She had forgotten that he was so tall, so broad-shouldered and wide-chested. Forgotten how his gaze could burn into her. Forgotten how easily he wore his well-cut clothes. Forgotten? The truth was she had remembered everything about him against her will. Remembered that he had been Sofia's lover. Remembered that he had a wife. Remembered how she had recognized a dawning of love for him within herself during the whirlwind bliss of his kisses and hard embrace.

With difficulty she found her voice. "I'm well. I suppose Gabrielle told you I was here."

"That's right." He nodded approvingly around at the decor. "I like all you've done to this shop. I wish you every success."

"Thank you." For want of something to do with her nervous hands, she set aside the lamp she was holding and began to unpack the second one. He came to crouch down facing her, his forearms resting across his knees.

"Do you mind that I've come to see you?"

"No. Are you going to be long in Monte Carlo?" She did not halt the unpacking.

"A few days."

Was he on business? Had he come south especially to see her? She did not dare to voice the questions aloud. "These lamps are to give the final touch to the showroom. I think they're just right, don't you?"

"Perfect. Shall we gauge the effect?" He picked up one and set it on the counter. Then he plugged it into a socket and switched it on. The light streamed forth, the lampshade's opal colours making a gentle motif of their own across the walls and ceiling. She gave an exclamation of delight, springing to her feet.

"It's even better than I had hoped! Let's switch them all on."

Each lampshade held a variation of hues that added to the pastel glow while at the same time the direct light would be concentrated on whatever jewellery was being offered for sale without shining in a customer's eyes. She stood poised in the middle of the floor and thrust out her hands as if dabbling them in the patterned glow. He watched her and loved her and knew he could not leave Monte Carlo again until he had broken through every barrier of restraint that she had set up against him.

"Irene." He spoke her name as if it were an expression of endearment.

She folded in her arms almost defensively, her hands coming to rest one on top of the other against her chest. "Yes?"

"Leave everything and spend the rest of the day with me."

"I can't. There's too much to do."

"Play truant just for once."

That made her smile, but she still shook her head. "It wouldn't be fair to Arthur or to Jacques. They're working like slaves at their benches. We're getting stock from my designs ready for sale, and we have only the rest of the autumn left in which to do it."

He was not to be deterred. "Tomorrow is Sunday. Don't tell me that you're such a hard taskmaster that you make your goldsmiths work a seven-day week!"

"No, of course not."

"Then I'll hire a boat for the day, and we'll go sailing along the coast. Have you been to the Casino yet? No? This evening we can dine together and visit the tables afterwards."

She had been wanting to go to the Casino, not so much to try her luck at the tables, but to observe the setting where great fortunes were lost and won. As for the sailing trip, it was enticing beyond all measure. She had worked long and exacting hours for as far back as she could remember, or so it seemed at times, and probably never harder than during these past weeks. With effort she tried to summon up some resistance, to remind herself that she would be going into a danger greater than any risk she had ever taken, for her whole heart would be put at stake. Yet she was weakening. It was easier to be resilient and wise in London and Paris, but in the champagne air of Monte Carlo there seemed to be a bewitching element weaving its own spell. Almost with a sensation of surprise, she heard how she answered him.

"I'll be ready this evening by eight o'clock." She went to the lamps in turn and switched off each one. The resulting gloom of the showroom, created by the drawn-down blinds, was dusklike. Inwardly she marvelled that there should be no return to sanity with the dousing of the curiously magical light given off by the lamps. As if compelled by some force over which she had no control, she went into his arms as he moved towards her, their lips meeting in a deep kiss that made her cling to him as if drowning.

When they broke apart breathlessly, she pushed his

arms from her. "Go now."

He made no protest. "Until later, Irene."

She heard him talking to Arthur in the workshop while she folded the tissue paper and brushed up the scattered wood shavings in which the lamps had been packed. Being out of earshot, she supposed he was being told something about the work in hand. It was not important to her. All she knew was that the thrilling restlessness which possessed her was being aggravated by his still being on the premises.

When she could no longer hear his voice and knew with every nerve and fibre that he was gone, she felt relief in the sense that she could concentrate on work again. What had had its beginnings in a mere awareness of his nearness had increased to a tumultuous, empathic state such as she had never known with any man before. She was in love. Deeply, exultingly, and maturely in love. This was no springtime sweetness with dreams to shatter and fade. This was love without illusion. She was going into it with the full realization that it could only lead to heartbreak. But there was no going back.

There were two ways of entering her apartment. One was by a staircase situated between the show-room and the workshop, while the other was by an exterior flight of stone steps at the rear of the building. At exactly eight o'clock, she opened her front door into the moonlit night and stood by the iron balusters. A *voiture* with lamps aglow was drawing into the courtyard. Gregory alighted and looked up at her. Her beauty struck at him. Not even the moonlight could dim the brightness of her hair brushed up smoothly into its topknot, a single hair ornament winking like a star. A soft, white shawl was wrapped about her and over one shoulder in matador fashion because however mild the daytime was, the September evenings were often cool once the sun had gone down. There were diaphanous points to her dress which wafted as she began to descend the stairs, a pointed satin shoe showing with each step.

"It's been a long wait for me since this morning to see you again," he said smiling. "Now I'm rewarded."

"The flowers you sent were lovely," she replied. She had taken time to arrange the bouquet that had been delivered from a florist's shop shortly after noon, breaking away from a task at her place at the workbench to do it. Already he had had a disrupting effect on her schedule. She had found it difficult to give her time to anything in hand with her thoughts running forward to this hour of seeing him again.

He took her to Ciro's, which was renowned throughout the Riviera for its superb food and equally famous cellar, so that during the fashionable winter season even royalty had to book tables well in advance. Monsieur Ciro, a rotund little Neopolitan with a waxed moustache, welcomed them effusively. "Good evening, Monsieur Burnett. Good evening, mademoiselle. 'Ow nice to see you in Monte Carlo again, sir. This way, if you please."

They were shown to a well-placed table, which like all the rest shimmered with orchids and gleamed with Florentine goblets. Then there began the procedure in which Monsieur Ciro delighted, which was to boast extravagantly of the rare specialties that he had to offer his valued clients, wanting to impress them with the infinite pains taken to serve only the best of the best for the delight of their tastebuds. Gregory was used to the elaborate routine, and Irene was intrigued by it. When their order was finally given, they looked at each other across the table in shared amusement.

"It will be just as good as he says it is," Gregory assured her, "although that may be hard to believe."

The right note of happiness had been sounded for their evening in each other's company. They talked of many things. For the first time there was no discord in their being together. Each had accepted the inevitability of loving each other.

Hand in hand they went up the steps of the Casino in the glow of suspended lamps under the glass canopy, and entered there. Irene gazed at the gilt and stained glass, the ornate ceilings of great height, murals of voluptuously thighed women reclining on clouds, and the spinning brilliance of the roulette wheels. She won a few francs and lost them again. Once Gregory won without realizing it, looking at her instead of listening to the croupier or caring where the wheel stopped, which made them both laugh as the chips were pushed towards him across the green cloth. They left the Casino as they had gone into it, no richer and no poorer in financial terms. As for their feelings for each other, that was another matter. Every passing second was bringing them closer together.

Yet he did not spend the night with her. He did not even enter her apartment but only opened the door for her with the key from her silver chain purse, which she had dropped in sudden agitation. He realized that unexpectedly she had found herself facing ghosts from her past as well as his. It was not wholly surprising. He felt that when they had talked more intimately than they had done this evening, which had been a mere prelude to all that would ultimately come about between them, there would be no more shadows to darken the path that he intended they should follow together. Drawing her into the curve of his arm, he bent his head and kissed her with a passionate tenderness, whereupon she in turn stood on tip-toe to press her face briefly against his in a swift demonstration of deepest affection. Then she bade him good night. He watched the door close.

When the same thing happened the following evening, he wondered how long he could endure being shut out. With a sigh he thrust his hands flat into the pockets of his evening coat and, with a rueful compression of his lips, surveyed the secluded courtyard from the landing where he stood. Then he began to descend the stone flight. He thought he had cleared everything between them that day. And what a day it had been, she full of gaiety and high spirits, he wonderfully content to be with her. The boat he had hired was a small yacht with a crew of three, which meant that he and Irene were able to lounge in

353

cushioned basket chairs under a canopy and enjoy the sight of the rocky coastline with its exotic foliage sliding by. The cobalt blue of the sky was matched by the sea with its sun-diamonds sparkling across the surface. Iced drinks were served to them, a phonograph played, and later they ate a luncheon of seafood and salad. He pointed out the Empress Eugénie's villa at Cap Martin, the Rock of Monaco looming up behind it. There were many other fine villas to be glimpsed where the rich and the famous and the infamous took up residence in the season, and he told Irene of the change she would see in the resort when it came.

They had brought bathing costumes with them and swam twice during the day while the yacht lay at anchor. One of the crew let down a ladder to the lapping water to facilitate their coming aboard again.

Towards evening, when golden lights began to cluster along the darkening shore, they talked long and seriously. They spoke of Lillian. He told her as much as he could of his marriage and its disintegration.

"When did you meet?" she asked, her voice quiet. The sky and sea behind her were as flame-red as her hair.

"In the spring of '94. We married shortly afterwards in New York where she had accompanied me on a visit. I had business there. She wanted a vacation. We came back to London as husband and wife."

"That would be four years before you and I met at Milton Square."

He considered briefly. "Yes, that is right. Lillian was a music hall artist then, a singer of folk songs from her native Lancashire, bright, saucy, and flirtatious, a favourite with the gallery. She thrived on praise and applause, literally and figuratively, and she still does. It feeds her excessive vanity. She revels in being loved but is incapable of loving to any depths in return."

"Why is that, do you think?"

"It is no fault of hers, none whatever." He spoke with understanding and compassion. "Her beginnings were hard. She was raised in squalor and without being shown the least affection. She can care only for herself. At heart she is insecure and quick to be frightened when things go wrong for her. Her pet fear used to be that some disaster would drive her back to the slums from which she came. It still haunts her today, although she would never admit it. I always know when she contacts me on some pretext that she is in a panic of one kind or another, and I can usually sort everything out for her."

"You feel no animosity towards her?"

"None at all. It was different when nothing was going right with our marriage and I was hot-headed and jealous." Different, he thought to himself, when he discovered that she had no conception of faithfulness, having long used her body as a means to cement auditions or higher billing or anything else that would further her career. Their wretched marriage had finally fallen apart. "The adulation of the audience means more to her than anything else has ever meant. It is a constant reassurance to her that she is lovable, and she preens in the glorification of stardom."

"Why have you and Lillian never divorced?"

"She has an almost pathological fear of scandal. Since proof of adultery is necessary in our English courts in order to obtain a divorce, she would not consider going through the ordeal of a hearing. At the time it did not matter to me. I decided that I had made my one and only venture into marriage while she had no thought beyond her good name in connection with her theatrical career. The newspapers would have fallen on the divorce case with unholy relish, anything about a Gaiety Girl making news, and they would have started digging out corners of her humble origins that she did not want investigated."

"Has she no wish to marry again?"

"At the present time she finds it useful to have a husband at a distance. She can play one stage-door johnny off against another by reminding them of my existence."

It was then that Irene had shivered, drawing a wrap closer about her, although whether at all that he had told her or the chilling of the sea air at the day's end he did not know. Getting up from her chair, she had gone to stand at the yacht rails, looking shorewards. He went to lean his arms on the rails beside her. The harbour was drawing near. They spoke no more of Lillian.

Ashore they had supper in a simple harbourside restaurant, neither of them being dressed for more formal surroundings. Her face had caught a golden tint from the sea breeze, and her hair was tangled by salt water, giving a new facet to her beauty in his eyes. She drank quite a lot of wine, which was unusual for her, and her lightheartedness returned as if the serious talk between them had never been. They danced with local couples on the handkerchief-sized floor to the music of a piano and a concertina which would have won no prizes for harmony but made up for it in exuberance. He sent the two musicians a bottle of wine each through the waiter, and the music continued at an even faster pace. Irene danced with her butcher, who was lightfooted in spite of his vast size, and the floor cleared while everyone applauded them as they whirled round and round. Others would have danced with her afterwards, but he had claimed her back again, holding her close to him. Then, at her doorway, she had flung her arms about his neck to kiss him soundly, her salt-scented hair whipping against his face, and had withdrawn behind her door once more.

It came to his fifth and last evening. By day she had worked, adamant about not deserting Arthur and Jacques at the bench when there was so much to be done, and it had never been earlier than seven-thirty before she allowed him to call for her again. He had plenty to occupy his time, for he had brought diamonds by arrangement for Cartier's, and he went by train one day to Cannes and drove himself by hired motorcar to Nice on another day, where he had business with private clients. It was on his final morning that he hailed a *voiture* and was driven the short distance to the Cap d'Ail village where a number of villas, set spaciously apart, were being built on the sloping hillside, each with an unimpeded view of the sea. He took a liking to the property and consulted the agent in the village with satisfactory results. He told Irene about it that evening during the interval of a concert to which he had taken her.

"I have secured the plot and discussed plans with the architect."

"I can see that it is a good investment," she said sagely. "Before long, anything purchased today should double its value, or even triple it in years to come if Monte Carlo continues to be a gambling Mecca for the rich."

He wanted to tell her that he saw his villa as more than an investment, secure though he believed it to be. For him it was the home that she would eventually share with him. Her shutting the door against him was simply a minor delay that time would overcome. He knew well enough that she was not tantalizing or teasing him. She was simply settling matters with her own heart and conscience before she took the step from which there would be no return.

As always, he saw her up the flight of steps to her

door and unlocked it for her as he had done since their first evening. He fully expected her to turn to him for their last good-night kiss with no change in the procedure to which he had become accustomed. But this night, when the door swung inwards, she simply entered the narrow hallway of her apartment, leaving the way open for him to follow her. She had kept a wall light burning in its tulip shade for her return, and she paused in its glow, half turning to look back at him, her shawl slipping down from her shoulders to hang looped from her elbows. Her shadowed green eyes were luminous as the night sea; her moist lips parted slightly as if she held her breath at what was to come about as a result of the decision she had made to bar him no longer.

He closed the door behind him and shot the bolt. As he approached her, she moved ahead of him again to reach her bedroom door, which she pushed open with the flat of her hand. Within was a wide brass bed with a white lace spread. The curtains at the window were already drawn. Letting her shawl drop onto a chair, she went to switch on the tasselled lamp at the side of the bed, and the greater part of the room was illumined softly in its creamy light. Neatly she removed the lace spread from the bed before folding back the sheet of snowy linen and smoothing the frilled pillows. He watched her every movement, although not once did she look again in his direction. Half-turned away from him, she put up her hands to commence unfastening the back of her high-necked dress.

"Allow me to do that," he said quietly.

She stood quite still, bowing her head to aid him in the release of the little hooks below her hair-line. The dress parted as hook after hook gave way down the length of her spine. He kissed the nape of her neck before sliding his hands under the shoulders of the garment to draw it down and away from her. As it fell to the floor, she stepped out of it and stooped to pick it up and put it aside, thus turning to face him again. She was left in a silk chemise and waist petticoat, her nipples high against the slippery surface. Taking one end of the ribbon bow at her deep cleavage, he untied it so that the chemise slid downwards and all the beauty of her breasts was revealed to him. He realized the extent to which his admiration of her showed in his face when almost in wonderment she touched his cheek with her fingertips and drew them gently across to the corner of his mouth. He made an encircling bracelet of his hand about her waist and kissed every one of her fingers.

"You are my one and only love, Irene." He had thought such a declaration long lost to him. There had been words of passion and of lust uttered often enough over past years, but never since the days of his disillusionment had he spoken the language of the heart. It was like being reborn.

She looked away from him with lowered lashes and her whisper was barely audible. "I have been loved before."

He understood that she wished to spare him disappointment. Perhaps she half feared his jealousy. But the very innocence of her confession was endearing to him. "No. You have never been loved as I shall love you this night with my heart, body, and soul."

Her eyes came back to him with a new serenity and an inner joy as if a last doubt had faded away. Then her head tilted back, and she shook her hair free so that it went swirling down her back. As he cupped her breasts, she closed her quivering eyelids on the delight of his caressing. He kissed the nipples lingeringly, and she held his head between her hands, burying her fingers in his hair. Tremour after tremour went through her as he scooped away from her waist the rest of her silky garments until garters, stockings, and all else lay at her bare feet. He was dazzled by her. Putting his arms about her thighs, he picked her up in a kind of exultation, and she rested her hands on his shoulders, looking down at him, her hair wafting in a red-gold curtain around them. He carried her thus to the bed. Moving one hand upwards to support her back at the shoulderblades, he lowered her down onto it, her head sinking a little into the soft pillow. He smoothed a wayward tendril of her bright hair away from her brow, leaning over her.

"I've been waiting for this time ever since the evening I first saw you," he whispered ardently. "Somehow, for a while, I lost you along the way."

Her gaze followed him as he went to the opposite side of the bed to discard his clothes. His whole body was absorbed in a great shout of passionate desire for her, but he intended to exert control over himself, for her pleasure would be his, her ecstasy his, and he would bring her as he had vowed to a peak of love and loving such as had never been hers before. Strong, muscular, and powerful, he entered the bed beside her. Her arms were waiting for him. He gathered her to him, and his mouth found hers in a rapturous onslaught that was both fierce and tender.

Then he kissed every curve and plane of her body in a ravishing exploration, until there was no sweet and secret part of her that had not become known to his lips, his tongue, and his stroking caresses. He could tell that he had brought her to a full knowledge of her own sensuality, maybe to a comprehension at last of the eternal association of her own red hair with the wildest realms of passion. She caught her breath again and again in delicious torment, writhing erotically, captive within his loving embrace, while her hands clutched spontaneously at him or, in quieter moments, drifted over his body with a voluptuousness of touch that made him tremble against the force of longing that possessed him. When the time of penetration came, with all the fragrant bouquet of her anointments making his head spin, he thought he must die from her unleashed response. Suddenly her eyes opened abruptly and widely for no more than a second or two as she looked up into his elated, passion-torn face, but it was long enough for him to see her pupils dilating exultantly on the brink of a sensation never previously experienced. He closed home on her with a groan of glory. Ecstasy broke forth, and they soared together into a oneness that seemed to unite them for all eternity.

It was sometime in the night that she, lying within his embracing arms, her head on his shoulder, gave a sigh of utter happiness. He stroked back her hair and tilted her love-bruised lips to his again. As her mouth blended with his, he felt himself reassailed by passion and moved once more to arch his worshipping body over hers.

If it had been possible he would have cancelled everything to stay longer with her when dawn came, but that could not be. He would have travelled many miles and voyaged across the Atlantic and back again before he could return to this apartment and to this woman whom he loved as he had never loved in his life before.

When he was dressed and ready to leave, she slipped on a robe and went into his arms for a last embrace. "Take care of yourself," he urged solicitously, holding her close. "I'll be back at the first chance. Write to me. Write all the time."

"I will," she promised fervently.

She saw him out of the apartment, hugging her trailing robe to her. He turned once before reaching the gates of the courtyard, walking several paces

363

backwards to keep his gaze on her. She stood there in the sun shadows at the top of the stone steps, the morning light in her hair. He was reminded of the first time he had carried a last image of her away in his mind's eye. This time she blew him a kiss from her fingertips.

Thirteen

Sofia appeared unannounced on Irene's threshold. It was the day before the shop's November opening, which had been timed to coincide with the commencement of the winter season.

"My dear child, at last, at last," she exclaimed with arms outflung.

"Stepmother!"

They hugged each other, both of them talking and firing questions and laughing in the joy of reunion. Sofia had been travelling in Russia and visiting old friends there ever since she and Irene had parted from each other in London. When she had a chance to draw breath, she viewed the interior of the shop with approval, exclaimed at the variety of attractive jewellery and other items of adornment made up for stock, and enthused about how comfortable and pleasing Irene had made the little apartment. She herself had booked into the Hôtel de Paris, having known there would be no room for her and her maid under her stepdaughter's roof.

"What news of Maria?" Irene asked. "I received a wedding invitation only yesterday. Do you like the man she is to marry?"

Sofia, who was wandering around the sitting-room to look at some paintings Irene had bought from a local artist, swung about with an uncertain smile. "Leon is very handsome. Very rich. And very arrogant. There is little more to say about him."

Irene rose in concern from the chair where she was sitting. "Don't you think she will be happy?"

Sofia gave a little shrug. "She is head over heels in love with him."

"What does her grandfather think of the match?"

She sighed heavily. "My uncle is greatly changed since you saw him. His heart is not good, and he has deteriorated into a sick and feeble old man. All he wants is to see Maria married before he goes. To him this union is a splendid match." Opening her purse, she took out a flat package, which she handed to Irene. "Maria asked me to give you this latest photograph with loving greetings."

Irene removed the wrapping. In a delicate frame of shell-pink enamel and silver, which she recognized instantly as the work of Fabergé, there was such an excellent head-and-shoulders likeness of Maria that she could only conclude that it was equally good of Leon, whose gaze was turned towards his betrothed. He was every bit as handsome as Sofia had stated, romantically hollow-cheeked with a marvellous jaw and a nose chiselled to perfection. But unlike his future bride, whose beautiful face radiated an innocent joyfulness, there was cynicism in his smile and bored disdain in the heavy-lidded eyes. It was not the expression of a man in love. With an anxious frown, Irene's gaze returned to her stepmother.

"Is there no chance that Maria will change her mind?"

Sofia gave a rueful smile. "Ah, so you can see through to the flaws, too. No, Maria thinks him quite perfect. She views her wedding day as the gateway to living happily ever after." Briskly she straightened her shoulders. "Dreams do come true sometimes. Let us hope for the best. Shall you attend the marriage with me?"

Irene, who had placed the photograph on the counter, still studying the faces within the frame, turned in surprise. "Are you going to make that long journey back again next month? Why didn't you stay a little longer whilst you were there?"

"And miss the opening of your shop? Certainly not!"

Irene shook her head in affectionate resignation. "I should have known that you would make sure you were here to give me moral support, no matter at what inconvenience to yourself." It had been her hope that Gregory would be present, but he was far away in New York, staying with the Tiffanys. He wrote to her frequently. She had a stack of letters in her chest of drawers. They were tied together with a blue ribbon, which was not out of place. There was love for her in every line he penned, either directly or indirectly. Sooner or later she must break it to Sofia that in spite of all the well-meant stepmotherly advice which had been given her, she had fallen in love unwisely and with the last man whom either of them would have expected to take over her life. Moving across to a shelf where the wedding invitation stood propped against a vase, she picked it up. "It couldn't be at a worse time for me. I can't possibly leave the shop so soon after its opening."

"What a pity! It will be a long time before the chance to see Maria comes your way again, quite apart from the importance of the wedding day. I understand that she and Leon are to spend their honeymoon cruising in Caribbean waters."

"I wish her every happiness and will write that message to her," Irene said, hoping that her stepmother's obvious misgivings would prove to be without foundation.

Irene had a new dress for the opening of the shop the next morning. Not a classical black this time, but a soft, white chiffon blouse and a slim, grey skirt. Beribboned garlands of flowers decked the exterior of the shop in celebration of the occasion. The effect was charming, even though the florist had not included a single carnation, which was considered an unlucky flower by Monte Carlo gamblers and might deter superstitious people from entering the premises. In the window for dramatic effect, Gabrielle's collar of cabochon sapphires with its butterflies glowed against the drapery of creamy velvet. It had taken many hours of Arthur's time to create the lovely piece, and the chance to display it as an example of what the shop could produce was too good to miss. He and Jacques came into the showroom to watch Irene raise the blind from the window and unfasten the entrance door for the first time. Sofia had arrived a few minutes before, not wanting to be absent from the great moment.

"There!" Irene straightened up from slotting back the lowest bolt. The three with her broke into applause. Then Sofia kissed her cheek warmly.

"Congratulations, my dear. You've worked so hard for this day. You deserve every success."

"You're right, Mrs. Lindsay," Arthur affirmed. "I remember all the questions about goldsmithery that Miss Irene used to ask me every time you brought her to Old Bond Street in those days. Nobody could have studied more or worked harder towards this occasion."

Smiling Irene went to the counter where she had poured out four glasses of champagne. She handed them round, and they drank a toast to the shop. No sooner had the two craftsmen returned to their workshop than the shop door opened. It was not a customer. It was a delivery boy in a brass-buttoned uniform from the florist. He handed a long box tied wtih a large satin bow to Irene and departed.

"They must be from a well-wisher!" Sofia exclaimed. "How kind!"

Irene lifted the lid. At least three dozen long-stemmed dark red roses. She took the little card from its envelope, but she knew the donor's name already. It was signed with a single initial: G. He had said everything through the flowers themselves. She looked at her stepmother. The time of breaking the news had been thrust upon her.

"They are from Gregory. He must have ordered them before he left Monte Carlo."

Surprise flickered Sofia's eyelids. "He was here? You saw him?"

"More than that. Much, much more."

Sofia had gone white to the lips. "You mean that you and he—?" The words would not come out. Something odd had happened to her throat. Sofia saw her stepdaughter nod in answer to her. Then she heard the most terrible, primeval wail rend the air and knew that she herself had uttered it. In a kind of wild disbelief, she saw that her hands were clenched and her arms were bent rigidly at the elbows, digging deep into her own bowed waist.

"No, no, no!" Irene cried, wanting to dispel such a terrible reaction. She put her arm about Sofia and guided her to a chair where she sank down. Fortunately the doors between the showroom and the workshop were closed so that the curious groan of anguish had gone unheard above the noise of the tools in use. Swiftly Irene fetched a bottle of smelling-salts, which was kept in a first-aid box, and wafted it under her stepmother's nose. It was thrust aside almost immediately.

"I am all right," Sofia said with regained self-control, pressing a hand against the upper part of her

abdomen as she took in a few deep breaths. Her heart
was dead, she thought, but she would go on living. It
had perished on a shaft of love that had somehow
escaped all her careful clearing-out of false hopes and
dreams that had been built on her own foolishness
and nothing more. The numbness that she felt
within was welcome. She would never know heartache again. Nothing was now left of the past. Not
even herself.

"I had no idea you would be so upset," Irene said
desperately, crouching beside her to look up into her
face.

"Should I not be distressed at hearing that you
have given yourself to a married man?" Sofia knew
she was being unfair. It was the first time she had ever
been harsh with the girl, but somehow their
relationship had become blurred. She saw her not as
the stepdaughter whom she had always cherished
maternally, but as the woman who had taken from
her the only man she had ever really loved, no matter
that her brief hour had long since faded and gone. It
was an old truth that a hurt inflicted within the
family circle, whether intentionally or unintentionally, gave far, far greater pain than anything an
outsider could inflict. "So he spoke of a new-made
decision to divorce Lillian Rose, did he?"

"No."

"But he talked of marriage to you, I am sure."

"No."

"Then it is as I always believed. He still cares for
his wife more than for any other woman."

371

"I don't believe that."

Sofia corrected her pedantically. "You mean you do not want to believe it."

Irene rose from beside the chair and drew back a pace. "Once I loved Derek, but it came to nothing. Once Gregory loved Lillian, and there was a similar outcome."

Sofia sprang to her feet. "Have you lost all your senses? There is a world of difference between the two cases. He is legally bound to another, and you are not. You are no more than a passing fancy to Gregory. He has treated you dishonourably. Without his freedom he had no right to make love to you or you to allow it!"

The criticism of Gregory stung Irene to defensive anger. What had been said about her mattered less. "You have no cause to talk self-righteously of such freedoms to me! In Nice you were still my father's wife!"

No sooner were the words out than she clapped the fingertips of both hands over her mouth as if what she had said could be thrust back and never heard. If Sofia had been ashen-faced before, she now took on the look of a corpse, and she swayed on her feet.

"How did you know?" she questioned hoarsely. "I never mentioned Nice when I told you that Gregory had once been a good friend to me."

"Someone spread a rumour." It was the only truthful way Irene could think of in which to answer her.

"Did your father know? Do you think it ever

reached his ears?'' She was as close to panic as if he were still alive and liable to enter the room at any second.

Irene took the hand she stretched out for support. "Would he have kept silent about it if he had known?'' she said evasively, hoping for no more questions on such a delicate issue.

Sofia shut her eyes tightly in thankfulness at such a sensible viewpoint. "No. He was too jealous-natured not to challenge me. Oh, thank heaven! I would not have wished to cause him any sadness.'' Tears brimmed her eyes when she opened them again. "Or you, my child. You did right to rebuke me. We have never quarrelled so fiercely before, and I pray it never happens again. I think for a few minutes I must have been out of my head.'' She withdrew her hand and went across to look down at the roses in the box. "How have you not hated me for once loving the man you love?''

Irene gasped. "How could you ever imagine such a possibility? It is I who should ask you that question! I've no excuse to offer for falling in love with him, and if I hadn't weakened in my resolve never to become emotionally involved with him, perhaps you and he—''

"Do not say it!'' Sofia shook her head firmly. "Do not ever think it. He and I were never destined for each other. What is more, I do not want anything that happened between Gregory and myself to haunt you in any way.''

"Be reassured on that point. Everybody's past is

made up of pieces from other people's lives. Like a jigsaw puzzle. I hardly knew Gregory at that time. I had met him once."

"That is right. It was the first and only time that Edmund invited him to the house. Your father told me quite a long while afterwards that Gregory had advocated your being allowed to go to the School of Handicraft. He tipped the scales in your favour."

"Did he really? I never knew. He has never said."

Sofia picked up one of the roses, holding it by the stem while she rested the bud against the palm of her other hand. "There is something else you do not know. When I found myself unable to raise the money at the last moment to see you into this venture, it was Gregory who volunteered a handsome loan which I have just recently repaid."

Irene's expression was ecstatic. "Can you still doubt his love for me? You have this minute given me double evidence on another plane."

Sofia's gaze was gently sympathetic. "Do not search so hard for confirmation, my dear." She returned the rose to the box, which she then picked up and held out to her stepdaughter. "Put your beautiful flowers in water. I should not like to see them fade before time."

Irene cradled the box in her arms. "I have changed since I confessed to you in London that I feared to love him without the hope of some permanence to the relationship. I'm more courageous now. When he came to Monte Carlo, I knew that whatever the right or wrong of the situation, the choice was entirely mine. I could take what Fate was prepared to offer me, accepting the consequences responsibly, or I could send him away without ever knowing how it would be to lie in his arms. But I won't believe that at this present time he doesn't love me more than any other woman alive."

Sofia looked down unseeingly at the box lid, playing absently with the satin bow. "Has he told you that he loves you?"

"Yes."

"Then perhaps you have more cause to back your belief than I would have assumed originally. I will tell you that he spoke no such words to me."

"I appreciate your unselfishness in telling me that."

Taking another deep breath, Sofia raised her head high. Almost as if reverting to Irene's nursery days, she made a quite playful gesture of shooing her along. "Now get that vase for your roses before any customer comes into the shop."

As Irene went upstairs to find what she required, Sofia leaned weakly back against the counter and let her arms drop limply to her sides. The one great fear at the back of her mind had been that she would find herself hating her stepdaughter if anything serious should come about between Gregory and Irene. Mercifully hate had passed her by. She had been saved by the total disintegration of her own heart.

No customer came into the shop that morning to catch by chance the sight of the crimson roses vivid against the pale walls. Yet there was plenty of activity in the resort. Because it was the first day of the season, people were arriving by train and carriage, a shift in the social status of those taking up accommodations in the villa and hotel to match the prices that had increased overnight. Horse-and-carriages loaded with trunks, chests, and hat-boxes went rolling by. It was as if the whole of Monte Carlo was being stirred like a Christmas pudding, drawing in silver charms and lucky threepenny pieces and all manner of other good things to produce a rich and extravagant result. Quite a number of people on foot paused to look in the window of the shop, staring with admiration at the spectacular sapphire collar, but nobody was enticed by it across the threshold to see what else might be offered within.

Throughout the afternoon it was the same unrewarding stillness within the showroom, while outside the bustle continued. The garlands festooning the exterior began to fade, petals drifting across the window to fall onto the pavement and end up in the gutter. It was dusk, and one minute was left till closing time when the door burst open and a well-dressed young Englishman strode into the shop.

"That sapphire collar in the window," he said in crisp, cultured tones, smoothing with a crooked finger one end of his sandy moustache. "I should like to take a closer look at it."

Irene went to fetch it on its gilt-tasselled cushion from the window, and set it before him. He was intrigued by the intricate workmanship that made the butterflies look as if they were poised for flight.

She explained to him how the collar fastened at the back of the neck.

"This piece is not for sale," she went on, "but is an example of what can be designed and made for individual requirements."

He gave her a cynical glance and spoke scathingly. "Do not attempt that kind of foreign market-stall argy-bargy with me, young woman. I know the sort of selling tricks that are used abroad. If you had ever served in a decent English jeweller's, you would know that a good piece of jewellery sells itself if the craftsmanship and the price are right. How much is it?"

Irene kept her patience. She had had experience with rude and difficult customers before. It never failed to amaze her how many seemingly well-bred people kept their good manners for each other, with none to spare for those who waited upon them in whatever capacity. "I regret having to disappoint you, but it has no price except to the client concerned. It was made up for her out of her own gems."

He groaned with exasperation. "Then fetch me another one. You are wasting my time."

"There is no other in that style. Everything I design is unique. Nothing is duplicated. Would you like to see some design sketches of other collars?"

"Not unless one similar to what I want could be made up within an hour," he snapped sarcastically.

Irene ignored the barb and took from a cabinet another collar, which was of turquoises, fastening at the front with an ornamental silver clasp. Beside it she placed one of crystal pendants and a third of pink pearls. She could see that each one impressed him, but he came back to his first choice with disgruntled agitation.

"I have to have this one." He prodded a finger at the sapphire collar. "It's those damn butterflies. The lady for whom I am buying it saw the collar from her carriage not more than an hour ago and showed a liking for it. No other will do. Can you not let me have it and make another almost like it for your other customer?" He leaned an elbow on the counter, his tone becoming persuasive and confidential. "It is essential that I have it for this evening."

She shook her head firmly. "All I can suggest is that I design a butterfly collar in another style to be ready at a future date."

He drew back and slammed down a fist on the glass surface, his face ruddy with temper. "You have no right to display wares that cannot be purchased!" he shouted at her. "You can be sure that I shall let it be widely known that this is a most disobliging establishment!"

The door slammed after him with such force that she rushed across to make sure that the stained-glass panel had not been cracked. The young man's shouting and the banging of the door had brought Arthur hurrying into the showroom, Jacques behind him. Both had been in the process of putting on their coats to go home.

"What happened? Are you all right, Miss Irene?" Arthur enquired anxiously.

Briefly she explained what had happened. "I've been taught a lesson. Never again shall I display wares that are not for sale to the general public. Tomorrow I'm despatching the collar by special messenger to my grandmother. I'm quite amazed by that customer's persistence. He was positively aggressive."

"Maybe he had cause to be," Jacques commented with a Gallic shrug.

"Why? I offered to design him another collar, but he was not prepared to consider it."

A salacious twinkle showed in the Frenchman's eyes. "The *demi-mondaines* are arriving back in Monte Carlo. Some of them are in great demand. I think that your customer hoped to win a particularly popular one with that expensive trinket. He will be a lonely and disappointed man tonight."

"You've said enough, Jacques," Arthur intervened with a frown.

Jacques smiled, shrugged again, and said good night. Arthur went about the padlocking of the grid across the door and taking other security measures, while Irene put the sapphire collar and various items of particular value in the safe. She was thoughtful.

"Do you think Jacques was right in his deduction, Mr. Lucas?"

"I'm certain he was," Arthur replied stiffly. Although he had seen much of life, he and his wife kept to their faithful path together.

"Then, if one of the *demi-mondaines* liked what she saw in my window enough to drop a hint that she would favour it as a gift, she should be back to look again. I shall try to make the display a little more spectacular each day.''

Half an hour later she went to dine with her stepmother at the Hôtel de Paris as previously arranged. It was a handsome hotel, and the lobby was thronged with faces that might have been flicked from the society pages of every international newspaper and magazine.

Before going up to her stepmother's suite, she went to look at the equestrian bronze of Louis XIV that stood against a background of potted palms. The horse's raised fetlock was supposed to be a fount of good luck, and in the few minutes that she stood studying the famous piece, any number of men and women touched it in passing. She knew she was no less a gambler than anyone on his or her way to the Casino, but she had not the least desire to gather her fortune from such a fickle source. Her stakes lay in the inventiveness of her designs and her ability to win on her own fortitude. She turned away as a golden-haired woman trailing a pink marabou boa and asparkle with diamonds came tripping forward with a white-gloved hand outstretched towards the fetlock. She was laughing over her shoulder with the young man who was with her and did not notice Irene, who recognized her instantly with a sensation of dismay.

"I never go into the gambling rooms without placating my luck first," Lillian Rose proclaimed liltingly. The superstitious little ceremony took no more than a few seconds, and then the couple went on their way. Irene drew a deep breath. She turned to find that Sofia had come in search of her.

"Can you guess whom I have just seen?" Irene asked her.

Sofia gave a nod. "Lillian Rose arrived today. Two or more of her stage-door admirers are with her."

Irene saw Gregory's wife again after dinner when Sofia suggested that they go into the Casino for a little while. Lillian was playing roulette, and it looked as though Louis XIV's horse had justified its reputation in her case. She was winning and was excited about it, a young man on either side of her. A third man, standing behind her chair with a bored and disgruntled air, obviously being ignored by her, was the customer with whom Irene had dealt earlier.

Irene marked the little scene with interest before she and Sofia moved on to take seats at another table under the low, silk-fringed lights. The necklace had not been required for a *demi-mondaine* after all, but for an English actress with no less expensive tastes.

Sofia spent ten days in Monte Carlo before deciding to return to St. Petersburg by way of Paris, where she intended to get an outfit for the wedding. It was the day after Irene had seen her off at the railway station when Lillian Rose came into the shop. She was on her own, but her personality was such that she seemed to dominate her surroundings. Irene had just served a customer, who had departed, and was putting away a tray of rings. So far sales had been sparse, but at least a trickle of people had come in from time to time. Lillian, after taking a sharp look around at what was displayed, came to the counter. She exuded an expensive scent, and her clothes proclaimed their Paris label. She spoke without preamble.

"You were wearing an emerald brooch at the Casino a few nights ago," she said to Irene. "Was it your own design?"

Irene was surprised. She had served Lillian once with a Fabergé cigarette case but did not expect to be remembered. It had never occurred to her that she, observing Lillian at the gambling table, had been observed in turn. Her brooch had caught glances, but with so many magnificent jewels adorning ears, throats, wrists, and bosoms, she had not expected it to have the same effect as at a private gathering or when seated in the direct gaze of people passing the table where she had sat at Maxim's.

"Yes, I designed it."

"As you have designed everything else you sell?"

"Yes."

"Then I have a business proposition to put to you." Lillian sat down on a chair by the counter. "It will be profitable to us both. I shall select a piece of jewellery, which you will put aside for me. Then someone of my acquaintance will come in to buy what I have described to him—"

"As with the sapphire collar?" Irene interrupted.

Lillian frowned and flicked her hand impatiently. "The foolish boy jumped the gun. I was most annoyed when I heard that he had rushed in then and there to get it for me. I had only been instilling the idea into his head, fully intending to speak to you first.''

"Well?"

"The procedure is quite simple. You will sell the jewellery I have chosen to the gentleman concerned. When it is displayed on my person at the Casino or the Opera House or anywhere else of importance, it will be a greater advertisement for your shop and your wares than you could gain from any other source. I can make your name for you. I'll let it be known to everyone whence it came. In return you will allow me a percentage on all the sales that come to you through me. Ten percent should be fair.''

"I couldn't think of it!"

Lillian misunderstood. "Very well. Eight percent. That is being generous. I'll be staying in Monte Carlo until Christmas, which means I should bring an exceptional amount of business your way in the build-up to the festive season.'' She saw Irene's increasingly astounded expression and raised her eyebrows questioningly. "Is this the first time you have come across such arrangements? I can tell you that it is quite a common practice when a woman is as much in the public eye as I am. In London I have a special understanding with a number of dress houses. Sometimes I have garments completely free of cost. Usually I choose several dresses, keep one, and send the rest back the next day. The money is then refunded to me, less a small discount, out of the account that a gentleman will have settled in full.

You see how practical these arrangements can be. I suggest we do the same with any jewellery given personally to me that I do not particularly want to keep."

Irene could see that Lillian had no idea how distasteful she found the proposition, quite apart from any other factor involved. "I could never be party to such a scheme!"

Lillian regarded her disdainfully. "Am I to understand that you're turning down the privilege I'm offering you?"

"Yes!"

"And you expect to establish yourself in Monte Carlo?" It was said mockingly.

"I shall do it in my own way and in my own time."

"Oh, I see." Lillian stood up and took a pace or two across the floor before she half turned to look back derisively at Irene behind the counter. "Are your principles at stake? Or is it because I happen to be Gregory's wife?"

Irene tautened. "I would not enter into such dealings with anyone."

Lillian continued to regard her cynically. "I'll never divorce him, you know. Or allow him to divorce me. Don't be deceived into believing that pursuit by my admirers brings them any reward. I enjoy being at the centre of their rivalry, but I preserve my good name above all else. The Guv'nor would soon hear about it at the Gaiety if I did not."

"Even in Monte Carlo?"

Lillian slewed her eyes sideways at Irene, her

mouth pursed on a little smile. "He has eyes and ears everywhere, which is why he likes his Girls to be seen in smart places and to be well to the fore at any international social event. I usually come to Monte Carlo when there is a winter break between shows, or I'm allowed a short vacation for health reasons during a long run. This time there was an added incentive. I wanted to take a good look at you. After seeing your jewellery, I was even prepared to enter into one of my business deals with you, because I don't believe in sentiment when there is a chance of money to be made. You see, Gregory has had many women in his life since he and I separated. I don't doubt that when he gets over you there'll be many more to follow. But you are the first one to make him reconsider his marital status. When he came to me four or five weeks ago to talk of divorce, I could scarcely believe my ears."

In spite of the ugliness of all that was being said, Irene bloomed on the one piece of vital information that meant so much to her. Four or five weeks! That meant he had taken the first steps to regain his freedom before coming to her at the shop. But the way had been blocked by Lillian's selfishness. She tried to keep an emotional quake from her voice.

"Why did you refuse him? You don't love him. You don't want him."

"And you do?"

Irene came around to the front of the counter, her hands clasped. "With all my heart."

Lillian tilted her head archly. "My, my. Such

devotion. Well, you are doomed to disappointment. The Guv'nor has no objection to my being married. In fact, he quite favours it, because it reassures wives in the audience, but he would never stand for my appearance in a divorce court, not even as the innocent party. So there you have it. My career comes first. Accept your brief hour and leave it at that." She moved towards the door to leave.

"You haven't brushed me aside!" Irene spoke vigorously. "I'll fight you for him somehow."

Lillian paused again. She was quite unruffled, almost amiable. "It is not I whom you have to fight. It is Gregory himself. He promised me once that if ever we would sever the tie between us, it should be my decision alone. That is why he came to see me before his lawyers. He wanted me to release him from his bond. I refused, and I shall go on refusing. In any case, I shall need him one day. When my stage career is over and my beauty is fading, he will be there to take care of me. I'll never be lonely. That is a good insurance, don't you think? To know that loneliness can always be kept at bay. I was Gregory's first love. That kind of spell is easy enough to revitalize. So I intend to be his last love as well. There is nothing you can do about it."

The door closed behind her. The draught caused a petal to drop from the facing crimson roses in their vase on one of the display shelves. Automatically Irene went to pick it up from the floor, and she held it cupped in her hand against her breast. Gregory had said that Lillian had an obsessive need of adulation, and proof had now been given. Such a woman would take and take in her insatiable greed for emotional and financial gain, while giving nothing in return. In some ways there was a parallel between Gabrielle and Lillian. Both had had humble beginnings, both needed the reassurance of wealth, and both used men for their own ends. Yet there were vital differences. Gabrielle cared nothing about scandal, except when she had taken steps to protect her daughter from such taint. But otherwise she laughed at gossip and thrived on it, whereas Lillian feared it as a weapon of self-destruction. Gabrielle had chosen her path in life and followed it, letting the devil take the consequences, but Lillian's need for total security showed a lack of individual courage and an inherent weakness of character. She hid her passing affairs behind the respectable façade of being a Gaiety Girl, while Gabrielle had always taken her lovers flamboyantly for all the world to know about. The King of England when he was still the Prince of Wales had passed through Gabrielle's bed, as had the Kaiser, the Czar while still heir to the throne, King Alfonso of Spain, and a host of statesmen, poets, and other writers, from Briand to D'Annunzio. She had loved them generously from the heights and depths of her voluptuous nature. How did Lillian's lovers fare? Was she as mean and sparing in the sphere of love as she was in the rest of her ways? There was little doubt of it in Irene's opinion. Lillian was incapable of feeling anything for anybody except herself. Yet that self-love fed on and was sustained by the devotion and adulation of others. It was a sorry state of affairs.

Business improved towards Christmas. Quite a lot of repair work flowed in, which helped the day-to-day expenses, and occasionally there was a sale of minor importance. Gregory's letters came at frequent if irregular intervals. He hoped to get back to see her early in the New Year. Sofia wrote a lengthy description of Maria's wedding day. The bride had looked beautiful, and her bridal head-dress had dazzled. Then, less than a week later, there came the sad news that Maria's grandfather had died in his sleep. Finally it was Christmas, and Irene knew a sense of relief that Lillian would have gone back to England. It was as if a cloud had lifted away, however temporary the respite might prove to be.

Fourteen

January brought the peak of the elegant season to Monaco. More yachts sailed grandly into the small harbour to lie alongside those already sleekly at anchor. The Romanovs, the Vanderbilts, the Astors, and many more internationally known names booked into the hotels, taking over whole floors, the Grand and the Metropole rivalling the Hôtel de Paris. Villas were reoccupied; entourages of mistresses and servants were installed. The Hermitage teemed with beautiful women as if it were a harem in its own right, and these breathtaking creatures, gloriously attired, appeared everywhere like the pale magnolias coaxed forth by the gentle climate, bowers of lemon and orange-blossom, and violets over all. Live-pigeon shoots went on all day, the poor frightened birds with clipped tail feathers having been delivered in basket crates for endless slaughter against the azure sky. Shooting of another kind took place when the first duel of the season was fought in a villa garden at dawn; both parties were slightly injured, and their honour was satisfied. Later there would be other duels—the French, the Hungarians, and the Russians being notoriously quick to fling out a challenge. Tragically, there was a suicide, a man who shot himself after losing everything he owned at the tables. On the whole these tragedies were rare, the management of the Casino preferring to allow extended credit and to pay the unfortunate gambler's fare home, but there were always those who refused to be helped or to heed warnings.

The traffic doubled and then tripled with the influx of new arrivals. Highly polished carriages of every description were driven along the narrow streets, the flanks of the horses as smooth as satin. When handsome, white reins were in use and the coachmen and grooms were in cockaded hats, this proclaimed that the owner of the carriage was a Romanov, and several such sets were to be seen, the resort abounding in grand dukes and duchesses as well as in lesser ranks of the Russian nobility. Their excesses and their extravagances were legendary. They had their own luxurious compartments attached to trains, and servants slept on the floor outside the doors of their sleeping quarters. The St. Petersburg to Nice express train was slowed down to half its usual pace all the way whenever the Czar's cousin travelled, for he did not think it good for his heart to journey faster. He was one who still made his servants bow their heads to the ground when he passed by, in the old custom that had once prevailed in his country. Another nobleman with a health fetish had baskets of fresh strawberries brought daily to his gold-lined bath, where he bathed in their juice. A count had the garden of his villa replanted every night in order that he could look out on a fresh vista of colour each morning. It was he who had a dish of oysters sent to his courtesan at the Hermitage, and she found a fabulous pearl necklace nestling amid the shells. When one *demi-mondaine* could not decide which of a collection of Cartier diamond bracelets she liked best, her Romanov lover swept the whole lot into her lap. It was a common sight to see the Russians thrust mille notes into a candle flame in order to light their cigars, although other nationalities matched this ostentatious disregard for money, and the Romanovs were only a flamboyant part of the wealthy stream of those who came to squander fortunes beyond calculation at the tables of the Casino.

It was an elderly Russian lady of distinction who summoned Irene to her suite at the Hôtel de Paris one afternoon, the instructions being that she should bring designs for a pendant suitable for a young goddaughter who held to all the new twentieth-century ideas on how things should be. It was exactly the kind of commission that Irene had been hoping for, and she took along some of her most original and startling design sketches. Madame Borisvinsky, who was short and plump with an amiable face and grey hair, had come to Monte Carlo to benefit her arthritis by sitting in the sun on her balcony and taking beneficial mineral baths, for she could only walk with great difficulty by leaning heavily on two sticks. But she had a lively sense of humour, a taste for gossip, and smoked one Turkish cigarette after another in a mother-of-pearl cigarette holder. Before she talked business with Irene, she ordered Russian tea and offered her chocolates from a large box.

"My goddaughter was bridesmaid at Maria Romanov's wedding," she explained to Irene, "and could talk of nothing but the bridal head-dress that had been designed by a jeweller of distant relationship by marriage to Maria and who was presently in business in Monte Carlo. I decided I could not do better than to order from you a pretty gewgaw for Natasha's forthcoming birthday in March, which meant I should get to know you at the same time. How soon could the piece of jewellery be ready?"

"In plenty of time," Irene promised her. If the period had been shorter, she knew that Arthur and Jacques would work all hours if need be. She had a fine team in the two of them.

"Then let us decide on the most outrageous of your designs," Madame Borisvinsky said sardonically. "The young these days seem to want to be different from their elders in every respect."

The design chosen was asymmetrical, using gold and enamel with a single baroque pearl. Madame Borisvinsky held up her hands and shook her head in good-humoured mockery at the change towards such unconventional designs, saying that her goddaughter would preen like a little peacock when the pendant was hers. She was reluctant to let Irene go, for like most old people she enjoyed a captive listener to regale with tales of the past.

"Come and see me again," she invited. Then she made sure that her invitation would be taken up by giving Irene a rope of pearls to be cleaned and rethreaded.

Irene had the pearls safely in her purse as she came down the staircase in time to witness a spectacular arrival. The newcomer's name reached her in the whispers of others nearby: La Belle Otèro. Irene slowed her pace, her curiosity aroused. So this marvellously striking woman sweeping into the Hôtel de Paris was Caroline Otèro, the courtesan whom Gabrielle detested.

Caroline Otèro was about thirty-five, her magnetically beautiful face round and olive-complexioned, proclaiming her fiery Spanish blood; her brows were thick and black, as were her lashes. She graced the boards of the Folies Bergère from time to time, performing flamenco dancing with a sensual intensity that was akin to a sexual encounter with every man watching her. She had the most perfect hour-glass figure, her waist a handspan, her hips generous; and her breasts, which were full and pointed, had been the architect's inspiration for the twin cupolas of the Carlton Hotel at Cannes.

How the staff members were running about her, bowing and scraping! With her was her current lover, Baron Ollstreder. Perhaps she was tired from the journey, because the attention she was receiving appeared to irritate her increasingly.

Suddenly she snapped in furious exasperation at the manager of the hotel, who had been there to receive her. "What *is* all this fuss about? Anyone would think I was royalty! I'm a paid whore and nothing more!"

In the stunned silence that followed, everybody in the vicinity having heard her discordant shriek, her high heels tapped sharply across the marble floor towards the staircase. She passed Irene without a glance, staring haughtily ahead with her black eyes flashing, her nostrils dilated. Baron Ollstreder came imperturbably in her wake, seemingly well used to her tantrums.

Within days Monte Carlo rang with tales of La Belle Otèro's customary sensational behaviour. She was gambling like a madwoman and losing recklessly. In the evenings she sometimes wore a jewelled bolero of such value that two armed guards never let her out of their sight. Late one night, at the height of a party, she had kicked off her shoes, dispensed with her dress, and danced barefoot in diaphanous lingerie out into the square.

When Irene returned the pearls to Madame Borisvinsky, she found her in a state of high excitement. "What do you think? Diane de Chandel has arrived in Monte Carlo. She and Caroline Otèro are deadly rivals. Oh, how the sparks will fly when they meet!" The old lady chuckled with glee.

No doubt to the relief of the management of the

Hôtel de Paris and a good number of other people, De Chandel had taken up residence in one of the most palatial villas with her own entourage, consisting of a wealthy lover, maid, hairdresser, masseuse, and all the other people that such women kept in tow. Madame Borisvinsky came to the shop, during one of her rare and difficult outings, to describe how Otèro and De Chandel had come face to face at the Casino.

"Each was wonderfully bejewelled and splendidly gowned. It was impossible to judge which of them looked more beautiful, and they both knew it. If ever two women breathed fire and brimstone in a moment of rivalry, they did! Yet they simply acknowledged each other with the most gracious of nods and went to their respective seats at different tables. I know what is going to happen. From now on, every evening at the Casino each will try to outdo the other in dress and valuable adornments."

It was as the old lady predicted. Irene wished she could have afforded the subscription for admittance to attend the tables every evening in order to watch these two lionesses at bay—not so much for the trauma of the scene, but to see the fabulous jewellery that each had collected as trophies along their individual paths.

Then, unexpectedly, a cryptic message was delivered to Irene by the housekeeper of her grandmother's apartment, who left again without a word. Irene read it through: *Tell no one I am here. Come at once. —Gabrielle.* Puzzled, she obeyed the request. She arrived to find the blinds down as if the apartment was not being used, and the housekeeper, after admitting her, showed her through to the sitting-room in the servants' quarters where lace curtains let in the sun. Gabrielle was waiting for her there.

"Irene, my dear! I knew you would come!"

"What is all this mystery?" Irene asked when they had kissed each other's cheek and seated themselves at the table.

Gabrielle patted a polished wooden box that she had placed before her. "This is the reason." She lifted the lid, showing that it was crammed with any number of unset stones from her collection. "I have half a dozen more boxes with me. You must design me a parure—tiara, earrings, everything—incorporating as many gems as possible and unlike any other ever made. And quickly! There is no time to be lost!"

"I'll design you whatever you want, but tell me for what purpose and why the secrecy. Are you afraid of the gems being stolen?"

"No, no. It is just that I don't want Otèro or De Chandel to know I'm in Monte Carlo. I want to hold on to an element of surprise for when I do make an appearance. You must have heard that the two of them are trying to outdo each other at the Casino? Yes? Well, sooner or later each will spring a masterstroke in an attempt to outshine the other completely. In its way it's a fight to the death. I want to compete." A deep seriousness had come over her. "Some of the *demi-mondaines* hate men, you know.

That has never been my sin. I have loved each and every man for as long as our liaison lasted. If sometimes I loved them a little longer, they never knew. Every jewel given to a *demi-mondaine* is a tribute. I want to show Otèro and De Chandel that if they are queens of love, then I am the empress."

Irene thought it was probably the strangest commission ever given to a jewellery designer. It was somehow sad and incongruous all at the same time.

"Allow me a free hand," she suggested. "I have an idea already, but I want to give it some thought."

"Whatever you do will be right, I'm sure," Gabrielle endorsed huskily, suddenly overwhelmed that the support she needed had come to hand.

Irene worked all through the night. She had completed her sketch designs in detail when Arthur rang for admittance at the workshop door. Jacques arrived almost at the same time, and the two men stood side by side to study the drawings she laid out on the bench for their inspection. Neither said a word. Then Arthur, who never said anything was impossible, raised his head and gave her a long look.

"I'll have to take on more hands if we are to get it done in the short time you have stipulated, and it will mean everyone working night and day."

"Can you find the right craftsmen?"

"Yes. I have a source I can tap in Nice and another in Paris."

"Then get them here as soon as you can, Mr. Lucas."

"What about the rest of the design that doesn't

come into my field?"

"I'm counting on your wife. She has nimble fingers."

He nodded, looking pleased. "Then all we have to do now is to clear the decks for action, Miss Irene."

During the day a storeroom was converted with another bench into an additional workshop. By the evening two goldsmiths were at work there, and a third joined them the next day. Whenever there was a break between customers, which was often an hour or two, Irene worked herself alongside Arthur and Jacques. She was serving in the shop when the fourth man arrived and did not see him until a little later in the afternoon. He was seated at the place she usually took when she was free, his back towards her, his head bent over his work. She came to a halt in the doorway, knowing him with such a poignant pang of the heart that she could not speak. Jacques alerted the newcomer to her presence with a word or two, and he turned on the stool to regard her without a vestige of surprise.

"Hello, Irene," he said with a smile. "It's been a long time."

Derek had come back into her life.

It was after ten o'clock that night when the day's work came to an end. Derek did not leave with the others but waited to see her on her own. There had been no chance to talk before. She was tired and exhausted, feeling the effect of no sleep the night before, and she led the way up the stairs to her apartment. She indicated that he should help himself to a glass of wine while she sank down in a chair. He looked around at her little sitting-room with approval.

"Very nice. But then you always did have good taste." He poured the wine and would have handed a glass to her, but she declined. "You've come a long way, literally and figuratively, since we last saw each other."

She set an elbow on the arm of her chair. "I assume you worked with Arthur Lucas in Paris, which is why he was able to call you here."

"That's right." He sat down opposite her. "When I left Lindsay's—or was thrown out, which is a better description—I decided to make a complete break. Your father would never have given me any kind of testimonial to see me into another London jeweller's, in spite of it not being my work that was at fault in his eyes. I didn't want to move to a lower grade of shop or return to the provinces, and so the very next day I took the steamer across to France. When I arrived in Paris, I went to see Arthur Lucas."

"But how did you know him? Oh, I suppose you met when you first came to Lindsay's."

"Yes, briefly, and then it happened that one of the older men had sent on one of Arthur's tools that had been overlooked when he left, and once in conversation there was some mention of his having gone to work at a particular jeweller's in Paris."

"At Siegfried Bing's?"

"No. He wasn't there then but at a smaller place. I told him that I had left Lindsay's through temperamental differences with your father, whom he knew to be a difficult man, and that I wanted to try my luck in France. He arranged some minor outwork for me while, as he told me later, he checked with his former fellow craftsman at Lindsay's that I had not been dismissed for dishonesty. The reply said I had left of my own accord and that my work was of the high standard required by any jewellers of repute." He took another sip of the wine. "That was good enough. Arthur spoke to somebody about me, and I was in full employment again."

"I find it odd that Mr. Lucas never mentioned that there was another of my father's former employees working in France."

"Why should he? He and I never worked in the same place or saw each other except by chance. He did know that some while ago I set up my own workshop to do full-time outwork on my own, which was why I was able to come to Monte Carlo when he sent for me. It's probably the only time he has given any thought to me since he gave me a helping hand. Now when he needed one on your behalf, he looked in my direction for one in return. In any case, he would never have expected you and me to have known each other."

"I hadn't thought of that."

"So there you have my adventures in a nutshell. I have yet to make my fortune, but you look well on the road to achieving yours, if the commission I'm working on is anything to go by."

"It's true that I may stand or fall by it. Time will tell." She leaned her head back against the cushions of the chair and regarded him steadily. After all this time, and although she was deeply in love with another man, something of his former attraction for her gleamed through. Perhaps, as Lillian had said, the effect of first love could never be wholly dispelled, even if, as in Derek's case, deceit and lovers' lies destroyed its original sweet magic, leaving betrayal in its wake.

"There's one more thing I should tell you," he said, looking at the wine in his half-emptied glass as if he did not want to meet her eyes as he divulged what he had to say. "I'm married."

It was on the tip of her tongue to ask him bitterly if he had returned to England once after all to fulfil his obligations to his former landlady's unfortunate daughter, but she decided against it. She knew him now. He had left England as much to escape that consequence as to make the fresh start he needed. It would feed his pride and his ego to learn that she had humiliated herself by going in search of him in the early light of a London morning with dreams of their going away together.

"Is your wife with you?" she asked instead.

He faced her again. "I left her in charge of the workshop. She is not a craftswoman, but she keeps my accounts and is very efficient. She was serving in a milliner's shop when I met her. Her name is Brigette."

401

"That's a pretty name," she said sincerely while not wanting an awkward silence to fall in their conversation.

He finished his wine abruptly and put the glass aside. This time he did not take his gaze from her. "I loved you, Irene," he declared intently. "If it had not been for your father—"

She stood up quickly. "That is something in our lives that is over and done with."

He rose to his feet with far less haste. "Do you still have the pendant?"

Such anger consumed her that her voice shook as she answered him. "No. I do not greatly care for the work of Obrist!"

He had the grace to look somewhat discomfited. "I suppose I should have told you it was not my work. I would have, but you assumed when I gave it to you that it was something I had made you, and I hadn't the heart to cause you any disappointment. I was afraid of losing you, Irene. If you had married me when I wanted you to, we would never have parted."

She stiffened involuntarily. Too much anguish was being unwillingly recalled. "Let us be sensible, Derek. You are to be working here for a short, indefinite period, and we shall be seeing each other all the time. There is nothing of any significance between us anymore, and the best thing we can do is to forget there ever was. Now we'll say good night. I'll see you out and lock up again after you."

A sudden similarity with the past hit them both in the same instant. He looked hard at her as if compelling her to hold his gaze. "That used to be my task when we were together in days gone by."

"Times have changed, and everything with it." She went down the stairs ahead of him, driving poignant memories from her. When he had gone, she leaned against the secured door and put a hand wearily over her eyes. The last thing she wanted at this time was to be torn by a painful intrusion from the past. If only Gregory were here! Never had she needed or longed for him more.

She made sure in the days that followed that she and Derek were never alone together again. In the workshop everything was organized to a degree, and all went well. Another goldsmith joined the team on a temporary basis, and he was as handpicked as the rest whom Arthur had chosen. The sawing, filing, snipping, and polishing continued in the workshop without pause. The furnace glowed, melting gold pouring from the crucibles, and on a special bench gems were being handled in what appeared to be organized chaos as the jewelled piece began slowly to take shape.

Time was fast running out. Gabrielle was beside herself with anxiety that the adornment would not be ready in time. It added to her frustration that she must remain closeted in the blind-shaded apartment with little to distract her. When she was bored with reading, she played cards with her lady's maid or chess with her chef, who was also her housekeeper's husband. She was frequently cross and ill-tempered, a great trial to the three who waited upon her. Since a visitor to a seemingly closed apartment might have attracted attention, Irene kept away after taking the necessary measurements from her grandmother for the piece that was to be made. In any case, she could no longer spare a moment away from the workshop, working as hard at her place at the gembench as anybody else. Yvonne Lucas, after completing the initial silk work that was to provide the backing of the piece, had taken over at the counter in the shop, freeing Irene from any other calls on her time. It was therefore with some exasperation one afternoon that Irene received a summons delivered by Yvonne to see a customer in the showroom, who would not state her requirements to anyone else. After unhooking her leather bench apron and hastily removing the linen overall that she wore, Irene smoothed her hands over her hair in an attempt to make herself presentable as she hurried from the workshop. To her surprise she found Madame Borisvinsky's middle-aged maid waiting to speak to her in confidence. The message was short and sharp. The old lady had discovered through a chance remark that the following evening at the Casino was to be the time and place of confrontation between Otèro and De Chandel. She wanted to be sure that Irene would be there.

"I'll be there," Irene said fervently, sending the maid back, with the reply. Then she hastened back to the workshop. "Listen, everybody! We have to be finished with our work within twenty-four hours. Tomorrow evening what we have been making here is to be worn.''

There came a roar of protest and shouts of it being impossible. Then Arthur rose from his stool and spoke out. ''We can do it if we work all through the night. I for one don't intend to disappoint Miss Irene, and I hope you will all follow my example.''

Derek was the first to answer. ''I'm with you!''

Irene flashed him a grateful glance, and he grinned, sticking up his thumb in a gesture of triumph as everybody else gave their support.

Yvonne kept the coffee-pot replenished all through the night. At intervals she produced a variety of good cheeses and some bread for quick snacks. When morning came, those who felt unable to go on without some rest for their eyes snatched some sleep in Irene's sitting-room chairs. Then they were awakened, and somebody else took a turn. Early afternoon came. Still the pressure did not ease, but towards four o'clock one by one the goldsmiths sat back on their stools, allowing Irene to set the last stone.

Slowly she lifted her head, letting her hands drop limply into her lap, and she smiled tremulously around at all who had stood by her. ''It's done.''

They all cheered, the men clapping each other on the back. Derek, in his exuberance, took her by the shoulders to swivel her around on the stool where she was sitting and kissed her full on the lips. In the general rejoicing nobody else took any notice, but he drew back quickly, his eyes growing serious, and let others crowd forward to shake her hand. She wished she had not felt his mouth on hers again. It made her feel disturbed and uneasy. When she glanced in his direction again, he was still watching her, the skin taut over the bones of his face, his cheeks hollow.

The packing of the finished piece now began. It was placed in a box, which in turn was padded well before being placed in a laundry bag. Yvonne took it to the servants' entrance of Gabrielle's apartment, where she handed it over to the housekeeper as if indeed the bundle contained nothing more than clean linen.

It was dark, and all of Monte Carlo glittered like a spread of jewels itself when Irene slipped quickly into Gabrielle's apartment. There she helped her grandmother to array herself in her jewelled splendour before going herself to the gambling rooms where all was to take place. Derek was posted strategically outside the apartment building where in co-operation with Arthur and Jacques he would signal the right moment for Gabrielle to cover the short distance in her carriage to reach the steps of the Casino. It was essential that she should be the last of the three courtesans to arrive.

Irene felt tense with nervousness as she waited in the marble-pillared approach to the rooms. She had dressed to blend in with her surroundings in an evening dress of pale pink chiffon, the skirt composed of handkerchief points, and she wore some of the shop jewellery around her neck and on her wrists. All around her, women in elaborate gowns, jewels and feathers and flowers in their hair, their escorts with them, drifted into little chattering groups and then dispersed again in a colourful swirling that was never still. The alertness of everybody's glances, the quick turn of heads, and the general air of mounting suspense made it obvious to Irene that rumours of some kind must have been circulating throughout the day. At least Gabrielle's secret had been well kept.

Suddenly an almost tangible ripple of excitement ran through the whole Casino. Irene found her view blocked as people went forward, but she heard what was being said. "It's De Chandel! Look at her! Oh, bravo! Bravo!"

Irene eased through in time to see Diane De Chandel advancing gracefully from the lofty hall beyond in a white satin dress and a searing blaze of jewels. She was covered in precious gems from head to toe. It was not enough that she wore a magnificent tiara, but beautiful pearls were entwined in her hair and hung in loops to her shoulders. Her throat was encased in a collar of rubies to which had been attached a great number of pendants for the occasion. Her bosom bore the weight of several marvellous necklaces, while bracelets and bangles encased her wrists and arms, her fingers beringed to the knuckles. Around her waist were gem-studded belts, while girdles of emeralds, sapphires, and diamonds swung and glittered about her hips. In a way it was difficult to see exactly what she was wearing, for the lights of the chandeliers struck such fire from the jewels that she seemed to move in a twinkling aura of light, out of which her bewitching face glowed as pale as ivory.

She was wearing every important piece of her jewellery in a public proclamation that she had had more ardent lovers and had received higher and more costly tributes than her hated rival. It was obvious to everyone that whatever Otèro wore that evening, it would be lost in comparison with the spoils of love being flaunted by De Chandel.

Play had stopped in the gambling rooms. Everyone wanted to see what was happening. Even those playing in the exclusive private rooms appeared in doorways and came to swell the growing crowd of spectators. Then, as word spread that Otèro had arrived, women began to stand on chairs to get a better view.

A gasp went up. Otèro was not wearing a single piece of jewellery! She was making her entrance in a low-cut, black velvet gown that accentuated her superb figure, her raven hair simply dressed in a waved pompadour and with not so much as a pearl in her ears. At first it seemed to all who watched her approach that she had capitulated. Defeat had been admitted. Then those spectators nearest her began to titter and then to laugh. Soon Irene was able to see why. In Otèro's wake came her elaborately coiffured maid, who was more adorned with fabulous pieces of jewellery than De Chandel, even to the point of wearing the famous bolero that spent most of its time in a bank vault. As if that were not joke enough against Otèro's rival, the maid was weighed down by the large jewel case that she carried, the lid open to reveal its dazzling treasure trove of gems. The laughter soared.

Irene saw that De Chandel had gone crimson with humiliation and rage. Otèro's red lips curved with a smug smile of triumph, but when she expected the crowd to close behind her to follow her into the gambling rooms, there came exclamations of astonishment that caused her to swing around swiftly and look behind her. Her eyes flew wide with disbelief and fury. A third contestant for supremacy had arrived.

Where De Chandel's walk had been graceful and Otèro's sensual, Gabrielle's pace was stately. With her head held high, her gleaming, blood-red hair held in place by a pair of gold filigree combs, she wore an elegant tunic gown of gold tissue with a cloak of the same rich fabric flowing from her shoulders into a train behind her. As she passed by and the full magnificence of her bejewelled cloak came into view, applause began to break out. Here was no higgledy-piddledy profusion of gems in vulgar display, but an Art Nouveau design of taste and artistry in jewels and baroque pearls in every hue, with nymphs and winging birds rising from flowers an foliage that spread out into an exotic border, the whole reinforced by a network of gold. The applause became thunderous. Gabrielle's sensitive and soignée appearance could not be faulted. Otèro and De Chandel were forgotten. It was Gabrielle's night. Total triumph was hers.

As people followed after the victoress into the gambling rooms, Irene was left practically alone. She smiled to herself as she leaned a hand against one of the marble pillars, letting her head drop back a little in exultation that all had gone even better than she had dared hope. More applause came from the distance as Gabrielle took a place at one of the tables. Then Irene began to realize that someone, who had been kept away from her in the crush, had been left alone much as she had been on the opposite side of the carpeted path that the courtesans had taken. For a few seconds she savoured the delicious anticipation of when she would turn her head and meet his eyes, her body tremblingly aware of him. She did not have to be told that he had come in amorous search of her.

"Irene!"

She could hold back no longer. On a spin of her foot, she swung around, her own appearance nymphlike as the soft chiffon moulded itself to her slender body. An exclamation of joy broke from her as she was caught up in Gregory's arms.

Fifteen

For Irene it was a night of love in the truest sense of the word. They walked arm in arm to her apartment over the shop. Gregory had brought her a special keepsake. Not diamonds, which was what might have been expected considering his position in the diamond world, but something he knew would mean far more to her. At first sight it was a charming, unassuming ring of matted gold with filigree work such as was popular in the first decade of the nineteenth century.

"Read the inscription," he breathed, watching her face. "It is said to be the ring that Nelson gave Emma Hamilton a few weeks before the Battle of Trafalgar."

She turned the ring slowly and read the words that had been engraved there long since: *My love for all eternity*. Then the letters *E* and *N* were closely entwined. Instantly the tears gushed from her eyes, taking her as much by surprise as it did him. She had heard that women wept at the sight of the Taj Mahal, that great monument to faithful love, and the ring had had the same effect. Speech was beyond her, her joy too deep. He gathered her to him in understanding, and for a while he just held her, the back of her head cupped in his hand.

When she did lean away to look at him, her voice came huskily. "How ever did you find such a love token?"

He took the ring from her and slid it onto her finger, kissing her at the same time. "It's been in the family for a great number of years. It came into my great-grandfather's possession in the days when he still had a pawnbroker's shop. Nobody knows who parted with such an heirloom over a counter. It has been kept ever since in the original little box that housed it during the transaction, and for a long while the unredeemed ticket was attached to it. It may be that until this moment it has never been worn since the day it left Emma Hamilton's finger."

He kissed her again. Then he made love to her more sweetly and tenderly than before. They were consumed by an adoring passion for each other that shut them away from all else into a world of their own. It was a time of rediscovery, renewed wonder, and fresh delights, their limbs entwined, their breath and bodies blending, their whispering of such tenderness that it was as if they had invented a love language of their own.

At the Casino, Gabrielle was making amends for

having failed to give her granddaughter financial support when it was needed, her conscience refreshingly cleared as she let it be known by whom her jewelled cloak had been made. The word carried as if from flashpoint to flashpoint. Gabrielle Roget's breathtaking array had been designed and created by Irene Denise at the little shop that lay in a narrow side street not far from the square.

From the shop's opening hour, that same street was blocked with carriages. Many women sprang out of them in impatience and went on foot to join those already crowded into the small shop. Design sketches were snatched from Irene's hands, and more than once one was torn down the middle as two would-be customers grabbed it at the same time. They wanted everything from necklaces to cloaks and capes similar to what they had seen the previous evening. Irene and Yvonne were rushed off their feet. Finally Irene sorted out the immediate confusion by making appointments to see each woman customer at her hotel or villa, where requirements could be discussed in a civilized and leisurely manner. The names of gentlemen were also on the list, for Irene pitied their expression of helpless incredulity as female elbows dug them out of the way, and she made sure that she secured their names before they escaped the crush in relief.

Arthur wisely retained his temporary workforce, putting them back into their places at the benches when they had come in merely to collect their pay and gather up their own tools before departure. He was able to tell them that the orders taken during the first hour were enough to keep each of them in full employment for many months to come. The success of the business was assured. From now on, the young woman whom he had known since childhood and whose talents he had acknowledged a long while ago would be fully established. She would be able to take her place proudly alongside Fouquet, Gautrait, Lalique, Vever, and Tiffany in the field of Art Nouveau jewellery.

He also had another reason for wanting to keep a larger workshop. Sooner or later he would have to appoint a successor to take his place, and there was a highly suitable candidate among those who were there originally on a temporary basis. At the first opportunity he would put the fellow's name forward to Irene. As for himself, the pressure of work on the jewelled cloak had made him realize that he was an old man. He could no longer cope as he would wish with such intensity of concentration and the intricacy of the task at hand. Worst of all, he had known for a long time that his eyesight was failing him, and tiredness was making the condition worsen.

But whereas the jewelled cloak had been instrumental in making him come to terms with his age, it had given his wife, who was ten years younger, a new lease on life. She had thoroughly enjoyed getting back to her needle in the sewing of the cloak and had agreed to take on making the foundations of all other jewelled garments that were ordered. This meant that she was no longer at the counter, which she had not much liked, but was sitting at home all day surrounded by silks and satins, happy as a lark.

Irene was another who had never been happier. She thrived on hard work, and to have her jewellery acknowledged by the *monde* and the *demi-monde* in a single stroke was so wonderful to her as to be almost beyond belief. As if that were not enough, she was thrillingly and excitingly in love with a passionate man whose adoration of her seemed to open new realms with every meeting. Her only regret in the present rush of business at the shop was that it took her away from him when she would have preferred to spend every moment in his company. He did have business of his own along the Riviera, and when he was away she crammed her hours by fulfilling appointments and designing at her drawing board. Arthur had told her that on a previous visit Gregory had offered to supply diamonds to the workshop if they should be needed, which enabled her to broach the subject to him at a business level. Steeped in the finer aspects of Art Nouveau, she had long used many comparatively inexpensive materials in her designs, such as glass, ivory, bronze, and mother-of-pearl; and this was why she was able to keep a range of handsome wares that did not touch top prices. But certain women did not appreciate a piece of jewellery unless its value could be measured commercially rather than in terms of its intrinsic artistry. This meant she had to use jewels of the standard that she had handled in her father's shop. Fortunately she had the unstinted financial backing of her stepmother, which enabled her to unleash a supply of the stones that she needed, not only from Gregory, but from other gem dealers known to Arthur and herself. At times the amount of money involved made her turn pale when she thought about it, but luckily people did not expect to owe money to jewellers as they did to their tailors or their milliners or others who catered for their requirements, and bills were settled without much delay, ensuring a ploughing back of funds to offset some of the everlasting outlay. Quite a number of customers brought their own jewellery to have it reset to one of Irene's designs, and some supplied their own gems, which meant profit without much cost to herself; but whichever way the work came in, there was no easing up of the continuing flow.

Before leaving Monaco again, Gregory took Irene to see the villa at Cap d'Ail. The roof was in place, but the interior was still a maze of unfinished walls and floors and unglazed windows. When they had made their way carefully through it, he telling her what each room was to be, they came out onto the terrace that between long established date and coconut palms gave a splendid view of the peacock-blue sea. She sat down on a pile of planks.

"It's going to be a lovely house," she declared enthusiastically. "It's a pity you won't be able to live in it all year round."

He sat down on the planks beside her and took her hand into his. "You could, Irene."

She smiled at him gently, shaking her head. "I

can't. You know and I know that we must not look beyond each hour we spend together." She had let down her guard briefly when Lillian had spoken of his asking for a divorce, allowing herself to hope against hope that a closed way was about to open up for them. The disappointment had shocked her back into reality. All the time he and Lillian were bound together legally, the element of insecurity about the future must remain. "If I should move into this villa, it would be a surrender of the independence for which I have striven for such a long time."

"You would still have your freedom to do whatever you wished."

She shook her head. "No, I wouldn't. Neither would you."

"I don't understand you."

With a sigh she twisted her hand around to link her fingers affectionately with his, looking at him with loving regard. "If we lived together under one roof, I would begin to change. Not in loving you, but in wanting more than we share now. In a house I would want to go to sleep in your arms as your wife and to wake up as your wife. I would start yearning for children and a fulfilled family life, which can never be. The stigma of illegitimacy brings down the full force of the world's cruelty on a child and its path in life, which I could never let happen through any personal indulgence on my part. I should become more demanding of your time in compensation, probably not wanting you to leave me. I'm not possessive now, but I know my failings, and it might happen."

"I'm willing to take that risk."

Again she gave a shake of her head. "No. It would be unfair." She leaned towards him to place a kiss lightly on the corner of his lips. "As we are, we make no claim on each other's lives. There are no recriminations and no agonizing over what can't be changed. We have to bear partings, but only in the knowledge of what our sweet reunions will bring us. This is how our relationship has to be. We are responsible people who love each other. Let us never forget it." With her hand still locked in his, she stood up and looked down the length of him. "Shall we go now? Don't look sad. We'll know happiness in the villa, even though the situation won't be as either of us would have wished it."

Side by side they wandered back down the track that the builders' cart had made. Before they reached the dusty road, he told her that he had approached Lillian a while ago with a request that was in effect a demand that she must allow him a divorce.

"Lillian told me about it when she came into the shop one day." Irene went on to tell him much of what had been said, only holding back Lillian's belief that with time she and Gregory would be reunited again. It was almost as if a superstitious fear kept her from voicing it.

For Gregory it was somehow doubly painful to hear further endorsement from the woman he loved, of his wife's implacable attitude. It left him no choice but to reveal details of the final breakdown of the marriage. "It was strange, but Lillian never saw herself as being unfaithful to me. She was as fond of me as it was possible for her to be, probably caring more for me than for anyone else she had ever known, but gradually her behaviour pattern of doing anything to further her career came to my knowledge. It created an intolerable state of affairs. We were on the point of splitting up when she discovered that she had inadvertently become pregnant by me. I suppose every man hopes for a son at some time in his life, and I thought that this unexpected turn of events might prove to be the remaking of our marriage. At three months she was still doing a singing turn at one of the better music halls when she happened to be seen from the audience by the Gaiety's Guv'nor. She was called to audition quite legitimately and was successful. That same day she had a back-street abortion."

"Oh!" Irene could tell by the tightening of his expression the shock it had been to him.

"She came home and collapsed, already haemorrhaging. A doctor came at once. During the fight to save her life, I held her hand while she begged me not to divorce her, concerned only with her future at the Gaiety. She knew that what she had done was the final straw, and there would be no going back for either of us."

"Then that is how she extracted the promise from you."

"Naturally I would have promised her anything to help keep her alive. As soon as the danger was past and her recovery was certain, we parted. I went to Holland and took over the Amsterdam office. I made it my base until my father's death brought about my return to London. I'm afraid I was not surprised that Lillian should hold me to that promise. Even if she had not, there would still be no way to overcome the impasse at the present time. As you know, divorce is the last thing she wants, and since appearing at the Gaiety, she has taken the greatest care never to let the slightest suspicion be cast against her name."

"At least nothing can stop us from loving each other," Irene said in gentle reassurance.

He brought her to a standstill in their walking and held her by the shoulders. "You are everything to me, my sweet Irene."

She smiled blissfully at him and put her ring-finger against her cheek. "I know," she whispered, causing him to smile back at her. Then she slipped her hand into the crook of his arm, and they continued on their way, still looking at each other.

At the end of the week, they had another of the partings that were becoming all too familiar to them. When he had gone, Irene worked twice as hard to make up for the time she had lost in being with him, welcoming the yoke of it again, for it helped to ease the anguish of never quite knowing when she would next see him. She had taken on two able young women assistants in the showroom, both of them dressed in white chiffon blouses and grey silk skirts. She herself now wore whatever she wished, always elegant, always in pastel tones. Often for the greater part of the day, she would be upstairs at her drawing table with an overall protecting her clothes. It was a great thrill for her on the day she came downstairs to find Empress Eugénie in the showroom. As always the old lady was in black, with a bunch of Parma violets at her waist.

"Ah, Miss Lindsay. I heard that you had opened this shop. I wish you success."

"Thank you, ma'am." The appearance of the Empress was the golden seal of approval on the business. Irene was delighted. Even the simple replacement of a safety chain on the Empress's piece of jewellery was of importance in itself, being a piece that she always wore. It was a shamrock brooch of emeralds, which had been her first love gift from the late Napoleon III.

Irene, handling the task herself, thought how men all through the ages had sought to express their feelings with jewellery to the women they loved. Her own love gift from Gregory had come already steeped in a lasting passion that had taken no heed of scandal, war, and other adverse circumstances. It shone on her finger, catching the light as she completed the fastening of the safety chain with a pinch of pliers. To her, Gregory's ring seemed to have regained a full lustre through the new love that had made it a special keepsake for the second time around.

There proved to be two sidelines to the main business of designing and selling jewellery, and they were to take a steady place in the running of the shop.

One was the choice of some customers to have a valuable piece of jewellery copied in cheaper stones, which they wore on occasions, while the original remained in safe-keeping. Her father had carried out this type of commission, and she herself had dealt with such orders for replicas many times when behind his counter. But the other sideline was less familiar to her. It was one that her father had always handled with his head salesman in privacy, and when she first had to deal with it, she was unprepared for the request that was put to her. She had been called down to the showroom from her drawing table by one of her assistants to face a haughty-looking woman who demanded to speak to her in private. There was only the small office in which to receive her. It would not have been businesslike to invite her into home surroundings.

As soon as the door closed, the woman took a slim leather box out of her purse and opened it to reveal a finely jewelled aigrette in the form of a sprig of lilac. "How much will you give me for it?" she demanded. Then, mistaking Irene's hesitation of surprise to mean a reluctance to purchase, she thrust her face forward aggressively. "Do not pretend you are not interested. Every jeweller in Monte Carlo tries that trick when he knows the seller needs money for the tables! And do not imagine that I do not know the true value of this piece!"

Irene regarded her coolly, pushing the box back across the desk and rising to her feet. "This is an honest house, madame. Nobody is cheated here.

Take your jewellery elsewhere."

The woman's face crumpled, and her whole attitude changed. "I apologize. I spoke out of turn. I should have known that Empress Eugénie would not patronize a jeweller whose reputation was not impeccable. That is why I came to you today. Make me an offer, I implore you. The Casino will soon be opening its doors, and I have nothing to stake today!"

Slowly Irene sat down again. She thought it tragic for anyone to be so obsessed by the tables, but it was not for her to judge others. Taking the aigrette out of its velvet bed, she examined it through her jeweller's glass. The stones were good, although the piece in itself was of no interest in her. She named what she knew to be a fair price. The woman was grateful. After receiving proof of identity and ownership, Irene wrote out a bank draft, which was snatched up. The street door banged shut after the woman before Irene could emerge from the office.

That evening, when everyone had gone home, she told Arthur of the incident. He took a close look at the aigrette and agreed that she had hit the right level with the price she had set upon it. Privately he thought she could have obtained it for much less, but he knew better than to suggest that she take advantage of anyone's misfortune. She was like her father in that respect, scrupulously honest in all dealings.

As it happened, he was glad that the purchase of the aigrette had given him a chance to talk to her on her own. He raised the matter that he had long had in mind. After breaking it to her that his time in her employ would be shorter thàn he anticipated due to his increasingly poor eyesight more than to his age, he put the suggestion forward as to who should be the one to take his place as head of the workshop. He was taken aback when she received it with some hostility.

"Not Derek Ryde, Mr. Lucas! I don't think he would be suitable at all."

"I beg to disagree. He is an outstanding craftsman, and it would be a great shame to let him leave at the end of the month." He saw she looked startled. "I'll remind you that he has only stayed on for the length of time that he has in order to oblige me. I would have been hard put to find a goldsmith equal to him during that first great rush of work that came upon us. If he is not offered some inducement to stay on, he'll be going back to Paris on the very day the verbal agreement made between us comes to an end. After all, he has a wife awaiting his return."

She bit into her lip, frowning. "The trouble is that I'm used to working with you now, Mr. Lucas. I don't know that Mr. Ryde and I would see eye to eye on how the workshop is run. What about Jacques taking your place eventually?"

"He is far too young. He has all the restlessness of youth that has not yet tried its wings. We gave him his first job after his apprenticeship. He's not ready to settle down in the same workshop for years to come."

"You think Mr. Ryde is?"

"I'm sure of it. He said to me himself a while ago that he would never return to Paris if he had the chance to stay in Monte Carlo."

"Hmmm. I suppose he favours the proximity of the Nice racetrack."

Arthur glanced at her sharply. She was like her father again at that moment, knowing all that went on without anybody realizing it and coming out with a shrewd observation when it was least expected. "He's a wagering man, I grant you, but that is nothing to hold against the standard of his craftsmanship. He never cuts short his hours and never stints his share of work; he has an easy manner and is able to get on well with people."

She sighed resignedly. Derek was the same in her workshop as he had been in her father's, interested in what he was doing, his outside distractions having no place at his bench. Since his work could not be faulted and his personal life was entirely his own, she should not go against the advice that Arthur had given her about marking him out for special promotion. It was strange, but she could still tell just by walking through the workshop whether Derek had had a successful gamble or whether he had lost. The glittering look of triumph in his eyes when he glanced up at her, the jauntiness of his attitude, and the cocky set of his shoulders were as revealing now as in the past. At times it was perilously disturbing to be attuned to his jubilation, almost as if in a moment of madness she might forget all that had happened in between and throw her arms around his neck in congratulation as she had done many times in days gone by. In reality she knew she would never give way to such an impulse, but she rarely worked at one of the benches during these times, usually finding something else to do.

"I'll do as you suggest, Mr. Lucas. But I hope you will stay long enough to see me through the expansion of these premises. The next-door property is coming up for sale, and my stepmother is willing for the purchase to go ahead."

"When do you plan to start this expansion?"

"As soon as the season is over. The work can take place during the slacker summer months. It will give us extra room in the workshops, increased storage space, a more spacious showroom, and I can enlarge the apartment upstairs."

"What about a pleasant ante-room where you can receive people who come to sell to you?"

"I've thought of that. It can be adjacent to the office once the space is available. What do you say, Mr. Lucas? Will you stay until the alterations are completed?"

"I'll stay for as long as you need me, have no fear. As for Mr. Ryde, will you speak to him?"

She nodded. "Tomorrow. I'll see him in the office as soon as he arrives for work."

Derek found her writing at her desk, but she put down her pen as he took the chair opposite her. He had an idea why she wanted to see him. He had heard that Arthur Lucas had retirement in mind and knew himself to be the obvious choice as a successor.

"I understand that your time with us is almost at an end, Derek," she said as an opening. Then she went on to explain the situation and to offer him the position of chief workmaster. All the time he was listening, he was also aware of the old desire for her pulling at him. It was the same every time she passed through the workshop, paused to speak to him at the bench, or had any reason to come near him or to appear within his range of vision. He had experienced a keen and quite unreasonable jealousy at the realization that she was well and truly in love with Lillian Rose's estranged husband. He knew Lillian. They had grown up in the same slum street of Manchester. She had not been particularly pleased to see him when he had first turned up at her Gaiety dressing room, but when she discovered he had no intention of divulging anything about her early days to the press or anyone else, they had resumed their acquaintanceship, and she had been good for a loan now and again when he had been short of cash to settle with his bookmakers. Through visiting her at the theatre, he had met and dallied with one of the chorus girls, whom he had treated to everything when he had money in his pocket. She, poor bitch, had complicated matters by falling in love with him. What a tangle he had been in during those last few months in London! Everything had gone wrong except his relationship with Irene, until even that was terminated unexpectedly. He had been thankful to leave London and get away from everything. His only regret had been losing Irene in the process. It was still a regret. He could visualize her body now under her neat clothes. She had concluded what she had been saying and was looking at him questioningly.

"I would like to take over from Arthur Lucas," he conceded willingly. "I can see this business growing until you have branches elsewhere. I hope to prosper along with it and maybe to manage one of those branches for you one day."

"Your confidence in me is flattering," she said, smiling.

"I always did tell you that you had exceptional talent."

She did not want to be drawn into talking about the past. There was a way to settle it once and for all. "You told me that Brigette keeps your accounts and is extremely capable. I'm willing to offer her the same job here if she would like to take it."

"I'm sure she would."

"Then you had better have some time off to go to Paris and settle everything there. Will it take long?"

"No. The workshop and our living accommodations are rented. Brigette and I should be able to move here within a matter of days."

"I look forward to your return," she said, closing the interview.

He pushed back the chair and stood up to lean both hands on her desk. "I was drawn to Brigette because she reminded me of you."

She had taken up her pen, intending to resume her

writing, her gaze already on the papers before her. For a moment or two, she did not reply. When she did, it was to glare up at him in a blaze of fury that took him by surprise.

"Don't ever say anything like that to me again!"

He stared at her. "What are you afraid of? That in spite of everything, somehow we still care for each other?"

She sprang to her feet. "I stopped caring for you long ago! I love someone else."

He gave a half-grin, narrowing his eyes at her. "I don't dispute your loving Burnett. He's attentive enough when he's here, and you're as transparent in your feelings towards him as you could be. But that has nothing to do with what was between us and is still between us. It has never quite left you, and it has never left me. If you are to be honest with yourself, you will know that I'm speaking the truth."

Her lips parted in denial. He saw her draw in a faltering breath, and then she rephrased what she had been about to say. "Let the past lie forgotten, or I have no alternative but to withdraw the offer of future promotion for you when Mr. Lucas leaves!"

He saw that she meant what she said. Straightening up away from the desk, he let his hands drop casually onto his hips. "Now it's my turn to be honest on another track. I don't want to lose that position, and I bow to your stipulation. Does that meet with your approval?"

She gave an abrupt nod, her colour high. He moved away to the door, looked back once over his shoulder at her, and then went out. Sitting down again, she put a shaking hand across her eyes. He had made her face up to the fact that one small part of her heart was still vulnerable as far as he was concerned. It was not love, not fondness, but a curious bitter-sweetness that lingered on from what had been good in their relationship. And it had been good in laughter and certain shared moments, no matter what had come afterwards, no matter how devious with her and with other women he had proved to be. She found it particularly galling that she should still find herself able to believe him when he said that he still cared for her.

Now and again Irene went to see how Gregory's villa was progressing at Cap d'Ail. She wrote to him about it, even though she knew he had lost a certain amount of interest in the project since she had made it clear that she was not prepared to live in it. He sent her news of London. Fabergé had renounced all ideas of a foreign branch in Paris or anywhere else except London, where he was to open in Duke Street, Grosvenor Square. She recalled what Derek had said about the day when her name would be above branches everywhere. He had put her secret dream into words.

She had returned from viewing the villa one Sunday afternoon when Derek came to see her with his wife. He and Brigette had arrived from Paris the previous day and had moved into an apartment of two rooms and a kitchen, which Arthur and Yvonne had made on the top floor of their house, following a source of income that they had found profitable in their previous abode.

"I am enchanted to meet you, Miss Lindsay," Brigette said when Derek carried out the introductions.

"It is a pleasure to make your acquaintance," Irene said in reply to her, feeling astonished. Derek had said that there was a resemblance between them, and she could not deny it. They were not alike in features, but they were of the same height, their skin of the translucent pallor common to redheads, and whereas her hair was red-gold, Brigette's was a rich, dark auburn, naturally wavy, and of equal luxuriance. Their eyes were a different colour. Brigette's were a dark brown, faintly mysterious, for she had a mannerism of looking through her lashes at the person to whom she was speaking. Not that she said much in Derek's company, seemingly content to let him do the talking whenever they were together. Irene was able to see why Derek had been able to come away to Monte Carlo for as long as it suited him, leaving Brigette to manage on her own in Paris, because her devotion to him was obvious. She would do unquestioningly whatever he wanted. He had found a woman who wanted nothing more than to be his adoring slave. To Irene the thought of such a state of mind was abhorrent. She believed that a woman should love within the framework of her own being, qualities and faults enriching the love she gave; such submissiveness as was to be found in Brigette belonged to past decades and not to the first years of a whole new century when women were beginning to assert themselves for the first time.

Yet in the office Brigette came into her own, proving that she could easily have been independent and earned her own living, if the need had arisen. Irene discovered that Brigette was practically a genius with figures, and everything Derek had said about her efficiency proved to be true. She wore alternately one plain and one striped, high-necked blouse with a dark, ankle-length skirt for her work, and moved about as quietly and unobtrusively as a shadow. In her neat, unassuming way she took the burden of managing the office and all that was involved from Irene's shoulders, leaving her free to design, take a spell at the workbench, or deal with particularly important customers, either by appointment or in the showroom.

Irene could not quite like her. She told herself it was probably due to some unacknowledged, utterly irrational resentment that Derek should have found consolation with Brigette while she herself had been still fraught with disillusionment and despair, for it had come out that he had married Brigette after being in France less than three months. He had admitted openly that his bride's dowry had enabled him to equip his own workshop. If there was anything left from the sale of that equipment after their leaving Paris, it had not reached Brigette's purse. As week after week went by, she appeared in the same clothes, always immaculate, the blouses washed, starched, and ironed after a day's wear, but never a variation.

Her eagerness to receive her own wage packet after making up the wages for all the rest of the staff was always obvious. Her eyes gleamed, and she tucked it away in her purse in an almost miserly fashion. Yet she spent every sou of it during the week as methodically and practically as she dealt with the office work.

"I buy vegetables from a peasant's garden before they come to market," she confided one day, "which means that I get them at a lower price." On another occasion she revealed that she met the fishing boats on the quayside in order to bargain over a purchase. She baked her own bread, cooked cheap cuts of meat with an equally cheap wine with plenty of fresh herbs to a standard of which she was proud, and made salads with the addition of leaves from wild plants that she gathered herself. Gradually it became apparent to Irene that Brigette's wages covered rent and food and necessities. Derek's money was his own. Brigette had come to terms with a gambling husband. She kept the roof safe above their heads and starvation from the door while he indulged his obsession within the rise and fall of his own finances. In its own curious way, the marriage was a complete success.

Irene could not help but admire Brigette's stamina. She thought it was as well for Derek's own good, quite apart from the extra burden of anxiety that it would have put on his wife, that he could not play at the Casino. In its beginnings, anyone had been free to gamble there; one room had been known as "The

Kitchen" because of the number of servants that had gathered there, but all that had changed long since. Applications were vetted carefully, full evening dress was *de rigueur*, and the gambling rooms were barred to workmen and servants, which was the category into which Derek as a craftsman would fall ignominiously. There were others who were barred as well because of the very nature of their employment: anyone dealing with public or private funds, such as tax collectors, bank clerks, public notaries, and so forth, whose presence might have inhibited the careless rapture of gamblers at the tables, was forbidden to enter the precincts.

Irene went to the Casino about once a week—either with Gabrielle, who wanted to show her off as the designer of the cloak, or with Madame Borisvinsky, who liked to have her as company. When with one she could not talk to the other, even if the three of them were in the same gambling room, for Madame Borisvinsky would not acknowledge a courtesan, and Gabrielle had learned over the years to ignore completely anyone who might snub her. Through them both Irene was introduced to a great number of men, many wishing to further the acquaintance, either honourably or with lesser principles, according to whether the introduction had come through Madame Borisvinsky or Gabrielle. She wanted none of them. Her love for Gregory was such that she knew if fate were ever cruel enough to part them, she would lead a solitary existence until the end of her days.

She did meet one man whom she liked immediately as a friend. He was Sergei Borisvinsky, the second son of Madame Borisvinsky, a widower for many years with a grown-up family. Grey-haired and distinguished, with twinkling blue eyes, he came to visit his mother at Monte Carlo while staying elsewhere along the Riviera. He had the same quick sense of humour.

"I hope you are not letting my mother bully you," he said to Irene, making sure that his mother was within hearing. "She is a Tartar when she wants her own way, you know."

"Nonsense!" Madame Borisvinsky intervened cheerfully from the chair where she was sitting. "I am a dear old lady. Everyone knows that except my obstinate sons."

To Irene's delight his visit to Monte Carlo coincided with Sofia's return to see her. Sergei and Sofia had never met before, but they had many mutual acquaintances. When the four of them dined together and went to the Salle Garnier afterwards to hear the great Sarah Bernhardt recite some monologues with all the fire and verve at her disposal, Madame Borisvinsky seized an opportunity during the interval to whisper in Irene's ear. "Let us do a little matchmaking. Sergei has been alone far too long."

Irene looked towards her stepmother, who was engaged in conversation with Sergei. It was easy to see that they liked each other. But Sofia's eyes had a shadow of sadness across them at all times these days. Irene feared that it would not be easily chased away.

Sixteen

Throughout the summer the alterations to the shop in conjunction with the newly acquired neighbouring property took place. Irene was able to keep one section open to deal with business, and routine was only interrupted in the workshop for a few days when the dividing wall was being opened up and reinforced to make it doubly as large. She gave everybody a holiday at this time but could not get away herself. She had received an invitation early in June that she had had to refuse. Maria had written from St. Petersburg that she and Leon were to spend the summer months cruising in the Norwegian fjords in their yacht and had asked if Irene would join them. There were eight cabins, and all would be occupied by Leon's friends if Irene did not come to keep her company.

The letter worried Irene. There was a note of desperation in it. The special reference to the loyalties of the fellow passengers suggested that Maria expected to feel lonely and shut out. All Irene could reply was that she had to go to London in September and would plan her trip to coincide with Maria and Leon's visit before they returned home.

At Cap d'Ail Gregory's villa was completed, and Irene saw to the furnishings as they had previously arranged. She followed the new note in Art Nouveau, as she had done in the decor of her shop from the beginning, which was leading the style out of its floreated extravagances into a calm asymmetry. She sent for furniture with vertical lines, which she knew Gregory liked as much as she did, and used delicate colours against the natural wood panelling that caught and diffused the bright daylight into a restful glow. A photographer took some pictures of the result, which she sent him, and she planned to take more with her to show him the progress of the newly planted garden when she made her London visit.

In late August the shop was ready to cope with a new rush of business when it came again. Work from the last season had kept everyone busy, and there had been a steady sale at a more moderate level during the resort's off-period. Arthur retired. He had new thick-lensed spectacles, but they did little to ease the effect of the cataracts that were causing the dimming of his sight. Irene had one last business discussion with him before he left, mapping out her future policy; he approved it and wished her good luck in everything she did. Yvonne would now be the breadwinner in their little household, but he had saved all his life and faced no financial problems.

In her enlarged office, which was separated from Brigette's new domain, Irene told Derek of her intention that he should be more than head goldsmith. "I want you to be the manager here. I need to be able to leave a responsible person in charge of the showroom as well as the workshop whenever I'm absent."

"Say no more," he said, grinning. "I accept the new appointment with pleasure. I told you once before that I looked forward to managing one of your branches for you. This is a good beginning. However, there's one condition I must clarify. On the day I make my fortune, I intend never to work again."

She shook her head indulgently at him, as she sat back in her chair. "Haven't you discovered yet that you're never going to get rich at the races, Derek? You should have been a bookie. They're the ones who make the money."

He shrugged cheerfully. "Where's the excitement in taking wagers from others? I need to gamble, Irene. It's passion of another kind and no less satisfying."

"Only when you win," she pointed out.

He raised an eyebrow cynically. "I don't know. There's a dreadful thrill in losing too. It makes one's heart stop and one's teeth ache, but out of the blackness there shines the certainty that the next time one will be lucky again." His lids narrowed at her. "I view you in the same light."

She looked displeased and exasperated. Since her last warning to him there had been no further talk in such a vein, and she did not want it now. "You force me to say the same to you as I said last time. Forget the past or you can't stay on here."

"I'm not talking about the past. I'm looking to the future."

She regarded him angrily. "You're gambling at this very minute, aren't you? It amuses you to create a situation where the dice may or may not fall in your favour. The stake in this case is your future in this business. Well, I call your bluff. You shall stay on as manager for Brigette's sake if not yours!"

His eyes were full of laughter. "Accepted! I have a black morning coat and striped trousers awaiting collection in readiness for my appointment."

"I hope you ordered a new coat for Brigette at the same time!"

His face darkened. "I'm generous to Brigette when I have a win, but she's mean as hell. She salts away every sou."

"For your protection and for hers!" Irene countered. "Can you honestly tell me that you haven't been glad of her thrift and prudence when you have found yourself in debt again?"

He glared. "Has she been talking to you about me?"

"No, no. We only discuss business. You forget I know you well."

His good humour returned. "Indeed you do, my lovely Irene."

She allowed the remark to pass, letting its significance lie unprobed. In a business-like manner she told him what his salary would be, and then they discussed various other matters connected with the workshop and the showroom without bringing their personal relationship to the fore anymore that day.

It was with an untroubled mind that Irene was able to leave Derek in charge when she left for England. When she stepped off the boat-train at Victoria into the hustle and bustle of the platform, she saw that Gregory and Sofia had both come to meet her. They were standing side by side. As far as she knew, neither had been face to face with the other since the development of her own special association with him. Sofia was looking very brittle and bright, Gregory calm and smiling. For Sofia's sake Irene did not run into his arms as she would otherwise have done; but in the brief kiss of greeting that they shared, each conveyed to the other the special joy of being together again.

"There's someone else here to meet you too," Sofia said.

Irene had had eyes only for the two most important people in her life, and she turned almost without recognition to the fair young woman whom she had not realized was standing with them.

"Maria!" she exclaimed in astonishment, in which pleasure mingled with an inner dismay. Maria was so changed, so thin and drawn with none of the happy exuberance that had characterized her when they had first come to know each other.

"Dear Irene! How well you look! It is wonderful to see you again."

"I thought you weren't arriving until the end of the week," Irene said as they embraced affectionately.

"Leon became bored with salmon fishing, and his friends grew quarrelsome. To my relief, the holiday was cut short a little earlier than expected."

It was enough to confirm Irene's earlier fear that the marriage was not turning out as Maria had expected. She recalled what she knew of the behaviour of some of the Romanovs at Monte Carlo. It sounded as if Sofia's first misgivings about the match had been well founded.

"I have yet to meet Leon," she said.

"This evening. You shall see him this evening. Gregory has arranged that we all go to Covent Garden and out to supper afterwards."

Irene was to stay with Sofia at Milton Square. Back in her old room, where nothing had been changed, she marvelled that so much had happened to her since the day she had come home from her Swiss school to find that Sofia had given her a larger and far better appointed bedroom than the nursery quarters she had previously occupied on an upper floor. That same fateful evening her path and Gregory's had crossed for the first time. Now convention was separating her from him, when she wanted nothing more than to be with him by night and day while she was in London. Instead, for Sofia's sake, she could not stay under his roof. It would slight her stepmother's hospitality and desire for her company,

441

quite apart from any private pain it might cause Sofia to know that they were together in endless intimacy.

Gregory called at Milton Square in good time that evening. He found Irene attired in mint-green satin, a princess line that moulded her to the hips, her only jewellery the special emerald brooch. Sofia was statuesque in deep blue velvet, sparkling in a parure of diamonds. At the Opera House they had to wait a few minutes for Maria and her husband to arrive. When the couple did appear across the crimson-carpeted foyer thronging with people, Maria's bravely smiling face could not disguise the tear-swollen pinkness of her lids, and Leon, although not drunk, was not completely sober. He was, Irene thought at first glance, the most handsome man she had ever seen, with a profile of god-like splendour, marvellous bones, and a smile to charm birds out of a tree. But the sensual mouth was cruel, and his eyes under black brows, apart from a flicker of lustful appreciation at her looks and figure, were as stony as their colour.

"You live in Monaco, I understand," he said to Irene as they went up the wide staircase together.

She raised her eyebrows questioningly. "Surely you must know from Maria that I have a jeweller's shop at Monte Carlo?"

He snapped his fingers in forced recollection. "Yes of course. Didn't you make her a necklace or brooch or some other trinket for our wedding day?"

Irene glanced sideways at him. Was he mocking

her? Surely he had not forgotten completely what his bride had worn for their marriage. "I designed the bridal crown."

"So you did. I remember now." His temporary spate of forgetfulness appeared to have been quite genuine. "Shall you be in London long? Maria made me bring her to England mainly to renew her friendship with you."

"I'm only staying ten days. I'm here to buy gems."

He regarded her with a frown of disbelief. "Don't tell me you live at the resort all year round? It must be a dreary place out of season."

"I don't find it so. It's quieter of course. Several of the hotels close, but the Casino has a summer season for those prepared to face the hotter weather."

"God! I can picture that dreadful herd. Peasants aping their betters at reduced rates in third-class hotels and playing sous at the tables. Mercifully the Salon Privé is never opened to riff-raff."

Irene breathed deeply. "That depends on how you define *riff-raff*. To my mind it encompasses anyone who is ill-natured and inconsiderate to others, whatever their station in life."

His jaw hardened. "Am I to believe that you hold rebellious social views, Miss Lindsay?"

"Many women do. Unfortunately too many of them are afraid to voice their opinions."

"But you are not?"

"No." She tilted her chin in exhilaration. "I can say, do, and think what I like. I'm a working woman holding my own in a man's world. It's what I always wanted and what I have achieved."

They had reached the head of the staircase, and she drew aside to join Gregory as he came level with her. He gave her an expressive look that ignited a swift and familiar flame within her. It brought home to her the knowledge that she would have staked all her achievements in a bid to belong to him for the rest of her life. So much for female emancipation, she thought wryly to herself. Its Achilles' heel was the power of love.

When the superb performance of *La Bohème* was at an end, the five of them travelled in two carriages to Rules in Maiden Lane. There was a slight hold-up outside, because a royal personage had arrived to sup with a lady, but by the time they entered he had gone through a secluded entrance with her to a private upper room.

They were shown to a table that had been reserved for them. The decor was richly red and gold with ornately framed mirrors at a level that reflected the aigrettes and jewelled hair-pieces of the elaborately coiffured women. It was an exclusive restaurant popular with high-society and theatrical personalities alike. Leon ate little and drank a great deal but seemed able to hold his wine well. Maria and Irene, having many snippets of news to exchange, talked to each other as much as they could, although on the whole the conversation at the table was general, covering a range of topics. It was when they were leaving that events took a disastrous turn. Suddenly filling the inner doorway through which they were to depart, was Lillian, fresh from her appearance that evening at the Gaiety. Her aigrette of pink ostrich feathers stroked the gilded lintel overhead, and since she was standing with arms akimbo, her silk-gloved hands resting on her hips, her ruched boa brushed against the mahogany jambs of the door on either side of her. With her sumptuous figure, as much revealed as it was concealed by diaphanous silver-beaded chiffon over pearly satin, she was a glorious, voluptuous sight. There was not a head within range that did not turn in her direction. Behind her loomed her escort, a tall man with a monocle on a black silk ribbon and a large black moustache.

"What a surprise!" she trilled mischievously. "Miss Lindsay! Gregory! You're not leaving! Allow me to present Herr Jurgens." She half turned, just enough to allow him to bow before filling the aperture with her floating furbelows again. "He insists that you and your delightful company join us for champagne, cognac, liqueurs, anything you please." It was a blatant ignoring of the fact that the gentleman in question had not opened his mouth on the subject. She similarly ignored Gregory's mannerly refusal of the tasteless invitation, fastening her violet-blue eyes on Leon, whose smiling appraisal made her preen. "You, sir!" she cried winningly, fluttering a hand prettily and theatrically in his direction, "you carry out the introductions. I am Lillian Rose of the Gaiety Theatre. Who are you?"

Leon recognized her for what she was, realizing that she was wreaking some savage little vengeance on at least two of those with him, and saw no reason to spoil her fun. If he was not mistaken, there would be something in it for him if he indulged her malicious little whim and if he saw what he had expected to be a dull time in London with his wife being considerably enlivened. Lillian Rose was like a ripe peach. She would taste as delicious as she looked. Bowing to her in his most courtly manner, he put her hand to his lips.

"I am Count Leon Romanov. At your service, madame. I have the honour to present my wife, Countess Romanov and Mrs. Lindsay."

"Charmed." Lillian gave one of her most graceful curtain-call curtseys, making an even greater travesty of the whole encounter.

Irene was fuming. Maria had gone deathly white. Sofia remained pale and dignified, inclining her head. "Good night, Miss Rose," she said pointedly, moving forward at a sweeping pace that gave Lillian no option but to draw aside.

The innocent Herr Jurgens, whose knowledge of the English language was limited and who had grasped nothing of what had taken place, bowed as the older woman and the two younger ones went past him. He received a sharp nod of courteous intent from the Englishman, whose face was furious as he stalked by. The Russian delayed long enough to whisper in Lillian's truly shell-shaped ear. Whatever he said made her purse her lips coquettishly, such a fashionable coyness in her attitude that Herr Jurgens took umbrage at this impertinent intrusion upon what was his evening with this lovely actress. It had already cost him a not inconsiderable outlay on a pair of superb ruby ear-rings purchased at Garrard, the Crown jewellers, which he had sent earlier to her dressing room, having ascertained that the acceptance of a piece of jewellery by a Gaiety Girl meant that she would at least sup with the donor, if nothing more. He glared after the Russian, who went hurrying away to catch up with the rest of the party. It was a further annoyance to him when he was informed that a while before his arrival, the King of England had taken the last private supper room.

There were no more evening engagements for Maria with her husband after his encounter with Lillian. He was at the Gaiety every night, where after watching the show from the same box, to which Lillian threw special glances, he would wait with a carriage at the stage door to take her out to supper. Crowds of top-hatted mashers with bouquets of orchids or roses besieged the area, and every beautiful girl who emerged, whether she was from the chorus line or was one of the "Big Eight," made her own special contribution to the scene. All paused on the stage-door steps—some to blow kisses with both hands; others to wave, take a bouquet, bow from side to side like a slender reed in the wind, and generally dazzle and inflame the hopeful stage-door johnnies. Lillian was particularly in demand. In the present show she had a leading part, appearing in one scene in a pair of pink silk pyjamas, which was highly daring. Each night when she appeared at the stage door, a roar of approbation went up. She acknowledged it by uncurling her arms and flinging them high above her head, arching her body as if for flight, her appreciation of the homage being both sensual and gluttonous.

It happened that Irene and Gregory were at Romano's when Lillian and Leon arrived together late one evening after the show. The orchestra struck up the song she had made popular in the pink-pyjama scene, and she smiled and nodded to the right and to the left as if she were royalty, following the bowing head waiter through to the table that Leon had reserved for them. Unfortunately it was not far from where Irene and Gregory were sitting, although due to some screening by potted palms, the newcomers had not sighted them.

"I'm sorry this had to happen, Irene," he said regretfully to her. "We seem to have been ill-fated on this London visit of yours. Don't let it spoil our last evening together."

"I won't," she declared stoutly, but they both knew that a blight had been cast across their last hours in each other's company. They had had far too little time alone. Nothing had gone right. It made her nervous and afraid. Maybe they had known too much happiness in their loving, more in a short while than most human beings had in a whole lifetime, and by the mere pattern of events, things were beginning to turn against them. It gave her a sense of foreboding that made her dread her parting with him on the morrow as much as if she were never going to see him again.

It could not be said that Sofia had tried to keep them apart. She was not of that nature in the least degree, but she had quite excitedly committed Irene ahead of her arrival in London to a number of meetings with old friends and entertainments given specially in her honour and to which Gregory was not invited; even if their relationship had been known, which it was not, his uncomfortable status as a married man without a wife would have precluded him. Then Irene's own business appointments took up a number of hours. Finally there was Maria, who found in Irene a sympathetic listener, being desperately in need of someone in whom she could confide. With Leon absenting himself from her side to go his own way in London, she made lonely demands on Irene's time that were impossible to refuse.

"There is no one at home I can turn to for advice," Maria had said. "Leon has cut me off from everybody I used to know, and we move only in his circles. The women despise me because I'm younger than the rest of them, not sophisticated as they are, and my interests are simple and childish in their eyes. As for the men, they go hunting and shooting and drinking and womanizing as if they and Leon had no homes or wives or, in some cases, children as well." She burst into tears. "I hate being married. It's a wretched and lonely state, not at all what I thought it would be. I loved Leon so much. I still love him."

"Have you had no joy in your marriage at all?"

There was a tearful nod. "For a few weeks of our extended honeymoon, everything was wonderful.

Then he became bored with me. He gets bored with everything and everybody after a while. He must always have new excitements, new diversions and"— her voice faltered—"new mistresses." A cry of appeal burst from her. "What am I do *do*?"

It distressed Irene that she had been unable to offer any solution to Maria's problem. She had let her friend talk and talk in the simple therapeutic release of long pent-up misery and despair. All she had heard made her loathe the man, who was presently sitting only a few yards away from her under cascading chandeliers, who held the sensitive and warmly loving nature of his young wife in such brutal disregard. She felt suddenly that she could no longer endure being under the same roof with him. He and Lillian were two of the same ruthless kind.

"Let us go," she said suddenly to Gregory, passing her fingers across her brow. "I want to walk in the fresh air. Just with you."

He summoned the waiter for the bill for their interrupted supper. As they rose from their chairs to leave, people also began to rise up at the tables nearby, a ripple of applause being taken up all around the restaurant. Irene gasped at what she saw. Leon was giving Lillian the ultimate accolade that any Gaiety Girl could receive from an admirer. He had removed her silver satin slipper from her foot and leaped onto a chair to drink champagne from it. Cheers and laughter and increased applause greeted his showy gallantry as he downed the contents and refilled it again. Irene and Gregory left without another glance.

Lillian regarded her champagne-soaked slipper ruefully as Leon knelt on one knee to slip it back onto her foot. "It's ruined," she pouted playfully, delighting in the sensation that had been caused. It added to her satisfaction to know that some other members of the Gaiety cast were present. Everyone would have heard about it by the morning. She was one of the esteemed few who had had a titled aristocrat drink from her slipper. All the world loved her! One day Gregory would love her again.

Leon was still kneeling in front of her, her damp slippered foot supported by his hands at her ankle and toe. "Tomorrow morning I shall see that you have a new pair of satin shoes for every year of your life so far."

"Twenty-five!" she said quickly.

"Each one shall have a diamond buckle."

Then Lillian regretted not having been able to state the extra few years she had held back.

Irene and Gregory walked along the embankment, his arm about her. The black water of the Thames lapped silver and gold with reflected light. "I know now that I can never return to live in London," she said sadly. "It's been my dearest hope that eventually I might leave Derek in charge of the Monte Carlo shop while I opened a head branch in the West End where I could be near you all the time."

"I've been sharing the same hope."

"I think we both know it would be a mistake. There's too much of your other life to come between

451

us in this city. I can't foresee our ever being together for more than a few days or a few weeks at a time."

"There is always the villa where we could make our home."

She shook her head. "I've told you why that is impossible. My opinion has not changed and it will not. I love you too much to court disaster."

"Remember that," he said in such a fervent tone of voice that she looked up into his face enquiringly and he gave her his explanation. "That you love me. As I love you."

Then she realized he shared her unspoken fears that outside influences were gathering to draw them apart against their will. She clung to him as he kissed her with a kind of passionate desperation as if she were already half lost to him.

It was no better next morning on a platform at Victoria Station as they faced each other in goodbye. Neither Sofia nor Maria suggested accompanying her, and she had been thankful to have the last minutes with Gregory on her own.

"Don't cry," he said softly.

"I'm not," she replied bravely. "It's just some of the morning dew from Hyde Park on my lashes."

They had driven that way to the station. He smiled at her courageous little joke. "That is what I thought it was," he gave back in the same vein. "But I didn't like to say."

Along the platform, doors were beginning to slam. The moment of departure had come. He kissed and hugged her so hard that her feet left the ground. Then the guard blew his whistle, and she sprang up into the first-class carriage. Gregory shut the door, and she let down the window to reach out a hand to him. He walked with her as the train began to move until their clasp loosened and parted. Their eyes still held. They watched each other out of sight.

All had gone well at the shop in her absence. Derek told her that the ante-room had proved invaluable. Although it was still off-season, several people had brought pieces to sell, all wanting cash for the gambling tables, and he had been able to conduct the deals in privacy. She looked at what he had bought, and Brigette showed her the entries in the ledger. He had kept to her policy of a fair price, and she expressed her satisfaction with everything.

"How did you enjoy the trip?" he asked her when she had finished telling him of the orders for stones that she had placed.

"It will be a long time before I go again," she said with a frown and did not elaborate. He looked at her keenly. She supposed he was making a guess that all had not gone well with Gregory, but naturally he refrained from saying anything more.

The season came again, the hotels reopening like great oysters to lavish luxury on all who came to stay within their portals. Madame Borisvinsky returned to her same balcony suite at the Hôtel de Paris. Once again she began to gather in gossip and all the new scandals as if she were able to be here, there, and everywhere, instead of being mostly confined to a chair within her own suite. She wanted to know when Sofia would be coming to Monte Carlo again. She had not surrendered her matchmaking efforts for her son and was disappointed when Irene was unable to give her any dates.

Without even seeing his villa completed and furnished, Gregory arranged by post with an agent that it should be rented out for the season. It was taken immediately by an Austrian baron and his wife. Irene, passing it once, felt a great wave of sadness when she reflected that she and Gregory had never known love within its walls. Now she was sure they never would, and the spacious villa would be a seasonal home for strangers forever more.

It was no fault of Gregory's that he had been unable to make the journey to view the villa. Fabergé had called on him again for advice and guidance throughout the first months of the London branch's opening. Gregory wrote half seriously, half jokingly that she should throw up everything and return to London to be his right hand at Fabergé's again. In its way it was an expression of a deep longing that they should make a fresh start, taking up at the very point when they first began to acknowledge to themselves their love for each other. But the clock could not be turned back. She knew that if there were the least chance of their being able to do so, she would have gone to him by the next boat and train. Unfortunately the reality of how it would be for them in London was too painful to consider ever again.

She concentrated on her work. Her designing absorbed her thoughts and prevented them from drifting. Derek, since becoming manager, promoted another craftsman to his place on the bench. He excelled in his new role. Customers liked him. He knew how to sell; he was consultant in the workshop during any emergency, always ready enough to don his bench apron if his skills should be needed; and he also took over completely a task which Irene had never liked, that of buying jewellery from gamblers with nothing left to stake. He spared her from unpleasantness when one seller returned to buy back her own jewels after a win and was outraged at having to pay a little more than she had been allowed originally on the items—which was an accepted and fair procedure. There was a further scene into which Irene was drawn, alerted at her drawing table upstairs by the uproar, when a drunken man mistook her shop for another, insisting that he wanted to buy back his Fabergé cigarette case. She knew that no such item had been entered in the books, because she and Brigette went over the books together each week, and everything was accounted for in detail; but the man would not be persuaded and afterwards reeled about in the street, still shouting abuse. Derek was upset that he had not been able to protect her from the drunken insults.

"Don't worry about it, Derek," she said to him. "Such incidents are bound to happen in a place like Monte Carlo. I just hope the poor man remembers where he left his cigarette case when he is sober again."

It seemed as if her wish came true, for the

obstreperous man never returned, and the smooth running of the shop was not disrupted again. She began to appreciate even more having Derek in charge with Brigette's clerical efficiency as an extra bonus, since it allowed her to spend quiet hours designing and to keep appointments at any time when important customers wished to see her at their hotels or villas or, not infrequently, on board their yachts.

It was due to a delay in her being ferried back from a yacht lying at anchor when she arrived late at Madame Borisvinsky's suite. The old lady liked a flutter at the tables on Saturday evening, and Irene was told by the maid that Madame Borisvinsky had become impatient with waiting and had gone ahead to the Casino, hoping Irene would join her. But when Irene approached the roulette table where her elderly friend usually sat, there was no sign of her. Moreover, the table was *créped* completely in black, a sign that the bank had been broken by a lucky punter. The air was still vibrant with the excitement of those who had watched the play, but who had now withdrawn to other tables.

"Irene! Come here!" She turned to see Madame Borisvinsky leaning on her two sticks, a little distance away and hurried over to be greeted with an account of what had been happening. "My dear child! You missed such a sight. One of your countrymen had staked modestly when the Casino opened at four o'clock and had been playing ever since I arrived here an hour ago. I found people piling their chips on his numbers. He took such chances. We all held our breath, but it seemed he could not lose. The wheel was positively charmed by him. Then he broke the bank!'' The old lady chortled with delight. "Everyone wanted to buy him drinks and make a fuss of him. They always think a winner's luck is going to rub off on them. He drank one glass of champagne, refusing any more and settled down at *trente-et-quarante* but with less luck I am afraid. Let us go across and see how he is faring now.''

As they approached the *trente-et-quarante* table where a thick crowd of spectators had gathered, a groan and a shaking of heads showed that the punter's luck was truly on the wane. At least he was having the good sense to withdraw. People parted, a chair was pushed back, and the punter in full evening dress came into view, a couple of *demi-mondaines* keeping close by, for there was always a number of them on the lookout for gamblers who had come into the money.

"Derek!" Irene exclaimed in disbelief.

The *demi-mondaines* dropped back as he came to her, his face flushed with excitement and gave her a warm kiss. "This is it, Irene! I'm on to it! I've just lost rather heavily, which was a foolish error of judgement. I should have withdrawn at the first setback. I'll know another time.'' He patted his evening coat at the chest level of his wallet pocket. "I'm still seventeen thousand pounds the richer for a stake of four hundred pounds in good English money. What do you say to that?''

"I congratulate you," she said, still amazed. Then she presented him to her companion, who congratulated him in turn. He bowed to Madame Borisvinsky. He had always known how to conduct himself in polite society, and in his white bow tie and silk-lined coat he looked as if he truly belonged to the Casino setting or any other of equal opulence.

"You may help me to a table, young man," the old lady said to him. "Then I will allow you to have Irene's company for a little while." She wagged a finger at him. "On condition that you bring her back to me."

When this was done, Derek and Irene took seats on one of the brocaded sofas in another room, more champagne being brought to him with the compliments of the management in view of his success. When it had been served, he raised his glass to her, and she responded.

"You're wondering how I gained admission," he said with amusement. "I have you to thank. As soon as you moved me from the craftsman's bench, I went up a notch socially. Not, I grant you, high enough to gain an *entrée* to the Casino on my own merits, but one of the shop's customers, for whom I had some special work done quickly to oblige her, smoothed the way for me with a word of her own."

"When did this happen?"

"Yesterday."

"You've lost no time."

"It's what I've been waiting for ever since I came to Monaco."

"Is that why you came in the first place?"

"No. There was another reason."

She did not want to hear him say it. For her, all that had been between them might have happened in another age, another century. "I suppose you'll be leaving now that you've made a little fortune."

"Oh, no." He shook his head firmly. "Tonight was only the beginning."

She felt suddenly hollow with apprehension. "Derek! This is perilous ground. Haven't you learned anything from all the disasters that have beset you each time you've found yourself in debt? Do you think I haven't been able just by looking at you to tell whenever a horse at Nice hasn't won? You're no more lucky these days than you were in London."

"I've had a number of wins. How else do you think I found an adequate stake to start me off here?"

"Yes, but it's always been like that. Up and down. Mostly down."

His mouth set stubbornly. "What about tonight?"

"A fluke! Beginner's luck! Call it what you like."

"I'm only a beginner at the Casino," he corrected her. "I've played other wheels in my time." His gaze roved back hungrily in the direction of the gambling rooms. "But here I'm going to really make it. I feel it in my bones. It's something a gambler knows. I've worked it out exactly. A system in which luck and common sense play an equal part. It's different with racing. There one has to rely on some damn jockey not pulling it or a horse retaining its stamina over the last stretch. At the Casino it is between the wheel and me.'' He spoke through his teeth with savage satisfaction, his eyes glinting on a sense of power.

She put a hand on his arm. "There isn't a foolproof system for anyone. People have tried everything before you. There was the Yorkshire engineer who knew that machines always have a bias, and he had only to take a record of the winning numbers of each roulette wheel to discover the secret of success. He did win unceasingly until the wheels were switched at the tables. Now they're all manufactured in the Casino's basement and checked every day before the Casino opens. Some people had tried pushing losing stakes onto a winning number after the wheel stopped. Shortly before you came to Monte Carlo, a man staked on the hymn numbers at church the previous day and broke the bank. Afterwards so many went to the church to write down the numbers to follow suit, that the hymn numbers are now only announced during the service. It's a crazy kind of gold rush. Take your winnings and stay away. Then you will really be a winner."

He smiled at her in a way that showed nothing she had said had had any effect. "I've told you. I know exactly what I'm doing. I'll increase my stakes when I'm winning, as I did this evening, and I'll stop as soon as my luck shows sign of waning or if I sink to half my starting capital."

"But you didn't stop. After changing your chips at the *caisse*, you went on to lose at *trente-et-quarante*."

"I'll not do that again. It was a slip." He grinned at her. "A Casino beginner's slip, shall we say? An over-eagerness."

"It's that which could be your downfall!"

His confident air remained unassailed. "Look at it this way, Irene. Most punters who double their stakes on losing, invariably find themselves beaten at the post by the bank's maximum. I'll not let that happen to me. This evening I had no worries, the ivory ball was my devoted friend, but suppose I had to make a brave stand? It's simple. Double up to the limit for the next three turns of the wheel, whatever the result, win or lose, and then revert to one's original stake. It's simple, isn't it? All it needs is luck, and that can be wooed by one who dares."

"That system isn't new, so don't pretend it is. It was tried out about thirteen years ago by Charles de Ville Wells, who became the subject of the song about the man who broke the bank at Monte Carlo. You've forgotten one ingredient essential to that sort of success."

"What's that?"

"Self-discipline. De Ville Wells had an iron will and didn't allow himself to be tempted into one false move."

"Neither shall I."

"Derek, please," she urged, utterly unconvinced by his boast, "invest what you have won this evening into shares that will give you an income for the rest of your life. You can even buy into the business, if that would give you a better incentive, or start one of your own. Think of Brigette, not of yourself. She worries about you. Sometimes for days she is pale and anxious and hardly opens her mouth. Now more than ever she needs to know that the endless threat of insurmountable debts is removed from her once and for all."

Some of his ebullience was ebbing from him. She thought her argument had got through to him, but when she would have continued to press home her advantage, he silenced her with an impatient gesture, his face quite changed. "What did you mean? Now more than ever?"

She hesitated. "Surely you know that she is pregnant?"

He snapped his head back in a menacing glare of disbelief and spoke in a dangerously soft voice. "That's not true. It can't be. She's not very well at the moment. Strain and overwork, she told me."

"I doubt if that would cause her to be nauseous for the first couple of hours in the morning. I've told her to rest and come in a little later, but Brigette is too conscientious for her own good."

He looked for a moment as if he might die of the force of rage that went through him. His hands balled into fists on his knees, and his colour surged and receded. "The damn silly cow!" he ground out.

Her anger flared. "Don't talk about your wife like that!"

"My wife?" He sprang to his feet, standing over her. "She's not my bloody wife! I'm not married to her! I would as soon put my neck in a hangman's noose! You're the only one I've ever wanted in my whole life!"

She got up from the sofa quickly and hurried after him as he went charging away from her, ignoring those newcomers offering their belated congratulations on his earlier triumph, the news of it still circulating. The next day it would be in the press. The Casino management liked to publicize the breaking of the bank, for it was encouraging to others who came to the tables.

She caught up with him in the terrace gardens, tugging at his sleeve to bring him to a reluctant halt. "You owe me an explanation," she demanded. He heaved a great sigh. There was a wrought-iron bench nearby, and he sank down on it, resting his elbows on his knees and propping his head dejectedly in his hands. "I've been a fool. I should have told you everything in the first place. Brigette and I were living together in Paris. What I spoke of as her dowry was, in fact, some money she had saved. She was good to me. She has always been good to me. Coming from a strait-laced background, it was natural that she should want it to be thought that she and I were husband and wife. It was not important to me, just as long as I wasn't committed to the fatal step of marriage. I suppose it's something to do with wanting to retain a sense of freedom, of always knowing that if worst came to worst, nobody had the power to tie me down. Yet I tell you again, Irene, I would have married you if you hadn't put your principles and your career and everything else before your feelings for me. Maybe I'd have changed too. Given up gambling. Been the sort of man you wanted. Who knows?"

"I put nothing before my feelings for you at the

time. I only wanted everything to be open and above-board when we did marry. Why did you lead me to believe that Brigette was your wife when we met again?"

He let his hands drop and raised his head to turn a weary face towards her. "Pride. Conceit. My damned ego, perhaps. Call it what you like. Arthur Lucas had told me there was some man in your life to whom you were engaged. He's a romantic old fool. Complicated relationships are beyond his understanding. I suppose I had some idea of letting you think I hadn't been lonely after you let your father throw me out of your life." His voice became bitterly accusing. "Why didn't you come with me that night?"

She sat down slowly on the bench beside him. "I don't know. I suppose I was too shocked and frightened to reason properly. But at dawn next morning, I left the house with a piece of hand luggage to go anywhere in the world with you."

"Irene!" His tone changed to a note of wonder, and he half reached for her until he saw there was nothing tender in her expression.

"I uncovered a web of your bachelor existence that I had not known about." Now it was she who was looking back with anguish to that time of hurt and disillusionment.

"Oh." He frowned and pressed his lips together.

"In addition to passing your time with your landlady's daughter, who has good reason never to forget you," she said succinctly, "I discovered you

464

had alternated your time between a Gaiety Girl and me."

"She meant nothing to me," he protested. "Nothing at all. I knew Lillian Rose. She and I were kids together in the same street. It happened that I'd called at the Gaiety now and again for a chat with her about old times, and maybe I did flirt a little with one of the girls in the chorus. It wasn't easy to get past the stagedoor keeper, and I liked to saunter in at Lillian's invitation while all the mashers had to wait outside."

She was staring at him. "You know Lillian?"

"Yes."

"Then you must know that the man I love is her estranged husband."

"Yes. I didn't know it until I heard Arthur mention him by name in the workshop one day. Then I began to grasp the situation. What went wrong when you were in London in September? Is it over?"

She shook her head, looking down at the filigree ring she was twisting on her finger. "No. I love him more than ever. But we're drifting apart, not through any wish of his or mine. Lillian won't agree to a divorce. His life is centred in London, and mine is here. There is no future that I can see."

"Then you'd better accept the situation as it is. Lillian will never allow a stick to stir up the muddy waters of her past. She is married, and she wants to stay married. In her poor little mind, she adores respectability, which makes her much like Brigette in that respect. You wouldn't think to see Lillian on the stage these days that once she went without shoes on her feet. At the age of ten she was put in an orphanage. I suppose I'm the only one anywhere who knows her from those days, except—" he broke off.

"Except whom?"

"Somebody she cared about once. A seaman twice her age. His old mother was in the workhouse, and when Lillian was fifteen, she was put to scrubbing floors there. The seaman took her away with him to Liverpool. Then he went back to sea, and she tried her luck at singing, first in the streets and then at some questionable theatre. That's where her career on the stage began. Now you can understand why she has a past she wants to keep under the carpet."

"None of that need ever come to light."

"It's a risk Lillian would never take."

Irene straightened her spine where she sat. "After all this talk, my affairs are the same as before. What of yours? Have you decided to follow any of my advice?"

"I'm making no promises."

"What about a promise to Brigette?"

"Marry her, you mean?" He was spared having to give an answer. There was a tap of approaching feet, and Brigette herself came along the path. She slowed her pace with surprise at seeing the two of them on the park bench. She had a short cape over her shoulders, neat as always in a light blouse, dark skirt, and stockings. It would have been easy to mistake her for a nursemaid attached to one of the grand families staying in the resort. Her oval face was very pale and tense.

"What happened, Derek?" she asked agitatedly. "I couldn't wait at home any longer. I wasn't going to try to enter the Casino dressed like this, but I wanted to be near you."

Derek rose leisurely from the bench, no longer ill-humoured. Irene was glad that their talking appeared to have calmed him down. But then he had always been like that, a volcanic flash of temper which usually went as quickly as it had come. Reaching Brigette, he put up his hands and removed both the tortoise-shell combs from her hair, causing it to cascade in its dark auburn splendour over her shoulders and down to her waist. Then he took her face between his hands, burying them into her hair, and looked down into her face.

"I won—and lost. But I've enough left to buy you anything you want in the whole world."

She blinked at him in half-frightened bewilderment as if she had lived too long in uncertainty to accept that her scrimping and saving might be temporarily abandoned. He kissed her tremulous mouth and then flung an arm about her shoulders to lead her away. Irene looked after them. Derek was a strange man; there was much good in him, much weakness, and a great deal of conceit and deceit. Maybe he had met his match in Brigette. No doubt the baby was a trump card, and no matter what he might say, in Brigette he had found the anchor that he needed.

Seventeen

As always when the season hit Monaco with its full force, the resort's character changed overnight. The lives of those who lived there all year round, including the quiet colony of British residents existing on moderate means, some of whom had become Irene's customers, were completely disrupted as if an exotic wave made up of golden *louis* had come up from the harbour to engulf the whole principality. Derek took advantage of the rush of business at the shop, together with his own overtime in the workshop when the showroom was closed, to avoid any arrangements for a marriage with Brigette, who became if anything quieter and more taciturn as her pregnancy gently advanced. She wanted a name for her baby, but she did not want to lose Derek through such a demand. He had come into her life unexpectedly, disrupting her conservative, moral existence, and he was likely to take off with the same speed if she pressed too hard. Only he knew what she had done for him. Every standard and principle to which she had held dear she had sacrificed for him, and she was so conditioned to obeying his every whim that she thought it was well he had not told her to walk to the end of the harbour and jump in the sea after learning that she was pregnant.

Irene, realizing how many hours Brigette spent at home on her own, was uncertain whether she should condone Derek's long periods of overtime, even though it was highly beneficial to the business. He often worked until midnight. Sometimes Irene was in bed reading when he finally left, Brigette usually coming to meet him, and she would hear their voices in quiet conversation when the final padlocking was done and they walked away out of the courtyard. He was always first for the unlocking in the morning, usually managing to do some work before the rest of the goldsmiths arrived. Shortly before nine o'clock, he would change his working overall for his morning tailcoat and check that everything was as it should be in the showroom.

The only reason why Irene hesitated to question his enthusiasm for work was that when not at the workbench he was at the gambling tables. His system had come to nothing, and within a month he had lost the large sum of money he had won. With the eternal optimism of the habitual gambler, he was working out another system which he declared to be entirely foolproof. How much Brigette had been able to salvage from the original winnings, Irene had no idea. There was certainly no change in her attire to indicate any personal indulgence, and her working skirt had been let out slightly at the waist to accommodate the increase of an inch or two that was not yet obvious to those who did not know of her condition. Irene decided to sound her out on whether or not she wanted Derek's overtime curtailed.

With this purpose in mind, Irene went to the office one morning. Derek had just gone into the ante-room with a woman customer whose neatly costumed back she had glimpsed briefly, which meant there would be no chance of her talk with Brigette being interrupted by him. Whenever he was present, the woman became more and more incapable of answering for herself.

"How are you today?" Irene inquired.

"Quite well, thank you," Brigette said in her reserved manner.

Irene sat down and after a preliminary discussion about how some letters should be answered, she spoke to Brigette of Derek's long hours. "I had no idea he would want to continue to such an extent in the workroom," she said. "At first he only helped out in an emergency. Now it appears to have become part of his daily routine."

"He has to do whatever he wants." Brigette spoke in her flat, subdued tones. "Being in the showroom and wearing nice clothes suits him very well, but if he chooses to spend time at the bench there is nothing whatever I can do about it." An expression of mingled despair and resignation passed over her face.

"I thought when we came here from Paris that it would be a chance to put everything of the past behind us with the Longchamps racecourse far away, but Derek can't change. The only difference here is that we haven't had creditors screaming at us for money. What will happen if he loses far beyond his means at the Casino?"

Irene had found Brigette's veiling of lashes over every glance somewhat irritating, but now she comprehended that the mannerism was a shield against the exposure of inner distress. "Derek will be given a spell of grace in which to settle his debts," she explained, "particularly in view of his having once broken the bank, but if he fails to pay in full within an alotted time, he will be barred from entrance. Is that what you're hoping for?"

Brigette gave a weary shake of her head, looking downwards as she linked and unlinked her fingers. "It would make no difference. He would simply revert to wagering on horses as he did previously. I've seen Derek crying and desperate and shaking at what he has lost, full of resolve never to gamble again, but his promises mean nothing. He is forever trying to gamble his way out of the very problems he has gambled himself into, but he can't see it in that light."

"I realized a long time ago that you are ensuring that a home is kept together with your wages."

Brigette nodded. "He sees his own earnings as gambling money, never in terms of food, rent, or other responsibilities."

"That is why he works such long hours then? Simply to earn more to gamble more."

Brigette's long-lashed gaze shifted. "I never get a sou of it."

"Would you like me to restrict his overtime? Then maybe you would benefit by his spending more hours with you instead."

"He would only reduce his stakes at the gambling tables, not increase his time with me. When not at the workbench, he is at the Casino. That is why I come to meet him late at night as I do. Quite often I can persuade him to go straight home with me; otherwise he goes to the tables."

Irene sighed with exasperation at Derek's feckless-ness. "Don't you ever lose your temper with him?"

"It would do no good. I've learned never to argue. It only drives him from me. At the back of his mind, he knows that if he ever gave up gambling he would be left with things he didn't like about himself, his life, and even his past. Now he has the extra burden of fatherhood to face, which he bitterly resents as a threat to his freedom."

"Is there anything I can do to help?"

Brigette's reaction to the offer was alarming. Seemingly caught off guard, her brown eyes met Irene's gaze in a direct stare, the pupils dilating as if in guilty horror at the idea. "No! Nothing!" she exclaimed harshly, moving sharply in her chair as if on the point of taking flight at the prospect.

Irene was taken aback. "I wasn't trying to interfere."

Brigette recovered herself, lashes lowering again. "I realize that. Please let us speak no more about Derek."

Irene left the office feeling uneasy. Why should Brigette have reacted with such vehemence to her wish to help? It was as if the young woman's conscience had been assailed. But for what reason? Shaking her head in puzzlement, she went upstairs to resume work, picking up some personal mail that had been left on a side shelf for her.

Instead of going straight to her drawing table, she went across to the window seat, opening the first letter eagerly, having recognized Gregory's handwriting. She began to read even before she sat down, her gaze glued to the page. He was coming to see her shortly. Joy mingled with sudden apprehension. How would it be between them when they were together again? Would the shadow of circumstances beyond their control fall across them as it had done in London? She wanted to believe it would be otherwise, but the nagging doubt remained, exacerbated by his warning in another paragraph that there was every likelihood that Lillian would be in Monte Carlo at the same time. The current show at the Gaiety was closing, and she would be at liberty to return to her favourite resort.

Irene lowered the letter pensively. She knew a little more than he did in that respect. Maria and Leon Romanov were due to arrive soon on their yacht for an indefinite sojourn at Monte Carlo. Maria had written a while ago that her husband had been in correspondence with Lillian Rose since meeting her in London. It was her dearest hope that nothing would come of it, but she feared that they planned to meet again at the first opportunity.

A slight shiver made Irene turn as if to close the open window by which she sat, but she refrained, knowing it was not the draught that had set a chill upon her. It was something more, a curious premonition that events were gathering towards a decisive and traumatic time in her life. Even the people closest to her, or with some other influence on her fate, had come or were about to come back into her existence. Gabrielle had just reinstalled herself in her grand apartment. Sofia, presently in St. Petersburg again, was due to make an appearance on the Côte d'Azur at any time. Most important of all, she and Gregory were about to face their ultimate future. She shut her eyes quickly as if to keep at bay any imagined portent of disaster that might be hovering. When she opened them again, the room was as it had been before. Nothing was amiss. Only her strained face reflected back at her from a mirror on the wall.

Out in the street below, footsteps were emerging from the shop. She glanced down automatically. The customer from the ante-room was being seen into her carriage by Derek, who was giving his best managerial bow, coat-tails swirling, the sun glinting on his fair hair.

"It is always a pleasure to do business with you, Mr. Ryde," the woman said, her face hidden from

Irene's view by the wide brim of her feathered hat as she seated herself. Then her white-gloved fingertips danced lightly against the side of the leather purse that she was holding upright on her lap. If Irene had not been at window height, which enabled her to look directly down into the carriage, she would not have seen the little gesture that implied satisfaction.

"I'm honoured, madame," Derek replied.

The carriage drew away, and he went back into the shop. Although Irene's mind was more on her letter than anything else, she registered that he had undoubtedly bought a piece of jewellery from the woman in what had obviously been a transaction agreeable to both sides in the shop's best tradition. The arrangement with Derek was that if Irene was absent or otherwise engaged, he should conduct minor transactions himself on her behalf. He knew the limit she would go to on moderate pieces. Truly expensive items were another matter, and they would consult together on these, the final decision always being hers.

She was at her drawing table at work when Derek came upstairs to her at closing time, bringing an order that had just been confirmed for one of her designs. Taking the paper from him, she glanced through the details. Knowing that the male customer wanted the item for his courtesan, she was unintentionally reminded of what she had seen from the window at an earlier hour.

"What did you buy today?" she asked, almost as a matter of course.

"I bought nothing today," he replied. "Why do you ask?"

She glanced up at him in surprise. He was leaning both hands on the edge of her table, his arms straight, his expression faintly puzzled at her query. She sought to refresh his memory.

"You were showing a woman into the ante-room this morning as I came downstairs to go into the office."

He nodded casually. "Oh, you mean Madame Clementi. That's right. But I didn't buy. She had a few pieces to sell, but the gems were not up to our standard."

She returned her gaze to the order in her hand, but the writing danced before her eyes and she could no longer focus. Derek was lying to her. Lying to her as he had done in the past, when there had been other women in his life and she had gullibly assumed herself to be the only one. Now he was lying in another sphere, but with the same aplomb, the same devastating plausibility. She did not doubt that he was on tenterhooks at her unexpected question, but none of it showed in his pleasing face or in his relaxed stance.

A sick dread, which had been with her ever since she had received Gregory's letter, was seeping through her veins. If she had not witnessed that significant tapping of fingers made by the woman on her purse, she would not have doubted his statement for one moment. For all his faults, Derek had always been honest in dealing with the costly stones and precious metals within his charge. He had been honest in her father's employ and honest in hers. She knew of innumerable times when it would have been easy for him to have acquired something valuable without the least suspicion falling on him, but he was always scrupulous in accouting for everything. What he had done this day was an old trick in the jewellery trade, one that was not expected of trustworthy employees, still less from one whom she thought of as an old friend. He had secured a good purchase, probably at a bargain price and had paid for it out of his own pocket, thus depriving the business of its rightful share of the transaction. It was a petty fraud. Judging by the remark she had overheard, it was not the first he had carried out.

"Has Madame Clementi been to the shop before?" She was giving him the chance to open up, to tell her the truth.

"Yes, I think she has. Not to sell though or I would have remembered." He came to stand closer to her, looking over her shoulder at the paper she held. "Is there any great rush for that order?"

He had changed the subject. She wept inside, angry and disappointed with him.

That night, when everything was shut up and silent, she went down to the office and looked through the ledgers that kept account of purchases from customers. Everything was in order. Naturally Madame Clementi's name was conspicuous by its absence. She closed the ledgers again and sat thoughtfully for a while, mulling over her conversation with Brigette. It became painfully obvious that Derek was being protected by the woman who loved him. After showing Madame Clementi out from the ante-room to her carriage, he must have gone into the office to let Brigette know that on this occasion there was nothing to be entered in the books.

Abruptly Irene sat forward in the chair and slammed a fist down on the desk. How dare he! How dare Brigette pander to this sideline! No wonder she had had the grace to look discomforted when given an offer of help. They were in league together! Then Irene's rage ebbed again, and she heaved a great sigh. Considering Brigette's complete devotion to him, how could anything else be expected other than her willingness to fall in with anything he wanted to do. It also gave full explanation as to why there had been no debt-collectors screaming at his door, as Brigette had phrased it. With private transactions going on, he was able to keep abreast of his debts, selling his purchases elsewhere and using the cash to keep his creditors at bay, even if he was not able to pay them in full.

Leaving the office, Irene went slowly back upstairs. She was heavy-hearted. She could not challenge Derek without proof, for he would deny or evade everything as he had done today. At least he did not appear to be taking advantage of people's need to sell, which would have meant an unwarranted loss of goodwill towards the shop. Or was he? She recalled the anger of a woman a while ago, who had returned to repurchase her jewellery, which fortunately had not yet been disposed of, and who was livid at having to pay more than she had received. The question now was how much more? Was it in excess of the token cost of handling? If so, it meant there was a false entry in the book. Then there was the drunken man who declared, apparently in error, that he had sold his Fabergé cigarette case to the shop and wanted it back. But there had been no record of the deal. Admittedly, Madame Clementi had sounded satisfied. Excessively so, now that the matter was considered in a new light. Had Derek charmed the woman into believing each time he bought from her that he was paying above the market value? No less harm could result if she should discover that she had been duped.

Finally, Irene had to face the fact that the woman might have been disposing of stolen goods. Greed abounded in any place where money was won and lost so easily as in Monte Carlo; jewel thieves were active anywhere in the world when valuable jewellery was flaunted and displayed.

She could not take on the hateful task of awaiting concrete evidence that Derek was not giving her the loyalty she had expected of him. For his sake and her own, she would take the step of eliminating the opportunity for him to make private deals, which would give him warning at the same time. Nothing would make her believe that he intended any harm towards her by purchasing goods he suspected of being stolen, but if he was taking such a risk now and again, he was endangering not only her livelihood but the good name of the business she cherished so dearly.

Early next morning, she confronted him in the workshop before the rest of the craftsmen arrived. He was at the workbench.

"After what you told me yesterday about Madame Clementi bringing a brooch of poor value to us," she said to him, "I have decided that no more purchases shall be made of jewellery below the line that needs my consent. In that way, I can maintain my high standards of buying and selling."

He looked up from the filigree work he was engaged in, his attitude one of complete unconcern. "Very wise. I had thought several times of advising you to make that stand, but you don't always take kindly to suggestions on policy." His grin was disarming, and his eyes twinkled.

Derek, Derek, she thought, have I made a mistake about you after all? Then she said, "One of my chief worries is that stolen goods might penetrate our security if too much buying from outsiders continues."

If he was aware of being severely warned, he did not show it, simply giving a dismissive gesture to emphasize that it was an unlikely possibility. "I don't think you have any need to worry on that score," he assured her. "The reputation of this shop shines forth, as Shakespeare would have said, like a good deed in a naughty world. There are plenty of receivers of stolen goods on the Riviera without tricks being tried on honest traders."

Her doubts about him were ebbing, but she could

not leave the matter there. For her own peace of mind, she would check on the identity of Madame Clementi and try to discover if she moved in circles that were at all dubious.

At the first opportunity she asked Gabrielle if she knew a certain Madame Clementi. Her grandmother pondered and then shook her head. "She is not a *demi-mondaine* as far as I know. Where is she staying?"

"I've no idea. It is just that she came into the shop, and I'm interested in finding out more about her."

As she might have expected, she had more luck with Madame Borisvinsky.

"I know whom you mean," the old lady said at once. "A nice enough woman. She is staying at one of the minor hotels and comes to the Casino more to be seen at the tables than because she can afford even a modest stake. I have sat next to her a couple of times. She is one of the unhappy and usually respectable band of husband hunters that haunt the Riviera resorts."

"Whatever do you mean?"

"She's on the lookout for a well-to-do husband. I can recognize the type immediately. Monte Carlo in particular is full of such women. Many are widows; some are divorcées tired of being ostracized in their own social circles. They eke out their savings for a season, some going as far as to sell their inferior jewellery piece by piece, and even their clothes as the weeks progress, simply to settle their hotel bills and stay long enough to catch their prey. A good many impoverished and disappointed women leave Monte Carlo at the end of a season with nothing to show for the saddest gamble of all.''

"You are sure Madame Clementi is one of these?''

"I am positive. She is already wearing the same evening gown far too often, which suggests that most of those she arrived with are at the pawnbroker's.''

Irene was overwhelmed with relief that her worst fears as to why Madame Clementi had been at the shop were banished. Derek had not been lying after all when he said that the brooch the woman had offered for sale had not been up to the shop's standard. That did not excuse him from buying it himself for a small return elsewhere, but it did absolve him completely from any link with stolen goods.

Madame Borisvinsky had delivered the welcome information while they were seated in the glassed-in section of the terrace of the Hôtel de Paris. They were awaiting the arrival of Maria and her husband Leon, whose yacht had anchored in the harbour a few hours ago.

The last rays of the setting sun had faded long since, the lights of Monte Carlo rivalling the stars. The old lady was, as usual, full of the gossip of the day. Lily Langtry had broken the bank two nights ago by winning twenty-five thousand pounds. A financier had been almost as lucky the previous evening, but he had been attacked in his room by an unknown assailant who had escaped with the loot. A Hungarian count had given a dinner party for a hundred guests, all of them dining off gold plates, some of which the Hôtel de Paris had had to borrow in haste from another hotel. She also informed Irene that Lillian Rose had arrived that afternoon with her entourage of maids, chauffeur, secretary, and the usual complement of young *beaux*.

So Lillian had come. Irene sighed to herself. It made her uneasy to know that Lillian was in the same resort, but perhaps it was even worse for Maria. Even as Irene thought of her friend, she saw her appear in one of the open doorways, glancing about searchingly with a despairing air. As Irene sprang up from her chair to hurry across to Maria, it struck her that her friend had the look of a dejected little ghost with her pale face, her whispy white chiffon gown and a boa of gossamer-light, silver-threaded ruffles that trailed from her arms.

"Dear Maria!" Irene exclaimed affectionately. "I've been looking forward to seeing you again. How are you?"

Maria was barely able to respond to Irene's greeting, her throat corded with the effort of keeping back tears. "I am on my own this evening. Leon bluntly refused to accompany me. He left the yacht earlier to meet Lillian Rose."

It was easy to see that she was on the brink of breaking down. Irene spoke encouragingly to her. "Be brave. Don't let anyone see you cry here. We can talk later."

Maria nodded, drawing on Irene's supportive strength, and together they went across to Madame

Borisvinsky. The old lady tactfully pretended not to notice that anything was amiss. She could be kindly in moments of crisis towards those she liked, just as she could be unmerciful in gossip about others whom she disliked. Keeping to safe ground, she talked to Maria about people whom they both knew at home, exchanging news and giving an air of normalcy to the evening.

Later, when the three of them were crossing the hotel lobby at the slow pace necessary for Madame Borisvinsky's awkward gait, it was unfortunate that Leon and Lillian appeared in the midst of those milling about, making their way together out of the hotel and seemingly with eyes only for each other. Maria jerked to a halt and stood as if transfixed, shaking so violently that even her teeth began to chatter. Irene grabbed her.

"Is your maid in your suite?" she said swiftly to Madame Borisvinsky.

The old lady nodded. "Yes. Quick! Get Maria up there at once. I will follow at my own speed."

Irene guided Maria to the nearest lift. The girl stumbled as if in a trance. Once inside the suite, Irene sent the maid running for a blanket and helped Maria to lie down on a *chaise longue*. She continued to shake after she had been covered up, and the tremours of shock were only beginning to ebb when Madame Borisvinsky appeared to find Irene holding a cup of warm tea for Maria to sip.

"Dear me, dear me," Madame Borisvinsky said, sitting down stiffly, resting her hands over the heads of both her sticks which stood propped together in front of her. "Men are the cause of all the trouble in this world. They never grow up. Always wanting a fresh toy, whether it is a better gun, or a faster carriage, or another woman." She looked sympathetically at Maria. "I went through exactly what you are going through now when I had been married less than a year."

"I wish I could die," Maria moaned in her distress. "I cannot go on."

"You can and you must," the old lady replied. "A sense of duty will sustain you. It means putting away many cherished, romantic dreams and coming to terms with your life as it is and how it has to be lived. Nothing is ever exactly as we would like it to be on this earth, but that does not mean it is impossible to know some happiness."

"There can be none for me." It was a desperate cry.

Madame Borisvinsky remained calmly reassuring. "It will come and in unexpected ways. I know what I'm talking about. I would give you a simple guideline, a golden rule that should never be broken. It is simply that you must keep your personal dignity inviolate. Never lower yourself to useless recriminations. That achieves nothing. The more guilty a man knows himself to be, the more angry he will become, blaming you for his troubles and his own weaknesses. Indeed, he will welcome the chance to make you his scapegoat and then will despise you for it. But," she added, holding up her forefinger, "if you keep your dignity as his wife and the mother of his

485

children, he will come to see you as his refuge, his haven, and his defence against women of whom he has tired, women who will attempt to keep his love by committing all the follies that you will have so carefully avoided. I tell you that you will win over them through retaining your own self-respect. Then your daily life with your husband will always be agreeable to him and to you. Moreover, it will be enriched by blessings impossible for you to visualize at this hour of betrayal."

Irene had turned away, drifting across to the window to look out at the moonlit sea while Madame Borisvinsky was delivering her homily. It was probably far better advice than she could have given Maria herself, spoken as it was through the voice of age and long experience. There was also a certain rapport between the two of them through inbred conditions of class, upbringing, culture, and customs. Maria, her face still a mask of anguish, had propped herself slowly up on one elbow and was beginning to question her elderly adviser falteringly. Irene knew that she herself could never subdue her spirit to such a compromise as Madame Borisvinsky was putting forward, but within the rigid framework of Russian society, it was probably the only way women in their position could retain their sanity and survive.

It was suggested that Maria should stay the night at the hotel, but she had recovered enough to insist on returning to the yacht. It seemed as if she wanted to be there when Leon returned, not to cause a scene, but to take the first step along the path she had been advised to follow. Irene stood by the harbour wall to watch her being ferried back to the long, white yacht, the dinghy crew as smart in their brass-buttoned uniforms, ribbons fluttering at the back of their sailor hats, as if they were from a warship of the Czar's own fleet. Maria looked small and very feminine in the midst of them. She waved twice before being lost to sight.

Irene turned her footsteps homeward. As she entered the courtyard at the rear of her shop, she saw there was a light glinting through the closed shutters of her apartment window. Only Gregory held a key other than herself. Her heart told her he was there. Yet she hesitated at the foot of the stone steps, afraid and uncertain, not knowing how it would be between them.

Almost as if he knew she must be there, the door opened abruptly to release a shaft of light and he came down the steps to stand half illumined by it, looking down at her. For a few moments neither of them spoke. Then he said, "Could you live in Holland? I'm thinking of closing the Hatton Garden office and relocating the main business to the diamond centre of Amsterdam."

She leaned back weakly against the stone wall, enervated momentarily by joy at what he had conveyed. He had found a way by which they could be together! Then she reached out as he came hurrying down to her in the moon shadows and took her in his arms. He kissed her until she wondered why such dark, premonitive fears had plagued her over the past months, for it seemed that after all there had been no grounds for them. All the way up the stone steps, he continued to kiss her lips and face, murmuring endearments to her, telling her that he missed her, longed for her, ached for her, and above all loved her with such intensity that he could not endure another parting such as they had just been through. She let him guide her into the apartment, her eyes shut in delicious rapture at their reunion. Then she surrendered gloriously to his love-making.

When morning came, the whole of Monte Carlo was gossiping about the latest scandal. Lillian, propped up by satin pillows in the sumptuous bed in her suite at the Hôtel de Paris, scanned the morning papers to see if a mention of it had come into print, even though common sense told her that the party at the Hermitage had reached its disastrous climax long after the local printing presses had closed down for the night. When her breakfast tray had been brought to her, she had been able to tell at once by her maid's face that word of it was circulating like wildfire throughout the whole palatial hotel. Not that the girl dared to say anything. Lillian was not above striking out in a fit of temper, and her personal servants had learned not to speak out of turn. But the sly glance before the respectful good-morning greeting and a settling of the tray on its supports across her knees had been like a shouted proclamation that all was known as far as she was concerned.

Letting the newspapers slip from the bed to the

floor, Lillian poured herself a cup of coffee and held it with both hands as she took a sip. If the Guv'nor got as much as a whiff of the scandal, he would be down on her like a ton of bricks. Why, oh why had she agreed to go to the party in the first place!

But she knew why. Her gaze went greedily towards the dressing table where, flanked by her Lalique crystal flagons, a white hollywood box gleamed its origins as Fabergé. Within reclined the most magnificent diamond necklace she had ever seen. When Leon had given it to her, fastening it about her throat, she had known orgiastic exultation in its glittering splendour. Her eyes had widened at her own reflection in the mirror. She had almost fainted with pride of possession and the enhancement of her own beauty. She had worn her golden hair high in its fashionable coiffure, leaving her long, swanlike neck free for the anticipated adornment that he had promised her. A necklace from Fabergé, he had said. Yet still she had been unprepared for the high collar of marvellous diamonds that had descended into a radiating spread of briolette pendants, the whole set in white gold, until not only her throat but her shoulders and the upper swell of her breasts sparkled dazzlingly. One exquisite pear-shaped briolette hung enticingly at her very cleavage, blazing like an icicle in the sun.

Only one thing spoiled the moment of presentation. She had seen his reflected face hardening with desire for her. So far she had kept him at bay. He should understand that Gaiety Girls had to be wooed long before they could be won. That banner of respect was her protection, her shield against persistent advances that she did not want to meet. Sex had never been anything more for her than a means to an end, this attitude going as far back as when she had first escaped drudgery in a workhouse, and it was entirely separate in her mind from love. Love was romantic, spiritual, and pure, content with a kiss, a languishing glance, a holding of hands, and above all that special quivering of adulation that came across the footlights to centre on her alone. All this was why her favourite swains were very young men, who were prepared to treat her as an unattainable goddess of the theatre, stealing a glove from her as a keepsake, removing the horses from her carriage, and manning the shafts themselves to pull her through the streets, and sending her innocent love poems in which they poured out their hearts. It was these youths she liked to keep in tow, for they were prepared to give her expensive gifts as expressions of their undying devotion without thought of reward and were easy to restrain if their feelings should overcome them.

Older men were less gullible and more demanding, but even they kept to the rules in their treatment of a Gaiety Girl—or did if they were gentlemen in the true sense of the word. Only Gregory had been able to make her glimpse a garden beyond the trees, but even he had not realized that his love alone could never assuage her hunger to be loved as only an audience could love her, her rightful place a pedestal with the stage-door johnnies at her feet.

If she could answer honestly when asked—as she so often was by reporters eager to interview a Gaiety Girl—who was the man in her life, she would not have said her husband, as she usually did for convention's sake, but the Guv'nor. He had taken her from the lowly boards of a humble music hall and set her in the limelight of the Gaiety without wanting anything in return. He was her ideal. Her own Greek god. And as far removed with his portly figure and rough looks as he could be from the handsome Romanov who was fondling her.

"We mustn't be late for the party," she had chided playfully, scooping his hands away. "You are the host, and I'm going to be the most envied woman on the Côte d'Azur when I appear in my necklace. You are the dearest man. Lillian is going to kiss you for her lovely, lovely gift."

She had known that the party was to be at the Hermitage and in its grand restaurant where she had dined before amid its pink marble pillars and gilded medallions. What she had not expected was that the other five Russian gentlemen present, two of them also of the Romanov clan, would have brought *demi-mondaines* to be their partners. She was deeply offended. No Gaiety Girl could sit at a table with whores. It was obvious that Leon, being a foreigner, had not understood the etiquette of the situation. She explained it all to him very prettily, saying that she would willingly dine alone with him at another table but could not join his present party.

He flew into a rage. She would have stalked away from him, but he seized her and with both hands on her shoulders had thrust her down into a chair at the table. It was then that she understood the contempt in which he held her. She was no more to him than someone to bed. He had estimated her price and paid it in the necklace. Now he would extract the full value, commencing with this hateful party.

To show her displeasure, she would not talk to him and ignored the others. Leon, in his disappointment with her behaviour, became very drunk. The best champagne was being served. The corks popped continually, and the waiters danced attendance. The party became increasingly rowdy, the *demi-mondaines* laughing in vulgar outbursts. Leon was so drunk he could hardly keep from falling out of his chair. Lillian felt sickened. Most harrowing of all for her was the knowledge that she had been recognized and was being whispered about by the other diners. The humiliation was terrible for her. She attempted to escape on the pretext of going to the ladies room, whereupon Leon came and leaned against the door, waiting for her, a glass of champagne in his hand. When she emerged, he escorted her back to her chair, and as she sat down, he bent his head to whisper in her ear exactly what he would do to her on the spot if she had any thought of slipping away from him.

Such was his drunken mood that she did not disbelieve that he meant what he had said, and so she shuddered with disgust. All inadvertently, he had mustered up old degradations for her, echoes of the past that no one had any right to revive for her again. She hated him. Hated and loathed him and, worst of all, feared him for the cruelty that lurked behind his handsome looks, something she had not suspected before the start of this dreadful fiasco of an evening.

The hour grew late. The restaurant emptied, some diners wanting to escape the vulgarity emitting from one section of the room and leaving before they had intended. Eventually only the Romanov party remained.

"Bring the rest of the champagne I ordered," Leon suddenly shouted to the head waiter. "Every bottle of it."

It came on trolleys. Leon seized an unopened bottle by the neck and hurled it against the nearest pillar where it smashed as if against the bow of a ship. He gave a wild whoop of triumph and gathered up another while his companions followed suit and the *demi-mondaines* cheered and clapped. The waiters stood by helplessly. At least the Romanovs always paid for any damage. Leon aimed next at a chandelier and scored a hit, crystal shards descending in showers. Another bottle hit the first of the mirrors, each of which he smashed in succession, the falling glass adding to the din.

Lillian seized her opportunity to edge away unnoticed in the uproar. Then she turned and ran as fast as she could on her thin silver heels into the lobby and down along the underground corridor that connected the Hermitage with the Hôtel de Paris.

She did not stop running until she reached the sanctuary of her own suite. As her maid helped her undress, she sobbed noisily with rage and humiliation, ignoring the girl's inquisitive expression. Never had she had such a terrible evening! Her only consolation was her beautiful necklace. She put it lovingly against her cheek for comfort and balm to her injured pride before she locked it away in its box.

Now going over the events of the night before as she lay propped against her satin pillows, she moaned aloud at the awfulness of everything. How could she have allowed herself to become involved with such a brutal man! His whispered threat in her ear had been enough to forewarn her that he would expect things of her that he would never demand from his wife. How dare he imagine that she, Lillian Rose of the Gaiety, was to be treated like a common doxy. She wanted to avoid meeting him ever again, but she was not going to leave Monte Carlo before she was ready just because he happened to be in the vicinity.

An uncomfortable thought struck her. What if he should demand the necklace back when he discovered that what he had expected to receive from her in return would not be forthcoming? Nothing on earth would make her surrender the necklace. It was a gift given freely to her without any stated obligation, and therefore it was her legal property. But would he see it in that light? For him it had been half of a bargain, her body to provide the other half for his lustful pleasure. Never!

Yet there was the dreadful possibility that he might waylay her and resort to physical violence of another kind in disappointed outrage. She put trembling fingers to her cheeks, always fearful of damage to her beauty. Suppose he should beat her face beyond repair. Her voice broke forth on a pent-up screech of horrified protest as though such danger already threatened her.

"No! No! No!"

Suddenly she knew what she must do. Even as her maid came running in to see what was the cause of such a shriek, Lillian thrust the breakfast tray aside and leaped out of bed. Ten minutes later she was emerging from the hotel into the sunshine. The mimosa trees were in full bloom, bobbing in a faint breeze as bright as her own golden head. The distance she had to cover was short, and she hurried there on foot. She reached Irene's shop and went inside quickly.

"I wish to see Miss Lindsay," she told an assistant.

Irene was in the office with Brigette and came at once. She was surprised to see Lillian and spoke coolly. "You have something to say to me?"

"Yes. In private."

Irene showed her into the ante-room. As soon as the door closed, they sat down opposite each other at the table. Irene, who had been expecting Lillian to launch forth on personal matters regarding her relationship with Gregory, was amazed when it appeared that she had simply come on a business basis. She set the Fabergé box on the table and opened it to reveal the marvellous necklace of immense value.

"How soon could you make me an exact replica? One that I could wear without the difference being spotted?" she demanded.

Irene removed the necklace from its velvet bed and examined it closely through the jeweller's glass that she always kept in a special pocket sewn into the side seam of all her daytime dresses and skirts. The request was not unusual. "It won't be easy," she said truthfully. "This is the work of one of Fabergé's best workmasters, and the quality of the stones is exceptional."

"But you can do it?"

"Yes, of course. The French have reached an amazingly high standard in the manufacture of paste jewels. The sort I should get for this piece would deceive anyone but a jewellery expert actually handling it."

"How long would it take?"

"Is it so urgent? I think we could do it in two weeks."

Lillian thumped a clenched hand impatiently on the table. "Too long! I want it done in two days. Three at the most."

Irene gave her a long look, seeing that she was desperate. "Just a moment while I consult on the matter," she said.

Derek had been called into the workshop and had not seen Lillian arrive. He was surprised when Irene told him who was in the ante-room and what was required. "I have no idea why there is such a rush," she continued, "but Lillian Rose looks really frightened. I suppose it's a case, as it is with so many women, of being too nervous to wear a fortune around their necks in case of robbery. My guess is that once she has the copy, the original will go straight into the bank vault."

"You're probably right," he agreed. "I'll take a look at the necklace. We can always stamp or cast the setting instead of carving it out of the solid metal. What is it? Gold or platinum?"

"White gold. The diamonds are colourless, free of carbon inclusion, and quite magnificent."

In the ante-room, Lillian looked up in displeased surprise when Derek entered with Irene. "Derek! I had no idea you were in Monte Carlo! The last I heard was that you were in Paris. Are you working here?"

He grinned a little maliciously at her. "Yes. Derek the Unexpected—that's my title, wouldn't you say?"

She was in no mood for light banter. "You must get this necklace copied for me in the shortest possible time. It would not hurt you to work night and day to oblige me for once. After all," she added bitingly, "I have helped you out a number of times. You still owe me two hundred pounds from the last time we met."

"Trust you never to forget anything where money is concerned, Lillian," he taunted acidly. "Would you be willing to wipe the slate clean if I should oblige you in this matter?"

She looked at him viciously. "You don't change, do you!"

It was becoming abundantly clear to Irene that in spite of their long acquaintanceship, each disliked and despised the other for individual reasons. She spoke up. "This is not the place for personal bargaining," she said sternly. "The point is, Derek, whether or not we can complete the work within a short time."

He shrugged casually, half smiling to himself. It obviously amused him to keep Lillian hanging onto his words for a decision. He put a jeweller's glass to his eye, and his whole face relaxed its expression in appreciation of the quality of the stones and the workmanship itself.

"How important is this replica to be?" he asked Lillian. "Is it simply for general appearance?"

She did not quite grasp his meaning, and her mind raced for a plausible answer. "I shall wear it for display, but I want to keep the original in a safe place."

He explained in more detail. "The point is that if you want to deceive completely, the setting should be handmade, and that will take as many hours as it took to make the original, a long and painstaking task."

"Impossible!" She wrung her hands. "I can't wait that long. Isn't there a short cut to gain the same effect?"

"Then it won't come under close scrutiny?"

"No. Only I shall know the difference."

"In that case we can take the short cut you request. I can guarantee the result will make it necessary for a special mark disclosed only to you to ensure that you never muddle them up."

"You still haven't said how quickly you can do it for me."

"Preliminary work can start right away, but it will still take a week from the time the paste stones are received from Paris." He was enjoying her anxiety.

Lillian thought her head must split with stress. Somehow she would have to stave off Leon for that length of time. "I can rely on absolute secrecy, can I not?"

Irene answered on her own and on Derek's behalf. "That is the jeweller's code. Even the messenger I shall send to Paris for the paste stones will be a retired goldsmith accustomed to keep silent on all matters concerning the handling of valuable jewellery. His name is Mr. Lucas. When the work is completed, he will deliver it to you in a package disguised as some other purchase which will eliminate any connection with me or anyone in my employ."

While Derek took the necklace in its box to a security room to begin the measuring and listing of what would be required for the replica, Irene asked Lillian a question herself. "Why did you come to me for the work you want done when there are several other jewellers in Monaco?"

Lillian blinked. "I'm not sure. I don't know why, but I didn't think of going to anyone else. I suppose it is because you are English, no matter the personal differences between us, and furthermore," she continued with a rare lapse to her origins that was an indication of her acute anxiety, "I'm sick to my guts of foreigners at the moment."

With this cryptic statement she hurried away as quickly as she had come. Once back in the hotel, she was genuinely overcome by a return to fright and distress at what might happen if Leon should suddenly force his way in to see her. In panic she changed her suite, giving strict instructions that nobody should be informed of her new whereabouts in the hotel, the only exceptions being the doctor, whom she sent for, and a certain Mr. Lucas who could be expected in a few days time. The doctor found her in bed, weeping profusely, the reason for which she did not divulge to him. To think that she, the idol of the Gaiety, should have to hide away from a hateful man in such an ignominious fashion!

The doctor was used to the hysterics of spoiled, rich women. He prescribed a sedative, said he would install a nurse by day and night to minister to her needs, and suggested that she rest on the *chaise longue* instead of lying in bed. Lillian became more relaxed once the sedative began to take effect. She thought she might even indulge herself during the period of her retreat from the social whirl, being comfortable in a loose *négligée* all day without the constriction of whalebone stays, eating her favourite chocolates, enjoying her favourite drinks, and letting her maid dress her hair in different coiffures until she found one dramatically suitable for whenever she would leave her so-called sickbed to reappear in public again.

Since incoming phone calls were being stopped on her behalf at the hotel's exchange, she simply received a list twice a day of the names of people who had rung her, as well as those who had come in person. She glanced through them in panic. On the first day Leon had phoned twice and then called at the hotel where he had been given a note from her to say that she was indisposed through reaction to the disgraceful dinner party and that she never wanted to see him again. When a great basket of red roses was delivered an hour later, she had viewed them with abhorrence, her hand trembling as she took up the attached card. But they were not from Leon. She laughed aloud in her relief. One of her young *beaux* had sent them. Two of her other swains, not to be outdone, sent her hothouse fruits and more flowers which, with more red roses, proved to be daily offerings for her speedy recovery from the mysterious malady that had struck her down; and love letters came in abundance from them.

Leon made no further attempt to get in touch with her after receiving the note. She gained confidence. He must have come to his senses and realized that his behaviour had been inexcusable, accepting that no decent woman would have anything more to do with him after what he had said and done. Unfortunately it was no consolation to her that not a word of the disastrous incident had appeared in the press, for gossip spread like wildfire back to England from any resort abroad that was popular with English society. To try to forestall the Guv'nor's being informed by others that she had allowed herself to become embroiled in a drunken orgy, she wrote him a long letter of explanation, making light of it all, which should make him dismiss any more spiteful version.

Over and over again she reminded herself deliberately that in its own way the dreadful dinner party had been a blessing in disguise. It had saved her from submitting to Leon in appreciation of the necklace, which would otherwise have been her fate. Instead the necklace was without taint. More than that, from her first sight of it she had known it to be the fulfilment of her dreams—not only beautiful, but worth thousands of pounds, an insurance against ever having to go without luxuries for the rest of her life. She loved it with a passion she had not known herself to be capable of experiencing, a feeling deeper than she had ever felt before for anybody or anything. She would die before she would ever let it go back to the man who had given it to her.

On the appointed day for its redelivery to her, she was dressed and waiting impatiently when she was informed by telephone from the hotel desk that a Mr. Lucas had called to see her. "Send him up," she instructed eagerly.

Arthur was carrying what appeared to be an ordinary brown paper parcel as he went up in the lift. It pleased him that he was entrusted by Irene with small tasks to carry out for her. When he was admitted to the suite, he bowed courteously to the customer and set down his parcel on a table where he proceeded to unwrap it.

Lillian fumed inwardly at his slowness, but she caught her breath when he lifted the lid of the Fabergé box and then that of a plain red leather box to reveal two seemingly identical necklaces, which blazed and dazzled as if white fire had been released into the room.

"Which is which?" she exclaimed in awe.

"Would madam care to guess?"

"This must be the original." She indicated the contents of the Fabergé box simply because she assumed it would be returned in the same container as that in which it had been handed to Irene.

Arthur shook his head. "For safety's sake, the replica and the original are in reverse boxes." He took a powerful lens from his pocket and handed it to her. "Look on the back of the gold clasp of the replica. You will see the mark you were told about."

She did as he had said and was able to discern it. He gestured that she should examine the clasp of the original to see that it was clear. Then, asking her to accept the lens with Miss Lindsay's compliments for any future identification, he took a step back discreetly while she picked up the bill. It was no higher than she had expected. She wrote out payment straight away, and he departed with it.

Left alone, she took out her beloved necklace and held it to her throat. If anything, it was more beautiful and precious to her than ever. She wished she could have worn it that evening, but that would

be madness and might make worthless all the trouble
she had gone to in order to protect her valued
possession. Instead she would wear the replica for the
first time. Sooner or later she would meet Leon, and
if she was wearing it, she would simply unclip it and
hand it over to him with a grand gesture of dismissal.
If not, she would collect it from the hotel's vault in its
Fabergé box and give it to him with similar aplomb.
With the necklace apparently returned to him, he
would be powerless to make demands on her. By the
time it was discovered to be a copy, she would be back
in England and far away from him. If ever questioned by any authority on his behalf, she would
point out that the necklace had been a gift to her, and
it had been a little joke on her part to let him have the
replica as a reminder of their brief acquaintanceship.
There would not be a single thing he could do about
it.

Irene went hand in hand with Gregory to the
Casino that evening. It was their last outing together
before he left on the morrow for England again. They
had made plans for their future together. After he
had transferred his business fully to Amsterdam, she
would be with him throughout the summer months,
designing in a studio that he would incorporate with
his premises for her. When she had established a shop
and workshop there, making it a centre from which
Irene-Denise jewellery should go out to all the

corners of the world, she would sell the Monte Carlo shop.

As always, the Casino was in full swing. They met Madame Borisvinsky on her way to the tables, and while they were talking to her she suddenly shielded the side of her mouth with her closed feather fan.

"That is Madame Clementi," she whispered to Irene. "You were asking me about her."

Irene glanced in the direction she had indicated and saw for the first time the face of the woman whose innocent selling of a brooch had inadvertently given away Derek's sideline, which might otherwise have never come to light. She was a pleasant-looking women, although there was nothing remarkable about her; her hair was dark, her complexion olive, and her evening gown of green velvet in a style of quiet, good taste. A woman easily lost in a crowd. Yet something about her made Irene take a second glance in her direction, although she did not know why. She guessed that she had glimpsed Madame Clementi on her previous visits to the shop to sell to Derek and had been too busy to register anything positive about her.

"Shall we go to the tables?" Gregory suggested, offering Madame Borisvinsky his arm to help her along.

The old lady accepted his support gratefully. "Poor little Maria is not here this evening," she confided to Irene on her other side, "but Leon is in the Salon Privé gambling like a madman, I have heard. And winning!' Then with that sixth sense she had, which alerted her to any kind of social excitement, she began to look back over her shoulder. "Something is happening. What is it? I cannot see."

Gregory guided her around in order that she could peer in the direction from which a rustle of attention was causing other heads to turn. There was Lillian, greeting acquaintances charmingly as she came along, the marvellous necklace spitting fire from her throat and bosom. She wore no other ornament to detract from it; her golden hair was sleekly coiffured, her gown of clinging white lace. Her tall young *beaux* were with her, strutting like cocks, proud and protective in their escorting of their favourite Gaiety Girl.

"Lillian is in her element this evening," Gregory remarked drily to Irene. "What a necklace!"

Irene made no reply. She was unable to tell whether Lillian was wearing the original necklace or the replica. If it was not the real necklace, as was most likely, then it was no mean achievement of the French paste makers that even a diamond expert could be deceived without close examination. Gregory had not been told of Lillian's visit to the shop, secrecy having been promised and kept, Derek himself working night and day to get the copy done in the short time that had been allowed.

Then from the direction of the Salon Privé there came another stir. Leon must have left instructions that he was to be informed at once whenever Lillian put in a reappearance at the Casino. He advanced towards her, his face hard, his eyes flashing with temper. Everybody could tell that something dramatic was about to take place.

Lillian saw him coming and did not quail. She was no longer afraid of him with her *beaux* at her side and so many people around. She regarded him with the slightly amused, slightly superior air with which she received the ovation of an audience when she appeared on stage for the first time at a performance, knowing that such worship was her due.

Only those still in the Salon Privé knew that Leon had snatched up a fistful of golden *louis* from his winnings before dashing from the room. As he reached Lillian, he brought his clenched hand up to chest height and flung the coins into her face with full force in a gesture of utter contempt. She cried out in painful astonishment, throwing up her hands to defend herself, and reeled back. He hurled himself after her, breaking through the young men who had leaped to her defence. Grabbing at the necklace, he tore it from her throat, snapping the clasp; and at the same time he shoved his hand full in her face, giving her a vicious thrust that sent her staggering backwards to collapse screaming on the floor.

Then Leon felt himself swung around by the arm by Gregory, who let fly with a left fist, catching him under the ribs and doubling him up. The necklace fell from his hand and skimmed underfoot, his heel crushing two of the paste diamonds into glittering powder, the deception at an end. A tremendous right-hander, with Gregory's full weight behind it, thudded home under Leon's eye. He went crashing down full length, blood spurting from his nose.

Gregory stood for a few moments, breathing heavily, but there was no sign that Leon was able to rise to his feet. In any case, gentlemen and the Casino's staff were coming between them, two or three seeking to bring the felled man into a sitting position. Gregory shook off the clasp of those who imagined he had to be restrained and turned to find that Lillian, weeping and hysterical, had been helped to her feet. With a great sob she threw herself into his arms. Signalling to Irene to keep close to him, he led the distressed Lillian out through the staring throng, and eventually the three of them reached Lillian's suite. Then she broke free from his aid.

"I must get away from here," she shrieked, possessed by panic. "I can't stay in this place another second!" She refused to be calmed down, her only thought being to get away. Stamping her foot at her gaping maids, she ordered them to pack. Then she herself rang the hotel desk for her chauffeur to bring her motorcar to the entrance.

Gregory calmly poured himself a drink, Irene having refused the offer of one. She wanted to get away from the suite almost as much as Lillian did, but he seemed to consider it his duty to see the frantic woman safely on her way. In the bedroom, Lillian was changing into a travelling costume, shrieking orders that one of her maids was to follow by train with the trunks. As soon as she was dressed and the porter came for some hand luggage, she ran to

Gregory, flinging her arms about his neck.

"Come with me," she appealed urgently. "Let bygones be bygones. I need you, Gregory. You still love me; I know you do. We can make a fresh start."

Irene felt herself go cold with dread. Lillian, beautiful and tearful and appealing, looked capable of melting any man's heart. Gregory was half smiling at her, setting his hands on her waist.

"You don't need me, Lillian. You never did. You were in a state of panic when you agreed to marry me in New York, much as you are now. You had lost a couple of bookings before we left London, and then you failed to get a Broadway stage part that you had been hoping for, am I not right? You could not face returning from your so-called American vacation without some security."

She drew back, glowering at him. "I'm still your wife. All the time I'm alive, you'll never be able to call any other woman your own. One day you'll come back to me. Irene knows it and I know it! You'll see!"

Turning on her heel, she stalked from the suite to go downstairs and collect her precious Fabergé necklace and some other jewellery from the hotel's security vault.

Gregory saw Irene's taut expression and drew her into his arms. "It's not true, you know," he said to her. "You are my own and always will be. Nobody shall ever part us. We belong together."

Irene pressed herself close to him, trying to be comforted. The dread that Lillian had reawakened in her would not be banished.

It assailed her again as they were leaving the hotel. Two gentlemen in evening clothes came after them at a swifter pace to confront them on the steps. "Mr. Burnett?" one of them enquired. "Mr. Gregory Burnett?"

"Yes," Gregory replied.

"You are the husband of Madame Lillian Rose?"

"I am."

"Are you aware that she cheated Count Leon Romanov by retaining a valuable necklace and substituting a paste one for its return to him?"

"I was not. But I did not see a necklace returned. I only saw one snatched from her."

"That is not the issue in question."

"How did the necklace come into her possession in the first place? Was it loaned or was it a gift?"

"It was given to Madame Rose on a certain understanding which is not to be fulfilled."

Gregory's mouth tightened cynically. "This discussion is a waste of time. The property is hers since it was given to her. The ethics of the case are nothing to do with you or with me." He took Irene by the elbow to continue on their interrupted way, but again the two men moved to block their advance.

"The matter is not concluded, sir. I have a message to deliver to you of the utmost importance."

Gregory's eyes narrowed as if he suddenly comprehended what was about to be forthcoming. "Well?"

"Count Leon demands satisfaction. Not only have you offended his honour and assaulted his person, but you are, sir, the husband of the woman who has cheated him most abominably!''

Irene gave a little moan of dismay. Gregory showed no sign of emotion. ''When is it to be?''

''The hour is already after midnight. Therefore it will be today at dawn, the venue the gardens of Villa Lunel. As the challenged, the choice of weapons is yours. Swords or pistols?''

''Pistols.''

''A doctor will be present. Shall you be able to arrange a second? If not, this gentleman with me, Monsieur Devereaux, would be honoured to carry out that duty.''

Gregory bowed to the second man. ''I'm obliged to you, sir.''

''Then all arrangements are made. Good night to you, sir. Good night, mademoiselle.''

The two men returned to the hotel. Irene could not believe that she had seen or heard aright. It was like being drawn deep into a nightmare from which it was impossible to wake. ''You can't!'' she cried desperately. ''It's stupid! It's archaic!''

''I agree,'' he said evenly to her, gathering her trembling hands into both of his. ''But I have never turned my back on a challenge, and to refuse the one I have just received would be to belittle my nationality in the eyes of others. In other words, I would be betraying my king, my country, and everything I believe in. That is something I can't do, not even for you, my darling Irene.''

She saw that no argument would move him. All

she could do was to try to match her courage to his. "May I go with you at dawn?"

He shook his head. "No. Wait for me at home. Meanwhile there are a few hours left before I have to leave you."

As they turned homewards to her apartment, she realized that this cruel twist of events was the culmination of the sense of premonition that had been haunting her for the past weeks. The life of the man she loved was being put into grave danger. She had never been more afraid.

Eighteen

Derek, arriving for work in the early light of day, was surprised as he entered the courtyard to find that Irene had been watching out for him at the door of her apartment. She came running down the steps at once, a shawl flung around her shoulders of her light woollen dress. He dropped the leather bag in which he had brought his noonday snack and caught her by the arms with both hands when she reached him, her face distraught.

"Whatever is the matter?" he exclaimed.

She clutched the lapels of his coat in her desperation. "There's been a duel between Gregory and Count Romanov in the gardens of the Villa Lunel! It was over Lillian and her diamond necklace. Will you go and find out what has happened? I've had no word yet."

He had gone ashen. "What happened about the necklace?"

She told him as briefly as she could, explaining how Leon had attempted to regain what he considered to be his property and then describing Lillian's panic-stricken flight. "It has been like a nightmare for me ever since. Say you will go and make enquiries for me! Gregory forbade me to appear anywhere near the place."

He seemed unable to concern himself with her lover's fate. "Will Count Romanov try to get the original necklace back by other means, do you think?"

She drew away from him, her face compressed into incredulous shock at his heartless disregard for her present feelings. "I don't know if Gregory or the count is still alive. For all I know, they might both be fatally wounded. If you will not do what I ask, I'll go myself, no matter that Gregory has forbid me!"

He caught hold of her as she swung away. "Wait! I'll go! I'm sorry if I didn't understand the urgency at once. Wait indoors. I saw a *voiture* at the kerb around the corner. I'll take that."

Then he did break into a run to do as he had said, but before he could reach the outlet of the courtyard, a closed carriage swung into it and drew up alongside where Irene was standing. Monsieur Devereaux jumped out.

"Prepare yourself, mademoiselle," he said gravely. "I have bad news."

She thought her heart had stopped. "What has happened?" she whispered with pale lips.

"Mr. Burnett has suffered a severe wound. He was

taken to the hospital in the doctor's care, bleeding profusely." He held out a hand to guide her into the carriage. "I will take you there at once."

Derek, who had come running back, overheard what had been said. "Shall I come with you, Irene?"

She shook her head, barely knowing what she was hearing in her pounding fear that she would not get to the hospital in time. As Monsieur Devereaux followed her into the carriage and took his seat, Derek held the door ajar to ask a question of him. Whatever it was, no answer was given. Monsieur Devereaux was not prepared to discuss anything with a stranger and reached out himself to jerk the door shut.

"Is there any hope?" Irene asked him.

"Mr. Burnett was taken straight into the operating room. We must hope for the best."

Suddenly she thought of Maria. "What of Count Romanov?"

"Unharmed. As the two duellists turned to fire at each other, Mr. Burnett deliberately aimed his pistol wide. He is a courageous and honourable gentleman."

Irene shut her eyes, biting deep into her lip. She should have known that Gregory would never take advantage of being a good shot, even though his opponent was probably no less skilled. But no tears now. This was a time for being brave, as he had been.

She stayed all day at the hospital but was not allowed to see him. A doctor informed her that the operation had been performed, and that its ultimate success depended on the strength of the patient. He was dangerously weak from loss of blood. The nuns in their starched white robes hurried up and down the corridor and in and out of doors as they went about their nursing duties, and each time she would look up in hope that one or the other of them was coming to tell her that she could go to Gregory's bedside, but they never so much as looked in her direction.

Not long after midday she turned her head to see Arthur Lucas making his way along the corridor to where she sat. In spite of his thick spectacles, he did not see her until she sprang up and ran to him.

"Miss Irene!" he exclaimed. "I looked into the workshop this afternoon, and Derek told me you were here. I was sorry to hear that Mr. Burnett is in such a poorly state. Is there any better news?"

"Nothing yet." A shuddering sigh escaped her. "All I have been told since this morning is that his condition has not worsened."

Arthur led her back to the seat and sat down beside her. "How did it happen?"

She told him the whole story. He listened quietly. It always saddened him that diamonds, the most beautiful of all stones in his opinion, should arouse such greed and ugly passion from time to time. He had been interested in Lillian Rose's necklace and its copy, and he had thoroughly enjoyed the trip to Paris to collect the paste stones.

"What has happened to the replica now?" he asked, seeing that it was good for her to keep talking.

She let her shoulders rise and fall. "I've no idea."

"Maybe Count Romanov will want it repaired. There are some extra paste stones in the workshop."

"I shouldn't think he would want to set eyes on it again. It will remind him too much of the humiliation he suffered when Gregory floored him."

Arthur wagged his head. "These Russians are touchy folk and full of pride."

"Not all," she contradicted. "I've never met a gentler person than Maria Romanov. She will be suffering as much as anybody through all this trouble."

A nun was approaching. "Miss Lindsay?" she queried.

Irene looked at her, reaching blindly for Arthur's hand. He held hers tightly as she rose slowly to her feet, not knowing what she was to hear. "Yes."

"You may see Mr. Burnett now, but only for a minute."

He was conscious and knew her, but he looked terribly ill. "Irene, darling," he whispered, "I knew you would be here."

She bent over and kissed his forehead. "Don't tire yourself with talking. I'll be here all the time."

He smiled faintly, closing his eyes. The nun indicated that she must leave again. Looking backwards over her shoulder at him, she went reluctantly from the room. In the corridor she resumed her vigil. The fact that she was not advised to go home was indication enough that Gregory's life was still hanging in the balance. Arthur stayed with her until the late afternoon. Then he had to leave, knowing that Yvonne would have started to worry about his absence.

One of the nuns brought her a bowl of soup and some bread, urging her to eat. She obeyed simply because she did not want to sink into a state of collapse, realizing that she had not eaten anything since the previous evening. What kind of soup it was and whether the bread was brown or white, she did not notice, but only choked it down, her throat constricted by anxiety.

Towards ten o'clock Gabrielle arrived at the hospital. She had not been out all day and only received the news of the duel and its results when she reached the Casino. In her bright blue satin and lace, adorned with jewels and her hair a shrieking red, she appeared like a gaudy parrot amid white-clad nuns as she advanced upon her granddaughter.

"I've only just heard! How is he? Still alive? Thank God! I heard the worst at the Casino, and my first thought was to find you."

She was exhausting company. Several times she was hushed by the nuns for talking stridently, but she was incapable of remaining unobtrusive wherever she was, and when a final reprimand came from a doctor, she got up in a huff to leave.

"What a place! I can't imagine anybody getting better here," she announced tactlessly. Then she kissed Irene effusively, covering up her thankfulness at getting away and considering her duty done. "Let me know if there is anything I can do. Remember that I'm your grandmother, and family is all-important at these times.'' Her sweeping departure proclaimed that she had no intention of coming back. To Irene there was something curiously final about her going. It was like the re-severing of a link that had been joined only briefly.

In the early hours there was some concern that Gregory was weakening. Irene was called to his bedside, and she sat holding his hand as it lay on the coverlet. But he rallied. Compassionately the doctor allowed her to stay by him until dawn. He was sleeping peacefully.

"Now go home and have some sleep yourself," a nun advised kindly. "Somebody is waiting in the corridor to see you safely there."

Unable to think of whom it might be, Irene went back to the corridor. On the seat where she had sat herself for so many anxious hours, another woman was waiting, her face gaunt with tiredness, her eyes red-rimmed with private tears. It was Sofia, still in travelling clothes from wherever she had come. She stood up as she sighted Irene, who was deeply glad to find her there. They moved swiftly towards each other and embraced, each momentarily speechless in thankfulness that the man they both loved was going to survive.

"How did you know I was at the hospital?" Irene asked her as they went from the building together, both tired to the point of exhaustion, their pace slow.

"It was sheer chance that I should have returned to Monte Carlo on the train that arrives after midnight.

Sergei Borisvinsky met me at the station as arranged, and it was he who told me what had happened. His mother was most anxious that I should know that my stepdaughter's *beau* and my nephew by marriage had been engaged in a duel with such unhappy results. When I failed to find you at the apartment, Sergei brought me to the hospital. He would have waited with me, but I sent him away. I was told that you had just gone to Gregory's bedside because a moment of crisis had come."

"You have been waiting all that time?"

"One of the nuns came to tell me when the danger was past. Did you know that Leon and Maria have left Monte Carlo?"

"No, I didn't."

"Their yacht sailed as soon as Leon rejoined it after the duel. Although duels are still generally accepted as a way for gentlemen to settle their disagreements in this part of the world, there would have been some police enquiries if Gregory had died. By getting away from Monaco, Leon avoided any aftermath, and I fear the matter will soon have faded and been forgotten by all concerned."

In Irene's tired mind there came the echo of something else which she had heard said about Leon, but at the present time it was impossible to recall what. She felt as though she had been years without sleep or rest.

She slept until midday. Sofia awakened her as requested or else she would have slept longer, but she wanted to get back to the hospital to see Gregory

again. There began for her the frequent daily visits
that were to become part of her routine. At first she
could only sit a little while at his bedside, and she was
the only visitor permitted, for he was still extremely
weak, a state that was to last for quite a while. But as
he began to make progress, Sofia was allowed to see
him for short periods.

When at last his recovery was assured, Sofia made
arrangements to return to England. On her last
afternoon, she and her stepdaughter said goodbye at
Gregory's bedside. Then Irene left the two of them on
their own for the final hour or two before Sofia
caught the early evening train.

As Irene drew near her shop, she saw Madame
Clementi emerge from it and go off on foot in the
opposite direction, not seeing her. Irene's heart sank.
Was Derek taking advantage of her frequent absences
to resume his individual buying practice again? She
might be misjudging him. It was possible that
Madame Clementi had called in vain.

Irene followed the woman with her eyes. She was
dressed in the tailored costume that she had worn the
first time Irene had seen her but was wearing a
different hat. It was as fashionably wide-brimmed as
the first one, and as she crossed the street a few yards
distant, her profile showed that it was trimmed with
a veil that was drawn in flatteringly under the chin. A
shaft of recognition pierced Irene's memory. She
knew her! For a matter of seconds the narrow Monte
Carlo street dissolved into her father's ante-room in
Old Bond Street when a certain Mrs. Duncane

switched a valuable ring under his very nose! The name of Madame Clementi was another alias for the jewel thief, Ruth Williams, who must have come straight to the Riviera after serving her sentence in a London prison.

Irene held her breath at this revelation. It had been the veil and the lowered angle of the head that had unlocked the faintly tantalizing impression she had had of having seen the woman somewhere before; otherwise the dyed hair and reshaped eyebrows, the deeper tone of complexion, and the perfectly assumed role of the slightly impoverished husband hunter would have continued to deceive indefinitely.

Without changing her pace, Irene continued on until she reached her shop, going in by the street entrance. Both her assistants were serving, and Derek was showing to a couple a selection of diamond bow-brooches. He glanced at her, as he often did when she came through the showroom. Perhaps something of what she had felt in recognizing Ruth Williams still showed in a pallor of complexion, for as soon as his customers were gone he followed her into the workshop where she had gone to check on how a new piece was progressing.

"How was Gregory today?"

"Getting better," she answered, sliding the pins from her hat before removing it. "He is allowed to sit up now. I'm going back again this evening."

"I have a couple of Arthur Conan Doyle books he may like to read."

"I'm sure he would."

"I'll bring them with me tomorrow."

She went upstairs to her drawing table, but she did not work. With her elbows on its surface, she sat with her head supported by the spread fingers of both hands. Derek was dealing in stolen jewellery. She was sure of it. He was certainly only the middle man, for the money needed in such transactions would never stay long enough in his pocket for him to be able to establish himself as a profit-making "fence." Nevertheless, her respected business was being used by him in the most abominable way. He had thought her safely at the hospital that afternoon. Normally she would not have been home for another hour at least, but she had made arrangements with Sofia that had not been known to him.

It must have been the ultimate triumph for Ruth Williams when she knew herself to be fully seen and unrecognized by the one person in Monte Carlo able to denounce her. Irene now recalled how the woman had lingered casually near her, glancing around as if looking for somebody, but in reality gathering proof that her disguise was entirely perfect.

An hour went by, and still Irene sat on. All the time while the worry about Gregory's eventual recovery had closed her mind to all else, she had let many half-registered incidents slip away. Now she was letting them return. At first it had been a higgledy-piggledy collection of happenings that appeared to bear no relation to each other, but gradually they were beginning to slot together in a way that was frightening to her, but there was no going back.

Finally she stirred. Downstairs the assistants were leaving, their day's work done. Derek had commenced the locking-up and security measures. She went downstairs to him.

"Are you working this evening?" she asked.

He smiled at her. "No. I'm going to have a flutter at the Casino. Why do you ask? Was there something you wanted done?"

"Nothing of importance. You know I'd prefer you not to put in all those extra hours at the bench, for Brigette's sake."

A look of displeasure showed in his glance. "I won't be tied to any woman's apron strings. Brigette tricked me by becoming pregnant. It was her way of getting me to put a ring on her finger, but it hasn't worked."

"Does she know that you have no intention of marrying her?"

"Yes, I've told her. I became sick to death of hints and finally let her know once and for all that she will not get me to sign my freedom away."

"What of the child?"

"I'll keep Brigette and the baby when it comes. Nothing will change. She should be thankful for that."

Irene, recalling the London girl whom he had abandoned in a similar condition, thought that at least it showed he had some feeling for Brigette since he did not intend to leave her high and dry.

He had locked up the workshop after the craftsmen had departed and was gone himself by the time she was on the point of leaving for the hospital. She delayed long enough to go into the office and take an important paper from the files which she put safely away in her purse.

"Is anything wrong?" Gregory asked her after they had kissed and she took the chair by his bed.

"A little business worry, that's all," she said cheerfully. "I thought I had left it behind at the shop. I didn't realize that it still showed."

"Anything I can help you with?"

She laughed happily, his returned interest in the outside world confirming the good medical reports she was being given each day. "Not at the present time. I may need to consult you later."

When she left the hospital, she did not go straight home. Instead she went to Arthur's address. She glanced up at the top floor where Derek and Brigette had rooms, but it was in darkness. He would still be at the Casino, and no doubt poor Brigette had gone to bed. That was as well. Irene had no wish for either of them to know about her visit. When Yvonne answered the door, she requested quietly and in a note of urgency that she might speak to Arthur on his own.

"I'll take you through to him," Yvonne said, copying unconsciously the same tone of voice as people do on such occasions. Arthur was seated at the lamp-lit table in the sitting-room, reading his newspaper, which he folded and put aside. Irene came straight to the point.

"When you sat with me in the hospital on the day

of the duel, do you remember mentioning some paste stones? You said they could be used to repair the damaged replica of Lillian Rose's diamond necklace if need be."

"Did I?" he replied vaguely. "I don't remember, but I know there must be some in the workshop. Why? Did you need them?"

"Would they be part of the order you collected from Paris?"

"Yes, those are the ones I meant."

She took from her purse the original order that she had taken from the office files and showed it to him. "Is this what you fetched?"

He pulled the table lamp nearer and peered closely through his spectacles at the paper in the full light. His forefinger followed the list down to the bottom, muttering the descriptions of the items as he checked them. "Fifteen briolette pendants . . . pear-shaped . . . nearly spherical . . . ovid . . . pear-shaped again. Mmmm. Asymmetric rose cut. Cushion brilliant. Mmmm. Mmmm." Finally he looked at her. "The list is correct except that this is not the paper I was given. The order I handled was for two of each item written down here."

She sat forward sharply. "Do you mean that you fetched this listed amount in duplicate?"

He nodded, handing the paper back to her. "Isn't that what you wanted? Derek gave me all the instructions."

"Didn't you think it was a large number of stones for a single necklace, however ornate?"

"I was given no details. When you asked me to go to Paris on your behalf to collect an urgent order of paste stones, you didn't state how many were required. I suppose, after seeing the finished replica, it must have struck me that Derek had been extra cautious in ordering over the number in case of any unforeseen flaws, which is why I assume there must be some left suitable for repair work." He frowned worriedly. "What is wrong, Miss Irene?"

It was the second time she had been asked that question this evening. She feared something was terribly wrong, but she had no proof yet. "It may be nothing, Mr. Lucas," she said, standing up in readiness to leave. "I would be grateful if you would keep it from Brigette and Derek that I was here this evening."

"Whatever you say, Miss Irene," he replied seriously. He was drawing his own conclusions. It looked as if Derek was doubling up on orders and making a dishonest profit on the side. If true, it was a despicable abuse of trust.

Unknown to either Irene or the old man, Brigette was aware of the visit. She had been standing in the darkness of her top-floor room, looking through the lace curtains in the hope of seeing Derek coming home from the Casino and had seen Irene arrive. Leaving the window and going out onto the landing to look down the stairwell, she had been struck by the low and urgent tones of Irene's voice. It was no social visit. Ever protective towards Derek, she had gone down to the next landing and stayed there in the shadows. The house was quiet, and the door of the sitting-room was thin. She had heard enough to tell her that an order was being checked and questioned. She returned to her room as silently as she had left it. Only the baby in her womb thumped about. Putting on her hat and coat, she dropped the door-key in her pocket and went back down the stairs and out of the house. Derek would not be pleased at being called away from his gambling, but it had to be done.

As soon as Irene reached her apartment, she made herself a pot of strong coffee. Revived by it, she took a second cup with her down the stairs that led to the shop. There she switched on the office light and sat down at the desk to go through the ledgers as she had done once before. She found the entry for the paste stones. The full amount she had paid the supplier was there, but the paste items themselves had been listed under the jeweller's term: *a parcel of stones (paste)*.

Leaving the ledger open, she went into the storeroom and began a thorough search. There was no place where she did not look. If she could just find the duplicate set, or even half of it, she would know that at least on one score she was misjudging Derek. Nothing came to light. She went through the cupboards and drawers in the workshop. All in vain. Although there was no reason why they might be in the showroom, she left no corner there unchecked. Finally she wandered back into the workshop and stood, tired and saddened, knowing that what she most feared must be true.

"You don't look as if you can find whatever it is you're looking for," Derek's voice commented from another doorway.

She gave a gasp, instinctively drawing back a step. He stood leaning an arm against the jamb, immaculate in his evening clothes, obviously having come straight from the Casino. She realized he must have let himself into the employees' entrance without a sound and watched her from the dark passageway where coats were hung by day and working overalls by night.

"How long have you been there?" she demanded.

"Long enough to see that you were going through the whole place as if with a toothcomb. Why?" He came forward into the full light.

"I was foolish enough to hope that I might find a second set of the paste stones to match those used for Lillian's necklace."

"And you haven't." It was a statement, not a question.

"That's right." She drew in her breath. "You used the duplicate set to make a second replica, didn't you, Derek? You deceived me by letting the original necklace lie in the crimson box until the last moment. When you turned away to pack both boxes up for Arthur's delivery, you substituted the second replica for the original."

His expression did not change. "Your assumption is correct. I knew that if you were to deliver the necklaces, I wouldn't get away with it. Just handling them for Lillian would have been enough at close quarters for you to become suspicious, but poor old Arthur wouldn't have been able to see if I had made them both of bottle glass."

She passed a hand over her eyes as if his attitude was beyond her comprehension. Then she gave her head a little shake, looking directly at him again. "I was too upset the morning of the duel to think about it at the time, but afterwards it came back to me that you had only wanted to know about Leon. Even to the point of asking Monsieur Devereaux if he was still alive just as we were about to drive off to the hospital. You were afraid that Leon would persist in trying to get the original necklace back, which meant danger to you. I believe you hoped that Gregory had killed him."

"It would have solved everything as far as I was concerned. I was most anxious when you told me he had made an issue of the necklace at the Casino, something I could not possibly have anticipated since Lillian was so guarded in her request for a replica."

She leaned back wearily against the edge of one of the benches. "How did you imagine you would ever get away with such a deception?"

"What do you mean? I have got away with it. Count Romanov knows the trick Lillian pulled on him, but that's the end of it as far as he is concerned. It was a relief to me when he sailed away on the same day as the duel. With Lillian also gone from Monte Carlo, it meant I had nothing to worry about."

"Haven't you forgotten something? As soon as

Lillian goes to have her necklace insured, the truth will be out."

He gave a half laugh. "That would not have happened if she hadn't lost the replica at the Casino. I know Lillian. She is as mean as hell as far as money is concerned. With the original, as she thinks, in a bank vault, she won't pay out for insurance."

She stared at him incredulously. "Do you imagine that I'm going to condone theft?"

He raised an eyebrow. "Theft? Who is going to back your story? Not Lillian. She won't want the sordid details getting into the press, no matter how much her greedy little soul might grieve for the loss of her precious diamonds. Count Romanov? He might be interested in what you have to say, but what of his wife? She's your friend, isn't she? Would you subject her to the misery and humiliation that would be her lot if I stood trial over stealing a necklace that her husband had intended for his mistress? I think not." Seeing that she was aghast at his audacity, he smiled reassuringly, taking a few leisurely steps nearer her. "Such a chance as duplicating that necklace will never come my way again and frankly, I wouldn't want it to. It was a once-in-a-lifetime gamble I had to take."

"There was nothing in that vein about your passing on stolen jewellery to Ruth Williams, alias Madame Clementi!"

The bones seemed to stand out in his face, straining the skin. "You're talking nonsense."

She shook her head wildly. "Don't lie to me

531

anymore! I've had enough! It was remembering how she switched a ring in my father's shop that gave me a clue as to what you had done with the necklace. She has contacts willing to pay well, has she? I'm telephoning the police now!"

He snatched hold of her when she tried to pass him, jerking her close. "Listen to me, Irene. There's no need to give me away. I'm asking your forgiveness. Maybe I have done a few deals that I'm not proud of, but I've needed the money. You know how I am. When I first met Brigette, I tried to stop gambling. For a while I did. If I could conquer it again, I'd never need to do the things I've done. You know I've always believed that if you had married me when I asked you, none of this would have happened." His voice softened. "I love you as much now as I did when we first met. For all that you felt for me once, don't give me away."

Hearing his tender, cajoling tones, it was as if time had turned back. She came to an understanding as to why she had treated him differently from any other employee, despite his failing to give her the loyalty expected of him. It was because she had never totally banished some part of the deep affection she had once had for him. It had mellowed her attitude towards him over and over again, making her lenient and forgiving and quick to make excuses for him. In return he had lied and cheated and deceived and robbed. Her heart no longer had any will to intervene against reason on his behalf. Everything was over and done with.

"It's no good, Derek. I'm going to do as I say!"

He was agitated, unable to believe that he had lost the power to win her round. As she attempted to pull herself free of his hold, he tried once more. "Listen to me! I can tell you something that will make a great difference to your life. All I ask in return is that you say nothing about the necklace or anything else that you suspect me of. I'll go away. I'll take Brigette with me. We'll make a fresh start in Canada, Australia, or even New Zealand."

She beat at him with her fists in exasperation. "Don't try to bargain a lie with me!"

"I'm not lying! I'm telling you the truth. You must believe me. It's a secret I held on to, simply because I found it useful for getting money out of Lillian whenever I needed it."

Her expression became one of abhorrence. "Blackmail?"

"No! I would just tease her a little about what I knew of her early days, and she would open her purse and give me a loan when I needed it."

"Then don't tell your secret to me! I want nothing to do with it." She wrenched free and made for the office door where the telephone was located. His next words halted her at the door.

"You don't want to know that Lillian was married once before!"

She came to a halt with a sharp intake of breath and swung about, an expression of anguished stupefaction on her face. "Are you saying that she and Gregory are not legally tied?"

He gave a nod. "When she was fifteen, she ran away from the workhouse with a seaman, and they were married in Liverpool on her sixteenth birthday."

The fact that he should have withheld such knowledge from her was breaking her eyes into the exquisite brilliance of unendurable pain. "You of all people knew and did nothing to clear the way for me!"

"I always hoped that you and I would come together again."

She flung her arms over her head and began to sob with a terrible abandon. Her tears did not stop. Her physical strength seemed to give out with the violence of crying, and after leaning against the jamb, she sank slowly down to her knees, still sobbing. She wept for what she had been told. She wept for Derek's cruelty and betrayal. And she wept for a love that had once showed itself bright as the sparkle of a diamond in a jeweller's ante-room in Old Bond Street and which had gone from her life at last.

When finally she lifted her head, she was alone and knew that she had been from the first outburst of tears. Derek and Brigette were probably on their way out of Monaco. She got slowly to her feet and went through to lock the entrance door that he had left unfastened behind him when he went.

Gregory was sitting out of bed in his dressing gown when she arrived to see him at her usual time the next day. He was daily growing more impatient with his convalescence.

"You look like a spring morning," he greeted her admiringly. She was in primrose yellow with a straw hat. There was renewed strength in his arms as he held her for ardent kissing.

"I have some news," she said seriously when he had released her. "But first, didn't you tell me once that you and Lillian were married in New York?"

"Yes, it was a civil ceremony."

"Did she ever give you any reason to suspect that she had been married before?"

He stared at her, his eyes narrowing. "Never. What have you heard?"

She told him everything from how her early suspicions about Derek had culminated in his extraordinary revelation. Gregory leaned his head back into the pillow propped behind his shoulders, his hand gripping the arm of the basket chair in which he sat. "Is it possible? My God! Has she really tricked me all these years?" His voice shook convulsively.

She was afraid she had upset him too much, but he was stimulated by what she had told him. She had to summon immediately to his hospital room the English lawyer, Mr. Jackson, who was resident in the community.

It took Mr. Jackson three weeks to travel to England, gather the information required, and return to Monte Carlo. By that time Gregory was out of hospital and looking well. Mr. Jackson laid the facts before his client and Irene in her sitting-room above the shop.

"The lady presently known by the stage name of Lillian Rose was born Lily Potts. Since I had been given the approximate date of her birth, based on the fact that she ran away at the age of fifteen, it was easy enough to find the entry of her flight in the workhouse records. I spent the next ten days going through the Liverpool church registers. Finally her name came to light. She married a certain Harry Baldwin, seaman, a few months after running away with him. That suggested that it was on the eve of his taking ship, so I then examined mercantile records. Harry Baldwin was second mate on the *Seaward Star.*"

"Then my marriage to Lillian is null and void," Gregory said soberly. Irene's hand was in his, and he clasped it hard in the significance of what they had been told.

The lawyer pursed his lips regretfully. "There is a query, I am sorry to say. It has to be sorted out before such a pronouncement can be made. According to Miss Rose, her husband was drowned at sea long before she married you."

He saw that he had dashed the hopes of the couple sitting opposite him. They looked expressively at each other in silent communication. As for himself, the lawyer thought he would never forget the fury with which the beautiful, blonde actress had turned on him when he produced the evidence he had gathered. She had been in a bad mood when she received him, tossing down a newspaper which fell at his feet. He had retrieved it for her, placing it on a

536

table, his eye inadvertently catching a headline telling of a woman jewel thief caught with a Fabergé diamond necklace, which had been traced through the Russian jeweller's records to the ownership of Count Leon Romanov. Why he should have remembered that news item he did not know. Maybe it had become immediately associated in his mind with the amount of jewellery that Lillian Rose had been wearing. It was almost as if she had pinned on her person, or draped about her neck, the most valuable pieces of jewellery she owned to compensate for some quirk of personal disappointment. He had never seen a lady so lavishly adorned at such a commonplace morning hour.

"Harry Baldwin died before I married Gregory," she spat at him.

"Do you have a death certificate to substantiate your claim, madam?" he asked her.

"No, I haven't!" she spat at him, her eyes flashing. "I changed my name when I went on the stage. If any death certificate was sent, it never reached me. Now get out!"

He got out, thankful to leave her stormy presence. Patiently, he had resumed his enquiries. Now, having delivered the bad news to his client, he was able to put forward more information that had subsequently come to light from mercantile files.

"It is correct that a Harry Baldwin was lost at sea from a ship out of Liverpool at the time Miss Rose claims to have become a widow. However, my investigations showed that there was another seaman of the same name who transferred to a Scottish vessel. It is my considered opinion that Miss Rose heard, or read, of the seaman's drowning and assumed it was her husband. Perhaps his stated age, or a mention of his birthplace, or some such detail aroused a doubt in her mind that she was never prepared to investigate. By that time she was beginning to establish herself in a theatrical career and wanted no more to do with the past."

"Is it known whether this second seaman is still alive?" his client questioned.

Mr. Jackson allowed himself one of the faint quirks of his thin lips that for him amounted to a smile. "He is very much alive, serving on the ferry that plies between the Scottish mainland and the Orkney Islands. I have been in communication with him. He has agreed to travel down to London, with all expenses paid, to see if Miss Rose is the wife whom he lost contact with. Do you wish to be present when I confront her with him, Mr. Burnett?"

Gregory inclined his head. "For her sake, I must be there."

He and Irene travelled to London with Mr. Jackson. Irene, with a view to the time she had anticipated spending in Amsterdam, had already appointed a new manager who had come to her with a high recommendation from Cartier's. If Harry Baldwin should prove to be Lillian's husband, there would be no need for Gregory to transfer his business abroad. The lawyer had said that a notice inserted in the newspapers that the marriage between Gregory and Lillian was invalid was enough to re-establish his freedom publicly.

Irene stayed at Milton Square when Gregory and Mr. Jackson went to meet Harry Baldwin and go with him to Lillian's address. Mr. Jackson had arranged the appointment with her. What he had not told Gregory, anticipating some argument, was that he had given no indication as to a third person being with them.

They found Lillian in her drawing room. She, expecting further questions that she did not welcome, more fearful than ever of a stirring up of her past, faced them with hostility when they entered. Then her eyes widened and her mouth dropped agape as Harry Baldwin came forward, wearing his best bright brown suit and nervously rotating his cap in his hands.

"'Ullo, Lily," he greeted her. "It's been a few years since you and me last saw each other."

She became hysterical, throwing herself about, tearing her hair, and screaming. Mr. Jackson hurried Harry away, putting him back on the train with ten sovereigns for his trouble. Then he hastened back to Lillian's house. Gregory opened the drawing-room door to him.

Mr. Jackson found Lillian quiet and subdued, although her hair was still in disarray, and she had not changed out of the dress she had torn. She signed the papers he put before her which stated that she was the legal wife of another man and setting his client free of all the obligations she had previously imposed. He took the papers and departed.

"Well, that's that," she said bitterly to Gregory. She unfolded herself gracefully from her chair and went across to stand in front of the fireplace where she regarded her reflection in the framed mirror above it. Almost idly she began to tidy her hair. "I suppose you realize that this affair will finish me at the Gaiety? To the audiences I will have been living in sin with you. To the Guv'nor it will be the final straw. He did not like me being gossiped about for being with Leon Romanov in Monte Carlo. He liked it still less when word reached him of that necklace being snatched from me in a public brawl. He did not mind the duel so much. After all, you were my husband defending my honour, or at least that's how it appeared in the press. Now even that romantic event will be set up against me."

"What shall you do?"

With raised arms, she was repinning the knot high at the back of her head. "I've had an offer to star at the Folies Bergère, and I'm going to accept it before the Guv'nor can give me the boot. The French are less prudish than other people. They like to see a beautiful woman scandalously pursued. I intend to be an enormous success on the Parisian stage."

Gregory, preparing to leave, gave her reflected image an amused smile. All anger against her was long gone. He was already committed to the future. "I have no doubt that you will be. Good luck, Lillian."

She did not turn her head, but watched his

departure in the mirror. If there had been any way in which she could have called him back to her, she would have done so. "Goodbye, Gregory," she said at last. Her words sounded hollow in the empty room.

At Milton Square the waiting had gone slowly for Irene. Most of the time she had wandered about restlessly, giving Sofia no chance to broach a subject she had been saving up for the right moment. Finally Sofia felt unable to delay any longer.

"Would you mind if I sold this house, Irene?"

Irene turned with some surprise at the question but gave a little shrug. "Not at all. Why should I?"

"It was your childhood home."

Irene dismissed this sentimental point with a shake of her head. "You mustn't let that stop you. I can quite understand that you must find it a large and lonely place when you are on your own."

Sofia shook her head almost shyly. "That is not the reason I wish to sell. I'm going back to live in St. Petersburg. Sergei Borisvinsky has asked me to marry him."

"That's wonderful!" Irene exclaimed, darting over to hug her exuberantly. "He is a fine man, and I've seen that he is devoted to you."

Sofia nodded contentedly. "He is good and kind. He has helped me to look to the future again, and I love him for wanting to share it with me. Oh, my dear," she added on a gush of heartfelt yearning, "I hope all goes equally well for you."

The waiting continued. Both of them glanced again and again at the clock. The minutes passed with agonizing slowness. Then at last there came the sound of a hackney cab drawing up outside. Sofia, seeing that Irene seemed incapable of making any move now that the long-awaited moment had come, hurried across to the window. There she held back the filmy curtain to view the arrival.

"Is it Gregory?" Irene asked in a whisper, standing motionless, her hands clasped tightly in front of her in suspense. "How does he seem?"

Still holding the curtain, Sofia looked across at her with a radiant smile. "To judge by his expression and the lightness of his step, I should say that all is well."

With an exclamation of joy, Irene ran into the hall, jerked open the door, and flung herself into Gregory's arms before he could reach the threshold. He kissed her long and hard in the pale London sunshine. It was the beginning of everything for them.

SENSATIONAL SAGAS!

WHITE NIGHTS, RED DAWN   (1277, $3.95)
by Frederick Nolan

Just as Tatiana was blossoming into womanhood, the Russian Revolution was overtaking the land. How could the stunning aristocrat sacrifice her life, her heart and her love for a cause she had not chosen? Somehow, she would prevail over the red dawn —and carve a destiny all her own!

IMPERIAL WINDS   (1324, $3.95)
by Priscilla Napier

From the icebound Moscow river to the misty towers of the Kremlin, from the Bolshevick uprising to the fall of the Romanovs, Daisy grew into a captivating woman who would courageously fight to escape the turmoil of the raging IMPERIAL WINDS.

KEEPING SECRETS   (1291, $3.75)
by Suzanne Morris

It was 1914, the winds of war were sweeping the globe, and Electra was in the eye of the hurricane—rushing headlong into a marriage with the wealthy Emory Cabot. Her days became a carousel of European dignitaries, rich investors, and worldly politicians. And her nights were filled with mystery and passion . . . .

EXCITING BESTSELLERS FROM ZEBRA

HEIRLOOM (1200, $3.95)
by Eleanora Brownleigh
The surge of desire Thea felt for Charles was powerful enough to convince her that, even though they were strangers and their marriage was a fake, fate was playing a most subtle trick on them both: Were they on a mission for President Teddy Roosevelt—or on a crusade to realize their own passionate desire?

A WOMAN OF THE CENTURY (1409, $3.95)
by Eleanora Brownleigh
At a time when women were being forced into marriage, Alicia Turner had achieved a difficult and successful career as a doctor. Wealthy, sensuous, beautiful, ambitious and determined—Alicia was every man's challenge and dream. Yet, try as they might, no man was able to capture her heart—until she met Henry Thorpe, who was as unattainable as she!

PASSION'S REIGN (1177, $3.95)
by Karen Harper
Golden-haired Mary Bullen was wealthy, lovely and refined—and lusty King Henry VIII's prize gem! But her passion for the handsome Lord William Stafford put her at odds with the Royal Court. Mary and Stafford lived by a lovers' vow: one day they would be ruled by only the crown of PASSION'S REIGN.

LOVESTONE (1202, $3.50)
by Deanna James
After just one night of torrid passion and tender need, the dark-haired, rugged lord could not deny that Moira, with her precious beauty, was born to be a princess. But how could he grant her freedom when he himself was a prisoner of her love?

Available wherever paperbacks are sold, or order direct from the Publisher. Send cover price plus 50¢ per copy for mailing and handling to Zebra Books, 475 Park Avenue South, New York, N.Y. 10016. DO NOT SEND CASH.